# THE BURNING HOURS
*When the flower of youth perishes*

*Written by*
**Lawrence V. Stefanile**

*Dedicated to*

**Peggy**

*And*

**The Stefaniles, who served with honor and distinction in World War II**

**THE BURNING HOURS**
*When the Flower of Youth Perishes*

*Published by*
**Biblio Publishing**
**The Educational Publisher Inc.**
**1313 Chesapeake Ave.**
**Columbus, Ohio 43212**

ISBN – 978-1-62249-265-7

The Burning Hours: *When the Flower of Youth Perishes*
Copyright 2015 by Lawrence V. Stefanile
No portion of this book, either written or e-book may be used or reproduced in any manner whatsoever without written permission except in the case of brief quotations embodied in critical article or reviews.

First Edition
April 2015

# ABOUT THE AUTHOR

The latest offering from Lawrence V. Stefanile is a stunning drama of personal courage, devotion, self-sacrifice, perfidy, cowardice and duplicity, and love tested in the crucible of adversity. Mr. Stefanile is a life-long resident of New Jersey. A retired chief executive officer in the health care and management consulting fields, he holds advanced degrees in social science and educational administration. Mr. Stefanile is the recipient of the U.S. Department of Veterans Affairs Distinguished Service Award.

*They were young, the pretty girls*
*and the handsome boys,*
*Distant thunder faint in their ears,*
*They danced and laughed away*
*the burning hours of their youth,*
*Then, thunder roared,*
*And, like a flickering flame,*
*gaiety died in the wind of war*

Lawrence V. Stefanile
April 2015

# 1

**The Ardennes Forest, Belgium**
**Christmas Day, 1944**

Vince Farro blew warm breath onto his trigger finger and slid it back into his glove. His wet feet felt like two blocks of ice. He peered through a wool mask under his helmet, his breath hanging like a gray cloud before dissipating into the icy air. Vince swung his rifle to eerie sounds, whistling through the snow-choked forest before him.

Small arms fire erupted and then stopped leaving the night ghostly still.

"Somebody got it," he thought, dismissing the incident from his mind.

"The guys that daydream don't wake up," Vince recalled Sergeant Carroll Darling's warning in his thick Alabama drawl.

"There's one thing that might keep you all alive," Darling began, "we all liked Jimmy Wilson, but Jimmy's dead, one too many daydreams about his wife and kids and his farm in Idaho. Last night a Kraut infiltrator shoved his bayonet through Jimmy's heart because Jimmy wasn't paying attention. What I'm telling you jokers is you got to stay alert. You married guys this isn't the time to be thinking of your wives and kids. The rest of you clowns forget about your girlfriends inviting you into paradise. Damn it! Stay alert! It's all you need to know and maybe you will get out of here alive."

"I might be dead tonight," Vince thought. "At least, the guys that got killed when lost in their dreams died with sweet memories. Maybe, they're the lucky ones. I'm living like a trapped rat in a frozen hole in the ground."

The chatter of machine gun fire opened up, crackling through the night and then it stopped.

"No guarantees I'll get out of here alive," Vince murmured.

Machine gun fire started up, longer, more intense bursts, and then nothing. The snow swept landscape was again soundless.

Vince fired bursts into dancing shadows in the forest, their echoes disappearing into the night. He needed to dispel the fear that clung to him like the frozen wool mask on his face. He knew his only escape home was in his mental imagery. If he had no tomorrows, then Vince wanted to spend his mortal hours with the person he most desired. Vince closed his eyes, lifted his face to the falling snow and dreamed of Linda Conover.

# 2

**Jersey City, New Jersey
Autumn, 1942**

Linda Conover, an elegant young woman whose rich chestnut hair matched her warm brown eyes commanded the sunlit room that looked beyond the Hudson River to the New York Skyline. Her soft smile and unaffected personality endeared her to all who knew her. Vince was bowled over the first time he saw Linda. His eyes traced her every move as she came to him, her hips tossing ever so slightly, the scent of her perfume in his nostrils, her delicate hand extended in greeting.

"Hello, I'm Linda Conover."

"I'm Vincent Farro," Vince shook her hand.

"Hello, Vincent Farro," Linda smiled.

"I was just passing by," Vince explained.

"You're here now, please come in."

"No thanks I have to go."

"I won't force you."

"Is this your party?"

"Yes, we're celebrating my appointment."

"Congratulations."

"This is my husband, Derek," Linda said.

Neatly turned out in his Army uniform Derek exuded an air of self-importance. He sipped a beverage of unknown origin glancing everywhere in the room, but seldom resting his eyes on Linda, the way lovers' transmit intimate signals.

"You have guests," Derek pulled Linda's arm brusquely a conqueror's grin crossed his mouth.

"It was a pleasure meeting you," Linda smiled.

Vince nodded and watched her walk away.

# 3

**Jersey City, New Jersey**
**January 1924**

Vince Farro and Domenico "Tommy" Tomasso from their earliest days were inseparable. They lived next door to one another in the Italian section of Jersey City. Their births, two hours apart, in 1924 were legendary in their neighborhood. Now they shared a foxhole on a ridge in Belgium shooting at Germans who were trying to kill them.

The day in January was clear and cold. Julia Tomasso and Regina Farro commiserated over their visibly pregnant conditions. They moistened their lips with licorice tasting Anisette trying to forget their discomfort.

Julia's fiery personality was matched by her coal dark eyes and her razor sharp tongue. Conversely, Regina was reserved; of medium height, she had warm brown eyes and long black hair that cascaded over her shoulders and onto her bosom.

"We look like we swallowed beach balls," Julia laughed.

Regina nodded agreement, shifting into a more comfortable position.

"Wow! He's kicking like a soccer player. This kid wants out," Julia said, her breathing labored. "How are you, Regina?"

"A little better than you, I think," answered Regina, shifting back and forth in her chair. "You never heard from Cologero?"

"My mother warned me not to marry him. *Buona a nulla truffatore!* Good-for-Nothing crook, a bum, she yelled at me. I didn't tell you, Regina," Julia's voice grew somber between rapid bursts of breathing. "My mother prayed to the saints to stop the marriage. She wanted to slap me, to bring me to my senses. Instead, she bit her hand to keep from hitting me. I should have listened to her. Cologero thought I was pregnant with his baby. That didn't stop the little man with big plans. He took off faster than an Olympic sprinter. I never heard from him."

"She bit her hand to take your pain, Julia," Regina grimaced at her own pain, "Oh, God!" she exclaimed, placing her hand on her bloated stomach.

"Should I call? Should I call?" Julia repeated.

"He's calming, now!"

"How do you know you have a boy in there, Regina?"

"His name will be Vincent for my Vincenzo."

"I got a boy in here," Julia ran her hand over her protuberant belly, "Today is Sunday, Regina. I'll name my son Domenico, Sunday, the day of his birth.

"Julia! I have to get to the hospital!"

"Okay!" Julia knocked the candlestick phone off the kitchen table. It tumbled to the floor, out of her reach.

"I can't get it! It's too far from me! Regina, I can't reach it!"

"Pull it up by the wire!" screamed Regina. "Hurry, Julia, or I'll deliver on your kitchen floor!"

Julia tugged on the wire.

"It's like catching a fish at the shore," she laughed, pulling the phone to her.

"It's not funny, Julia. Get help!"

Julia dialed the phone her eyes tracing the agonizingly slow rotation of the disk.

"Blessed Jesus," I'm exploding!" exclaimed Julia.

"Sergeant Dugan speaking."

"Put Captain O'Malley on the phone!" Julia demanded.

"Who is calling Captain O'Malley?"

"Julia Tomasso! Tell him Julia Tomasso!"

"Captain! Some Italian dame wants to talk to you."

"What's her name?"

"Julie Tomato or something like that."

"Tomasso! You Idiot, Tomasso!" Captain O'Malley ripped the phone from Dugan's hand.

"Scram, Dugan!" This is a personal call.

"Where should I go, Captain?"

"Walk the beat, feed the horses, just get out of here."

"Shamus! Come! Now!" Julia screamed into the phone.

"Are you ready?"

Julia's undulating contractions rolled together, without let-up.

"What's that noise, Julia?"

"It's Regina!  She's ready, too! Hurry!" Julia doubled over in pain.

"What! Two of you! You think this is an ambulance service, Julia? What'll the boys think? The Precinct Captain taking two pregnant women to the hospital! These guys gossip like little girls. Word'll get to the Commissioner. Then, I'm ruined, Julia."

"I'm going to…," Julia choked. "I'm going to have your son!" She screamed into the phone. "On my kitchen floor if you don't get here, and soon!" Julia shrieked, breathing rapidly, heavily, in and out. "And, you're worried about your career! Is that what you want, Shamus? Is that what you want? Do you want your son born on my kitchen floor?"

Regina slid to the cold floor. She rolled onto her back. Her pelvis grew heavier. Her contractions came closer. Julia stretched obliquely in her chair, the phone receiver in her ear.

"Get here! Now! You dumb Paddy!"

"Control your temper," Shamus said, tauntingly.

"Control my temper!" Julia screamed into the phone. "I'll go to the newspapers! I'll call the mayor! If I have to I'll call the Pope!"

"I'll be there right away," Shamus promised, and hung up the phone.

"Are you all right, Regina?"

"I'm okay, I think. You okay?"

"We're okay, Regina," Julia said, her voice swallowed in unrelenting pain.

The Burning Hours

**The Ardennes Forest, Belgium**
**Christmas Day, 1944**

Tommy Tomasso's brain struggled to keep his body alert. His only sensation was a progressive perception of discomfort. As he and the men on the ridge knew death would come from the forest. He wanted to light a cigarette to experience the warmth of a flaming match and settle his nerves, but it was a dead give-away to German snipers. Tommy's heart beat like a clock ticking away the minutes to his oblivion.

"What's that?" Vince whispered.

"I don't know," Tommy tightened his rifle's trigger.

"Sounds like a bird."

"Can't be, not in this snow," responded Tommy.

"Flowers grow in the snow."

"You're nuts, Vince, where?"

"In the Alps."

"No kidding."

"It's true, Tommy."

"How many books have you've read, Vince?"

"I don't know."

"It is a bird! Listen, Tommy!"

"You're right," Tommy relaxed his trigger finger. "Do you think he's cold?"

"Maybe, he's lost; I guess he's cold."

"Lost and freezing! Like us, but, the bird can fly away, Vince."

Flares zoomed skyward followed by heavy machine gun fire.

"Germans tripped the wire," Vince observed.

Machine gun fire continued heavy and then it stopped and the eerie green flare died in the sky. For a short time it was quiet, then, machine gun fire erupted, again.

"They're raking the field."

"Lots of dead Germans," Tommy mourned.

The machine gun fire stopped. Only pelting snow was audible.

"What are you thinking, Vince?"

"Christmas at home, Bing Crosby singing White Christmas."

"The Germans call Crosby *Der Bingel*," Tommy said.

"Where did you hear that?"

"I heard some of the guys talking."

"If *Der Bingel* came here he wouldn't have to dream about a white Christmas," Vince said, ruefully.

"Plenty of snow here to make his dream come true," Tommy laughed.

"Can't hear the bird," Vince whispered.

"Yeah!" Tommy chimed in, "flew away, smart bird."

"Wish we could fly away."

"I'm with you, Vince."

Tommy and Vince lapsed into silence watching for enemy movements, listening for strange sounds.

Then Tommy felt a jab to his ribs.

# 5

"Next month, we'll be legal," Vince said.

"What do you mean?"

"Twenty-one, Tommy, we'll be able sit at a bar and order drinks."

"When we get home, let's go to Lisa's Tavern and get loaded."

"It's a deal."

"Kurt Schaeffer got killed," Tommy said, after a brief pause.

"I heard he got hit at Anzio after knocking out two machine gun nests."

"Kurt had it all, Football All-America, college scholarships, he didn't have to be in this war, Tommy," Vince lamented.

"Remember when Mr. Birkman took attendance in English class," Tommy reminisced. "I detect a hickory aroma from Schaeffer's German Pork Store, he'd say. Where are you, Kurt?"

"Right here, Kurt laughed and stood up, all 6'5" of him," Tommy said.

"Tell your dad to save me two knockwursts. You may take your seat, Mr. Schaeffer, he'd say." Vince smiled at the memory of Kurt's and Samuel Birkman's attendance ritual.

"How about Brady measuring javelin throws at the track and field meet? Kurt warned he was too close, but Brady didn't move. I still see that javelin sailing through the sky and Brady running around trying to avoid it," Tommy laughed, loudly.

"Shut up! Tommy!"

"Sorry," Tommy whispered. "A little higher and Brady would be talking like a soprano."

"Six more inches Kurt, you yelled, and you would have speared him like a fish! Everybody in the stands clapped and you had to stand up and bow."

---

The Burning Hours                                            Page 9

"Brady ran us around the hot gym because you shot off your mouth, Tommy," Vince paused, "Kurt could have gone to college or played for the New York Giants. He enlisted to prove he was a patriotic American. He didn't live to see his twentieth birthday."

Kurt Schaeffer's death was a reality neither Vince nor Tommy wanted to accept. Soon the snow-caked landscape would be stained red their youthful memories stolen by the drumbeat of war. In those brief moments of remembering Kurt Schaeffer and Samuel Birkman, Vince and Tommy forgot how cold they were.

# 6

**Grayson County, Texas**
**Spring 1899**

Enoch Darling, a circuit preacher in the fifth decade of life felt the swaying of his trusted horse Bathsheba beneath him. He traveled the roads of Grayson County, Texas searching for souls to save. The rhythmic swaying of Bathsheba inflamed Enoch's carnal desires. Fearing the loss of his soul he dismounted and fell to his knees. He implored the Almighty to deliver him from the lustful temptations that had captured his body and soul. Enoch waited, but no responses to his supplications came.

"Why have you abandoned your faithful servant?" he demanded.

Again, he heard only the menacing wind in the black woods.

"I am unfit to dwell in your House, Lord! Satan has snared me!" Enoch lamented.

Again, only eerie winds filled his ears. He mounted Bathsheba and galloped fast to Skitty Street. Enoch lashed Bathsheba furiously straight to the Pleasure Palace Social Club where he had prayed with fallen men and women. He jumped off Bathsheba and dashed through a row of statues of satyrs and naked women, feverishly banging a large brass ring until the front door swung open.

Inside the color red dominated the parlor where women lounged seductively on recliners awaiting the attention of palace patrons. Enoch ran to a room at the top of the dimly lit hallway and pushed its door open.

Lulu McCallister, nubile, no more than sixteen and smiling angelically, stood at her bedside. Beads of sweat glistened on Enoch's face, his eyes burned hot with desire. He picked Lulu up like a feather in his sweaty grip and pinned her shoulders to the bed, and then a voice thundered in his head, "Why didn't you wait for me?" it roared. Enoch rolled off Lulu and felt his flesh cooling.

"Get out of this house of iniquity!" the voice boomed, "Go and spread the good word!"

Enoch dragged Lulu down the stairs, out of the building. He mounted Bathsheba and pulled her up, behind him. The Madam's shotgun blast peppered Bathsheba; she reared up and spilled Lulu to the ground, Enoch pulled her back up and they galloped away into the night.

One year later, their son was born. Enoch baptized him Carroll, *a war champion for the Almighty.* In the passing years they traveled the back roads of Texas, winding up in Alabama. Enoch preached the Bible, Lulu sang hymns and Carroll passed the hat. When Carroll was seventeen Enoch handed him a silver dollar and told him to find his way. Carroll never saw Enoch and Lulu, again.

# 7

**Fort Dix, New Jersey**
**Summer 1943**

Carroll Darling recalled his first meeting in 1943 at Fort Dix, New Jersey with Vince, tall and thin, unruly black hair, circumspect and thoughtful, and Tommy, Vince's opposite, shorter but more powerfully built, his red hair a match for his hell raising temperament.

Sergeant Darling joined the army after Enoch and Lulu abandoned him. He served honorably in World War I where he was wounded several times in the Argonne Forest. Now in his forties Carroll Darling knew only life in the army; he was an army lifer.

"I'm Sergeant Darling!" He growled to a line of newly inducted soldiers, mostly eighteen and nineteen year old boys.

"I'm Private Sweetie-Pie."

"Who said that?!" Darling bellowed.

Tommy stepped forward, grinning.

Darling leaned into Tommy demanding his name.

"Domenico Tomasso," Tommy answered, "My friends call me Tommy."

"I'm not your friend! Tomasso is an Eye-talian name. So you won't mind if I call you Tomasso-Paste, smart ass!"

Before Tommy could verbalize his comeback, Vince told him to shut up.

"Get back in line, Tomasso," Darling growled.

Following Darling's order Tommy executed a sloppy about-face.

"Try it, again! Tomasso-paste!" Sergeant Darling ordered.

"Yes sir," Tommy said.

"Don't call me, sir, its sergeant, got it?"

The Burning Hours                                  Page 13

"Yes sir, I mean sergeant," Tommy executed a neat about-face and winked at Vince.

As he dismissed the line of newly inducted soldiers, Darling laughed to himself at the redhead from New Jersey who had the temerity to defy him.

# 8

**The Ardennes Forest, Belgium**
**Christmas Day, 1944**

As night inched to dawn, German artillery got louder and closer. Successive blasts shook the snow laden forest amputating tree tops exploding pine needles and wood splinters into massive clouds into the gray morning. Vince and Tommy covered their ears to blot out concussive waves rolling through the forest. Hours later the artillery bombardment stopped.

"It's starting!?" Tommy said.

"German artillery," Vince mumbled.

"Why don't they just come so we can get this over with?"

"Take it easy, Tommy, we all got the jitters."

"Yeah! We all got the jitters."

"What's that?" Vince leveled his rifle.

"Stay where you are or I'll blow your brains out!"

"Hold it!" Vince grabbed Tommy's arm, "It's Darling."

"Ready, Vince?" Darling said, pushing through the snow to the lip of Vince's and Tommy's foxhole.

"Locked and loaded, Sarge," Vince responded.

"What about me, Darling? Are you angry with me, honey?"

"Shut up! Tomasso-sauce," Darling countered, "How's baby?"

"She's sleeping," Tommy stroked his automatic weapon.

"She'll be ready, Sarge."

"Make sure you wake her up when the alarm goes off. Scuttlebutt says the Krauts are coming through our left flank, probably through your position."

"You okay, Vince?"

"I'm good, Sarge."

"Tommy?"

"Yeah, Sarge, hey, Sarge." Tommy called.

"What!" Darling answered.

"Nothing. Thanks."

"Good luck," Darling crawled through the snow toward the tree line.

"Sleet's letting up," Vince observed.

"Darling's a good man," Tommy said.

"The best," Vince agreed.

"If it wasn't for the wool socks your mother knitted for us, we'd have frost bite, like lots of the guys."

"I got the second pair in my pack."

"I'm wearing both pairs."

"Yeah," was the only comment Vince could muster.

"Who's the dame you're always dreaming about, Vince?"

"She's no dame, Tommy, she's a lady."

"I didn't mean it that way."

"I know you didn't, Tommy."

"Do I know her?"

"Yeah, you know her."

"Why won't you tell me?"

" Later."

"We're gonna be best men at our weddings, right, Vince?"

"Right, Tommy."

"So – who's the mystery woman?"

"It's kinda complicated."

"I need to understand. We're in church on your wedding day. I'm standing with you. The priest says anyone against this marriage speak now or something like that. No one comes forward because your bride is a mystery."

"Stop breaking my chops, Tommy."

"You know the first thing I'm gonna do when this is over, Vince?"

"You told me a thousand times."

"Marry Rosemary."

"You only kissed her once, Tommy. How do you know she's the right one?

"Sometimes, you just know," Tommy said reflectively.

"Yeah, sometimes you know," Vince agreed, and then both men fell silent.

# 9

**Academy for Young Women**
**Jersey City, New Jersey 1943**

Sister Tomasina Ambrose, Director of the Academy for Young Women looked at the wall clock moving inexorably to the 3:00 pm hour. Garbed in a black habit, a rosary with an enormous crucifix dangling from her waist belt, she instilled fear into the graduating seniors waiting for the dismissal bell to sound. A large woman with a cherubic face and pink complexion, she walked the corridor glancing at the young girls who studiously avoided eye contact with the nun's soulless gray eyes.

She stopped in front of her nemesis, "Do you have cigarettes in your bag?"

"No sister."

"You realize if you are lying, you will forfeit your place in the graduation ceremony."

"Yes sister."

"You won't mind if I look in your bag."

"No sister," the young girl complied.

Sister Tomasina examined the bag and finding no cigarettes she moved on. The young girl closed her bag and smiled at her victory over the dreaded nun. Earlier, she had passed the pack of cigarettes to her boyfriend from Hill Top High School who was participating in the track and field meet at Roosevelt Park. He secreted the pack in his sneakers getting it passed Thomas Brady, the most despised teacher at Hill Top High School.

"Remain after dismissal," Sister Tomasina ordered another senior girl.

"Yes sister," the young girl complied.

The clock moved to the 3:00 pm hour and for thirty seconds the bell clanged frenetically. The girls thundered out of the school most ran to the nearby Roosevelt Park.

"Look at them," Sister Tomasina observed, "they can't wait to fantasize over partially clothed public school boys," her facial expression required a response from Rosemary.

"Yes sister," Rosemary said.

"Review your books, Rosemary," Sister Tomasina said, "soon you will be a Novice."

"Thank you, Sister."

The track and field meet at Roosevelt Park ended. Hilltop High School prevailed against its competition. Kurt Schaeffer won all of his events, setting new scholastic records. For his crude remarks, Thomas Brady sentenced Tommy to twenty laps around the hot gym. When Vince defended Tommy, he got the same sentence.

"What you said about Brady was pretty bad."

"Yeah, I know," Tommy answered tugging at his perspiration soaked T-Shirt sticking to his chest.

"Bowing to the crowd really flipped Brady."

"It was worth it, Vince! Think of Brady, writhing on the ground screaming for an ambulance," Tommy laughed.

"I should know better than to stick up for you, Tommy."

"Let's cross now, before the traffic worsens," Tommy said.

"What's with you and Brady, Tommy?"

"Whatta' ya' mean?"

"I know he's a bastard, but he seems to have it in for you special."

"Come on, Vince. Let's go," Tommy evaded answering.

Across the street from the Academy for Young Women, Vince strolled nonchalantly, deep in thought, while Tommy whirled around, burning his warehouse of energy, conjuring up his next adventure.

"So, what's going on with you and Brady?" Vince repeated.

"It's a long story."

"I'll listen."

"Not now, Vince."

Tommy stopped, suddenly. His eyes riveted on a girl who had exited the Academy. He grabbed Vince's arm, bringing him to an unexpected stop.

"I'll see you, later, Vince," Tommy said.

"Where are you going?" Vince hollered.

Tommy didn't answer.

He dashed into the rushing traffic to the opposite side of the street. What Tommy didn't know as he darted between screeching vehicles his life was about to forever change.

# 10

Rosemary McNulty enjoyed the prospect of a weekend away from suffocating Sister Tomasina. She cradled an armful of books against her chest, walked slowly, relishing the sun on her fair, freckled face. Tommy wove through traffic bringing several vehicles to screeching stops ignoring motorists' angry protests. When he arrived unscathed at the opposite side of the street, he jumped onto the pavement, beside Rosemary.

"Hi, I'm Tommy. I saw you from across the street," he said, out of breath.

"Go away," Rosemary didn't look up.

"What's your name?"

"I said, go away."

"Give a guy a break. I coulda' been killed running across the street."

"You shouldn't take chances, like that."

"It was worth it. That's a lot of books for a small girl. Let me help you," Tommy held out his hand.

"I'm not a small girl!"

"Okay, don't get mad," Tommy smiled at the rise he got out of Rosemary.

"Don't laugh! I mean it!"

"Okay, I won't call you a small girl. I'm leaving next week for the army, won't you even look at me," Tommy beseeched.

Rosemary looked at Tommy, who was waiting, quietly hopeful.

"You are the prettiest girl I have ever seen," Tommy said, examining the contours of Rosemary's face, her strawberry blond hair, her sky blue eyes.

"I'm sorry you have to leave," Rosemary cast her eyes downward, ignoring Tommy's compliment.

The Burning Hours

"Please talk to me. This might be my last chance to get to know you. What is your name?" Tommy pleaded.

"My name is Rosemary. I'll pray for you," still looking down at her books shifting in her arms.

"That's my friend, Vince, across the street. We have the same birthday. He's two hours older than me. He's going to the library. Vince is always reading. He's a smart guy. Will you pray for him, too?" Tommy felt a need to tell Rosemary everything he could, as fast as he could.

"I pray for all the boys."

"Hey! Vince!" Tommy yelled, "This is Rosemary."

Vince stopped and turned. "Hello, Rosemary!" Vince waved from across the street.

"Isn't she a doll?"

"You're embarrassing me," Rosemary's face flushed pink.

"She sure is, Tommy! Be careful of that clown you're talking to, Rosemary. He'll break your heart," Vince joked.

"Thank your friend for the compliment," Rosemary requested.

"You can thank him, yourself," Tommy answered.

"I won't yell across the street, it's not ladylike."

"You're actually talking to me," Tommy said. "Vince!" Tommy yelled, "Rosemary said thanks. She would have told you herself, but she didn't want to shout over the traffic."

"Tell her, she's welcome," Vince continued walking.

It was the first time their eyes had met. Rosemary's books fell to the pavement. Tommy bent down and picked them up. Sister Tomasina watched from the Academy's main entrance silhouetted in black against the sunshine. Rosemary looked back, nervously and then to Tommy.

"Is something wrong?" Tommy asked, looking in Sister Tomasina's direction.

"Nothing's wrong," Rosemary said, still distracted, they resumed walking along the pavement.

The Burning Hours

"Your books are about saints and nuns," Tommy said. "Most of the girls I know read romance novels."

"I start my candidacy to become a nun in September."

"You're going to be a nun!" Tommy said, incredulous at Rosemary's revelation.

"I think so. I will work with the sisters before becoming a novice."

"Did you always want to be a nun?"

"I grew up around the sisters. I guess it was understood I would go into the convent when I was of age."

"Are you sure you want to be a nun?"

Rosemary looked at Tommy and smiled. "I guess so. I don't know. Sister Tomasina is my mentor. She's sure being a nun is right for me."

"Was that Sister Tomasina at the front door of the school?"

"Yes.

"Where do you live?" Tommy asked his sense of dejection lifting.

"There," Rosemary pointed to a white two-story wood frame building.

"That's where the …," Tommy fumbled.

"The word you are looking for is orphanage."

"Sorry, I didn't know."

"How could you know? The nuns brought me here when I was a baby, from Ireland. I never knew my mother and father."

"I never knew my father, I guess I'm a half-orphan," Tommy smiled.

"You're funny," Rosemary returned Tommy's smile.

"Do you know where Gruber's Drug Store is?"

"Yes."

"Would you meet me there, tomorrow? I'll buy you an ice cream sundae or whatever you like. I'll dress real nice for you. I'll be on time. What do you say?" Tommy talked non-stop.

The Burning Hours

"I don't know," Rosemary answered, and then she quickly agreed.

"Is noon okay?"

"Okay," Rosemary smiled.

"I'll see you tomorrow at Gruber's, at noon."

"I'll see you then," Rosemary responded.

"Okay, okay." Tommy repeated, excitedly.

"Hey! Vince! Wait for me!" Tommy dashed across the street, cutting between oncoming traffic.

# 11

**Gruber's Drug Store**
**Jersey City, New Jersey**
**June 1943**

Benjamin Gruber had two loves; Minnie, his departed wife and the drug store they opened in 1900. Depressively lonely, Benjamin felt the sting of his advancing years and painful arthritis. With Minnie's passing the spark in his life had dulled, he no longer slept well and when merciful sleep came, it was fitful. At the end of each day, Benjamin switched off the lights and climbed the back steps of the store to the second floor apartment he and Minnie had shared for over two decades. He'd set two places at the dinner table and imagine Minnie sitting across from him discussing the day's activities answering questions he knew Minnie was asking. "The lean years were the best," he said aloud. "It's not the same, my darling. Age is my enemy. Standing is hard, my hands hurt all the time. It's painful to work the soda fountain and grind chemicals," Benjamin drifted into silence. "The chemicals I mixed, in all those years, but I couldn't mix the right ones to save you," he sobbed. "It's the kids from the high school they keep me going, their energy and their laughter. This terrible war has changed everything. Benjamin didn't finish his dinner.

Gruber's Drug Store was a rectangle. On one side, the drug dispensary and laboratory, on the opposite side, an ice cream parlor with neatly spaced black slate tables and wire back chairs, and at its center, the soda fountain, its white marble counter lined with swivel chair stools, soda and syrup dispensers and a large red Coca Cola machine dominated the room. The floor to ceiling mirror behind the counter was trimmed with white lights and a Victory Ice Cream banner.

While preparing an ice cream Sundae, the door bell jingled.

"I'll be with you in a minute, Vince," Benjamin looked up.

"Okay, Mr. Gruber. Take your time," Vince said observing his painful struggle to scoop ice cream out of its cylindrical container.

"Is the Sundae ready?" a waiting customer asked, impatiently.

"Almost ready," Benjamin prevaricated.

"I'll give you a hand," Vince walked behind the counter.

"Thank you, Vince. Where's Tommy?"

"He'll be here, soon. He's got a date," Vince dug deeply into the vanilla cream.

"Tommy has a girl!"

"He's meeting her, here, at noon."

"Good luck to the girl who tries to tame Tommy."

"I think he's been tamed, already, you'll see what I mean."

"Finished," Vince announced sliding the tulip-shaped glass to Benjamin.

"We're a good team, Vince," Benjamin said, dispensing rich chocolate syrup over vanilla ice cream, topping mounds of whipped cream with a red Maraschino Cherry, then laying out a long stem spoon and napkins.

"All set," Benjamin announced. "That will be twenty cents."

The customer paid with two dimes and dug into Vince's and Benjamin's sweet creation.

"What can I get you, Vince?"

"I'll have a Coke."

Benjamin pulled the Coke machine's dispenser; a caramel colored liquid hissed into a fluted glass and erupted into bubbles before settling. He slid the glass to Vince.

"Float a scoop of ice cream, Vince. You're too skinny. If my Minnie were here, she'd fatten you up," Benjamin said, wistfully.

The Burning Hours

"I wish I could have known her," Vince said, touched by Benjamin's emotion.

"When do you leave?"

"Wednesday."

"You have a girl, Vince?"

"Nobody steady."

"Plenty of time. You'll see."

"I guess so. What do I owe you?"

"My pleasure," Benjamin patted Vince's face.

# 12

Tommy Tomasso nervously paced the pavement in front of Gruber's Drug Store. He looked up and down the street, but saw no sign of Rosemary. "I never felt like this," he mused, walking up and down the street, and then he heard the noon hour whistle. "She's not coming," he fretted.

Vince descended the steps, out of Gruber's Drug Store. "Look at you!" he exclaimed.

"Hi ya' Vince," Tommy said, distractedly.

"What has come over you, Tommy boy; hair combed, neatly dressed. What has this girl done to you?"

"Cut it out, Vince. She's standing me up."

"How could she ditch such a handsome little guy," Vince tweaked Tommy's cheeks, grinning broadly.

"Stop busting my balls, Vince. She's not coming. I'm going home."

"I don't think so," Vince said.

"What do you mean?"

Vince rolled his eyes upward. Tommy wheeled around.

"You look real nice, Rosemary."

"So do you, Tommy."

"You remember my friend, Vince."

"Yes, I remember Vince."

"Nice seeing you, again, Rosemary."

"I'm glad you came," Tommy said, excitedly.

"First, promise not to use the language I just heard," Rosemary demanded.

Tommy looked sheepishly at Vince who relished Tommy's discomfort.

"I'm waiting."

"Rosemary is waiting, Tommy," Vince teased.

Tommy glared at Vince, and then, softly, he said, "Sorry."

The Burning Hours                                      Page 28

"Sorry for what?" Rosemary queried.

"C'mon, Rosemary, don't rub it in," Tommy protested.

"I'll be going home."

"Okay you win, I won't use that language anymore, are you satisfied?"

"Tommy's word is good as gold, right Tommy?" Vince needled.

"Let's go inside and have ice cream."

"Make sure he keeps his word, Rosemary."

"Get lost, Vince," Tommy said and he and Rosemary went into Gruber's.

# 13

Tommy Tomasso was like the wind, restless and unpredictable. For Tommy the city was nothing more than a Petri dish to hatch his pranks. Vince helped him out of jams in school. Captain O'Malley bailed him out of scrapes with the police. Tommy wondered why. He dismissed the whispers he had heard. In the year of his departure to Europe Tommy would have his answer.

In their brief time, together, Tommy was sure he wanted to spend his days with Rosemary. When they climbed the steps into Gruber's Drug Store he felt a change come over him. Tommy ushered Rosemary past clusters of black slate tables to the soda fountain where they took seats.

Benjamin Gruber enjoyed witnessing the flowering of young love, their awkward moments, their shy smiles, and finally their sweet surrenders. For a fleeting moment Benjamin drifted back to his courtship with Minnie.

"You just missed Vince," Benjamin reported.

"We saw him, outside," Tommy replied.

"So, this is your lovely young lady Vince told me about."

"Vince has a big mouth," Tommy said.

"I thought he was very nice," Rosemary rebuked.

"I should have been the first to introduce you to Mr. Gruber," Tommy protested.

"It doesn't matter," Rosemary countered.

"It does to me," Tommy persisted.

"Where do you go to school, Rosemary?" Benjamin interjected.

"Academy for Young Women, I will graduate this year."

"That's quite an achievement."

"Thank you."

"My Minnie and I walked in Roosevelt Park near the school on days like this."

The Burning Hours                    Page 30

"Is your wife here, Mr. Gruber? I would like to say hello."

"I wish you could. Minnie passed away a long time ago."

"I'm sorry," Rosemary touched Benjamin's hand.

"Thank you, dear. Now, what can I get you?"

"Remember me," Tommy said, feeling neglected.

"Benjamin and Rosemary smiled at Tommy's pique.

"I'll have vanilla ice cream with cherry syrup and whipped cream on top," Rosemary ordered.

"A lot of whipped cream," Mr. Gruber, winked.

"A lot of whipped cream," Rosemary concurred.

"I'll have the same," Tommy said.

"You kids get a table near the window. I'll prepare your orders."

The day of Tommy and Rosemary's date was oppressively hot. Cars crammed with people returning from and going to shift work at defense plants rumbled along city streets disappearing into heat mirages shimmering out of boiling black asphalt surfaces. Defense plants and waterfront operations hummed around the clock. The city was alive, day and night. Soldiers and sailors from around the country many with southern and mid-western accents roamed the streets. They were welcomed into homes for lunch and dinner, and for news of the front. The doors of churches and synagogues stayed open night and day their priests, ministers and rabbis providing consolation to soothe the fears of relatives of young men and women fighting in Europe and the Pacific.

"That's Billy Schumacher and Joey Sharpe," Tommy said to Rosemary, who was looking through the glass window, "Billy and Joey are high school friends."

"Why are they in uniform?"

"They completed basic training; they'll be shipping out."

"Will they stay together?"

"I don't know, probably not."

"It would be good if they stayed together, wouldn't it be good?" Rosemary said, worry in her voice.

"It sure would be good."

"Will you and Vince stay together when you ship out?"

'I don't know I hope so."

"I hope so, too," Rosemary said, touching Tommy's hand.

# 14

Since Minnie's passing Benjamin had been dispirited and his advancing arthritis made his life difficult. However, this day was different. He felt renewed when earlier Vince worked with him. Tommy's and Rosemary's romantic dance made him forget his pain marveling at how the rambunctious boy he had known had transformed into a gentleman, totally at the command of the wisp of a young woman sitting opposite him.

Humming softly, Benjamin set his sweet creations before Tommy and Rosemary.

"They look wonderful," Rosemary congratulated Mr. Gruber.

"I don't know where to start," Tommy said.

Benjamin returned with a chrome-plated box.

"It's a portable radio, music for your first date."

"What do I owe you, Mr. Gruber?" Tommy asked.

"You two kids have brightened my day, that's payment in full."

"Thanks, Mr. Gruber…"

"Where are the dials on the radio?"

"Lift the plate and watch what happens. Lift the plate, Rosemary," Benjamin instructed.

"*In the Mood!*" she exclaimed, "I love Glenn Miller."

"The radio turns on and off when you lift and lower the cover," Benjamin said, "Enjoy yourselves; I'm going back to work."

"Thanks, Mr. Gruber," Tommy lifted and lowered the plate, starting and stopping the music, "This is the kicks," he enthused.

"Stop playing with the radio, Tommy," Rosemary scolded.

"Sorry."

"What's so funny?" Rosemary asked.

The Burning Hours                                    Page 33

"Nothing," Tommy brushed his fingers along his lips, then burst out laughing.

Rosemary's reflection in the radio's chrome-plated cover revealed the source of Tommy's amusement.

"It's not funny, Tommy," Rosemary said, wiping cherry syrup off her mouth, "If you don't stop laughing I'll leave."

"Okay, but you really looked cute."

"I'm having a good time, Tommy."

"So am I, Rosemary."

Benjamin Gruber was engrossed in preparing pharmaceutical prescriptions. He looked up and returned Tommy's and Rosemary's good-bye waves. The bell jingled and the door closed behind them. Benjamin flexed his fingers. His arthritic pain which had been obscured re-emerged and the bright sunshine had lost its luster.

The sidewalk across the street from Gruber's Drug Store was lined with well-kept bi-level houses many displaying small window flags with blue and gold stars. Tommy and Rosemary walked leisurely. The sun was hot, but they didn't feel its heat, instead they felt only its comforting warmth. Tommy didn't attempt to take Rosemary's hand. Instead, they exchanged silent smiles and continued walking.

"Are you afraid of going to the Army?"

"I wasn't, but I am, now," Tommy confessed.

"But, not before," Rosemary questioned.

"Before today, the war was a faraway thing. Everything is different, now."

"Why?"

Tommy stopped and looked directly into Rosemary's eyes.

"Now, I have something to live for," he said, "and the thought of losing you scares me."

"You hardly know me, Tommy."

"Some people know each other for a long time, but they never truly know each other. Then there are people who

The Burning Hours
Page 34

know each other for only a short time and it's as if they've known each other, forever. I feel as if I've known you forever, Rosemary."

Rosemary took Tommy's hand and smiled.

Sister Tomasina Ambrose stood on the front steps of the Academy staring malevolently at Tommy and Rosemary before going inside.

"Rosemary suddenly slid her hand out of Tommy's.

"What's wrong?" Tommy asked.

"Nothing," Rosemary lied.

"Why do you get nervous when that nun is around?"

"It's really okay, Tommy."

"It's not okay, Rosemary," Tommy clasped both hands around Rosemary's shoulders drawing her closer to him. "Listen to me; I don't want you to become a nun. When I come back from this war I want you to become my wife."

"Don't talk foolishness."

"Do you have feelings for me, Rosemary?"

"You know I do."

"Then tell me you love me."

"I do love you, Tommy."

"Is it okay if I kiss you, Rosemary? I won't be rough."

"I'd like that," Rosemary nodded her assent.

Tommy brushed Rosemary's lips, softly with his.

"That was real nice," Rosemary said.

In those moments it seemed to Tommy and Rosemary that the existential world ceased to exist that a transcendent quiet had enveloped the street and it held them in its thrall.

The Burning Hours

# 15

Except for the sound of artillery in the distance the night was ominously quiet. For a while, Vince and Tommy didn't speak. They looked through the falling snow at the forest for any kind of German troop movement.

"What do you think, Vince?"

"I don't think they left for Berlin."

"They'll attack before daylight I feel it in my bones."

"I think you're right Tommy."

"Lots of jitters, tonight," Tommy observed at the sound of scattered gunfire.

"There it goes, again," Vince said.

Tommy glanced at Vince and changed the subject.

"I was sorry about your father, Vince."

"Thanks, Tommy it seems like a hundred years ago."

"He always treated me good when I went for a haircut."

"Pop was gentle, he had a hard time with English, so he didn't talk much," Vince reflected, "He was a good man and a terrific father."

"Everybody who knew him liked him."

"I had a feeling something was wrong. When I got home that day the house was full of neighbors, Mom was crying, it was tough. A neighbor found pop. He was sitting in one of his barber chairs, real peaceful. The neighbor thought he was resting. He just died there, alone, Tommy. Christ, I miss him, I always will."

"Why do you think most of the guys visited their teachers before shipping out, Vince?"

"I don't know, maybe they're like second parents."

"If it wasn't for Mr. Birkman I'd spend the war in the brig," Tommy laughed sardonically under his breath.

"It might have been a good option."

"You'd be lonely without me."

"Wonder what happened to Brady?"

"I wonder," Tommy said swinging his weapon to a sound in the forest.

# 16

**Hilltop High School**
**Jersey City, New Jersey**
**September 1943**

Hilltop High School bristled with visiting former students now in military uniforms. Most joked they could roam the halls without passes. Now Privates First Class Farro and Tomasso Vince and Tommy visited Hilltop's administrative office for approval to visit their former teachers. Their army uniforms earned immediate authorization. The familiar corridors they walked were quiet the sound of their footsteps on the polished terrazzo floor acute in their ears.

"Who do you want to see first, Vince?"

"Mr. Birkman."

"Okay with me I always liked Mr. Birkman."

"I don't know if it is reciprocal," Vince poked Tommy.

"He gave me a passing grade so I'm sure he liked me."

Samuel Birkman, in his late sixth decade of life was the unofficial dean of faculty at Hilltop High School. A bachelor, he started teaching at Hilltop in 1900. His pleasant demeanor and objective views earned him the respect of fellow teachers and students, and his shock of white hair lent gravitas to his presence.

In the quiet of his classroom, Samuel Birkman sat at his desk looking out the window.

Vince knocked on the open door.

"Yes," Samuel answered without turning around.

"Vince Farro and Tommy Tomasso, Mr. Birkman."

"Come in, come in, I'm glad to see you boys," Samuel swung around and got up from his chair.

"Didn't mean to disturb you we thought we'd stop by and say hello before..." Vince stopped in mid-thought.

The Burning Hours

"Don't stand there, come in," Samuel greeted Vince and Tommy at the doorway.

"It seems like yesterday when Tommy and I were your students, Mr. Birkman."

"Your seat back there, Vince, and Tommy, you were here, first row where I could keep an eye on you," he laughed.

"Come on, Mr. Birkman, I wasn't that bad," Tommy said.

"You livened up the classroom, Tommy," Samuel hugged Tommy, "and Vince, always studious, it was a joy having you two boys in my class."

"We should go, now," Vince said, "It was good seeing you, Mr. Birkman."

"Likewise, Mr. Birkman," Tommy said.

"You boys take care of yourselves."

"We will, Mr. Birkman," Tommy replied.

"I enjoyed having you boys in my class," Samuel reiterated with an emotional quiver in his voice.

"Thanks for everything, Mr. Birkman," Vince said.

"Drop me a line when you can."

"Sure," Vince said.

"We will," Tommy added.

Samuel glimpsed Thomas Brady walking unsteadily in Vince and Tommy's direction from the opposite end of the hall. He thought his presence on the second floor strange since his station was in the gymnasium on the ground floor. Samuel noticed Brady's face was redder than usual and he appeared to sway.

"Who do you want to see next?" Tommy asked.

"I don't know. Who do you want to see?"

"Here comes Brady," Tommy said, "I hoped to avoid him."

"I heard you were in the building," Brady said, "the saviors of our county," he added sarcastically, breathing alcohol vapors into the air.

The Burning Hours

"Let's go, Tommy," Vince said trying to get around Brady.

"Not so fast," Brady blocked Vince's move.

"Back off," Vince said.

"What about you, Tomasso? The Irishman with a Dago last name."

"What the hell are you talking about, Brady?" Vince pulled Tommy back.

"Ask your friend," Brady slurred.

"Get out of our way!" Vince demanded.

"I'll keep an eye on your mother while you're gone, Tomasso," Brady winked, lasciviously, which would be his last semi-coherent utterance.

Tommy's fist splattered Brady's nose across his face, metallic tasting blood oozed into his mouth, his eyes had a faraway look as he slid down the hallway wall onto the cold floor.

Tommy pulled Brady up by his collar. "If you talk about my mother or even think about her, I'll kill you, Brady, count on it, I will kill you."

"Let's get out of here," Vince pulled Tommy off Brady who was mumbling incoherently and bleeding profusely.

Samuel heard the altercation and he went into the hall where he found Brady on the floor, his body twitching, and blood gurgling out of his mouth.

"I didn't want this to happen, Mr. Birkman," Tommy apologized.

"It's not Tommy's fault," Vince chimed in.

"I'll take care of this," Samuel said, "Go there's nothing here to concern you."

"Thanks Mr. Birkman," Vince grabbed Tommy's arm and they walked rapidly down the stairs out of the building.

"You got what you deserved, Mr. Brady," Samuel said, "I heard everything you said to that young man. You're a disgrace! If you know what's good for you, you'll resign, and if you don't I will report your behavior to the Board."

The Burning Hours

# 17

Following the Brady incident, Vince and Tommy went to the cannon mount, built during the Revolutionary War to protect the coastline from the English Fleet. Vince wanted to talk, but Tommy resisted. During their school days at Hilltop the cannon mount was the favored meeting place for seniors who had been given smoking privileges to meet and socialize. Tommy stared down the slope his thoughts far away clicking his Zippo lighter cap open and close, repeatedly.

"You don't have to tell me anything, Tommy."

"Captain O'Malley is my father," Tommy said, "I always wondered why he helped me out of jams. I didn't ask my mother anything about him. Because of going away, she felt I should know."

Tommy took a long drag on his cigarette, and then he turned to Vince.

"It wasn't a dirty thing between them, Vince. Captain O'Malley has real feelings for my mother. He made sure we were taken care of. "

"What about Mr. Tomasso?"

"He was in the rackets, arrested for numbers running, stuff like that; that's how Captain O'Malley got to know mom. I guess they just hit it off. Even though my father thought Mom was pregnant by him, it didn't stop him from skipping out on her. Later on, Captain O'Malley discovered he joined the Chicago Mob."

"Did your mom ever hear from him?"

"No."

"Do you know where he is now?"

"Yeah, he's in the Chicago River. He shot his mouth off one too many times and the big shots killed him," Tommy said, experiencing a sense of relief unburdening his secret to his closest friend.

The Burning Hours                                    Page 41

"You okay, Tommy?"

"This leave hasn't worked out like I hoped it would, Vince."

"I'm sorry Rosemary wasn't here to see you."

"I sent her a note; she had to know I was coming home."

"Things get screwed up, Tommy, don't worry."

"Yeah, I guess you're right."

"She's crazy about you, Tommy, it will shake out."

"Yeah," Tommy managed a smile.

"You want to go some place?"

"No thanks, Vince. I'll hang here for a while."

"What about you?"

"I'm going to spend time with Mom."

"What about that girl you won't tell me about?"

"There's nothing to tell."

"I'll see you later, Vince," Tommy said, flipping his cigarette butt over the cannon mount wall.

# 18

Darkness in the Ardennes Forest surrendered to early morning daylight. German artillery became more constant blasting the forest spewing wooden splinters and pine needles from treetops like swarms of locusts. Vince and Tommy knew when the lull came the expected attack would come. Their jitters drove them to check and recheck their rifles and ammunition clips. Then there was nothing more to do, but wait and hope they would be alive at the end of the day.

"Do you believe in fate, Vince?"

"I never gave it much thought."

"I've been thinking since meeting Rosemary."

"What about?"

"That day after the track and field meet if we left the park five minutes sooner or five minutes later I would never have met Rosemary."

"Then fate's been good to you," Vince said.

"I wonder if everything in life is beyond our control," Tommy ruminated.

"Like pieces on a chessboard being pushed around by some unseen hand?"

"Yeah, like that."

"Some people believe that."

"Do you think fate had a hand in Rosemary not seeing me before we shipped out?"

"If fate intervened I think it will be to your benefit."

"I sent her a letter telling her when I'd be back."

"I'm sorry you didn't see Rosemary, Tommy."

"I really wanted to see her, Vince."

"I know you did, Tommy."

"Did you see your girl?"

"No."

"Why not?"

The Burning Hours                                      Page 43

"It's not meant to be."
"Is that fate, Vince?"
"I don't know, maybe."

# 19

Sister Tomasina professed her vows at the end of World War I. Her ascendance to positions of power and influence was meteoric. As director of the Academy for Young Women she controlled the Order's crown jewel. Her native intelligence and political skills were indisputable and her cherubic image belied pervasive ethical, legal and moral failings. She plundered donations from the chapel's devotional candles, installed elderly lonely women in vacant rooms in the school building, and with a dishonest lawyer drafted wills, making her their sole beneficiary. Perhaps Sister Tomasina sunk to the lowest depths of moral turpitude when she sold for personal gain winter clothing donated by a garment manufacturer for distribution to needy families.

When Rosemary informed Sister Tomasina of her desire to marry and raise a family she displayed faux hurt. She prevailed on Rosemary to make a retreat before coming to a final decision. With knowledge of Tommy's intercepted note Sister Tomasina arranged Rosemary to be away during Tommy's leave.

On the day of Rosemary's return from the retreat, Sister Maria Fidelis was managing the reception desk. Young and professed she was well thought of within the religious order. Her olive complexion and brown eyes contrasted with the fair skinned, blue-eyed nuns at the school.

"Hello, Rosemary. How was your retreat?"

"It was good, Sister Maria."

"Did you change your mind?" Sister Maria whispered.

"I'm surer now than I ever was I want to marry and raise a family."

"I'm happy for you," Sister Maria squeezed Rosemary's hand. "I want to tell you something."

"Well," Rosemary said, taking a deep breath, "I'll go tell Sister Tomasina my decision."

"Rosemary," Sister Maria whispered.

"Yes."

The Burning Hours

"While you were on retreat your soldier came here."

"Tommy was here! What do you mean? When was he here?"

"Last week."

"Last week!" Rosemary cried, "Why didn't he tell me he was coming home?"

"He did," Sister Maria said.

"Sister Tomasina destroyed a note he left for you and arranged for you to be away when your soldier was home on leave. What she did was wrong, Rosemary. I'm so sorry."

Stunned and speechless, tears streaming down her face, Rosemary ran through the hallway and burst into Sister Tomasina's office.

"How could you do such a thing?" she demanded. "How could you be so cruel?"

Sister Tomasina came from behind her desk and said, dispassionately, "It is for your own benefit, Rosemary."

"What you did was not for my benefit!"

"This is the life for you, Rosemary, here, with me."

"All this time you were grooming me to be with you!"

"That's how things work."

"You are trying to destroy my life with Tommy!"

"Is that what you call a life? Bedding down with a ruffian and bearing his pups in pain. With me, you will experience none of that."

"My dream with Tommy and having his babies is beautiful. Your twisted mind can't comprehend that!"

"My child," Sister Tomasina cupped Rosemary's face in her hands.

"Take your hands off me!" Rosemary pushed her away. "Don't touch me! You're sick. You make me feel dirty!"

Rosemary dashed through the hallway past Sister Maria out of the building.

"Come back here, Miss McNulty!" Sister Tomasina screamed as nuns gathered in the hallway.

"You come back here! How dare you defy me?"

Rosemary didn't respond, she walked away, didn't look back and disappeared in the distance. Flushed with rage Sister Tomasina became silent, and then she summoned Sister Maria, "Report to my office, Sister, I have a new assignment for you."

"You should know, Sister, I petitioned the Mother House for a release from my vows. I leave next week for the Women's Auxiliary Corps. You will have to find someone else for your new assignment."

The nuns inside the building scattered. A solemn quiet descended on the landing where Sister Tomasina stood feeling strange and out of breath. The vehicles rushing along the boulevard seemed to move in slow motion. She reached for the large crucifix tethered to her belt for solace, but it was beyond her grasp. Swaying side-to-side like a metronome Sister Tomasina lost consciousness and tumbled off the landing.

She was dead before she hit the pavement.

Rosemary's mind was a brew of anger and despair. She didn't feel the warmth of the sun nor the summer breezes. She thought only of Tommy, tears rolling down her face, an unjustified sense of guilt at not seeing Tommy gnawed at her.

"I hope Tommy didn't think I stood him up?" Rosemary fretted experiencing an overwhelming sense of powerlessness. "What could I do?" she demanded of herself. She wanted to curse the evil nun, but didn't want to soil her mind with any thought of her. "Tommy has to know how deeply I love him." Rosemary paused at the spot where they first met. In her mind she began composing a letter to Tommy.

*My Dearest Tommy,*

*My heart aches that I did not see you when you were home. I hope you are well. I hesitate to burden you because you have enough on your mind. I want you to know nothing on the face of this earth would have kept me from being with you had I known when you were coming home. Sister Tomasina intercepted your letter and arranged for me to be away during your leave. Sister Maria told me you had asked for me at the school. If only, I could have been there for you. It seems like I am crying all the time. My heart is broken and will only be mended when we are together again. Words can't tell you how much I love you, Tommy.*

*Come home to me.*

*Your Rosemary.*

# 20

In the snow-laden forest trees by a trick of physics cast a glare onto the clearing as dawn appeared. The German assault was imminent, and like all of the men on the defensive perimeter, Vince and Tommy had only one thought, stay alive.

"That's Darling!" What the hell is he doing?"

"Looks like he's checking the wire," Tommy answered.

"He's dead if they spot him," Vince said.

In the clearing, Darling was a dark shadow slogging through the snow re-stringing sections of snow-covered wire. Then he heard a whistling sound above and froze in place. Within seconds a muffled *Wham* followed; its explosion blew Darling sideways, into the snow.

"Darling's down!" Vince shouted over a roar of gunfire that erupted from the forest.

"He's dead!" Tommy grabbed Vince's arm.

Vince pulled away from Tommy and crawled out of the foxhole. The snow slowed his dash to a slogging walk. His wet boots felt like concrete shoes. He fell and got up firing his rifle, cursing, bullets popping in the snow around him. He saw Darling's body a gray lump in the snow. Tommy opened fire in rapid arcs ripping into Germans converging on Vince and Darling. Vince shot dead three advancing Germans. His empty ammunition clip pinged out of his rifle. A German grenadier was on him. With no time to reload Vince batted away the rifle leveled at him. They grabbed each other engaging in a dance of death that only one would survive. As they struggled Vince smelled the German's last meal on his breath. He jammed his bayonet into the German's side hearing the tear of his uniform, feeling the bump of steel against bone, seeing the squirt of scarlet painting his white tunic. Vince saw impending death in the grenadier's eyes and before they closed and he slid to the ground, he said

The Burning Hours                                    Page 49

*Mein name is Hans*, My name is Hans. On the thin line that separates consciousness from unconsciousness and before shells ripped into his chest and he fell into the crimson splotched snow Vince saw his father.

Soldiers, bone weary from the fighting on the ridge marched in columns on a rutted road past a small farmhouse now the Army's field headquarters. A line of replacements marched on the opposite side of the road to the front line. In a corral two milking cows stood incurious. On the side of the road, the soldiers passed a life-size crucifix heavy with snow; some of the men knelt, said a silent prayer, and returned to the march to the rear.

"What's going on up there?" a replacement hollered.

"It's snowing," a bloodied corporal, yelled back.

Major Klaus Von Richter silently awaited the arrival of a senior American officer who would conduct his interrogation. At a windowless wall a few feet from Major Von Richter, Captain Hanley was talking aloud to himself about the soldiers who broke the German assault.

"I can provide added clarity to your question, Captain," Major Von Richter said.

"What do you mean?" Captain Hanley answered.

"I witnessed that action."

"Impossible," Captain Hanley said, "There were thousands of our guys fighting along that line."

"The assault you wonder about was under my command. That battle is now over, your line held. Without compromising my honor as a German officer, I tell you our assault was planned to penetrate your left flank. It didn't work because of two of your soldiers."

"What are you talking about? Two of our guys did all that. Has the Colonel gotten here?" Captain Hanley hollered to an orderly.

"Yeah!" a voice responded. "His jeep just pulled up."

Colonel James McLeod removed his helmet and banged it on a wood plank table sending wet snow into the air. 'Pete!" he shouted. "Put the supplies over here!"

"Okay!" Sergeant Pete Petrocelli answered.

"Colonel," Captain Hanley said, "The prisoner inside said he knows what happened in the action on the left flank."

"Baloney! No one man could know what happened up there. It's a waste of time, Hanley. Let's see what we could get out of him and then send him to the rear."

"He was the commander of that sector."

"This is the army, Hanley, it's not the Boy Scouts."

Major Von Richter stood saber straight and executed a crisp salute when Colonel McLeod entered the small room, he did not click his heels.

Surprised, Colonel McLeod returned Major Von Richter's salute.

"Have a seat Klaus."

"Thank you, Colonel."

"It's James, remember."

"Yes, thank you, James."

"Get back to work!" Colonel McLeod ordered. "What are you gawking at?"

For a few seconds dazed silence prevailed in the small farmhouse, and then as quickly as it came, it was broken.

"How are your parents?"

"They are well, in Switzerland."

"How is Renata?"

"She married a university professor; they have two children."

"I enjoyed their company when they visited in New York."

"And they enjoyed meeting my roommate from New Jersey."

"You know Klaus I had an all-time crush on Renata."

"You should have pursued it, James."

"A fireman's son from New Jersey and an aristocratic lady from Germany, it wasn't in the cards."

"You should have played your hand, James."

"It was a losing hand."

"You never tried so you don't know."

Suddenly Colonel McLeod's emotions were imprisoned by the sense of never knowing what could have been. He smiled wryly and said, simply, "Yeah, I never tried."

"Imagine my shock when I learned my roommate at Columbia is the son of a German Baron," Colonel McLeod said, changing the subject.

"And my surprise when I found my roommate is a fireman's son from Ridgefield Park."

"They were good days," Colonel McLeod said, nostalgically.

"Illusions of a better time."

"Where's Sergeant Petrocelli?"

"He's coming in now, Colonel," Captain Hanley answered.

"Pete!" Colonel McLeod shouted, "Bring me a pack of Camel's and two brandies."

"I got Old Gold, we don't have any brandy, this isn't Delmonico's, Colonel."

"What do you have?"

"Johnny Walker."

"Red or Black Label."

"Does it matter?" Sergeant Petrocelli retorted.

'Just bring whatever you have, Pete."

"Captain Hanley tells me you witnessed the action on the ridge's left flank. Is there anything you can tell me? I know you will not compromise your honor."

Sergeant Petrocelli placed a pack of Old Gold and two tin cups of Scotch on the table.

"Thanks, Pete."

"You tolerate that from a subordinate, James? It wouldn't happen in our command."

"You mean, Pete. There are some things even a command protocol can't control, Klaus. Do you recognize Sergeant Petrocelli?"

"Why should I recognize him?"

"Remember the break we took from studying for final exams."

"We drove on the George Washington Bridge into your home town," Klaus recalled.

"We rowed on the Hackensack for a while."

"It was hot and sunny I remember, a good day."

"Then we went to a tavern."

"Across the street from your town hall."

"Right."

"We drank wine and I had my first taste of pizza."

"A long time ago, now, recall the waiter."

Major Von Richter paused, "Sergeant Petrocelli!"

"His father owns the tavern. Pete and I have been friends from childhood. We were classmates in high school. Pete was an All-State running back."

"And that is…" Major Von Richter let the question hang."

"Football's best of the best."

"And you, James? What was your contribution to the team?"

"Second-string quarterback. I wasn't in the same class as Pete."

"Now, you are Sergeant Petrocelli's commanding officer."

"I don't know about that," Colonel McLeod laughed.

Major Von Richter and Colonel McLeod exhaled clouds of smoke into the room's frigid air followed by a silent pause.

"To those good days," James raised his cup.

"To those good days," Klaus repeated.

"Hanley! I need you to record Major Von Richter's witness."

The Burning Hours

"Okay, Colonel."

"What can you tell me, Major?" Colonel McLeod asked reverting to military protocol, dispensing with warm informalities.

"You know by now our plan was to penetrate lightly defended positions along your defensive perimeter. In the pre-dawn hours the plan was working," Major Von Richter said, twisting his index and middle finger signaling a desire for another cigarette.

Major McLeod slid the pack of Old Gold along the table.

"Keep it, Major," he said, leaning across the table lighting Von Richter's cigarette.

"It is the unexpected that upsets the equation," Major Von Richter dragged deeply on his cigarette, "this action proved that rule."

"Are you getting this, Hanley?"

"Yes Sir, Colonel."

"Go on, Major."

"Had that soldier not been checking your wire, and had our mortar shelling been less accurate, the outcome might have been different," Major Von Richter sipped his Scotch and then continued.

"When your soldier went down from our mortar blast another soldier came out of his foxhole to aid him. I saw him through my binoculars; he was more than 100 meters away. The snow slowed his charge he was an easy target for our grenadiers. Your soldier got to his fallen comrade at the wire firing into our advance until he was shot down."

"Get a map, Hanley. I want to get a clearer picture of the sector."

"Yes Sir," Captain Hanley answered and left the room.

Colonel McLeod lit another cigarette and toyed with his Scotch. True to his aristocratic bearing Major Von Richter puffed his cigarette and sipped his Scotch with the aplomb he had displayed numerous times at State dinners.

The Burning Hours

"Is this what you are looking for, Colonel?"

"Yeah, thanks, Hanley."

"Point out the sector you observed, Major?"

Major Von Richter drew a line with his hand on the map.

"Here," he pointed.

"Where along the line did the action take place"?

"Here," he pointed.

"Check the unit operating in this sector, Hanley," Colonel McLeod ordered.

"Yes Sir."

Major McLeod said nothing. He got up and went into an outer room of the farmhouse. He wiped cold fog from a window with the back of his hand and stared through it, past the milking cows, still motionless, past the field of giant spruce trees sagging from heavy snow, into the sulfur gray sky. Major McLeod was lost in the rare serenity of the moment when Captain Hanley approached him.

"The 24th, the guys took heavy casualties."

"Okay, Captain," Colonel McLeod returned to the windowless room.

"Please continue, Major."

"A second soldier came out of the foxhole. He charged through the snow firing his automatic weapon across our attack line, knocking down our advancing grenadiers. There was suppressing fire coming from your defensive line, but it didn't halt our assault. The soldier's weapon blazed relentlessly as he pushed through the snow to his fallen comrades. When his ammunition ran out he threw his grenades point blank into our advance and then he did what you cannot teach a soldier to do."

Major Von Richter sipped what remained of his Scotch and put down his empty tin cup.

"Go on, Major," Colonel McLeod said.

"He stripped grenades from the belts of his two fallen comrades and threw at close range exploding them into our

The Burning Hours                                    Page 55

advancing grenadiers who were only yards from him. And then, your soldier reloaded and attacked the center of our advance his rifle non-stop spewing red and purple flames until our assault broke in confusion."

Major Von Richter paused conflicted by the courage of his grenadiers and a few American soldiers.

"Your soldier kept firing until he got back to his fallen comrades. He was shouting something to one of the men. I wish I knew what he was saying."

*"Don't you die on me, Vince! Don't you die!"*

"Our artillery blasts unleashed a storm of pine needles and splinters off the treetops in the forest. They slammed into the soldier's face, blinding him, but he kept firing," Colonel Von Richter paused, "and then a mortar blast silenced him, its explosion lifted him off the ground, and he fell on top of his comrade, he was no longer moving."

"Call HQ, Hanley. I want to know who those three guys are."

"In a better time those men would be drinking and singing ribald songs, together in your tavern or in a *Rathskeller* in Heidelberg, wars make no sense, James."

"Yeah," James nodded in agreement.

"I can tell you the name of the second soldier."

"How could you know?" Colonel McLeod said, incredulously.

"The sector had quieted after our retreat. I went with my aide past the bodies of the dead and wounded to where the three men lay next to one our grenadiers. I had to know, James. I brushed the snow off the back pack of the young man who shattered our plan. I thought *Der Kampf wird verloren* - The battle is lost."

"What's the soldier's name? Did you check the others? Were they dead?" Colonel McLeod questioned, rapid-fire.

"PFC Domenico Tomasso. I do not know the names of the other two soldiers. I saw no signs of life."

"Dead! All three!"

The Burning Hours          Page 56

"I believe so."

" Christ Almighty!" Colonel McLeod slammed his hand on the table.

# 21

**The Conover Estate**
**Westport, Connecticut**
**Winter 1945**

Charles Conover folded *The New York Times* and placed it on his desk, its headline blared, "Yanks Take Bastogne." Now in his fifties Charles looked through the window of his Cuban Mahogany paneled library at the kidney shaped swimming pool on his estate's recreation area.

His mind drifted back in time to a sweltering June day in 1915.

From the estate's library Charles Conover then twenty five years of age, the youngest chairman of a major financial enterprise in America watched a shirtless young man cutting and carefully laying marble around a kidney-shaped blue water swimming pool. The artistry of manual labor intrigued Charles, noting mentally the heaviest thing he had ever lifted was his briefcase.

Charles went outside, to the pool.

"Good looking job."

"Thanks," Paolo Bellini responded without looking up at Charles.

"Can I get you something to drink?"

"No, thanks," Paolo answered, fitting a marble block into a curvature of the swimming pool.

"I'm Charles Conover please call me CC."

"How are you, CC? I'm Paolo," he said wiping glistening perspiration from his face and without missing a step he went back to work shaping and smoothing the edges of another block of marble.

"Can I call you Paul?"

"I prefer Paolo."

"Paolo it is. Use the pool, if you like; there are trunks and towels in the cabana."

"Thanks," Paolo responded.

"Maybe, I'll give you a hand, tomorrow and learn something new."

"You'll get blisters."

"That's okay," Charles said looking to a car he didn't recognize coming along the tree-lined driveway toward the recreation area.

"Are you expecting someone?"

"My lunch."

"Your lunch knows how to drive a car?" Charles laughed.

"You're a funny guy, CC, that's my sister."

A gray car pulled up close to Paolo's marble-laden truck. A young woman, her raven hair pulled back and gathered with a blue bow got out. Her fair skin was flushed pink, her hazel eyes sparkled in the summer sun. She handed Paolo a brown paper bag and a liquid-filled bottle. She smiled demurely at the tall slender young man staring at her.

"Thanks honey," Paolo said. "What's in the bottle?"

"Water, Paolo. It's too hot for anything, else."

"You are so smart for a little sister."

"I don't mean to be rude," Charles said his eyes locked onto Adalina. "Please introduce me."

"This is my sister, Adalina," Paolo said, "this is Charles Conover his family owns this place."

"Hello, Charles."

Charles shook Adalina's hand; it was gentle and soft, he held it longer than propriety dictated. Paolo leaned on his truck swigging water, laughing to himself at the uncomfortable scene unfolding before him.

"Don't you have to get back to class?" Paolo asked, sternly.

"Yes, nice to have met you."

"Where are you going to school?"

"Westport Women's College."

"What are you studying?"

"I'm studying to be a teacher."

"When will you graduate?"

"This year."

"Are you done, CC?"

"Sorry, Paolo."

"I'll get to class on time. Paolo is such a big brother," an easy smile crossed her face.

Charles was speechless for a few moments.

"Is it okay, Paolo, if I ask Adalina to lunch, here, tomorrow?"

"You're really fast, CC, what about me? She told you I'm her big brother."

"Of course you too, Paolo."

"If Adalina wants to have lunch with you, it's up to her."

"Tomorrow, noon, Adalina, okay?" Charles said, almost breathlessly, "Will you come, too, Paolo?"

"Gotta' look out for my little sister."

"I understand. Is tomorrow alright with you, Adalina?"

"Sure, Adalina smiled."

"Okay," Charles said.

"Okay," Adalina repeated.

"You're sure," Charles asked.

"I'm sure," Adalina answered.

"I'll have cook make us a light summer lunch."

"That will be nice," Adalina said.

"Yeah, real nice, now, get to class, Adalina," Paolo ordered.

"May I walk with you to your car?"

"Alright," Adalina smiled.

"I wish you could stay longer," Charles started for Adalina's hand, but pulled back.

"I really have to get to class," Adalina said, looking toward Paolo who was pointing to the road outside of the estate.

"I'm looking forward to seeing you, tomorrow."

"I am, too," Adalina smiled.

"Be careful driving."

"I'll see you tomorrow."

Charles stayed with Adalina until she drove away. She turned onto the estate's intersecting road and soon was out of sight. Charles stared at the empty driveway. Suddenly he felt an acute concern for the safety of a young woman he had just met.

Charles Conover was Westport's most eligible bachelor. His pictures in the *Westport Tattler* with New England's most desirable young women were fodder for gossip. Betting pools sprung up throughout the country club circuit on who would be the lucky girl. But, none of the women Charles dated had elicited the confusing sensation he felt for Adalina. For Charles Conover, tomorrow couldn't come fast enough.

"My sister's no plaything, CC," Paolo warned.

"What? Did you say something?" Paolo's voice broke Charles's spell.

"Yeah, I said my sister is no plaything," Paolo repeated.

"Why would you think that?"

"Adalina is a good girl," Paolo said, proudly. "Since mom and pop died, I've been looking out for her. As long as I'm around nobody's gonna' hurt her."

"I would never think of hurting her, Paolo."

"You got a reputation, CC you're all over the newspapers."

"The right girl could change a guy."

"Yeah, we'll see about that," Paolo raised a skeptical brow.

"I'll see you, tomorrow."

"Okay, tomorrow," Paolo said, he didn't look up.

# 22

Colonel McLeod's mind swum in a dark pool of nothingness. He didn't think of the victory on the ridge nor did he recall his exchange of memories with Major Von Richter, only quiet filled the vessel of his mind.

The banging of the field phone jolted him back to reality. Colonel McLeod looked across the room to Captain Hanley, who was recording the information coming over the phone.

Captain Hanley hung up the phone and turned to Colonel McLeod. "Sir, the other two men with Private Tomasso is PFC Vincent Farro and Sergeant Carroll Darling."

"What's their condition?"

"There's no report on their condition, yet."

"Keep me updated, Captain."

"Yes sir," Captain Hanley replied.

"You couldn't tell if these three men were alive, Klaus," Colonel McLeod reverted to the familiar.

"If there was life, James, the cold and fog masked it. I couldn't tell."

"Hanley!" Colonel McLeod shouted into the outer room.

"Yes sir," Captain Hanley came running.

"Write up Major Von Richter's eyewitness account for my signature. I'm putting Tomasso in for the Medal of Honor, Farro for silver and Darling for bronze. Prepare the paperwork for my signature."

"Yes, sir, Colonel."

"It's fitting, James."

"I hope it's not posthumous."

"Brave men," Major Von Richter responded.

"Pete!" Colonel McLeod shouted.

"Yes sir," Sergeant Petrocelli appeared.

The Burning Hours
Page 62

"Get your jeep ready. You're going to drive Major Von Richter to HQ."

"I'm set to go, Colonel I was waiting for your order."

Colonel McLeod stood up and Major Von Richter followed his lead.

"Sergeant Petrocelli will escort you to headquarters, Major," Colonel McLeod rounded the table and the two men shook hands.

"To better days, James," Major Von Richter saluted.

Colonel McLeod returned Major Von Richter's salute.

"Sooner than later, major."

"This way Major," Sergeant Petrocelli swept his right arm.

"I would like to know more about your football All-State, Sergeant," Major Von Richter said.

"Glad to fill you in, Major," Sergeant Petrocelli answered.

Sergeant Petrocelli's jeep started up and drove away.

Inside the small farmhouse Colonel McLeod barked orders for reports on the battle's aftermath. He couldn't forget the fates of Tomasso, Farro and Darling. He lit another cigarette and waited for the phone to ring.

# 23

At twenty five years of age, Charles Conover was the youngest board chairman of a major financial institution in America. Renowned for his fearless deal making Charles generated huge profits building a banking empire second to none.

The self-confidence that propelled him to the dizzying heights of corporate finance now abandoned him. In the seconds of their meeting a strange feeling overwhelmed him; Charles fell hard for Adalina. Unlike the women he dated she was sweet, gentle and genuine. The night before their luncheon Charles suffered the exquisite agony of a young man in love. Sleep eluded him. The prospect of rejection assailed him. Charles Conover was in free fall.

The day Charles had waited for was perfect, sunny and clear with gentle breezes and birds chirping in the tree-lined driveway. Inside, the Italianate estate's marble floors created a cool environment in the sun room that looked through floor to ceiling glass-faceted arched windows to an expansive garden of sculpted hedges, a flowering garden and to small spraying Bernini-like fountains sparkling in the sunlit afternoon.

Charles kept moving the table settings as if they were pieces on a chessboard. Satisfied with the seating plan that placed Adalina by his side, he went outside waiting for Paolo's and Adalina's arrivals. He kept checking his watch. It was past noon. He watched vehicles his emotions falling when none turned into the estate's driveway. As Charles checked his watch, again he heard the sound of an approaching automobile. He heaved a sigh of relief at the sight of Paolo's old Ford bumping along the estate's cobblestone driveway rounding the spraying circular fountain easing to a stop next to a burgundy Grand Paige touring car and a canary yellow Stutz Bearcat. Charles's emotional tangle unwound in his excitement of seeing Adalina.

"Is it okay if I leave the car here?" Paolo asked.

"Sure," Charles answered.

"I wanted to be sure, it looks like the poor relative next to these two beauties," Paolo said, switching off the idling motor.

"It's okay where it is."

Charles went to the car's passenger side and opened its door. He offered his hand to Adalina who wore a pale blue dress just below her knees and a gold locket around her neck, her black hair was swept back and ruffled with a matching blue ribbon.

They exchanged smiles.

"You look lovely, Adalina," Charles stumbled out the words.

"Thank you, Charles."

"I'm really glad to see you."

"I'm glad to see you, too."

"I like your dress."

"She made it, herself," Paolo interjected.

"It's really attractive, Adalina."

"She's not the only one who makes things," Paolo said handing a package to Charles.

"What's this?"

"A bottle of red wine I made myself."

"Thanks, Paolo that's real thoughtful of you."

"Go slow when drinking it, CC, it's young and powerful."

Adalina took a bouquet of asters and dahlias from the car, "I brought this for the cook."

"She grew them herself, CC," Paolo proudly said.

"You're a girl of many talents," Charles smiled.

"I have a small flower garden at the back of the house. I enjoy growing flowers. It's a refreshing break from my studies, chores and tending to Paolo's business.

"Shall we go inside?" Charles said, gesturing to open molded double doors that led into a vestibule of gleaming marble and a staircase of gold-finished banisters that spiraled upward culminating in spacious second and third levels.

At sixty years of age Maura Bailey was vibrant and sharp-tongued as the day she came to Connecticut from Ireland four decades earlier. For thirty years she served the Conover family as estate manager and cook playing an important role in the formative years of young Charles, who considered Maura an elder sister, a friend, and a confidant.

Normally, Charles would seek Maura's advice, but this time he was unusually reticent. From the estate's front entrance, she watched Charles, Paolo and Adalina come to the landing, and in that moment the source of Charles's uncharacteristic nervousness became obvious.

"Paolo, this is Maura Bailey, Miss Bailey has been with the Conover family long before I was born, Miss Bailey, please say hello to Paolo Bellini."

"Nice to meet ya'," Paolo shook Miss Bailey's hand.

"Pleased to meet you, Mr. Bellini, that's a powerful grip you have," and turning to Charles, Maura asked, "Who is this young lady, Master Charles?"

"Excuse us for a minute," Charles took Maura aside, "Don't call me Master, Maura, that was a long time ago, I never liked that name, anyway."

"You are terribly touchy, Charles, I was teasing," Miss Bailey whispered.

"Quit teasing, it's embarrassing," he whispered.

"If you insist, Master, I mean, Mr. Conover," Maura teased.

"Come on, Maura, I insist."

"If you insist," Maura promised.

Each time Charles smiled Adalina returned an enigmatic grin masking her enjoyment at his discomfort.

"This is Adalina Bellini, Miss Bailey, Paolo's sister."

"Hello, dear, I am glad to meet you."

"Here is an expression of our appreciation for lunch," Adalina handed her flower arrangement to Maura.

"You are thoughtful the flowers are beautiful," Maura said, kissing Adalina's cheeks while Charles looked on envious of Maura.

Inside the sunroom Charles ushered Paolo and Adalina to their seats.

"I thought you would like a view of the garden, Adalina."

"Thank you, Charles."

"If it's okay with Paolo I'd like to take you on a tour of the garden."

"I'd like that."

"It's okay with me," Paolo consented.

"I'll see about the wine," Charles said, and left the room.

A vase containing Adalina's flowers sat on a desk in the estate's kitchen where Maura busily plated summer salads of angel hair pasta, arugula and pear-shavings laced with a light vinaigrette dressing, luncheon rolls and butter.

"Come in," Maura acknowledged Charles's appearance at the kitchen's entrance.

"Everything looks wonderful."

"What is happening to you, Charles?"

"I can't say, now."

"It's that young woman."

"How can you tell?"

"How does one know the sun is in the sky? You know, because you see it."

"Is it that obvious?"

"It is to me; remember I have known you all your life."

"I've been in her company for only a few minutes, Maura. When she left for school, I wanted to take her hand and keep her with me. What if she's not interested?"

"It's the chance you take, Charles. She is adorable and she is real she is the best thing that could have happened for you. There's no comparison with the artificial candy you have been dating. I have a sixth sense about these things," Maura patted Charles's face. "You have a good heart, Charles, and you have grown into a considerate and thoughtful man, I think she will see your virtues, but it's up to you."

"Do you think so?"

"I do."

"If you say so, Maura."

"Was there another reason for your visit to my kitchen?"

"Yes," Charles tapped his temple. "I'd like a chilled bottle of white Bordeaux."

"An inspired selection, is there anything else?"

"Not that I can think of."

"Don't keep that young woman waiting."

# 24

Colonel McLeod's orders to join the push against the weakened German line arrived. Dismantling the farmhouse of maps, records and equipment was underway. Transports idled in the newly falling snow along the snow covered road. Men of the combat regiment, what was left of it, checked their backpacks, weapons and ammunition readying to move out.

Throughout the war, Colonel McLeod had seen death numerous times; several of the dead were his friends. After brief moments of remembrance he'd forget, because forgetting in combat was a mechanism for preserving one's sanity in a world gone insane.

For unfathomable reasons, Colonel McLeod couldn't discharge the three soldiers on the ridge from his mind. Each time the phone rang he looked to Captain Hanley who shook his head, negatively. He then lit a cigarette and waited as long as he could for the phone to ring, again.

Colonel McLeod went outside on the farmhouse deck. He watched Sergeant Petrocelli complete his check of the jeep's rear mounted machine gun. Heavy transports pulled onto the rutted road going to the front. Columns of soldiers, their weariness buried into their souls slogged in columns parallel to the transports.

"Ready to go, Colonel?" Sergeant Petrocelli shouted.

"Okay, Pete," Colonel McLeod crushed his cigarette, adjusted his helmet and descended the splintered stairs of the farmhouse into the idling jeep.

Sergeant Petrocelli rolled into the advancing motorized line back to the front.

"No news on the three guys on the ridge, Colonel," Petrocelli asked.

"Nothing, Pete."

The Burning Hours

"Here comes Captain Hanley!" Sergeant Petrocelli exclaimed.

"Hold up, Pete!"

Petrocelli pulled out of the column easing the jeep to a stop.

"Colonel! I had a call from HQ about the guys on the ridge."

"What did you get, Hanley?"

"Darling is okay, a concussion," he said, out of breath. "He'll be back on the line in a few days."

"What about Farro and Tomasso?"

"Farro got shot up, but he'll be back on the line in a few weeks and Tomasso…"

"What about Tomasso?"

"He's in real bad shape, Colonel," Hanley hesitated.

"Spit it out, Hanley."

"Tomasso is blind, Colonel," Hanley said, waiting for McLeod's reaction.

"What else do you have on Tomasso?"

"He'll be moved to the general hospital in Liege."

Colonel McLeod acknowledged Captain Hanley's report and then drifted into a protracted silence.

"Colonel," Petrocelli said, and with no response forthcoming, he punched Colonel McLeod's arm, "Colonel."

"Let's go, Pete," McLeod answered.

# 25

Maura Bailey rolled a serving cart into the sunroom parking it against the wall adjacent to the window looking out to the garden. After serving Charles, Paolo and Adalina she took a bottle of white Bordeaux from a silver cooler poured the wine into long stem crystal glasses placing a glass at each place setting.

"Enjoy your lunch and let me know if anything else is needed," she said, and returned the wine bottle to the ice cooler.

"Thank you, Miss Bailey," Charles said as Maura turned to leave the room. Paolo and Adalina added their gratitude.

"The Bordeaux is from the Conover Winery in Napa Valley," Charles said raising his glass followed by Paolo and Adalina, "I hope you enjoy it as I know I am enjoying luncheon with you."

"The Bordeaux is crisp I detect a hint of citrus aromatics, it's delicious. Your winery should be congratulated on the wine's balance," Paolo offered his congratulations and took a second sip of the Bordeaux.

"I'll be sure to let father and mother know," Charles said, impressed by Paolo's knowledge of wine.

"Your father and mother run the winery," Paolo asked, somewhat incredulously.

"It was always father's dream to own and manage his own winery. When he was confident I could manage the company's affairs, he and mother purchased a sprawling vineyard in California's Napa Valley and they are having the time of their lives."

"That's wonderful for them, Charles," Adalina said, wistfully recalling her all too brief time with her mother and father.

"You go easy on the wine, Adalina," Paolo admonished.

"I'm a big girl, now."

"You're barely twenty."

"Okay, start your lunch, Paolo, it looks delicious, Charles."

Between buttered rolls and bites of Angel Hair pasta Paolo had twisted onto his fork, he matter-of-factly said, "This is an Alexander Jackson Davis design."

"Yes, it is. You are familiar with Italianate architecture, Paolo," Charles asked.

"I am," Paolo answered, sipping his wine, "I'm gonna build these mansions, one day," Paolo said, heartily consuming his lunch.

"Paolo has his first big project in New Haven, next month, Charles," Adalina said.

"That's terrific, Paolo. What are you building?"

"A three-bay car service building, everything is arranged the crews, the equipment and the budget."

"Let me know if financing is needed," Charles said.

"I've taken care of that," Paolo paused and took another sip of wine, "by your bank," he added.

"I trust we gave you fair terms."

"Very fair, couldn't have gotten better, and I tried," Paolo chuckled.

"Paolo, the bank is expanding I'd like you to meet with our building department, if you are interested."

"I'm always interested in growing my business, but no favors, I insist on that CC."

"No favors," Charles agreed, turning his attention to Adalina.

"Are you enjoying your lunch?"

"Miss Bailey is a wonderful cook."

"She sure is," Paolo added. "However, I have one suggestion, CC."

"What is that?"

"In addition to butter, we Sicilians use virgin olive oil with a little salt and pepper for dipping."

"Don't pay any attention to him, Charles, Paolo can be a pest. The entire lunch is perfectly delightful."

"His friends call him CC," Paolo chimed in.

"I prefer Charles," Adalina smiled.

"Your locket is very attractive," Charles said.

Adalina took the locket in her hand, snapped it open and turned her body to Charles.

"It's a graduation present from Paolo," and showing it to Charles, she said, "these are pictures of papa and mama, they passed away a long time ago.

"I'm sorry, may, I?" Charles said, extending his hand.

With a silent nod, Paolo acknowledged Charles's expression of sympathy.

Adalina handed Charles the locket, and their hands touched, briefly.

"Your mother is beautiful, you are her image."

Adalina blushed.

"Your father is a handsome man, such a magnificent mustache, I wonder who Paolo takes after," Charles laughed.

"You're a funny guy, CC," Paolo retorted, and in an instant the room filled with laughter.

# 26

"Patience, patience," Maura Bailey repeated, as she responded to the constant banging on the front door.

Victoria Vandermere stood in the open doorway the sun at her back stunning in a cream-colored riding outfit with matching boots and a brown velvet bowler-type from which her blond pony tail streamed along the middle of her back.

"Who belongs to the flivver next to the touring car, Maura?" Victoria asked, quickly adding, "Charles should not permit tradesmen to park their vehicles at the front of the house, he's so egalitarian," she said, lightly tapping her riding crop against Miss Bailey's chest for emphasis.

"Is Mr. Conover expecting you?" Maura said, icily, flicking Victoria's riding crop off her blouse with the back of her hand.

"We have a 3:00 o'clock riding date," Victoria answered, stretching her neck in the direction of the sunroom.

"It's now 1:00 o'clock, Miss Vandermere. Mr. Conover has a luncheon engagement. I'll let him know you are here," Maura said, muttering artificial candy under her breath.

"Mr. Conover ..." Maura started.

Victoria brushed past Maura into the sunroom.

"I thought we could get a head start on our riding date."

Startled at her sudden appearance Charles rose from his chair. Paolo and Adalina glanced at each other, and then at Victoria, who eyed the sunroom's luncheon preparations before settling on Paolo, and particularly on Adalina.

"Are you going to introduce me, Charles?"

"Of course," Charles replied, "Victoria Vandermere, please meet Paolo Bellini and his sister, Adalina."

Paolo stood up and said, "Hello." Adalina remained seated and echoed Paolo's response.

The Burning Hours                                           Page 74

"You are quite a burly fellow, Mr. Bellini," Victoria said, and then with her scrutinizing gray eyes, "Your sister is darling," she added, acidly.

Paolo didn't respond.

As Charles began speaking Victoria cut him off condescendingly inquiring of Adalina, "Where did you buy that charming dress I don't recognize its designer?"

"I designed and sewed it myself."

"Do you take in work, Miss ...?"

"Bellini, my name is Adalina Bellini. I sew only for myself."

"My New York couturier will be relieved that his enterprise is safe from your talents," she mocked.

Charles grabbed Victoria's arm and with restrained anger, said, "I'll see you out."

# 27

After Victoria's departure Charles lingered outside seething at her insensitive barbs directed at Adlina. He wondered if Paolo and Adalina thought lunch with the immigrants' brother and sister was nothing more than an amusing episode in his privileged life. When he went inside Paolo and Adalina were in the vestibule waiting for him.

"Are you leaving?" Charles asked.

"It was a wonderful lunch," Adalina answered.

"Please, don't go. You must see the garden, Adalina," Charles pleaded.

"Adalina has bookkeeping and school preparations. I'll be back, Monday to finish the job," Paolo said, coolly.

"Okay, Paolo, I'll have a check prepared for the balance I owe."

"Thanks," Paolo responded.

"I didn't expect Victoria she was out of line. I hope you don't think I share her outlook," Charles tried to dissuade Paolo and Adalina from leaving.

"We had a wonderful time, Charles, didn't we Paolo?"

"Thanks for inviting us," Paolo said, adding, "Please thank Miss Bailey."

Charles looked pleadingly at Adalina, and then resignedly he said, "If you insist then you must go."

On the landing, Charles and Paolo shook hands.

"See you, Monday," Charles said.

"Monday," Paolo, confirmed.

"Goodbye, Charles."

"I'll see you, again."

Adalina managed a small smile.

Charles watched Paolo and Adalina drive away and went into the mansion.

# 28

The sunroom was quiet, only echoes of the recent conviviality reverberated in Charles's mind. He picked up Adalina's half-full wine glass and walked across the room to the window where he looked into the garden and the fountains sparkling in the mid-day sun.

"Shall I prepare desserts, Charles?" Maura inquired.

"They won't be returning, Maura."

"I'm sorry, Charles, you were having such a good time."

"Paolo and Adalina asked me to express their thanks to you for lunch."

"I can guess what happened. Will you see them, again?" Maura asked.

"Paolo will be here, Monday to finish work on the pool."

"And the young lady?"

"I don't know," Charles said, somberly.

"What do you mean, you don't know?"

"I have witnessed Victoria's acid tongue before, but never with such cruelty. She was appalling, Maura and Adalina was so dignified."

"You tolerated Miss Vandemere far too long, Charles."

"I know that, now."

"I'll clean up. You should get ready for your riding date with Miss Vandermere," Maura said, disdainfully.

"I canceled it," Charles said, swishing the wine in Adalina's glass.

"Do you have feelings for this young woman, Miss Bellini?"

"Isn't the garden beautiful in the sunlight?" Charles deflected Maura's question.

Undeterred, Maura repeated, "Well, do you?"

Charles didn't answer.

"*The Wall Street Journal* says you are a financial prodigy. How could you be so smart in business and fear the calling of your heart?"

"Do you believe in love at first sight, Maura?"

"Love is a powerful force, Charles it could happen in an instant."

"Out there," Charles pointed to the garden, "I planned to steal a kiss, and I hoped she would reciprocate, but it wasn't meant to be."

"You're impossible, Charles," Maura said, clearing the table.

Charles silently looked out the window to garden. Maura continued clearing china, glassware and flatware louder than usual to get Charles's attention.

At the sound of the moving cart, Charles turned to her.

"I love her Maura," Charles confessed.

"Then go after her, Charles; there's no substitute for the real thing."

# 29

Paolo Bellini was running late Monday. He drove Adalina to the school library and then picked up bluestone slabs at the quarry to finish the swimming pool job. Adalina was silent Saturday on their way home from their date with Charles. She nodded no when Paolo asked if she wanted to talk. After parking in front of their one-story wood frame house Paolo asked if she wanted to go for a walk. Again, she nodded no and went into the house to her room. There her emotions in turmoil, tears welling in her eyes, Adalina sat motionless for a long time on her bed. She undressed, pulled her pillow against her body and curling into a fetal position she cried herself to sleep. Adalina remained cloistered in her room for the rest of the day. She had no appetite, she couldn't concentrate on her school assignments and when Paolo knocked on her door, she didn't respond.

Throughout his weekend questions swirled in Charles's mind. How deeply did he hurt Adalina? Why did he agree to a riding date on the day of their luncheon knowing Victoria's vindictive nature? Racked with guilt Charles spent sleepless nights and woke each morning exhausted. When simple mathematical computations resulted in errors he quit working. He refused breakfast prompting Maura to tell him he was lovesick.

When Charles looked out the window of his library to the swimming pool Paolo was busy laying out the remaining bluestone slabs. Paolo heard him approach, but continued working without acknowledging his presence.

"Paolo," Charles said.

"Yeah," Paolo answered, he didn't look up.

"I have a check for the balance I owe you."

"Not until I'm finished."

"I trust you," Charles answered.

"When the job is done and you are satisfied, then I'll accept your payment."

"Come on, Paolo, can't we talk."

Paolo put down his trowel and stood up.

"Let's talk."

"I'm sorry about what happened Saturday."

"Yeah, so am I."

"I hope you and Adalina don't think I had anything to do with Victoria's behavior."

"You rich people aren't like the rest of us. I've seen people who were just trying to make a living made fools of by your crowd and then they'd laugh about it," Paolo said, returning to fitting and sealing slabs in place.

"Stunned by Paolo's observation, Charles said, "Do you think I'm like that, Paolo?"

"Remember, I told you my sister is no plaything."

"Do you think I would hurt Adalina, Paolo? Do you think that?" Charles repeated, and then said, "If you do, we have nothing more to say to each other."

Paolo stood up, and said, "My gut tells me you're a good guy, but I can't get out of my mind hearing my sister cry all night. Why in hell would you make a date with that woman so close to our lunch?"

"It was a mistake I wish I could go back. I was going to tell Victoria there was someone else. You have to believe me, Paolo."

"How was your ride?" Paolo asked, sarcastically.

"Give me a break, Paolo, there was no ride, I broke off with Victoria when we were outside, on the landing."

"Yeah, alright," Paolo continued working.

"How is Adalina?" Charles asked, concernedly.

"Ask her," Paolo snapped.

"Will she be here, today?"

"No."

"Where is she? I have to see her."

"She's in town."

The Burning Hours Page 80

"Where in town, Paolo?" come on, don't make me beg.

"She's at school."

"At school?" Charles queried.

"At the library."

Charles dashed to the front of the mansion to the Stutz Bearcat. He jumped into the car, turned on the ignition and gunned the motor.

"Where are you going?" Paolo asked.

"For Adalina," Charles said, and began pulling away.

"She wouldn't be caught dead in this car," Paolo warned, running along side of the moving Bearcat.

"I'll see you later," Charles said above the roar of the engine as he sped away.

The Burning Hours

# 30

The three-story red brick building in downtown Westport was home to the Westport Women's College and host to a bookstore and café frequented by artists, musicians and writers. On a quiet day faint sounds of the horns and whistles of ships plowing the Long Island Sound coastline could be heard. Electric transmission polls their power lines, sagging in the heat were visible as far as the eye could see. Across the street a scattering of people waited for the unpredictable arrival of the Main Street Trolley.

Charles slowed his Stutz Bearcat to a stop in view of the college drawing curious stares from onlookers wondering who piloted such an expensive piece of machinery. Each time the door to the building swung open and people emerged, Charles stood up in the Bearcat for a better view. When the heat became too oppressive he walked around never losing sight of the building's main entrance.

"Hey, mister! Get my ball before it rolls under your car!" shouted a rail thin freckled-face young boy with floppy red hair and a space between his front teeth.

Charles picked up the ball that bounced in his direction and tossed it to the young boy who ran to him from across the street.

"Is this your car?"

"Yes, it is," Charles answered.

"That's some car, 60 horsepower engine and all."

"You know a lot about cars."

"I read about Cannon Ball Baker's run in his Bearcat on my paper route and now I see one for myself," the young boy said running his hand along the silver external gear shift.

"What's your name?"

"Fredric Oldfield, everybody calls me Freddie, what's your name?"

"Charles, how old are you, Freddie?"

"Twelve," Freddie offered a handshake that Charles accepted.

"You're an enterprising young man with a newspaper route, Freddie."

"It helps so my mother doesn't have to work so hard."

"What does your mother do?"

"She used to clean rich people's houses, she's sick now and can't work too much," Freddie said.

"You're a good man, Freddie, helping your mother, like that."

"Yeah, I guess so. Are you waiting for somebody?"

"Yes, I am," Charles said his eyes focused like a laser on the building across the street.

"Is it okay if I sit in the Bearcat?"

"Sure, hop in."

In a flash Freddie was in the Bearcat.

"If my friends could see me now they'd be jealous."

"What's this?" Freddie touched a clear circular device on a moveable lever.

Charles turned to Freddie and said, "That's a windshield."

"Keeps the wind out of your eyes when you go fast," and looking past Charles, Freddie said, "Are you waiting for the lady coming across the street."

Charles turned sharply, and was momentarily speechless.

"Hello, Charles," Adalina said, her eyes still swollen from crying and lost sleep.

"Adalina," Charles held out his hand, and with a slight toss of her head Adalina rebuffed his intended comforting touch.

"You're pretty, lady. Why were you crying?" Freddie piped up.

"I wasn't crying. I have a cold," Adalina prevaricated.

"My sister and her boyfriend are always fighting and my sister gets a lots of colds."

"This is Freddie Oldfield," Charles interjected.

"Hello, Freddie; my name is Adalina."

"Did you make her cry?"

"I didn't mean to and I'm sorry," Charles said, his eyes beseeching forgiveness.

"If I had a pretty girl like her, I wouldn't make her cry," Freddie said coming around the Bearcat.

"You're right, Freddie."

"Why are you here, Charles?"

"Paolo said he dropped you off at school, and I thought I'd drive you home?"

"In that," Adalina pointed to the Bearcat.

"It's a short ride and I want to talk to you," Charles pleaded.

"Thank you I'll wait for the trolley," Adalina said curtly.

"You mean you don't want to ride in the Bearcat, lady," Freddie said, incredulously. "I'd really like to ride in a Bearcat."

Seeing the orange-colored trolley lumbering to them, the motorman sounding its gong, its electric pole sparking on the overhead power wire, Charles quickly said, "I'll tell you what we'll do, Freddie. I'll go on the trolley and if you watch the Bearcat, I'll take you for a ride in it, tomorrow, okay."

"Okay, but I have to be home later to take care of my mother."

"Alright, Freddie, you go home when your mother expects you, meet me here tomorrow morning at 8:00 sharp."

"You won't stand me up," Freddie said, a business-like tone in his voice.

" I won't stand you up," Charles assured Freddie as the trolley clanged and thumped to a stop.

# 31

William Williams pulled a lever and the trolley door opened. A scattering of people disembarked and crossed the street. Charles and Adalina boarded and sat quietly, a few rows behind the motorman. Within moments, conductor Titus Gladwell appeared.

"Hello, Miss Bellini. Got a summer cold? Titus asked, casting a skeptical eye at Charles.

"An allergy, it will pass, Mr. Gladwell."

"Five cents, please."

Brushing past Charles, who sat in the aisle chair Mr. Gladwell collected Adalina's fare, and then pulled an overhead wire that recorded its collection.

"Five cents, please, young man."

Startled, Charles looked at Adalina and then Mr. Gladwell.

"I don't carry money with me," he said.

"You will have to remove yourself from the trolley."

A silent pause followed.

"What's going on back there?" William Williams shouted.

"A fare matter Mr. Williams."

"Give me clearance to start up when you're ready, Mr. Gladwell."

"I will, Mr. Williams. Sorry, young man, you'll have to leave."

"Adalina," Charles supplicated.

Adalina didn't respond.

Charles got out of his seat. He looked back at Adalina who silently stared out the window and began walking to the front of the trolley.

"Wait, I'll pay his fare, Mr. Gladwell," Adalina said.

"Take your seat, young man, and don't forget to repay Miss Bellini."

---

The Burning Hours                                    Page 85

"I won't forget."

Titus recorded Charles's fare and called out, in a booming voice, "Clear to go!"

William Williams pulled the door closed, pushed the controller and the trolley rolled forward.

"Is this your first time on a public transit, Charles?"

"Yes, it feels like everyone is watching us."

"That's how public transportation is; you get used to it."

The summer heat in the trolley did nothing to thaw the frost between Charles and Adalina. Only a smattering of words passed between them. Charles wanted to touch her hand, but refrained.

"I thought you were going to let me walk out of your life, Adalina."

"Did that bother you, Charles?"

"I didn't want to believe you would do that."

"Well, I didn't."

What changed your mind?"

"You made me feel so terrible this past weekend, Charles."

"Will you give me a chance to explain?"

"Why did you bring that stuck up woman to our lunch, to humiliate me, like that," she said, her mouth quivering.

"It wasn't intentional, I didn't mean to hurt you, please believe me," Charles spoke softly, sensing eyes and ears in the trolley were on him.

The trolley thumped to a stop. William Williams swung open the door, a rotund middle aged woman dragging a large bag of laundry climbed aboard. A sudden surge of the car disrupted her balance.

"Sorry, Mrs. Kowalski," William apologized, "this controller is very sensitive."

"That's what you always say, Mr. Williams," Susie Kowalski burst into a hearty laugh.

"It went well," William quizzed.

The Burning Hours

"Your bet on the Red Sox paid off at three to one odds," Susie whispered, stuffing three dollar bills into William's breast pocket.

"Take your seat Mrs. Kowalski," Mr. Williams changed to an official voice.

Flushed with the excitement of winning his bet William inadvertently pushed the controller forward, again throwing Susie off balance.

"Mr. Williams!" Susie exclaimed, "You're not shoeing horses anymore. Go easy or you'll knock me out of the tram," she complained and hauling her bag behind her, she took a seat, and bumped her ample rump against a dozing passenger to increase her comfort zone.

"Move over, President!" she ordered.

Susie settled into her seat opposite Charles and Adalina.

"Here's my fare, Titus."

"Anything in your bag for me, Susie?"

"Nothing, Titus, you should have stuck with the Red Sox."

"Clear to go, Mr. Williams!"

The trolley moved forward.

"Hello, Miss Bellini."

"Hello, Mrs. Kowalski."

"You look like you've been crying," she pointed to Charles, "Is he your boyfriend?"

"It's an allergy, Mrs. Kowalski. This is Charles, he's not my boyfriend."

"Seems like there's an epidemic of allergies among the young women in this town," Susie said, gripping her bag of laundry, she leaned back in her seat and closed her eyes, which she surreptitiously opened now and then to see and hear what was going on in the tram.

The trolley's rolling sensation created a hypnotic effect on its passengers who were either dozing or blankly looking out the window. Titus Gladwell sat peacefully at the back of the car, President napped and Susie pretended to be asleep.

The Burning Hours      Page 87

A Mt. Everest of silence separated Charles and Adalina that both seemed incapable of surmounting. The trolley had one last stop to make before arriving at the turnaround.

"Here's your stop, President?" William Williams announced.

"Wake up, President!" Susie bellowed.

President shakily got to his feet, "Thanks, Susie," he said and exited the tram.

"Why do you call him, President?" Charles asked Susie.

"His family name is Washington, his daft mother named him George, his schoolmates nicknamed him President and it stuck."

"Really," Charles smiled.

"Really," Susie smiled back and then closed her eyes.

"This is for you," Adalina handed a five cent coin to Charles.

"What's this for?"

"It's for your ride back to town you needn't repay me."

"My ride back to town?"

"So, you can pick up your car."

"So, I can pick up my car."

"Yes."

"Look at me," Charles demanded, "this may be the end of the line for this ride and it might be the end of the line for us. I came to see you safely home and that's what I intend to do. Is that clear?" Charles said, as if conducting a contentious board meeting.

Overhearing the quiet conversation across the aisle, Susie arched open and then closed her left eye, "A lover's quarrel; the make-up is one of life's greatest pleasures. Just say yes, softly, Adalina, and then look down. Don't look out the window. If you do, he'll think you're not interested," Susie mulled.

Adalina looked at her lap, and in a meek voice she answered yes, to which, in a barely audible voice, Susie murmured, "Good girl! The smart money is on you, Adalina."

"End of the line coming up," William Williams announced.

"I'm sorry I sounded so cross, Adalina."

"I've been stubborn, Charles, I'm very sorry."

"Until I met you and Paolo, and now Freddie and the people on this trolley, I didn't know what life was like outside the bank and the country club," Charles touched Adalina's face, his voice suffused with intimacy. "The worst thing is to lose someone you care for and I don't want to lose you."

"Susie's ears perked up a mischievous smile curled her mouth. "Now is your moment, Adalina, put your head on his chest, let him see your tears, he'll take it from there," she mused as if transmitting telepathic instructions to her pupil.

Adalina rested her head against Charles's chest two pearl-like tears rolled down her face. "It's alright to cry, Adalina," Charles kissed her mouth as the trolley slowed to a halt.

"Good girl! I knew you could do it," Susie rhapsodized.

William came from the front of the trolley and Titus from its back. Susie got up dragging her bag of laundry behind her. They converged at the center of the aisle opposite Charles and Adalina who were now sitting quietly holding hands, exchanging smiles.

"Why do you carry that bag of laundry?" Titus asked.

"It's my bank of customer betting chits," Susie whispered.

"Wouldn't a purse be better?"

"The cops can look into my purse, but they won't spoil their hands, rummaging through dirty diapers and underwear," she laughed.

"Outwitted them, again," William grinned.

"They're not too bright," Susie chuckled.

"Put a dollar on the Red Sox for me," Titus handed Susie a crisp dollar bill.

"Here's a dollar from my winnings, on the Sox," William placed his bet.

Susie noted the bets and slipped their chits into her bag.

"What do you gentlemen think?" Susie inquired, looking at Charles and Adalina.

"I think another kiss to seal the deal is in order," Titus offered.

"Yes," William agreed.

"Absolutely," Susie Kowalski chimed in.

"Good day, Susie," Titus said.

"Likewise," Susie," William said.

"Good day, gentlemen," Susie exited the trolley dragging her laundry bag behind.

# 32

Freddie Oldfield waited for Charles at the trolley stop. Sparse traffic cruised lethargically along Main Street. Freddie was sure he would get his promised ride and he wasn't disappointed when the yellow Bearcat pulled up, Charles at the wheel and Adalina in the passenger seat.

"Hello, lady. I guess you like the Bearcat, now."

"Not, really, Freddie," Adalina responded.

"Then you must like him," Freddie pointed to Charles.

"Yes, Freddie, I like him," Adalina smiled.

"A lot," Freddie wanted to know.

"A lot," Adalina whispered.

"Hop in, Freddie," Charles invited, and in the blink of an eye Freddie occupied the passenger seat.

"I'll wait here for you," Adalina said.

"We'll go to the end of Main Street and when we get to the open field I'll let Freddie steer. Would you like that, Freddie?"

"Do you mean it?"

"Yes, Freddie, I mean it."

"Is that a good idea, Charles?"

"We'll be okay. There's no traffic out there. Freddie can lean against me. I'll have my hands on the wheel, at all times."

"Is it okay, lady?"

"Promise you'll be careful, Charles."

"Don't worry, I'll be careful?"

Charles engaged the gear shift, eased the Bearcat into traffic, accelerated along Main Street in the direction of the open field.

"Wow! This is great!" Freddie exclaimed, looking back and waving to Adalina who waved back as the Bearcat got smaller and smaller until she could no longer see it.

The Burning Hours

The passing minutes seemed like hours. The longer Charles and Freddie were gone the more Adalina worried. The trolley came to a stop and few passengers boarded. When William Williams asked if she was coming on-board Adalina said no. He pulled the doors closed and the trolley rolled forward, sparks flying off the overhead power wire. Adalina paced up and down now convinced she should have protested more vigorously Charles's offer to let Freddie steer the Bearcat.

Adalina sat on the trolley passenger bench and waited. Several minutes ticked away before a yellow speck appeared in the distance. As the Bearcat came into sharper focus Adalina's worry faded away.

Charles pulled into the trolley stop area and turned off the ignition. One look at Adalina and he knew the Bearcat's days were numbered.

"Thanks, mister, my friends will be jealous when they find out I rode in a Bearcat and steered it. Thanks, lady for letting me steer."

"Please let me have the booklet and envelope I gave you earlier."

Adalina reached into her purse and handed Charles a blue booklet and a cream-colored envelope.

"Freddie," Charles said, "this is a savings book with your name on it. When you open it, you'll see today's date and one dollar written after it. Do you know what interest is?"

"No, I don't."

"It's when your money earns money. So even though you could spend this dollar, it's better if you don't do that and add to it whenever you can."

"Then someday I'll have lots of money, right?"

"That's right. Do you know where the Main Street Clinic is, Freddie?"

"It's up the street in a big gray building."

The Burning Hours

"I want you to take this letter there and give it to the woman at the reception desk. She will give it to the doctor whose name is on the envelope and he will take care of your mother."

"We don't have money for doctors, mister."

"It's taken care of so you and your mother shouldn't worry."

"Is this your name on the envelope?"

"Yes, Freddie, that's my name."

"Instead of calling you mister I can now call you by your name."

"It's a deal, Freddie."

"Okay, thanks Mr. Conover," Freddie said.

In the Bearcat Adalina slid close to Charles and whispered into his ear.

"I love you, too," Charles said.

Freddie's voice rose above the rushing traffic.

"Are you married?"

"Soon, Freddie," Charles answered.

# 33

**The Conover Winery
Napa Valley, California
Autumn 1915**

In the autumn of 1915, when Charles was 26 years old and Adalina 20 years old, they married in a private ceremony held on the veranda of the family's Napa Valley winery overlooking endless lines of ripening grape vines. Paolo who had traveled to California with Charles stood in the place of his deceased father. Laura Conover, Charles's mother served as Adalina's Matron of Honor and Charles Conover, Sr. served as Best Man.

Following their marriage Charles and Adalina honeymooned in Napa Valley. The warmth of the California sun and gentle breezes rolling off the mountains instilled in Charles and Adalina a sense of immortality. They stayed in the winery's chalet and took long walks in the vineyard where Charles fed plump grapes to a delighted Adalina. They enjoyed intimate dinners and danced on the veranda beneath a starlit sky, hoping their days together in the valley would go on, forever.

Soon their honeymoon ended. They returned to Connecticut where Charles resumed his role as Chairman of the Board of Conover Bank and Adalina began teaching in a local grammar school. To her delight Charles sold his Stutz Bearcat.

The joy Adalina felt when she announced her first pregnancy was dashed when a baby boy was stillborn. She withdrew speaking only when necessary. Then one day Adalina blurted out the questions that had incarcerated her emotions.

"Why did my baby die, Charles? Was it my fault?"

The Burning Hours

"You did everything humanly possible to bring a healthy baby into the world, what happened was beyond our control," Charles consoled.

"I wanted to name him, Charles," Adalina burst into tears.

Years later, in June of 1920, Adalina gave birth to their only child, a healthy baby girl.

Charles and Adalina named their daughter, Linda.

# 34

**Union Station**
**New Haven, Connecticut**
**Autumn 1945**

Linda Conover traveled to Westport for a welcomed weekend. She looked into her cosmetic compact mirror and saw a young woman weighed down with worry. From the start of her marriage to Derek Reed, Linda knew she had made a mistake. Charles and Adalina, and even Uncle Paolo, who didn't hide his visceral dislike of Derek, advised against the marriage. Linda in the flower of her beauty graduated college. Derek, a graduate dentist and a newly minted Army officer met Linda at a fraternity party and was struck by her beauty. When he learned she was heir to the Conover fortune Derek rushed Linda and she succumbed to his blandishments.

Now on a chilly fall day watching the landscape roll by Linda couldn't come up with a cogent reason why she accepted Derek's proposal of marriage. Perhaps it was the war or her desire to marry and start a family or maybe it was her trusting nature, she didn't know. When Linda informed Charles and Adalina of her decision to marry Derek they reiterated their objections, but wouldn't stand in her way if she had made up her mind.

Following their wedding ceremony, Derek and Linda traveled to the Waldorf Astoria Hotel in New York City. In the early evening of their wedding day Derek exercised his conjugal right in a cold, mechanical union devoid of love or feeling. Afterward as Linda lay in bed, her face buried in her pillow to hide her shame, Derek left to meet friends in the hotel bar. For the next two days Linda's emotions plunged to their lowest depths. Alone and disbelieving she wanted to pack and go back to Connecticut. Several times she picked up the phone, but put it down unwilling to burden Charles and Adalina with the result of her disastrous decision. During the week following their marriage Derek departed for the Army Base at the Presidio in California.

The train was on its final run to the New Haven station. Linda lightly powdered her face and put away her compact. She looked forward to seeing Charles, Adalina and Uncle Paolo and dinner at the country club and continuing her volunteer work with injured and disabled soldiers at the Station Hospital in New Haven and for a time forgetting her troubled marriage. When the conductor announced Union Station the crowded train began emptying. Linda remained seated until the crush of humanity, mostly soldiers on their way home or to reassignments thinned out. She then got up and exited the train.

Cavernous Union Station echoed the chatter and footsteps of people rushing in all conceivable directions. Adalina waited at the USO Canteen radiant as the day she captured Charles's heart. She wore an understated rust-colored knee-length cloth overcoat cinched at the waist and a hat of matching color. Her black hair flecked with gray, her fair skin clear as a bell her hazel eyes glowing at the prospect of Linda's visit.

Linda wove through the crowd to the canteen. She waved to Adalina, who smiled and waved back.

"I'm so happy you could get away," she said, cupping and kissing Linda's face.

"It's good to see you, Mother," Linda said, embracing and kissing Adalina.

"Would you like to have breakfast?"

"I'm not hungry, Mother, is daddy here?"

"Your father and Uncle Paolo are at the office. We'll see them for lunch at Angelo's in Wooster Square."

"I can't wait to see them."

"They're anxious to see you, honey. I think your Uncle Paolo has been practicing his bear hug. You know how much he loves you."

The Burning Hours

"I love him, dearly, despite my broken ribs," Linda joked, "Will we be going to the hospital?"

"Yes, ready to go?"

"Ready," Linda answered, lethargically.

"Linda," Adalina grasped her arm, "You look tired. Is your job weighing heavily on you?"

"My job is fine, Mother, I love it, the train ride tired me."

"You will tell me if anything is bothering you."

"Yes, I will."

"Then let's be off," Adalina said, skeptically, a sense of unease for Linda suddenly growing within her.

# 35

Freddie Oldfield waited for Adalina and Linda in the comfort of the idling Conover Bank company car parked at the station's curbside. Now 42 years of age, balding, bespectacled and thick at his mid-section Freddie worked for the bank since his younger days sweeping floors, running errands, bookkeeping. With Charles's help Freddie earned a law degree rising to the position of bank secretary. In a frame on a wall in his office, Freddie displayed the savings book that Charles's set up for him in 1915.

Adalina and Linda walked arm-in-arm out of the Station. Freddie got out of the car and opened the passenger door. Before getting in Adalina kissed Linda again expressing her delight at having her home, even for a brief time.

"Hello, Freddie, it's good to see you," Linda said, smiling.

"I'm glad to see you, Linda," Freddie held open the passenger door.

"Ride up front, Linda I'll sit in the back."

When Freddie reached to open the back door he felt a light smack on his hand.

"Take care of Linda, Freddie."

"Congratulations on your promotion to secretary, Freddie."

"Thanks, Linda, your father knows how to keep a guy busy."

"He sure does," Linda agreed.

"Where to Mrs. Conover?"

"We're expected at the hospital."

Freddie merged into streaming traffic along Union Street. The drive to the hospital took a few minutes. Freddie brought the car to a stop at its main entrance and turned off the ignition. Before he could get out of the car Adalina told him to stay put and both she and Linda exited the vehicle.

"Shall I pick you up later?" Freddie inquired through the open passenger side window.

"No, thank you, Freddie, we'll take a taxi later to the restaurant," Adalina answered.

"Good to see you, Freddie," Linda said.

"Likewise, Linda."

Freddie turned on the ignition and drove away, back to the bank.

Archie Robertson was a nineteen year old boy from Minnesota, tall and handsome with sky blue eyes, he played the field of young love with the same skill he exhibited on the basketball court. In the waning days of the Battle of the Bulge Archie stepped on a concealed mine and lost his right arm and his legs above his knees.

Linda spent countless hours with Archie, taking his dictations for letters home, reading to him from newspapers and magazines, sitting in the solarium, sometimes silently looking out the window, other times talking and joking.

"Come, sit with me, Linda," Adalina patted a place beside her.

"What is it, mother?"

"This came for you," she handed Linda a letter, "It's from Archie Robinson's parents. The department also received one. The letter tells sweet stories of Archie growing up, they express their appreciation for how well Archie was treated by everyone in the ward, and they have special words for you, Linda."

"What are you telling me, Mother?" Linda interjected.

"Since you were coming for a visit I thought it best to wait to see you."

"Did something happen to Archie? Archie was just fine when I last saw him."

"Honey," Adalina took Linda's hand.

"I know what you are going to say and I don't want to hear it, Mother!"

"I know, dear."

"Archie's dead, isn't he?" Linda's voice cracked.

"I'm sorry, Linda, the doctors think Archie lost his will to live."

"I'd like to be alone, Mother," Linda said, tearfully.

Linda cried as she read her letter from Archie's parents. When finished, she put it in her pocket and for several minutes sat alone fondly recalling memories of Archie. Then emotionally composed Linda went to the Volunteer Services Department where Adalina was filing medical records.

"Are you sure you can work, today?"

"I'm fine, Mother," Linda unlatched her locker door and removed a gray volunteer smock.

"You're sure?"

"I'm sure," Linda answered, lifting the smock over her head, tying its cloth belt around her waist and slipping out of her high heels into a pair of heelless shoes she swept and tied her hair back.

"I'm going to the ward."

# 36

Jacob Seidman always wanted to be a musician. The sounds of music in his head were pure they blocked out the street noise of Manhattan's lower east side where he grew up. Imagining himself a violinist Jacob stroked the air above his extended left arm with his right hand; his eyes closed communicating with the vast ocean of his collective unconscious world where the music he heard in his mind was born.

Linda rolled the ward's library cart from patient to patient chatting and supplying books, newspapers and magazines. When she came to the bed formerly occupied by Archie Robinson she stopped feeling strange at the sight of another young man about Archie's age now occupying his bed.

"I'm Linda Conover," she smiled.

Her voice broke the young man's preoccupation and he looked up.

"Is there anything I can get you?"

Jacob lifted his arm from under the bed sheet revealing a stump where his right hand had once been, and asked, "You could get me a hand."

"Wrong question, I'm sorry."

Jacob covered his arm, hesitated, and then said, "That was unfair. I know you're here to help."

"Let's start all over, shall we?" Linda said.

"Sure."

"My name is Linda Conover."

"I know who you are," Jacob responded. "You're the spitting image of your mother; she comes here with your father, often."

"I'm told we Bellini women resemble one another."

"I'm Jacob Seidman," he extended his left hand.

"Nice to meet you, Jacob Seidman."

They shook hands.

"Would you like a book or magazine?"

"No, thanks."

"Can I get you a soft drink?"

"No, thanks."

"Would you like to go for a walk?"

"I'd like that," Jacob said, swiveling to the edge of his bed, he reached for his bathrobe.

"Let me help you," Linda offered.

"I can do this myself," Jacob said, struggling unsuccessfully with his robe.

"It's alright to accept help, Jacob."

"Yeah, okay," he said, getting out of bed.

Linda held open Jacob's robe he slid his arms into its sleeves and she tied the ends of the cloth belt around his waist.

"Okay, you're ready to go," Linda said.

They walked to the solarium past nurses and doctors tending to patients.

"Nice to see you again, Linda," a patient said as they passed his bed.

"How are you, Douglas?"

"I'm going home, tomorrow."

"That's wonderful."

"I'll be seeing your father and mother, tonight."

"My mother and father will be here tonight," Linda said, quizzically.

"They come to see the guys the night before they leave."

"I'm glad you're going home, Douglas, good luck."

"Shall we go, Jacob?"

"I guess you know your mother and father donated almost everything in the ward," Jacob said, matter-of-factly.

"I know."

"But, you didn't know they came to see the guys before leaving."

"I didn't know that," Linda answered in a low voice.

"They sit and talk with the guys about their families, girl friends, things like that, a real nice send-off. I'm leaving tomorrow. I'll see them tonight."

"Mom and Dad never cease to amaze me."

"When your mother and father heard we got a small government travel allowance they did something unexpected?"

"What was that?"

"Tomorrow a driver from his bank will be waiting to take me to Union Station. Tonight your father will hand me an envelope that has five, ten dollar bills in it, their gift for a new start. They've been doing that each time one of the guys is discharged from the hospital."

"They never told me."

"I guess generosity is best done quietly and unnoticed," Jacob said.

"I guess so."

Furnished with circular tables and easy chairs the solarium looked more like a cocktail lounge than a hospital room. An upright radio at its far end played the Mills Brothers, *Till Then*. Linda and Jacob eased into chairs facing high glass windows looking out to the street, below. Jacob lit a cigarette and blew a cloud of smoke followed by well defined smoke rings into the air humming and softly articulating the song's lyrics.

"You're talented," Linda smiled.

"You mean the humming or the smoke rings?"

"Both."

"Are you married?"

"I am."

"You use your maiden name."

"Yes, for professional purposes."

"Is your husband serving?"

"He's an Army dentist. What about Jacob Seidman?" Linda changed the subject.

The Burning Hours                                       Page 104

"Not much to tell," Jacob said crushing the last of his cigarette in an ash tray on the table, "Have you ever been to New York City?"

"Yes, I have."

"Do you know the lower east side?"

"I've never been to the lower east side."

"I grew up in the lower east side me and my father. Pop was a cutter in one of the garment factories. It's a lousy job, hot and noisy, threads flying in the air. For as long as I could remember Pop would cough up threads he inhaled, trying to clear his lungs. What about you?"

"Mother insisted I volunteer. When I was young, she took me to hospitals and food dispensaries in New Haven. I could always get around father, but not mother. You're a privileged girl, Linda," she would say, "you must give back to the less fortunate."

"You're lucky to have parents like that."

"I defied them, only one time, they were right and I was wrong."

"I won't press you further," Jacob said.

"You're quite the diplomat," Linda responded, "Tell me about your father?"

Jacob reached for another cigarette, but changed his mind and put down the pack.

"Pop is a broken man he has arthritic hands and congested lungs, but he never complains."

"I'm sorry he's not well."

"One day he came home with a broken violin he found behind a music store. He knew I loved music always pretending to be a violinist. Here Jacob, he said, fix it, play it, love it."

"And did you?"

"Music was always in my head. I fixed the violin and the bow. I'd close my eyes and play the music I was hearing. I'd go to the music store on Second Avenue where the owner let me listen to the classical and popular records. I could play all of them by the sounds in my ear. Do you play?"

"I can get through London Bridge on the piano without a misstep" Linda laughed.

"A fellow musician," Jacob smiled back, and then he said, "It was a boiling 90 degree day everyone was on their stoops, night and day trying to beat the heat. The Rabbi from the neighborhood synagogue heard me playing my violin, kinda' like serenading the people from the tenement, that's how it started."

"What started?"

"The Rabbi arranged an audition for me at Julliard. I got my degree and a job as a violinist with an orchestra. I was on the top of the world. I played the violin in a tuxedo that I didn't have to pay for. I had a steady girlfriend and I made enough money to help Pop."

Jacob reached for his pack of cigarettes flipped the Zippo, lit up and quietly exhaled several deep drags.

"Then the war came. I was drafted and here I am," he said before lapsing into reflective silence.

"I'll listen if you want to go on, Jacob."

"Tomorrow I go home with hook a violinist without a hand. The girl I dated, married the deli owner on Hester Street while I was away," Jacob said, before continuing, "When my hand was hanging off my arm a medic stopped the bleeding. He gave me a shot of morphine and then he crawled to another guy without saying a word. There were so many guys down. I thought it best that I die then Pop would get the insurance money and it would be right because I knew he'd be okay. When I woke up in the field hospital my hand was gone."

"What would your father say if he knew what you were thinking?"

"He'd slap me on the head and say, Jacob, stop with the crazy thoughts."

"I wish I had answers for you, but I don't. Maybe all I can do is listen and hope my listening helps. You must believe deep within you have reservoirs of strength that right now are obscure, but one day will serve you well."

"Yeah, maybe," Jacob said, "We should get back to the ward. I'm sure there are other guys who will want to talk with you."

"Okay," Linda nodded.

"You helped me, Linda."

"Linda nodded, again.

No other words passed between them on their way back to the ward. The mid-morning sky turned variable. Jacob undid the cloth belt around his waist, pushed the robe off his right shoulder and wrestled it off his left shoulder and got into bed.

"Good bye, Jacob Seidman."

"Good bye, Linda Conover."

# 37

Adalina hired a taxi idling in a line on the street outside the hospital. Its driver, garrulous and ruddy-faced assisted them in. During the short ride to Wooster Square he spoke of his daughter, an Army nurse who returned safe from the war, except for its memories. The taxi drove through the Wooster Square Arch. The driver pointed to an imposing church where he said he now attends Mass for his daughter and the men and women who didn't come home or came back wounded in mind and body. Within minutes he pulled up in front of Angelo's Restaurant.

Adalina and Linda lingered in front of the restaurant.

"Will the war ever end, Mother?"

"We'll remember and you will educate your children's generation and when we are all gone the turmoil we experienced will fade away and the war will be consigned to the history books."

"That's a long time from now."

"Yes, decades from now; time moves slowly, but inexorably."

The airy dining room in Angelo's Restaurant afforded maximum diner privacy. Deferential waiters impeccably attired in tuxedoes were serving or waiting to serve patrons. Autographed photographs of Hollywood celebrities, diplomats and politicians dotted the room's four walls attesting to the restaurant's cultural and international popularity.

Stylish in a blue blazer, his generous mustache neatly trimmed, his flowing salt and pepper hair combed back in thick waves, Angelo Pensare stood in the center of the restaurant's archway trimmed with glowing gold lights. The Arturo Toscanini of Italian cuisine as he was known throughout Wooster Square, Angelo conducted his restaurant as if it were a well-tuned orchestra, epitomizing old world

European courtliness. Angelo designed the restaurant's meticulous kitchen, he hand-picked chefs whom produced dishes so artfully that most diners felt it criminal to disturb them with knife and fork.

"*Buona sera, senora,*" Angelo greeted Adalina with a slight nod and a soft kiss on her hand. "And, your lovely daughter," he repeated Linda's greeting with courtly flair.

"Good afternoon," Adalina returned Angelo's greeting.

"Nice to see you, again, Angelo," Linda said.

"Are you home for good, Miss Conover?"

"A brief visit."

"*Senora,* your husband and brother will be delayed; you should go ahead with lunch."

"Did he say how long they will be?"

"No, *senora*, he did not."

"Shall we, Linda."

"Pietro will show you to your table, *Buon Appetito.*"

"Thank you, Angelo," Adalina said, her appreciation echoed by Linda.

"Sit there, Linda, I'll sit here to see when your father and uncle arrive."

"Very good, *senora*," Pietro answered.

"What will you have, Linda?"

"I'm not sure I'm not very hungry."

Adalina summoned Pietro and ordered two glasses of Barolo at room temperature."

"The wine will put an edge on your appetite, Linda."

"Would you like to review the menu?" Pietro asked, setting two glasses of ruby red Barolo on the table.

"That won't be necessary, Pietro, I'll have the medallions of veal in Angelo's white wine sauce."

"A good selection."

"I'll have the same," Linda said.

"Drink your wine, Linda, it's good for you."

"It feels warm," Linda said, sipping the aromatic liquid.

"Mother."

"Yes, dear," Adalina responded.

"Finish the story when you and daddy were on the trolley."

"You've heard that story countless times."

"Never how it ended, did he return your nickel?"

Adalina nodded no, relishing the Barolo's warm bouquet.

"He didn't return your nickel," Linda exclaimed, "Was he still angry with you?"

"No that ended when he read me the riot act and I gave into him."

"You liked that, didn't you?"

"Liked what?"

"Giving in to him."

"I didn't know much about life then, but I was over the moon about your father, and yes, my daughter, I loved giving in to him."

"What happened, then?"

"He asked me if I had another nickel."

"Doubling his profit without an investment, I guess that's expected from a banker," Linda laughed.

"I handed him another nickel," Adalina said, "It's good to see you laugh, Linda."

"How much money did you have left in your purse?"

"Twenty-five cents."

"Twenty-five cents!" Linda exclaimed.

"That was a lot of money in 1915."

"The ten cents was for your return trip."

"We rode back to town and your father drove me home in the Bearcat."

"You hated the Bearcat."

"That weekend changed my life and here you are, my lovely daughter."

"You're blushing, Mother."

"You shouldn't put your mother on the spot."

"Isn't that what daughters are supposed to do?"

The Burning Hours

"Yes, honey, that's what daughters are supposed to do."

Pietro set plates of golden brown veal medallions before Adalina and Linda, respectfully he said, *"Buon appetito."*

"Another work of art, please compliment the chef for us," Adalina commented.

Pietro nodded and went to another table.

"I love the story of how you and daddy met," Linda said, "I wish…" she did not finish her thought.

# 38

Adalina's eyes rested with maternal affection on her daughter. Linda seldom confided her marital problems berating herself over the folly of her one act of rebellion and the disastrous consequences it produced. Since marrying Derek Reed Adalina noticed Linda was a shadow of the lovely and vivacious daughter she had raised.

"Linda."

"Yes, Mother."

"Please look at me, honey."

"I'm sorry, Mother; I didn't mean to be rude, I guess I'm preoccupied."

"Tell me what's bothering you."

"I want to, Mother I really do."

"You didn't finish your thought a few minutes ago?

"What thought?"

"What do you wish for?"

Linda put down her fork, "I wish my marriage was as loving as yours."

"You mustn't measure your life by my life or anybody's life, for that matter."

"I know," Linda nodded in agreement.

"I suspected things were not right with you and your husband. Heaven knows, I can't bring myself to even say his name."

"I should have listened to you and daddy, marrying Derek was my mistake and I have to deal with it."

"You tell the boys in the ward it is okay to ask for help, don't you?"

"Yes, when I think I can help."

"Don't you think it's time to apply that advice to yourself?" Adalina reached across the table and held Linda's hand.

The Burning Hours

"You'll never know how any times I wanted to tell you, Mother."

"Do you love your husband?"

Linda shook her head no.

"I made a terrible mistake. My honeymoon was horrible. I won't dignify it by saying we made love. There was no love, there never has been. He abandoned me to be with his friends. I feel violated."

"If I could I would bear your pain," Adalina squeezed Linda's hand.

"I know you would, Mother."

"Do you hear from him?"

"Hear from him!" Linda's voice rose, "I never hear from him, but I heard from the base medical officer."

"Why did he call you?"

"To inform me Derek was being treated for venereal disease."

"My God, Linda! Have you had relations with him since your honeymoon?"

"No, that was the only time. After receiving the medical officer's call I wired Derek and told him I wanted a divorce."

"Did he respond?"

"Yes, he said if I go through with a divorce it will be dirty and daddy will pay big time to get his rich girl back."

"He said that," Adalina commented, her anger rising.

"When he didn't respond to another wire I contacted the base command and was told he was reassigned to a camp in Mississippi holding thousands of German prisoners. He didn't respond to my request to initiate divorce proceedings. I haven't had any contact with him."

"Your father and Uncle Paolo are here. I think it's best we go home you've had a trying day."

"Mother, I'm sorry."

"Don't worry, honey."

Angelo greeted Charles and Paolo effusively at the restaurant's entrance. Over the years through strategic investments and trusting his instincts Charles expanded Conover Bank into a nationwide force lauded by *The Wall Street Journal* as a dynamic financial empire.

Now a successful construction contractor Paolo operated on an international scale. A bachelor by choice and involved in the lucrative Chicago, Las Vegas and Los Angeles construction markets only Paolo's extensive labor union connections exceeded his romantic interests.

"Sorry, we're late, honey" Charles kissed Adalina.

"How are you?" Adalina greeted Paolo.

"I'm good," Paolo answered.

"How are you?"

"I'm well, thank you."

"Where's Linda?" Charles asked.

"She's freshening up," Adalina forced a slight smile.

"Is everything all right?" Charles asked, skeptically.

"It's been a long day for her, the train ride, the news about Archie Robinson, she's exhausted, we should go home, we'll talk tonight."

"Did you finish lunch?"

"Yes, as usual it was delicious."

"Here's my girl," Charles hugged Linda.

"Hi, Daddy," Linda kissed Charles, feeling a sense of security in his embrace.

"How's my favorite niece?" Paolo grabbed Linda in the bear hug she expected.

"It's so good to see you, Uncle Paolo."

"You look thinner than the last time I saw you, Linda, are you feeling okay?"

"The normal pressures of work," Linda dissembled.

"You'd let Uncle Paolo know if anything is bothering you, right?"

"Right, Uncle Paolo."

"We'll be on our way," Adalina said, "Enjoy your lunch."

"We'll talk, tonight," Charles said.

"Yes, tonight."

"You get some sleep young lady I want to see a rested daughter when I get home."

"Okay, Daddy, I will."

"Pietro will show you to your table," Angelo said, "Something from the bar, gentlemen?"

"I'll have a scotch on the rocks; what about you, Paolo?'

"Brandy, Angelo."

"This way, gentlemen."

"I don't like the way Linda looks."

"Her marriage," Charles answered.

"I never liked that guy," Paolo snarled.

# 39

**General Army Hospital
Liege, Belgium
March 1945**

Even the whining noise of Dodge medical trucks didn't distract Vince's probing thoughts of that early day on the ridge. He took a last drag and tossed his cigarette onto the cobblestone street, picked up his duffel bag and went into the hospital.

"Where can I find Private Domenico Tomasso?"

"Upstairs, first floor," the reception desk corporal answered.

"Okay if I leave this with you?"

"Sure, give it here. I'll keep an eye on it," the corporal responded.

"Thanks," Vince handed the corporal his duffel bag. For a few minutes he stood motionless, his mind glued to the action in the early morning on Christmas day blaming himself for Tommy's injuries.

"You all right, Private?"

"Yeah, I'm okay," Vince answered and started for the staircase.

The first floor ward was bright, everything in it was white, white garbed doctors and nurses, white walls, white frame beds, chairs and bedside cabinets; it coalesced in a white sanitized blur.

A doctor and nurse poured over the medical record of a patient whose facial expression was one of resignation that he no longer controlled his own destiny. With a flip of his wrist the doctor closed the chart and approached the soldier, his manner professional, but distant.

"You're aware that a part of your right leg has to be amputated."

"Yeah, I know," the patient, a sergeant answered.

"It's a rotten deal, but you're fortunate in one respect."

"No kidding, Doc," the soldier answered, "Tell me the good news?"

"The surgery will preserve your knee you will have greater mobility than if the amputation was above the knee."

After a brief pause the sergeant asked, "When do you want to do it?"

"Now."

"Whatever you say, Doc."

The doctor handed his medical chart to the nurse at his side, a captain.

"How long will the surgery take?"

"About an hour, and then you'll be in recovery for several hours."

"I'll get you something to make you sleepy."

"Will you be in the operating room, Captain?"

"I'll be assisting the surgeon."

"Where are you from?"

"Vermont."

"I'm from Montana, where the sky is as blue as your eyes."

"What did you do before the war?" the captain brushed off the sergeant's flirtatious remark.

"My family has a small cattle ranch I guess ranching is out, now."

"You'll be getting around in fine form."

"Fast enough to catch you, Captain?"

"I believe you're flirting with me, Sergeant."

"I'm glad you noticed."

"There is a regulation barring fraternizing of officers and enlisted personnel."

"It's a dumb regulation."

"General Eisenhower agrees with you, he said so in *Stars and Stripes*."

"Then I'm in the clear."

"Are you ready, Sergeant?" she handed him two tablets.

"Will you be with me when I wake up?"

"I'll be with you."

"Captain."

"Yes."

"You're a woman."

"Guilty as charged," her eyes crinkled into a smile.

"Do you think it's going to matter?

"What's going to matter?"

"A guy with one good leg?"

"You're asking for a woman's opinion."

"Yeah, that's what I'm asking."

"For some women it will matter, for the vast majority of us, it is the man that matters."

"If you say so Captain," the sergeant said, unconvinced.

"I'm right, Sergeant."

"Life is a mystery. I don't know the name of the medic who saved me. I don't know if he is alive, and yet, he is an important person in my life."

"I know the feeling."

"You're an important person in my life, but I'll never see you, again."

"Why do you say that?"

"Because life works that way."

"Sometimes life takes unexpected turns."

The sergeant had fallen hard for the captain. His heart raced when she came to his bed. Her figure was more alluring than Betty Grable's iconic million dollar legs. The captain didn't wear a wedding band.

Despite the fog in his head the sergeant believed it was the captain not the medication causing his sailing sensation. She sat on the edge of his bed and held his hand, "I am not married, now does that answer your question?"

"How did you know?"

"I could tell."

"Then there's hope for me," the sergeant's voice began drifting.

"I'd like to see the Montana sky and show you Vermont's autumn leaves."

"It's a deal," the sergeant said his battle to stay awake lost.

From the far side of the ward came the clicking sound of a gurney.

"Stop fighting," the captain whispered, "I'll be here when you wake."

# 40

Vince looked into the ward at Tommy, and Darling, who survived the mortar blast with a recurring headache. Except for Darling dressed in his olive drab uniform standing next to Tommy the ward was a sea of sanitized white. Vince touched the sites of his healed wounds. The medics and doctors did their jobs and got him back on the line. He walked along the corridor created by beds on opposite walls. He passed a bedridden soldier who asked if he was going home Vince nodded negatively.

"Hello Vince," Darling said.

"Sarge," Vince shook Darling's hand.

"Tommy, Vince is here."

"Vince, I'm glad you're here."

Looking at Tommy holding out his hand, his eyes sightless an ache caught in Vince's throat. His mind raced back to earlier days when Tommy was a daredevil, a dynamo of limitless energy. Vince took Tommy's hand and then buried his head against his shoulder.

"It's okay, Vince."

"Come on, Vince," Darling patted Vince's shoulder.

"I'm okay, Sarge."

"Hey Sarge, did you know me and Vince were born on the same day, minutes apart?"

"I didn't know that, Tommy."

"We're better than brothers."

"I knew you were right away, in basic training," Darling answered.

"I'm not like this because of anything you did, Vince so quit blaming yourself."

"If I didn't go out, you wouldn't ..."

"I was going out anyway, I couldn't leave sweetheart here out there in the snow by himself, he'd be lonely without me," Tommy laughed, his teasing elicited an audible laugh from Darling.

Vince was unconvinced with Tommy's exculpation.

"Always busting my chops, Tomasso," Darling said.

"It's what I was made to do," Tommy answered, "Sarge, straighten Vince out."

"What's Tommy talking about?"

"Artillery wiped out the line, Vince, a lot of the guys didn't make it. If you and Tommy stayed in the foxhole you'd both be dead."

"That's what happened, Vince, Sarge is telling it straight, right Sarge?"

"That's the way it went down, Vince."

"I didn't know."

"You two guys got medals, you deserve them," Tommy said.

"Tommy was approved for the Medal of Honor, Vince," Darling said, "A captured Kraut major reported the action to our CO and our guys who witnessed the action reported it to HQ.

"That's a great honor, Tommy."

"He wants to have the award ceremony here, not at the White House."

"Why not, Tommy?" Vince asked.

"When I'm home, that's it, I'm home," Tommy answered, and then deflecting further discussion of the medal, "Sarge tells me you're going home, Vince."

"First to Camp Lucky Strike."

"When do you leave?"

"Later today."

"I hear the war isn't over for the guys in Lucky Strike," Darling said.

"What are you talking about, Sarge?"

"The push to the Rhine, Tommy."

"I thought you were going straight home, Vince."

The Burning Hours                    Page 121

"Me and 30,000 other guys waiting for transport back to the states," Vince joked.

"God damnit, Vince, you did enough. Why don't they let you go home?" Tommy pushed forward in his chair.

"No big deal, the army wants to get a few more months out of me, I'll be all right."

"Damnit," Tommy murmured.

Darling received permission to stay with Tommy and escort him home upon his release from hospital. Although old enough to be his father Tommy was the kid brother Darling never had. The smart aleck he looked out for during combat. But on the ridge it was Tommy who saved him. Life mixes its own mysterious brew Darling thought, and while Tommy and Vince had an unshakable bond ordained by fate he loved Tommy as a brother. Vince dwelled on his inability to help Tommy in the action on the ridge. Had he been conscious and able to fight Tommy wouldn't be facing a lifetime of darkness.

"When you get home, Vince, will you see my mother?"

"You know I will, Tommy."

"Tell her I'm okay, tell her I love her."

"Sure, Tommy, I'll tell her."

"Tell your mother I love her."

"I will, Tommy."

"You gonna see Mr. Birkman?"

"Yeah, I'll see him."

"Thank him for getting me out of the jam with Brady."

"I'll do that, Tommy."

"Say hello to Mr. Gruber for me."

"Sure, when you're home you can tell them yourself."

"Yeah, when I get home."

"What about Rosemary, Tommy?"

Vince's question created an unsettling pause.

Then Darling broke the silence.

"Tommy, what should Vince say to Rosemary when he gets home?"

Tommy didn't respond.

"Tommy," Darling continued, "the feelings in Rosemary's letters are for you. They're wonderful letters from a girl who loves you and has hopes for your future, together. You can't cut her out, Tommy. This is a tough go for you, but it's rough for Rosemary, too."

"You would never hurt Rosemary."

"You know I'd never hurt her, Vince."

"Did Tommy ever tell you how he met Rosemary, Sarge?

"Not that I can remember."

"Go ahead, Vince, tell Sarge," Tommy's memory of that summer day brought a rare smile to his face.

"Come on, Tommy it's your story."

"Start for me, Vince."

"Okay, Tommy," Vince agreed, "We left a track and field meet, sweaty from the heat. It was rush hour. We crossed the boulevard. The traffic was flying in both directions. Then out of the blue Tommy says I'll see you later Vince and he dashed into the traffic."

"I almost got killed, but it was worth it," Tommy picked up the story, "the cars were jamming to stops not to run me down."

"Craziest thing I ever saw," Vince added.

"Do you believe in love at first sight, Sarge?"

"I'm too old for that sorta' thing, Tommy, but if it ever happens for me I think I'd know it."

"You had to see her, Sarge. I was bowled over. I had to meet her."

"In her letters she sounds like a strong girl," Darling said.

"In no time Tommy followed her around like a puppy," Vince laughed.

"She told me to stop bothering her. I begged her for a date. I guess I wore her down because she gave in."

The Burning Hours

"You had to see Tommy the next day, Sarge, he was scrubbed and clean, his hair combed, he looked like a choirboy."

"You know, Sarge, I kissed Rosemary one time, that's all it took, one time and I knew," Tommy said, and then he drifted into silence.

"Write to her, Tommy, think how she must be feeling," Darling said.

"When I'm home, I'll see Rosemary," Vince said.

"Yeah, I know," Tommy responded.

"You know what she's gonna' ask, don't you, Tommy."

"Yeah, I know."

"What do I tell her, Tommy?"

"Tell her I love her and I always will."

"That's it, Tommy, nothing more."

"I want to do what's right by her, Vince."

"I know, Tommy, but not hearing from you has to be tough on her."

In a low quivering voice, Tommy said, "Rosemary is nineteen she deserves more than taking care of an invalid the rest of her life. I won't be able to provide for her the way I want to. I won't be able to protect her the way a husband protects his wife and family. I'd be a burden for the rest of her life. That kills me, Vince, do you understand, it kills me."

"Yeah, I understand, Tommy."

"I'd trade the Medal of Honor in a heartbeat if I could get my eyesight back so I could see Rosemary and my mother, again. It's dark in here," Tommy brushed his hand over his eyes, "When I dream I see her, I hear her breathing, and then I wake up. It was a dream, but I saw her, and before I go back to sleep, I think of Rosemary and hope she'll come back to me, sometimes she does, sometimes she comes back to me, in my dreams."

The Burning Hours            Page 124

"Write to her Tommy, tell her what you're feeling, and tell her what you told Sarge and me. When you are home and together, you'll figure it out," Vince said.

"Vince is right," Darling agreed his hand firmly on Tommy's shoulder.

"Yeah, okay, I'll answer Rosemary's letters. I wish you were writing the letters for me, Vince, you're good with words."

"It's not the words, Tommy, it's the feelings they express, and nobody can say it better than you."

"Will you put on paper what I want to say, Sarge?"

"Sure, Tommy, whenever you're ready."

Along the cobblestone street truck motors hummed. At their sound Tommy grabbed Vince and for fleeting moments they held on to each other.

"Be careful Vince, if you die, a piece of me dies," Tommy whispered.

# 41

Linda and Adalina arrived at Freddie Oldfield's office at 9:00 o'clock in the morning on the top floor of the Conover Bank building next to a sprawling boardroom a few steps from Charles Conover's suite of offices. It was sparsely furnished. On Freddie's desk a picture of his long departed mother smiled benevolently at him. A stack of legal documents waited for his attention. Framed on the wall behind his desk now brittle with age hung the savings account Charles opened for him in 1915, his college and law school degrees all the result of an accident of fate, his ball that bounced to Charles standing near his yellow Stutz Bearcat waiting to see Adalina Bellini.

If a person's identity is a mixture of successes and failures, fulfilled and unfulfilled desires, then the picture on the doorway wall of a proud Freddie taken in front of the treasured cabin he built in his spare time in the Canadian Shield of Ontario would yield a clue to a dimension of his personality that eluded even his closest friends and associates.

When his tired eyes watered with strain Freddie removed his glasses, leaned back in his chair and gazed at the picture of his log cabin waiting for his return to rekindle the warmth that awaited him there.

The stuttering sound of his intercom roused Freddie from his contemplative excursion. He slid his tie knot into his white collar, picked up the receiver and answered with a monosyllabic yes. And then said he would greet his visitors in the hallway and returned the receiver to its cradle.

In the hallway Freddie watched Adalina, dressed in a gray long-sleeved jacket and full skirt, and Linda attired in a rust-colored cable knit sweater and black skirt coming to his office. They wore gold lockets around their necks containing pictures of their parents. Linda's striking resemblance to Adalina never ceased to amaze Freddie.

Earlier Charles had briefed Freddie to use his legal skills and connections to end his daughter's marriage to Derek Reed. Freddie knew Linda was caring and sensitive and faithful to her upbringing and questioning her in the details of her unfortunate marriage pained him.

Deferring to the role she played in his life, Freddie greeted Adalina formally, he welcomed Linda's peck on his cheek and invited them into his office. Adalina waved off Freddie's attempt to seat her, as did Linda.

"Freddie, you know I won't be insulted if you call me Adalina."

"I know that Mrs. Conover, thank you."

"What's stopping you?"

"If it weren't for you and Mr. Conover I wouldn't be here, an attorney and board member of one of the largest banks in the country. It was your generosity that added longer, more comfortable years to my mother's life. Maybe, one day, but now, I think a respectful distance is in order."

"Alright, Freddie, I'll press you no further. Do you know how Freddie came to your father and me?"

"Yes, mother, I know," Linda answered, "Whatever happened to your ball, Freddie?"

"I lost it the next day threw it too high, missed the catch it rolled away. A boy picked it up and ran off with it.

"Did you chase after him?" Linda asked.

"I didn't I thought perhaps the ball could bring him the good luck, it brought me."

"You have a spiritual side, Freddie," Adalina said.

"Yes, I think I do."

"Your father provided me some details of your marital situation, Linda. There are questions I need to ask you," Freddie said in a lawyerly tone. Before he began the intercom buzzed, he lifted the receiver to his ear and listened.

The Burning Hours        Page 127

"Yes, Mr. Conover, Mrs. Conover and Linda are with me," a pause followed, "We're about to begin. I will Mr. Conover," Freddie hung up the receiver, placed a legal size pad and a pen on his desk, "All set, Linda?"

Adalina's expression was grave.

Linda's mood had shifted into seriousness. She wondered if her moment of weakness would be a millstone around her neck for the rest of her life.

"Yes, Freddie; I'm all set."

"You might find some of my questions distasteful and others insulting; however, in a proceeding such as this it is necessary to leave no stone unturned."

"I understand," Linda said.

"Okay, please state for the record, your full name and age?"

"Linda Bellini Conover, I am 24 years old."

"Where do you live?

"Hoboken, New Jersey on Garden Avenue."

"What is your husband's full name and age?"

"Derek Reed, he is 27 years old."

"In what state and town were you married?"

"Westport, Connecticut."

"In a church or civil ceremony?"

"A civil ceremony."

"Month and date of your marriage?"

"July 18, 1942."

What is your husband's occupation?"

"He's a dentist."

"Is he a member of the armed forces, if yes, the branch of the military, his military occupation and his present and past stations?"

"He is an army dentist, stationed at the Presidio in California."

"Currently serving?"

"Yes."

"Has he served overseas in any combat operations?"

The Burning Hours            Page 128

"His entire service has been in the United States at the Presidio."

"Did you honeymoon?"

"Yes, in New York City."

"For how long?"

"We planned on being In New York City for four days."

"Did you enjoy your time in New York City with your husband?"

"No, I did not."

"Please elaborate."

"Derek met friends in the hotel bar on the day we arrived. He left and did not return for the next two days. I had no idea where he was and he wouldn't tell me when he returned. He packed and without a word he left for California."

"Did your marriage produce children?"

"No."

"Are there any joint accounts, such as savings, checking?"

"No, none."

"Has your husband provided you any financial support?"

"No, he kept his army pay."

"You have been and continue to be self-supporting since your marriage, is that correct?"

"Yes, that's correct; he has not contributed to my support."

"Has he asked you for money?"

"Yes."

"Was it a large amount?"

"Several thousands of dollars."

"Do you know the reason for his request?"

"It was to support his drug addiction."

"Did you provide him the funds requested?"

"No I did not."

Freddie looked up from his notes and said, "Linda, you and Mrs. Conover are probably thinking why is Freddie asking me these questions. As your attorney I want to be prepared for any eventuality."

"I know Freddie," Linda responded.

"Okay, let's continue, do you own any property jointly with your husband?"

"No, there is no jointly owned property."

"Are there any insurance policies?"

"The only one I am aware of is the Army's life insurance policy."

"Are you named as beneficiary?"

"No, I am not."

"Do you know who is?"

"I don't know."

"I know you have a trust fund - and how do I know that -" Freddie warmed up, "I happen to be one its registered trustees."

"That's right," Linda smiled.

"I would know if there had been any withdrawals. It's good you have been supporting yourself. Now, I must ask – at any time, either verbally or in writing, have you indicated to your husband your intention to give him access to your trust fund or to add his name as a registered trustee. Think hard about this question, Linda, because if there is any discoverable verbal or written communication to that effect it would provide your husband a claim to the funds in your Trust."

"Linda," Adalina prompted.

After a short pause Linda responded, "I never gave him any reason to believe I'd make him part of my Trust Fund, I never expressed that to him and I never put in writing any such intention, although he asked me to."

"When did he ask you?"

"In New York City, before he left for California."

"Was your answer an emphatic no or did you give him cause to think otherwise?"

The Burning Hours                                     Page 130

"Before leaving he smiled, a malicious smile, and he asked me to name him a trustee of my Trust Fund."

"What did you say?"

"I told him under no circumstances would I agree to his request."

"How often did he make that request?"

"That was the only time. He never came home on leave. That was the last time I saw him."

"Were there any witnesses to this discussion?"

"There were no witnesses."

"What about his friends in the bar?"

"I never met them."

"And you never signed any document?"

"I never signed anything regarding my Trust Fund."

"Okay, that's good."

"Did you have sexual relations before your marriage?"

Adalina angrily interjected – "Freddie, how could you ask such a question?"

"I'm sorry Mrs. Conover these things are never pleasant."

"It's all right, mother. I never had pre-marital sex with Derek or anyone else. When I married I was a virgin. To this day I am sickened that he took that from me," Linda answered. "I feel awful. I'm sorry, Mother that I'm putting you and daddy through this, it's my fault," Linda said, sobbing.

Adalina took Linda's hand, "It will work out, honey, you'll see. Isn't that right, Freddie?"

"I'm sure it will. Would you like to take a break, Linda?"

"No, Freddie; I'm okay."

"You're sure? This next series of questions will be difficult."

"Go ahead, Freddie."

"For the record, Linda, I must ask did you have sexual relations with anyone, man or woman, other than your husband?"

"My God," Adalina said under her breath.

"I never had sex with anyone else," Linda took a handkerchief from her purse and dabbed her eyes.

"Did you go on dates with anyone, in his absence?"

"Occasional lunches and dinners with people at work."

"Male or female friends?"

"Both."

"Singly or in a group."

"Always in a group and then I went home, alone."

"Did you write notes to any males that could be construed as expressions of romantic interest?"

"The only correspondence I had was work-related."

Before Freddie could ask the next round of questions, Adalina said, "Linda is a good and decent young lady, Freddie, we both know that. I am boiling at what he has put her through. Freddie, you do whatever is necessary to rid...," Adalina paused concluding venomously, "this devil from Linda's life."

"Be assured, Mrs. Conover I shall."

"Last questions, Linda, okay?"

"Okay, Freddie."

"We need to establish grounds for your petition of divorce. Please tell me the problems that have made continuing life in a marital state with your husband untenable?"

"Go ahead, Linda," Adalina encouraged.

"I hardly know where to start," Linda said, "He never came home on leaves. He preferred the company of his friends. He contracted venereal disease and is a habitual drug user."

"Is there any proof of what you have just stated?"

"I was notified by the base medical officer of Derek's disease because it is sexually transmissible."

"Linda, let me stop you, have you had sexual relations with your husband since his diagnosis?"

"No, the only time we had sexual relations was in New York City, on our honeymoon."

"Was he clean at that time?"

"When the medical officer told me what Derek was being treated for I was frightened so I went to a woman's clinic in New York City and was examined and found to be okay."

"You should have confided in your father and me, Linda. We had no idea what you were putting up with," Adalina scolded.

"I'm glad you are in good health, Linda."

"Did you note the name and date of the medical officer's call to you?"

"Yes, I have it in my diary."

"Do you have your diary with you?"

"Yes."

"Please leave it with me."

"Okay."

"Has your husband ever physically abused you?"

"No."

"Do you want to restore your maiden name?"

"Yes, I want to forget everything and anything to do with the name Derek Reed."

"You can relax now, Linda. I'm sorry you had to endure this. I have everything I need should he contest the terms of your pre-nuptial agreement."

"What do you think, Freddie?" Linda asked.

"Everything you told me is grounds for dissolution of the marriage. The provable fact is you have been abused emotionally and the evidence is such that a persuasive case can be made for physical intimidation."

"Where do we go from here, Freddie?" Adalina asked.

"I will contact your husband and inform him of your intention to sue for divorce, according to the terms of your pre-nuptial agreement. If he has any common sense he will accept the generous terms of the agreement. I am licensed in New Jersey and thereafter will issue a Petition of Dissolution;

"And, if he doesn't," Linda asked.

"He might try to wait it out. That won't work for him since a legal action has been initiated. He might try to contact you to plead his case for reconciliation. Do not take his calls. You must not see him or be alone with him. Contact me and Mrs. Conover right away if he tries to communicate with you."

"I understand."

"Will I have to go to court, Freddie?"

"I discussed this with Mr. Conover this morning and he tells me he discussed this with you also, Mrs. Conover."

"Yes, that's right."

"If he doesn't contest our petition there will be an out of court settlement, it will be expensive, but it is the best solution, he goes his way and more importantly you are free of him, Linda."

"Is that alright with you, Linda?" Adalina asked.

"Yes, Mother."

"The fact that you are Charles and Adalina Conover's daughter and wealthy in your own right your husband may threaten to go public in an effort to extract a more substantial settlement than that in your pre-nuptial agreement."

"What are the chances he would do that?" Linda asked.

"A reputable lawyer would advise acceptance of the agreement. A publicity seeking lawyer might want to go public. It's hard to know."

"What's your best guess, Freddie?" Adalina inquired.

"I don't believe his case would be well received by a jury. He might think his pot of gold is in a public trial, but when he realizes there could be an unfavorable jury verdict my best guess he will not go beyond the pre-nuptial agreement."

A sense of emotional exhaustion pervaded Freddie's office, Adalina and Linda held each other's hand and smiled. Freddie looked up from his copious notes and asked if there were any questions or anything else to discuss, to which Linda and Adalina shook their heads no.

"I will prepare and issue a Petition of Dissolution of Marriage, per the terms of the pre-nuptial agreement, today," Freddie said.

# 42

Following his meeting with Linda, Freddie Oldfield sat back in his chair emotionally drained. Freddie knew Linda from her earliest days. She had grown into a beautiful, caring young woman and it pained him to witness her suffering because she said yes to the wrong man.

Impelled by his concern, Freddie went into the corridor and saw Linda before she and Adalina entered Charles's office suite. He promised her that he would do all in his power to expedite the divorce and apologized for the mechanistic nature of his interview. Linda said she understood and he was not to worry.

In his office Freddie mulled the unpredictable nature of human relations. He questioned how relationships for some people could be so right and for others turn out so wrong. He had little doubt that Linda aspired to a marriage like Charles's and Adalina's who on first sight knew they were meant to be together. He theorized Linda tried to emulate Charles and Adalina when she impulsively accepted Derek Reed's proposal of marriage, discovering too late that he was an abusive chameleon.

Each spring Freddie drove to Ontario's Canadian Shield to his cabin situated at the edge of a sparkling lake surrounded by soaring spruce trees, feeling the cool Canadian breezes and enjoying the magic of the Canadian sunset.

In his daydream Freddie recalled the Algonquin men and women who helped build his log cabin. When completed Freddie handed his camera to a lovely young Algonquin woman with eyes and hair as dark as the night and a shy smile that captivated him. Tentatively he asked her to snap his picture proudly standing in front of his creation.

Freddie had fallen in love with Kimi Fair Weather and she with him. Before a Canadian sunrise at the lake's edge they professed their union to be a marriage of desire. Soon afterward, Kimi gave birth to a son, Frederick Jr., now fifteen.

In his dream flight, Freddie envisions his arrival at the cabin where Frederick Jr. a physical mixture of Kimi and himself, is waiting. Frederick embraces Freddie with the simple greeting of "Father," then Freddie sees Kimi at the lake's edge, the sparkling water behind her, they embrace, Freddie whispers "My beautiful wife," Kimi responds, "My dearest husband."

Freddie often wondered why he chose to vacation in Ontario, build his cabin and in so doing he met Kimi. Or was it a predestined act ordained by an unknown universal power. Freddie had no answer and the question too profound for him to consider further. He loved Kimi and Frederick Jr. and they returned his love, unreservedly. He wished one day the same for Linda.

Freddie looked at the picture of his log cabin and envisioned his winter vacation.

# 43

Julia Tomasso's emotional state was an unforgiving knot of regret, despair and fear. The sound of the ringing doorbell brought a modicum of relief from her depression that appeared to deepen with each passing day. Her slippers nowhere to be found, she went to the front door on bare feet chilled by the floor's cold linoleum.

"Regina, come in. Are you all right?"

"I'm fine," Regina handed Julia a box.

"What is this?"

"It's a pound cake. I had some unused stamps for butter in my ration book. I gave up trying to sleep at 5:00 this morning. I don't sleep well, anymore."

In twenty years little in Julia's wood frame house had changed. In the kitchen, Julia brewed a pot of coffee while Regina sliced the pound cake. Within minutes the aroma of coffee permeated the room.

The gurgling of the coffee pot subsided and its caramel-colored liquid settled. Regina set two poured cups of coffee on the kitchen table.

"Have some cake, Julia."

"Do you have regrets, Regina?"

"Everybody has regrets."

"Regrets that bedevil you, night and day?"

"I can't rid myself of this awful feeling. I'm so ashamed, Regina."

"What's troubling you, Julia?"

"You know Tommy always got into trouble."

"I know, but Tommy isn't a bad kid, he was burning off energy."

"Before he was drafted," Julia said, "Shamus brought him home. He said can't you keep your kid under control. Then Tommy said how about our kid. I never told him Shamus was his father, but he knew. He looked at me with such disappointment and said thanks a lot, Mom. I didn't think. I slapped Tommy. I slapped my son and now he will never see," Julia said, tears streaming down her face.

"You never told me."

"I'd do anything to change what I did. I'll never forget the look on Tommy's face. He didn't say anything. He looked at me, Regina, he just looked at me. I told him I was sorry. I begged him to forgive me, but he turned away from me without a word and went into his room. I followed him. He was sitting on the edge of his bed, his back to me. I said, again and again I was sorry. I said please look at me, Tommy, I love you, I'm your mother, can't you forgive me? He didn't look at me. He had no words for me."

Julia shuddered and broke into breathless sobs, "I don't know if he ever forgave me. When he left for overseas I hugged him as tight as I could and told him I loved him. He said he knew; two icy words, Regina, that's all he said to me, two icy words. And, now he's blind. He'll never see the sorrow in my eyes for what I did or the love I have for him. Tommy got his temperament from me, Regina. When I slapped him I was punishing myself; I know that, now. I don't know what to do."

"Take some coffee, Julia. It's been a bad time for you. I'm sure Tommy forgives you and loves you. You have to stop torturing yourself."

Julia toyed with her coffee cup never raising it to her lips her thoughts remote in an inaccessible place. Regina couldn't discern whether or not Julia even heard her. "I'm sorry to burden you with my troubles, Regina when Vince is still away. Have you heard from him?"

"He writes when he can. His company is still patrolling."

"I didn't know, Regina. I'm so sorry. You never told me Vince is still in combat."

"He says I shouldn't worry, they aren't dangerous patrols," wistfully adding, "I hope he's telling me the truth."

The Burning Hours                                    Page 139

"Does Tommy know?"

"Vince told him when he saw him in the hospital."

"Tommy hasn't answered any of my letters. If he had written I would have known. You were always the strong one, Regina. I don't have your strength. I wish I did. I'm sure Vince will be okay. Soon we will have our sons home and safe, isn't that right?"

"Soon, Julia, soon," Regina reiterated.

"I'm worried about Rosemary," Julia pierced the quiet, "Did I tell you she calls me, Mom?"

"She does," Regina smiled.

"When she says Mom, I feel closer than ever to Tommy; is that strange, Regina?"

"It's a wonderful feeling, not at all strange."

"Rosemary loves Tommy when she calls me Mom, it's like I have my children with me."

"It's a good feeling, Julia."

Suddenly Julia's face was deepened with worry.

"Tommy hasn't answered Rosemary's letters."

"I'm sure she will hear from him."

"She's afraid of losing him."

"Has she confided that in you?"

"She thinks Tommy won't want to burden her."

"Tommy's life has changed in ways none of us will understand, Julia. He must be confused and scared. In time he will sort things out."

"I just want the best for them."

"I know," Regina squeezed Julia's hand.

Julia managed a small smile.

# 44

The doorbell's persistent buzzing ended Julia's and Regina's conversation, their eyes met, inquiringly. It brought back memories of a hot day in 1944 when they sat on Regina's porch sipping ice water as the sun went down. A Western Union bicycle boy known in the neighborhood as the Angel of Death peddled along the street in their direction. Paralyzed with fear, they clasped hands and watched as the he stopped across the street in front of the Marino residence. Oh, God! Regina gasped and Julia covered her mouth. They thought of Martin Marino when a small boy playing with Vince and Tommy. Within minutes the bicycle boy delivered a telegram and peddled away. Mrs. Marino's blood chilling screams of *Martin! Martin!* reverberated along the street, stopping only when she fainted. Julia burst into tears and Regina pressed her hands over her ears. Mrs. Marino aged overnight, seldom smiling, thinking each time she answered the doorbell Martin would be standing there, smiling and asking: "What's for dinner, Mom?"

"I'm not expecting anyone," Julia got out of her chair and anxiously went to the front door.

"Hello, Mrs. Tomasso. Thought I'd drop off your mail," the mailman said.

"Thank you," Julia said, her voice suffused with relief.

"Please get my mail, Julia, if there is any?"

The mailman confirmed Regina's mail and handed it to Julia.

"Thank you," Julia said.

"You're welcome," the mailman continued his route.

Julia anxiously separated her mail from Regina's looking for a letter from Tommy. She sat back in her chair, disappointed, "Only bills and advertisements," she grumbled. "You have a letter from Vince."

"I'll open it when I get home."

"If I had a letter from Tommy, I'd tear it open."
Regina went into the parlor.
"Don't worry, Julia, you'll hear from Tommy."
Regina opened Vince's letter and eagerly began reading.

*July 25, 1945*
*Camp Lucky Strike, France*
*Dear Mother,*
*I'll be coming home, soon. I thought I'd let you know that straight off. Right now, I am in Camp Lucky Strike. It's located in a town called Janville not far from LaHavre the departure port. Most of the camps that are the jumping off points for the guys going home are named for cigarettes, like Old Gold, Camels, Chesterfield. Since I accumulated enough points to go home, my war is done. I'm glad you forced me to do my arithmetic when I was a kid because I found an error in the command post's calculations (they forgot to add points for my battle star) and when it was added in I had enough points to go home, thank you, Mom. Now I just hang around, sleep late, gain weight and wait for a ship to take me home that could be one month or six months from now. I hope in time for Christmas. I won't know until the word comes down.*

*It's okay here, quiet and warmer than the foxholes. Tents as far as you can see are used for hospitals, kitchens, recreation, dormitories. You could buy things made by the local people. I sent you lace and other gifts. I hope they have arrived and if not you'll receive them soon.*

*In the field you sleep when you can because you're dead tired. I don't sleep too well. I thought it would be different now that it's quiet and I'm out of danger, but I wake up thinking about things I want to forget. A lot of the guys are bringing home war souvenirs. They have to register them with the command post before they are allowed to take them home. You should see the long line of the guys waiting with their souvenirs. I don't want anything that will remind me of this war so the only line I get on is the chow line. I'll probably be okay when I am home and I'm sleeping in my own bed. I never realized until now all of the things the word Home means. It's not just a word to me anymore.*

*I saw Tommy before shipping out to Lucky Strike. He's a celebrity at the hospital since the word is out about his being approved for the Medal of Honor. Sergeant Darling that I mentioned in my letters got permission to stay with Tommy and escort him home. What a relationship those two have. Darling is a big southerner from Alabama, twice Tommy's age and size, then there's Tommy, a smart aleck New Jersey kid tormenting him and Darling loving every minute of it. What a pair!*

*Tommy said to tell Mrs. Tomasso he loves her. When he told me to tell her he loved her I sensed in him a deep feeling that he really wanted her to know how he felt, he had tears in his eyes. He said he sends his love to you, too, Mom. I'll let you know my departure date as soon as I get it.*

*I love you, Mom and can't wait to be home.*

*Your Son, Vince*

Regina laid Vince's letter on the coffee table, tears spilling down her face. Julia looked worried. She asked if everything was alright. Regina said yes and in a trembling voice, "Vince is coming home," Julia rushed into the parlor and grabbed Regina in a tight hug.

"That's wonderful news, Regina," Julia said, tears flowing freely from her eyes.

"It's what I've been praying for."

Julia released her embrace and started back to the kitchen.

"Julia, there's a part of Vince's letter for you."

"There is, what is it? Read it to me," Julia slid next to Regina on the sofa.

As Regina read Julia became progressively breathless. "Tommy, my son, Tommy," she repeated in a low voice, knowing at last what she desired most had become her reality, and then in a rush of tears she slumped in Regina's arms.

# 45

Rosemary McNulty's melancholy lifted, supplanted with relief, an emotion she hadn't experienced in a long time. The radiant summer sun on her skin made her feel alive, once again, and the anxieties that had plagued her were gone. She wanted to dance and pirouette along the street, instead she ran.

"Rosemary!"

"Hello Mr. Gruber," she shouted back not breaking stride.

"Is something wrong?" Benjamin shouted from the front door to his drugstore.

"I'm fine, Mr. Gruber."

"Come inside, have a cold drink."

"Thanks Mr. Gruber," Rosemary waved, "I can't stop."

"What is it with today's young people, Minnie?" Benjamin looked heaven-ward. "I don't know," he answered his question dismissively waving his hand, "I know, Minnie, I was young once," he answered closing the door behind him.

Julia and Regina sat side-by-side on the sofa permitting their welcome news to evict the fear that had been their constant companions.

"I should go, now," Regina said.

"Don't go. I'd like you to stay; for once we have something to be happy about. I'll make another pot of coffee."

Regina assented, and Julia disappeared into the kitchen. As Regina re-read Vince's letter the doorbell rang; its incessant ringing shattered the sense of peace, Julia and Regina had experienced minutes before.

"I'll get it," Julia went to the front door as the unnerving ringing of the doorbell continued, unabated. When she

The Burning Hours                                    Page 145

opened the door, Rosemary removed her finger from the doorbell and the ringing stopped.

"My God! Rosemary."

Regina rushed into the vestibule.

Rosemary clutched an envelope in her hand.

"I received a letter from Tommy, Mom. I had to come to tell you," Rosemary's said, breathlessly.

"Settle down, Rosemary."

"Okay, Mom," Rosemary took a breath, "Tommy teases Sergeant Darling, who wrote Tommy's words. He says while he speaks Jersey Sergeant Darling writes in Alabama so he hopes I can understand what's in the letter."

"I'm delighted for you," Julia kissed Rosemary's cheeks repeatedly, "Very happy for you and Tommy."

"That's not all, Mom. Tommy told me to tell you he loves you."

"He did?"

"Yes."

"That's twice in one day," Regina said.

Julia was speechless.

"Tommy said I am his first and only girl," Rosemary's mouth quivered before she burst into another flood of tears.

# 46

Vince arrived at the Hoboken Bus Station mid-afternoon in early January 1946. The winter wind felt icy on his neck. He walked to the station building still decorated with Christmas and New Year ornaments where buses idled. Vince was glad to be home, to have survived the war, but conflicted by the deaths of so many friends. He believed he'd be able to sleep at Camp Lucky Strike. It was warm and there was no danger, but when Vince closed his eyes his relentless nightmares began.

The crowd moved at a snail's pace. Vince shifted his duffel bag back-and-forth for physical relief. He lit a cigarette and noticed a short soldier coming toward him.

"I'm going to Newark, where are you headed?"

"Why do you want to know?" Vince shot back.

"That taxi will take me into Newark, but I don't have the fare he's asking."

Vince looked at the soldier his face a combination of plea and hope. "I'm going to Jersey City, how much does he want?"

"Four bucks, how about it, we'll split?"

"Yeah, sure," Vince said, anything to get off this line.

"I'm Leo McGurn, everybody calls me Shorty."

"Vince Farro I guess I won the lottery."

They tossed their duffel bags into the trunk and got into the back seat. The driver gunned the accelerator and at long last Vince was on his way home.

"You live in Jersey City, Vince?"

"All my life. What about you?"

"California, Los Angeles. I'll be leaving from Grand Central in Newark. You'll be home before me," Leo said, his irrepressible personality contrasting sharply with Vince's reserved persona.

---

The Burning Hours                              Page 147

The long nightmare had ended. Life had awakened from the doldrums of the war years. Cars and trucks jammed the streets and highways. People rushed in all conceivable directions. The taxi ride was a milk-run, stopping and going, but it was preferable to a lumbering bus.

The cabbie drove to Journal Square where Vince had announced his intention to get off. After two years away his first sight of personal significance was Hilltop High School overlooking the street below.

"What's that building that's got your attention?" Leo asked.

"The high school I went to."

"The draft got me before I could graduate."

"Yeah, me, too."

"Journal Square!" the cabbie announced.

"This is where I get off," Vince said.

"Two bucks since you guys are splitting the fare."

Vince took five singles from his wallet, "That should cover the trip."

"You only owe two," Leo said.

"The trip's on me. I have a short walk home. You have a long ride ahead of you."

"I'll pay you back," Leo promised.

"Good luck, Shorty."

"Same to you, Vince."

"Okay, driver," with Vince's one-two slap of the palm of his hand on the passenger door, the taxi drove away. Vince hoisted his duffel bag onto his shoulder. Before starting home he looked around at familiar sights that seemed illusions of his not so long ago past. He walked past the theaters and the shops on the square. The massive brown brick multi-level hotel on the corner elicited memories of when he and Tommy were kids running along its wide flat top fence guarded by two concrete lions at its entrance.

Before he was drafted Vince didn't think about the Blue, Silver and Gold Star flags hanging in the windows of houses in the neighborhood. When he returned home from basic training and saw a flag with a single Blue Star hanging in his window and one in Tommy's window their meaning became personal. When he left for overseas the Blue Star was replaced with a single Silver Star flag. Down the hill Vince looked across the street at Kurt Schaeffer's house where a single Gold Star flag hung in the window. He put down his duffel bag, saluted, and then continued on his way; his desire to see his mother, to be home grew more powerful with each step he took.

The chill wind rose as dusk turned the day gray when Vince arrived at the porch of his home. He went up its steps, opened the unlocked front door and set his bag down. From the vestibule he saw Regina her back to him sitting at the kitchen table folding clean laundry. There was a pervasive quiet in the house.

"I'm home, Mom," Vince said, softly.

At the sound of his voice Regina stopped her chore, buried her face in her hands and with tears stinging her eyes, she said, "I won't turn around. I won't be deceived by another cruel dream. I heard your voice too many times and too many times I was disappointed. I won't believe it's you until you touch me, when I feel your touch, I'll believe."

Vince parted Regina's hands from her face, "See, Mom, I'm home," he said in a consoling voice.

# 47

Vince woke drenched in sweat at 3:00 o'clock in the morning. He sat in the parlor bathed in the soft blue light of the decorated Christmas tree Regina had left up for him. Unlike the noise in his head the parlor was serenely quiet. Vince wondered if the war would forever mold the rest of his life. He envied the guys who went home to their wives, girlfriends, children, to the family farm or their waiting jobs. He had no wife, no children and the woman he desired was beyond his reach.

Hearing Vince stir Regina emerged from her bedroom wrapped warmly in a terrycloth robe, "What's wrong?" she asked, her voice low and concerned.

"I'm okay, Mom, couldn't sleep."

Regina sat next to him on the sofa, "It's too cold sitting here."

"Sorry I woke you, Mom. Go back to bed."

"What's troubling you, Vince?"

"It's something a lot of the guys are going through; it will go away, don't worry."

"What will go away?"

Vince didn't answer.

"What will go away, Vince?" Regina repeated in a sterner voice.

"Mom, you should go to bed. I'll be okay."

"Until you say what's bothering you, you won't be able to deal with it."

"It's the nightmares. I see friends dead in the snow. I never wanted to kill anyone, Mom, but I did," Vince said, his voice cracking. "It haunts me that I did that. When I wake up, I can't breathe. It never stops."

Vince's turmoil cut Regina like a sharp knife. She put her arms around his shoulders and cried.

"I shouldn't have told you, Mom. Don't be upset, I'll work it out."

"Don't try to shield me, Vincent Farro," a maternal resolve flashed in her eyes, "You have to unburden yourself. The sooner you do the nightmares will stop. Now, try to get some sleep. Leave your nightmares in Europe, where they belong."

"The only times you called me Vincent was when you were mad at me."

"Heaven knows I'm not mad at you. I don't want you to be plagued by nightmares that you can chase away, if you fight them."

"Okay, Mom."

"I'm right," Regina said with an unwavering certainty. Now, try to sleep."

"I'll sleep here, tonight."

"Your bed will be more comfortable."

"Here is good, Mom."

"I'll get a pillow and blanket."

Vince fit his now 6'2" body on the sofa. Regina placed a pillow under his head and threw a blanket over him. She ran her hand through his thick black hair and kissed his forehead, "You will find a wonderful girl and your life will change. Now, try to sleep," Regina said, "I'll turn off the tree lights."

"Leave them on, Mom."

Regina nodded, but before leaving the parlor Vince called to her.

"Mom, tomorrow I'm going to visit Pop's grave."

# 48

In the early morning Regina was in the kitchen ironing Vince's laundered Army shirt and pressing a sharp crease onto his uniform trousers that she had reeled inside from the frigid air. As she swept the hot iron over Vince's shirt she smiled at the memory of Vincenzo and Vince, thirteen and growing like a weed, standing at rigid attention in the hallway, suppressing their laughter, waiting for her final inspection before leaving for Sunday Mass.

Now with Vince home safe and her anxieties expired the quiet morning was an incubator of memories and they flowed freely. Regina had graduated college, a rarity for a young woman in her neighborhood, and taught English to newly arrived immigrants. She was a young, attractive woman pursued by several suitors. But, it was the handsome young barber from Italy who stole her heart. She tutored him in English and their mutual attraction blossomed into love. Friends and colleagues were mystified at her rejection of the *"American"* boys, the WASPS who ardently pursued her, deciding instead on the barber who spoke heavily accented English. When she explained that she loved Vincenzo without reservation, her friends and colleagues accepted her decision, and yet, her reasoning eluded them.

Regina looked in on Vince sleeping, fitfully. She organized the ingredients of a hot breakfast. Before long the aroma of brewed coffee got Vince off the sofa into the kitchen where Regina was heating two skillets. From behind Vince put his arms around Regina's waist and kissed her cheeks.

"Good morning, Mom."

"It's good you are home, Vince, I prayed for this day."

"Breakfast smells good."

"Wash up, it will be ready, soon."

The Burning Hours                    Page 152

"I can't tell you how many times I thought about your pancakes and coffee."

"Stop wasting time and sit down, I'm putting the first batch on now."

"Okay, Mom, I prefer being ordered around by you, than the mess hall sergeant, and the food is a hell...," Vince stopped, "Sorry, I mean the food is a lot better here."

"Never mind," Regina said, "Enjoy your breakfast."

"There's only one place set?"

"I had something, earlier," Regina said, "I'm going with you to Papa's resting place."

"You miss Pop, don't you, Mom?"

"Every day."

"When I was wounded, Pop came to me."

"You never told me."

"I saw him before I passed out."

"I'll see him, again, Vince, I believe that."

"I know, Mom."

"I put Papa's razor, brush and soap mug for you in the bathroom," Regina said, a somber tone now in her voice.

"Thanks, Mom."

In the bathroom, following breakfast, Vince looked into the mirror his face lathered with suds recalling his father's shaving ritual when he was a boy. When finished, Vincenzo lathered Vincent's face with soap suds, and with his index finger, he shaved them off. Then emulating Vincenzo, Vincent cupped his face in his hands and exclaimed, "Feels good, Papa!"

When Vince left for the Army his face was relatively unencumbered with whiskers. Now as he shaved someone else appeared in the mirror. No longer was he the smooth face teenager who had left home. He slid his razor along the same route his father had taken countless times and when its rasping sound stopped, Vince cupped his face in his hands and whispered, "It feels good, Pop."

The Burning Hours                    Page 153

The gates of All Souls Cemetery opened at 10:00 o'clock every morning. Regina had dressed and was ready to leave. Vince finished dressing, and with a mischievous smile he said, "I'm ready for your inspection, Mom."

"Let's have a look," she said, "You'll do, except for this loose button on your overcoat."

"You're tougher than my sergeant, Mom."

"Yes, I think so," Regina smiled.

"Are you dressed warm enough, Mom?"

"Do you recognize my scarf?"

"It's the scarf I sent you from Belgium."

"I'll be fine."

"Alright, Vince said, putting on his hat."

"I have a very handsome, son; your father would be proud."

Regina pulled the front door closed. The sky was gray and overcast. Regina took Vince's arm and huddled close to him. They descended the porch steps on their way to All Souls Cemetery.

It was 9:30 in the cold morning

# 49

Half-an-hour after leaving home Vince and Regina arrived at All Souls Cemetery. They entered through its main entrance. The gates had been swept open at 10:00 o'clock by an ancient looking groundskeeper who completing his task disappeared into the warmth of a building at the far end of the cemetery. Vince and Regina walked along a curved path on frozen leaves that had fallen victim to winter's icy shears.

Off the path a young man and woman spread a grave blanket over the plot of their young daughter. Tenderly they smoothed the blanket as if tucking her warmly in bed. A chronological history of the three year old girl's brief life was engraved in a marble headstone.

Regina felt a pull in her heart at the sight. A three year old girl dying before her parents is not what nature intended, she thought. After Vince's birth she wanted a daughter to whom she could teach cooking and sewing and make frilly dresses, but she was unable to have another child.

The weather grew colder and Regina huddled close to Vince. Soon they arrived at Vincenzo's grave. Regina looked at Vince for his reaction. His eyes locked on the headstone's engravings: Vincenzo Farro, March 1900 – May 1941; Regina Farro, July 1903 - ). Vince didn't flinch when a surge of wind blew. He bent and kissed the marble headstone, which brought a rush of tears to Regina.

"Hello, Pop, I'm home, a couple of scratches, but I'm okay. I'm here with Mom."

"Good morning, my husband. These are my happy moments when I am with you."

Vince put his arms around Regina's shoulders.

"Remember the times we went to the park, Pop, when I swept the barber shop floor and you treated me to ice cream at Gruber's. I remember watching you shave and then you lathered my face with soap, and the times you saved me from

Mom's tender mercies," Vince said, pulling Regina closer to him.

"What are you saying, Vincent Farro? Don't pay any attention to him, Vincenzo," Regina reacted to Vince's last memory.

"Remember the time Tommy Tomasso and I got thrown out of Sunday Mass. When I got home, Mom asked if I had been to confession, I said I had. Then she asked if I had received Communion. I knew I couldn't lie. It would be worse for me if I lied, so I said no and then it began."

"That was a terrible thing your son and Tommy did and you, Vincenzo found it funny."

"It was Tommy's fault, Pop," Vince continued the story, "Mr. Gallo wore that hilarious toupee. When he came by with the collection basket I whispered to Tommy that it looked like a squirrel on his head. Tommy started laughing, and then I started laughing. Mr. Gallo told us to leave and you and Mom would hear from the Monsignor."

Vince paused, genuinely enjoying the memory.

Regina smiled, recalling that Sunday.

"Tommy and I were thrown out for laughing during Holy Communion. You said you didn't know if you could keep a straight face the next time Mr. Gallo came into the shop wearing his toupee. And you started laughing a real belly laugh," I loved hearing you laugh, Vince said wistfully.

"Mom said I was gonna really get it, but you got me off the hook."

"Your son and Tommy Tomasso were always stirring each other up, Vincenzo. They were masters at getting each other in trouble and you, my husband encouraged him. Remind your father why I added another week to your confinement."

Vince smiled, he was sure Vincenzo listened, enjoying the memories and despite the worsening weather, the feeling at the gravesite was warm.

"Mom confined me to the house for two weeks. It was tough to be in prison during summer vacation."

"You weren't in prison Mr. Farro! You were allowed outside with permission, but you weren't allowed to see or communicate with Tommy."

"Anyway, Pop, Tommy and I figured out a way to communicate."

"I'll finish the story, wise guy," Regina smacked Vince's arm. "The two jailbirds used my clothes line to write notes to each other about their schemes. When your son volunteered to reel in the laundry, I thought his punishment was doing him some good. That is until the day I took in the laundry and under a clothes pin there was a note to your son from Tommy."

"I got another week in the cooler," Vince laughed.

"And, you thought it was funny," Regina said, crying, "Everyday I miss you I'll never stop loving you."

"It's okay, Mom. Pop is here with us, laughing, enjoying these moments."

Regina placed her hand on the headstone.

Vince kissed the cold marble, "I love you, Pop," he whispered. Then he put his arm around Regina's shoulders, she tilted her head against his chest, her eyes moist from crying and softly Vince said, "Let's go, Mom?"

# 50

Visits to Vincenzo's grave always left Regina emotionally drained. It was after 11:00 o'clock by the time they reached home. Vince suspected Regina's lethargy to be more emotional than physical. She told Vince to go out and forget the war, and then she went to her bed, closed her eyes and fell asleep.

Vince decided to visit his former high school teachers. He walked along the inclining street that intersected Journal Square. By the time he arrived at Hill Top High School the building had largely emptied of students and teachers for the weekend. At its main entrance a cluster of young boys asked Vince how many Germans he killed. He didn't answer and went inside to the administrative office where he asked a receptionist if Samuel Birkman was on campus. The receptionist said he was in his classroom. Vince acknowledged with a nod, went into the corridor and climbed the staircase's squeaking steps to the second floor.

Samuel Birkman looked up from his book at Vince standing in the doorway.

"My God, Vince Farro!" He grabbed and held Vince in a bear hug.

"Don't mind me I'm a sentimental old fool."

"Good seeing you, Mr. Birkman."

"You look a foot taller than when I last saw you," Samuel exclaimed, "come in, sit down, let's talk," he spoke, excitedly.

"Not there, here, next to me," he patted a chair at the side of his desk.

Vince removed his hat and sat down.

"Thanks for your letters, Mr. Birkman they meant a lot to me. Sorry I didn't write back as often as I should have."

"You had more important things on your mind."

"Yeah, I guess so."

"You were wounded, Vince, how are you, now?"

The Burning Hours                                    Page 158

"I'm okay, a fraction of an inch the other way, and you could guess the result."

"Tommy lost his sight and Kurt was killed," Samuel reflected, solemnly, "I look around and I visualize you boys in your seats," he shook his head, "too many losses, all too soon the flower of youth perishes."

"I saw Tommy before coming home. He's got a rough road ahead, but you know Tommy, he's tough, he'll make it."

"Do you need money?" Samuel whispered.

"No, but thanks for asking."

"I have a question, if you don't mind."

"Ask away," Vince responded.

"Before your father passed, I was in his shop for a haircut. "Only your father had the skill to cut this mop," he smiled. "He mentioned how you told Tommy that Mr. Gallo's toupee looked like a squirrel on his head. Then both of you had seizures of laughter during Holy Communion and were tossed out of the church. Your father roared with laughter."

"It's a true story, Mr. Birkman."

"He said you were in major trouble with your mother, but he got you off the hook."

"Yeah, Pop saved me, more than once," Vince smiled.

"Your beautiful mother," Samuel reflected, "She had the pick of any eligible bachelor. But, when your father, looking the way you look now, walked into her class to learn English, smiled and said, *Buona Sera, Signorina,* your mother's eyes lit up like the brightest star in the firmament; the rest is history. A good and honorable man your father," he continued, "Too young," Samuel lamented, "much too young, a grave loss for us all."

"Mom and I visited the cemetery earlier today. We reminisced with Pop about the episode with Mr. Gallo. Strange you are mentioning it, only a few hours later."

"I knew you'd be here," he tapped his ear, "your father whispered to me."

"When I was wounded Pop appeared to me, he looked just like I remembered him."

"He's always with you and your mother, Vince."

"I want to believe that," Vince said.

"There are many unsolved mysteries in life. Now, tell me about your plans."

"I'm going to take it easy for a while. Then I'll look for a job. There might be openings at Western Electric. I'd like to follow up on your suggestion to teach English."

"Enjoy yourself, Vince, visit the shore, bake in the sun, and …," he winked, "make love to a beautiful girl. If you are still interested in a teaching career, I will prepare letters of recommendation to the college of your choice. How's that sound?"

"It's a deal," Vince stood up offering a handshake.

Instead Samuel grabbed him in another bear hug, "Go now, snow is on the way."

"Can I borrow some books from the library?"

"That won't be a problem, hurry before it closes."

"Tommy said thanks for helping him with Mr. Brady."

"It was nothing. Get on your way and let an old man get emotional in private.

# 51

Linda Conover pulled on her boots and re-applied her lipstick when the library door opened.

"I'll be right with you, Florence."

"If you're closing, I'll come back another time."

The voice that answered wasn't Florence Munson. It was masculine and deep. At first, Linda didn't recognize it, but there was something familiar in its resonance. She put away her lipstick tube and zipped closed her pocketbook.

From the doorway of the cloakroom she watched a tall uniformed soldier looking at her Mark Twain display. When Vince turned Linda was standing a few feet from him. He removed his hat and as he did a shock of dark wavy hair fell to the side of his forehead which he quickly swept back into place.

Everything Vince wanted to say to Linda was out of bounds. He wanted to tell her she looked more beautiful than when he last saw her, that her eyes could warm the coldest heart and her radiant smile light up the night. But, he knew it was unthinkable. Linda was older, she had been his high school teacher and she was married to the heir of the Conover fortune. So when they came face-to-face, after more than two years, all he could manage, was -

"Hello, Mrs. Conover."

For a moment Linda was speechless. The smooth-face teenage boy she had known came back from the war a ruggedly handsome young man. To her his transformation was nothing short of remarkable. Gone was her urgency to get home before the predicted snowstorm. She returned Vince's long look wondering if this man was once the teenage boy who had shown such an interest in books and literature. Suddenly she felt confused not knowing why or how to respond to him so she simply said -

The Burning Hours                                    Page 161

"Hello, Vincent. I hardly recognize you. You've grown so tall." And instantly, Linda wished she could start over. She knew her greeting was more like a mother saying to her son upon his return from summer camp that he had gotten to be a big boy.

"A war takes away your youth, you grow up fast," Vince answered.

"I didn't mean it the way it sounded, Vincent. I am glad to see you and happy that you are safely home. Please forgive my insensitivity," Linda said, feeling tense.

"It's okay, Mrs. Conover, I'm sorry I was rude."

"Not too many changes in the library," Linda changed the subject.

"Your Mark Twain display is attractive, like all of your displays."

Linda took Vince's hand, "I was upset when I read in the newspaper you had been wounded. But, you're all right, now. I'm so happy you came to see me."

"I'm all right," Vince said, softening the tense atmosphere, "How is Mr. Conover?"

Linda's mouth curled into a mischievous grin. "He's very well. I didn't know you knew my father."

"I mean your husband," Vince stammered.

"Oh, I know what you mean. I'm teasing you. My married name was Reed. I kept my maiden name for professional reasons. Dr. Reed and I have been divorced for several months, now."

"I'm sorry."

"Don't be sorry, it was for the best. So now you know. I'm the real Conover," she laughed.

"Oh," Vince said, uncomfortably.

"Oh," Linda needled, "Is that a problem for you?"

"Well ... No," Vince said, "It's just that I never knew a society girl.

"Well, now you know one," Linda rubbed it in, "I'm enjoying your discomfort, Vincent."

Vince laughed. "I guess we're even."

"Can we stop tormenting each other?" she extended her hand.

"Sure."

Vince took Linda's hand, squeezed it and reluctantly let go. The tension between them eased and they exchanged smiles.

Linda took a small book of poems from her desk. The note pinned to its cover read – *For Vincent Farro.* It was a book of Lord Byron's poems that Vince couldn't find in her library. Linda purchased a copy from a local bookseller and kept it on her desk expecting his visit. When Vince didn't show she put the book away.

Now her mood became serious as she handed the book of poems to Vince. She was still mystified as to why he hadn't visited her, knowing he had seen his other teachers. She was about to ask when Florence Munson came into the library.

"Could this be Vincent Farro," she exclaimed. "Come here give an old lady a kiss." Vince obliged and in return Florence planted a loud kiss on Vince's cheek.

"A five o'clock shadow to boot," she ran the back of her hand along Vince's stubble, exclaiming further, "Linda, don't you love the rasping sound of a man's beard? When did you shave last?"

"Early this morning; it grows fast."

"Well, you're not the teenage boy who said good-bye to me."

*"Everyone but me, Vincent; you visited everyone, but me."*

"With men like this, Linda, the war's outcome was never in doubt."

Cascading thoughts and unanswered questions flooded Linda's mind.

*"How did 70-year old Florence sense Vincent's needs? How could I have been so short-sighted? After what he had*

*been through, he was right to feel irritated with me. I waited for his visit, to give him the book I bought for him, to say good-bye, but he never came. When I looked at the book on my desk, I thought about him. When he was gone and I put the book away, he was never far from my thoughts. When I read in the newspaper he had been wounded and his condition unknown, I cried and I worried. Now, I feel like a stranger in his presence."*

Linda looked at Florence and smiled her agreement.

"It was good seeing you, Vincent. Ready to go, Linda?"

Vince and Linda didn't move.

"Let's go, Linda, before the snow comes."

"I'll see you outside, Florence."

"Vincent, why didn't you see me before you left? I thought we got along so well. Why didn't you visit me?"

"You were my favorite teacher, Miss Conover and I loved coming to the library," Vince stopped, "You should go before the weather worsens."

"You haven't answered my question, Vincent."

"Thanks for the book, Miss Conover. It was good seeing you, again," Vince stepped back, turned and walked out of the library.

The Burning Hours

Page 164

# 52

Leaving the school building, Linda saw Vince at the cannon mount leaning on the cold stone with his elbows smoking a cigarette. She bid Florence Munson good night and walked down the declining path to the cannon mount.

"Vincent," she touched Vince's shoulder.

"You should be getting home, Miss Conover, the storm is coming," Vince said, and turned away.

Linda remained still, she wanted to touch him again, but refrained. Vince continued looking into the distance, smoking.

Linda started walking away.

"It seems like a hundred years ago, the death and the misery."

At the sound of his voice Linda went to Vince.

"You are home now with the people you love and who love you," Linda consoled, unsure Vince had listened so she waited, quietly for a long time for any response.

"Death was a matter of inches, a fraction in either direction and I'd be nothing more than a ghost in your life," Vince said still looking away.

"That is an awful thing to say to me," Linda reacted.

"Sorry," Vince mumbled.

"What have I ever done that you would say such a terrible thing to me?"

"Vince flipped his consumed cigarette over the wall continuing to look into the distance.

"The least you can do, Vincent is look at me when I speak to you."

"You didn't do anything to me, Miss Conover," Vince said after a protracted interval.

"Then why, Vincent, why are you so distant with me?"

"I didn't mean to upset you."

"You succeeded, admirably," Linda said.

"The storm is coming you should go home."

"I don't understand. Why won't you talk with me? If I offended you in some way, Vincent, you must tell me."

"You didn't offend me."

"Is that all you have for me?"

"Yeah, I guess that's it."

"You're right the storm is coming," Linda began walking away, her eyes glazed with tears she was holding back.

"Wait," Vince said, walking to her.

"Please make me understand, Vincent, don't you know you're hurting me?"

"I'm sorry I never meant to hurt you, Miss Conover."

"Is it the war?"

"And other things I'm in a knot that I can't unravel."

"Maybe I can help, Vincent, if you let me," Linda offered as snow began falling.

"Thanks, Miss Conover, but there are things that can't be changed."

"I don't believe that, and stop calling me, Miss Conover, my name is Linda."

"Okay, Linda," Vince smiled.

"Walk with me to the trolley station?" Linda returned Vince's smile.

"Sure, I'd like that."

Linda took Vince's arm.

"You have a loose button on your overcoat."

"There wasn't enough time to mend it before Mom and I left the house to visit Pop's grave this morning."

"Does a loose button mean you are out-of-uniform?"

"Yes, it does. Mom will mend it when I get home."

"Tell me about your mother and father, Vincent," Linda asked as they walked to the main gate of the campus.

"Mom and Pop were great together. If you could have seen them you'd know what I mean. They both had

The Burning Hours                                    Page 166

humorous streaks, but Mom was the disciplinarian. When I was old enough Pop and I would scheme to set her off.

"You schemed against your mother?"

"It was all in fun. One Sunday before Mass Pop put shaving cream from his mug on the tips of our noses."

"How old were you?"

"Six or seven."

"Scheming against your mother when you were six or seven, I don't know about you, Vincent," Linda laughed.

"When Mom came into the vestibule we were standing at attention, trying not to laugh. She took one look at us and said, Good Lord, what did I do to deserve this? Then she wiped our noses with a handkerchief she took from her pocketbook and we left for Mass."

"So, Vincent, you were a bad boy."

"Pop bailed me out most of the times."

"Not all of the time," Linda smiled.

"Not all the time."

"Mom taught here, at Hilltop."

"I didn't know."

"She taught English in the day school and conversational English to newly arrived immigrants in the night school that's where she and Pop met; it was love at first sight."

The falling snow began accumulating as Vince and Linda walked to the trolley station.

"Mom miscarried, a baby girl. And then learned she couldn't have more children. It hit her hard. She often says Pop held her together during her difficult times."

"Your father sounds like a wonderful man."

"Pop is my hero a good and honorable man with a fabulous sense of humor. He was a barber in the neighborhood," Vince paused, and then he said, "He died when I was sixteen. It was sudden and hard knowing I would never see him, again. Everybody says I look like him," Vince said, wistfully.

The Burning Hours

"I'm sorry you lost your father, Vincent. I can't imagine losing my parents. It must have been terrible for you."

"Memories are good, but they are insufficient substitutes for his not being here."

"Your father must have been a very handsome man."

Vince smiled at Linda and said, "He was, should I take that as a compliment?"

"That is how it is offered."

Vince smiled.

"Are you cold, Linda?"

"A little, Vincent," she answered.

"Call me Vince," they exchanged smiles.

"I prefer Vincent."

"Okay, you win, Vincent it is."

"I usually do," Linda laughed, tugging playfully at Vince.

"Do you take after your mother or your father or a little of both?"

"My mother taught school, like your mother. Her first baby, a boy, died in childbirth. She was devastated for a long time and then I came long. She couldn't have any more children."

"We have something in common."

"What is that?" Linda asked.

"You're an only child and so am I."

"Is that good?"

"I hope so," Vince answered.

"I am the image of my mother."

"She must be a beautiful woman."

"That's nice of you to say."

"I meant it as a compliment."

"I accept in the spirit it was offered," they exchanged smiles.

The Palisade Avenue trolley hadn't arrived. The snow storm worsened. Vince looked at Linda her head pressed against his forearm enjoying the moments. And yet he knew soon they would end only to be preserved in his memory.

Vince looked again at Linda huddled against him as the approaching trolley slowed to a stop at the platform where passengers waited to board.

Linda tried to navigate the emotional currents running through her mind. Vince swept wisps of her hair that had escaped from under her wool hat, back into place. When he asked if she was cold Linda nodded, yes.

Vince slipped his arm around her shoulder and pressed her against him, "Is this better?"

Linda said yes without looking at him.

"You'll be warm in the trolley and soon you'll be home."

"Will I be as warm in there as I am here, now?"

Vince tightened his embrace and smiled.

"Do you have the book I bought for you?"

"It's under my coat," Vince placed his hand on his chest.

"Promise you'll keep it to remember me," Linda asked plaintively, no longer feeling like the privileged older woman, the high school teacher or the divorcee who survived an abusive marriage. Now she felt transformed into a young woman in the warm embrace of a special young man on a snowy evening she was about to lose.

"I promise," they stood in silence as the trolley filled with passengers.

Linda said good-bye, hurried into the crowd and disappeared into the trolley. She didn't look back.

Vince walked away from the trolley and he thought -

*Today was an affectionate hello and farewell. That's all it could ever be. One day I'll visit the library and I'll be greeted by a woman unknown to me who will tell me Linda Conover went back to Connecticut, to her life of privilege.*

# 53

On the trolley Linda sat in a window seat dabbing her eyes. A passenger in the aisle chair asked if she was all right. She answered yes, excused herself and went to the conductor.

"Please let me out."

"It's snowing, are you sure you want to leave?"

"Yes, I'm sure."

Before opening the door the conductor, a burly middle-age man said, "He's on the platform. I'll stay as long as I can, I'll whistle, twice when I'm ready to leave."

"I understand, thank you."

"No problem sweetheart. A pretty girl like you shouldn't be crying. Being young and in love is one of life's greatest joys."

"But it brings such pain."

"It doesn't matter if you are with the right person."

Linda walked off the trolley onto the platform.

When she came to Vince, he said, "You should go home, Linda."

"Why are you still here, Vincent?"

"I wanted to be sure you got on your way, safely."

"You're fibbing, aren't you, Vincent? Aren't you?" her voice rose, "I've cried more in one hour over you than I have in my entire life. I'm not going to cry anymore, Vincent. You're not being fair. Why won't you talk to me?"

Vince looked away, he didn't respond.

"You're infuriating, Vincent," she exclaimed, "don't you know I have feelings for you, can't you see that?"

Vince shuffled, uncomfortably, and then in a barely audible voice, he said, "I have loved you for a long time, Linda."

"Come with me," Linda tugged on Vince's loose button. "There is much we need to say to each other," she paused and lightening the atmosphere, "I'll mend your button and make us hot chocolates and we can talk the night away, okay?"

"That's a cute hat you're wearing," Vince teased.

"Don't change the subject, Vincent, will you come with me?"

"You know I want to."

"Not until you tell me," she looked into his eyes, "soon the conductor will whistle twice we'll either board together or I'll go home alone, what will it be?"

"Yes," Vince nodded, "Yes," he repeated.

"Did I hear you say yes?"

"Yes, I said yes."

"Was that so painful," Linda pushed Vince's shoulder, "Are you satisfied, now, you got me crying, again, and I promised myself no more tears over you."

"A society girl who sews and makes hot chocolate, what other talents do you have?"

"I knitted the hat," she laughed.

Inside the trolley curious passengers peered out the windows at the romantic drama unfolding on the snowy platform. A few men wagered on the outcome, and when Vince took Linda in his arms and kissed her mouth several women swooned while a middle-age man collected his winnings.

The trolley whistle sounded, twice, and its door swung open.

The conductor winked at Linda and she smiled, back.

"No charge, soldier," the conductor rejected Vince's fare, "You kids made my day."

# 54

Vince and Linda boarded greeted with smiles, handshakes and scattered applauses. They sat side-by-side, Linda in the window seat and Vince on the aisle. A middle-aged gentleman thanked Vince for coming on-board saying he won a ten dollar bet from his brother-in-law. As Linda beamed an elderly woman leaned past Vince and whispered she was glad that she went out and brought back her young man. She recounted how she practically had to kidnap Walter, her husband of happy memory, and lead him to the altar, continuing that men are such babies, too scared to fight for the women they love, and then casting a sly look at Vince, she told Linda that she indeed had a very handsome baby.

The conductor engaged the starter and within seconds the trolley rolled forward. Soon it was quiet inside. The trolley's rhythmic motion created a hypnotic effect on napping passengers as it drove through falling snow along the elevated trestle connecting Jersey City to Hoboken.

"When we get home I'll make hot chocolates and mend this," Linda twisted the button on Vince's overcoat.

"Then I'll be back in uniform, right?"

"You'll be the spiffiest soldier in New Jersey," Linda squeezed his hand.

"Snow's coming down hard," Vince observed looking past Linda out the window.

"It's a short walk from the station to the apartment I'll enjoy walking through the snow, holding onto to you."

Vince touched Linda's cheek and thought what a beautiful woman she is. Her brown eyes smiled warmly at his touch, she leaned her head against his chest and closed her eyes for a minute, and then said, "Daddy proposed to Mother on a trolley. Their courtship lasted one day from the day they met."

"Your father was fast," Vince said.

"Most of the unwed country club women were after him, but it was mother he wanted. They met on a Saturday when Mother delivered Uncle Paolo's lunch when he was working on the estate's swimming pool. In a single day, after a terrible misunderstanding, Daddy proposed marriage on a trolley in Westport."

"I'll bet you have a picture of Uncle Paolo and you," Vince said, "when you were a little girl wearing a construction hat with your name on it."

"I'll show you the picture when we get home. How did you guess?"

"It was easy you probably hung the honorary title of uncle on him when he was working around the estate, and you were chirping, in your little girl voice: Can I help, Uncle Paolo? Are you coming back, tomorrow, Uncle Paolo? And the title stuck. How's that? Bet I'm right."

"That's very good, Vincent," Linda's eyes narrowed, "You figured that out all by yourself. I'm impressed with your grasp of logic, but there's a problem, Einstein."

"Oh, yeah," Vince glanced at Linda, quizzically.

"You're wrong. Uncle Paolo is my mother's brother and for your information that makes him my blood relative," she shook her hand loose.

"Why are you mad at me?"

"Why would you think I couldn't be related to a man with the name Paolo? Can't you get over the notion that I come some rarified place?"

"The world you come from is different from …"

"From what, Vincent, from where you come from?"

"Mayflower men don't have names like Paolo, that's all I'm saying."

"That's not all your saying. I told you where I come from and where you come from doesn't matter to me," and then she leaned in and whispered, "because, I love you. If you must know Mother was nineteen when she and Daddy

The Burning Hours                           Page 173

got married. Mother's parents came from Sicily. I never knew them; they died when Mother was very young. Uncle Paolo looked after her until she married my father. Is there anything else you need to know?"

Vince shrugged.

Linda reclaimed his hand.

"Do you feel better knowing I am part Italian?"

Vince shrugged.

"You're such a dope, Vincent, but I love you, anyway."

# 55

Helmut Wagner was clearing snow off the sidewalk of his one-level, red brick apartment building when Linda and Vince arrived. A veteran of the Kaiser's World War I army, Helmut was a forthright gentleman who spoke his mind in a thick German accent. He had purchased his apartment building at the height of the Great Depression when it was uninhabitable. His imagination and hard work transformed it into a two-unit desirable rental property, one of which Linda leased when she came to New Jersey.

"It looks like we're in for a lot of snow, Mr. Wagner."

"I think so. God brings it and with a little help from me and this shovel, I help him take it away."

"This is Vincent Farro, Mr. Wagner."

"I know this young man from his picture in the newspapers," he removed his glove, "we are all proud of you, son."

"Nice meeting you Mr. Wagner," they shook hands.

"You treat this lovely young lady good, son. She's a delightful girl. If my *schatzi* had a daughter, she would be like this young woman, but," he waved his hand, "it wasn't to be, my *schatzi* is long gone, but my memories are warm."

"I will Mr. Wagner, if she gives me the chance."

"What do you think about this boy, Miss Conover?

"I like him very much, Mr. Wagner."

"Just very much?" he said with a twinkle in his eyes.

"Very, very much, Mr. Wagner."

"Then, there is nothing more to be said. Go in, now before you get cold."

Linda's apartment was cozy, functional and understated. Its walls painted a cheerful cream-color. A coat rack with equally spaced gold-colored hooks and a hardwood countertop was fixed to the foyer wall. With the exception of the bedroom and its bathroom the apartment was open and visible from the foyer. A double window looked out to the street. A rectangular coffee table separated a soft rust-colored sofa and a matching easy chair. A waist high partition divided the kitchen from the parlor. A small utility table at the far end of the kitchen brimmed with sewing and knitting supplies.

Linda hung her coat on a coat rack hook, slipped off and neatly placed her boots against the wall, took off her wool hat and put it on the countertop.

Vince hung his overcoat and jacket next to Linda's and put his hat on the countertop. Linda went to the kitchen where she took two mugs and a tin of cocoa from a cabinet above the stove and a bottle of milk from the refrigerator.

"I hope you like your hot chocolate with milk," she said, igniting a burner, "Make yourself comfortable, there are copies of *Life* and *Look* magazines." She then picked up a sewing box from the kitchen table and when she turned Vince still standing in the foyer.

"Are you coming in?"

Vince hesitated, then he said, "Until now the only places I lived in was home and in the army. When you closed the door behind us I felt different."

"Life changing experiences are powerful forces, Vincent. You are now in an intimate place with the woman who loves you," Linda said, softly and went into the kitchen.

Vince nodded.

"Get comfortable," Linda said. Within minutes she returned with two mugs of steaming hot chocolate. "Be careful!" she warned, "It is very hot." Sitting on her easy chair she pulled Vince's overcoat across her lap, snipped off the offending button, selected matching threads and began sewing.

With her thimble finger, she pushed a threaded needle through thick material securing the button. Incuriously Vince thumbed through the pages of *Life Magazine*, but was more interested in looking at Linda. There were no traffic sounds outside in the accumulating snow. A sense of tranquility pervaded the apartment, the kind of domestic atmosphere that Linda treasured. When she flipped Vince's overcoat to check her inside stitches its motion hiked up her skirt exposing her legs.

"Don't be fresh soldier, peeking is only allowed when I say so." She got up and hung Vince's mended overcoat on a hook in the foyer and then sat next to him on the sofa.

"I need to ask you something, Linda I hope you won't be upset."

"I don't want any unanswered questions between us."

"You might not want to talk about certain things and that's okay?"

"Tell me what's on your mind, Vincent," she sipped her hot chocolate.

"Why did you marry him? I saw the way he treated you at your party when you were appointed school librarian?"

"You remember that day?"

"I remember everything about that day, mostly about you, your smile, your walk, your brown eyes; I fell in love with you that day knowing it was an unattainable dream."

"Did you wake from your long sleep?"

"I did."

"What of your unattainable dream?"

"She is now my reality."

"To my everlasting shame I consented to marry him, an act of rebellion. I don't know what possessed me. My relationship with my parents is loving and respectful. Because of the war, many of the girls in my graduating class were getting married. I fell into that mindset. I never loved him, Vincent."

"Did you divorce him?

"Yes, I petitioned for the divorce," Linda answered, "I dated since my divorce, but nothing serious, and nothing happened."

"Did you live here with him in this apartment?"

"No."

"Why?"

"He preferred his friends, the drug dens and visiting prostitutes. I'm ashamed I didn't see the depth of his depravity. It was my decision that he not set foot here."

"He's out of your life now."

Linda placed her hot chocolate on the coffee table."

"What I am about to say might be painful. Please remember I love you, promise me?"

"Sure, I promise."

"You know I am not a virgin."

"I know."

"Does it matter to you?"

"You matter to me, Linda."

"I'm so sorry, Vincent," Linda burst into tears, "I wish I could have given you the gift of my virginity, but I can't."

"It doesn't matter," Vince consoled.

"Why didn't you see me before you left? Did I do something to anger you? If I did, you must tell me I want everything to be open and right with us," Linda pleaded.

"So many times I'd go to the library just to see you. You were always cheerful. I'd steal looks at you when you didn't suspect."

"Like before, when I caught you looking at my legs," Linda flashed a smile.

"There was a time in the library you helped me find what I was looking for. I couldn't concentrate when you were around. I thought you were the most beautiful woman on the planet. I knew even then that what I felt for you was more than a teenage boy's crush."

"Then why didn't you say good-bye to me? You saw everyone but me. When I read in the newspaper you were injured and your fate unknown I felt ill. If you didn't come back, I'd never know and the not knowing would be a wound that would never heal."

The Burning Hours                                          Page 178

"If I saw you Linda I'd tell you I loved you, an eighteen year old boy telling his teacher he had an incurable crush on her. I couldn't bear to hear you say I was a sweet boy, and then send me away with a peck on my cheek. I wasn't going to take that with me."

"I didn't know."

"You couldn't know I'm sorry I hurt you I never meant to."

"There is so much we would do over, if given the chance."

"Most of the guys in my squad were eighteen and nineteen; none of us had ever been with a woman. Our squad leader was twenty-two, we called him Pop. It's funny how war distorts everything. Earlier we drove a detachment of Germans from a village in France. Pop told us to expect a counter attack, which meant more of us would be dead. Some of the guys went to a house in the village to experience what it was like to be with a woman before they might die. A few of us went with chocolate bars, cigarettes and C-rations, payments for services we erroneously perceived to be love. I went Linda. I sat in the parlor waiting my turn."

"Vincent, stop; I don't need to know."

"One after one the guys came out of that room, it lasted a few minutes then a half-naked woman waved to me, when she said come I got up and …"

"Please, Vincent, I understand."

"I got up and left that place. No matter how impossible it seemed I thought how wonderful it would be if my first act of love was with you."

Linda fixed her gaze on Vince, a look of undisguised love in her eyes. She got up and rested her face on Vince's neck crying silent tears.

# 56

"I'm going outside for a smoke, Linda, is there anything I can do for you?"

"Dry the cups and saucers there are clean towels in the drawer."

"Kitchen patrol duty," Vince smiled drying and placing the cups and saucers in the kitchen cabinet as Linda instructed.

"Why are you smiling?" Linda asked.

"It feels good being here with you," Vince answered, "What brought you to Hoboken, Linda you could be living in Westport waited on by cooks and chauffeurs?"

"Are we re-visiting the society girl issue, again, Vincent?"

"No I'd like to know your motivation."

"The country club circuit is oxygen for most of my acquaintances, but I want my home to reflect who I am; does that answer your question?"

"But you are comfortable in either world?"

"It doesn't matter; do you know who you are, Vincent?"

"I don't know," Vince answered after a protracted silence.

"Think about it outside when you have your smoke. I know cigarettes were important when you were in the war, but you are home, now," Linda took one cigarette out of Vince's pack and handed it to him. "This is your last."

"You are a tough lady, Linda Conover."

"Only with the right man."

"Am I the right man?"

"You know you are."

"Are we clear about smoking?"

"Yeah, we're clear."

"You should call your mother, there's a phone in the bedroom."

The Burning Hours                    Page 180

"I forgot, thanks for reminding me."

Vince stopped at the doorway to Linda's bedroom.

"Don't be afraid, go in."

Linda's bedroom was airy. A large drape-covered window behind her bed looked out into a narrow side-street. Her bed was opposite the room's doorway and to the side of a bathroom.

Vince sat on the edge of Linda's bed.

"I'll close the door so you have privacy."

"I don't mind you hearing what I have to say," Linda smiled and went to the kitchen.

Regina answered the phone on the second ring.

"Hello, Mom, it's me, are you okay?"

"Weather weary, but I am fine."

"Do you have enough heat?"

"Yes, I'm warm, you just missed Julia Tomasso, she tells me you visited her, today."

"I did after we came home from the cemetery."

"She said your visit did her a lot of good."

"I won't be home tonight I'm staying with a friend."

"A female friend?"

"Yes, Mom, my friend is a woman."

"She's not one of those women."

"No, Mom she's a wonderful girl, the most beautiful girl in the world."

"Is she a neighborhood girl, do I know her?"

"No, you don't know her, you'll love her when you meet her, she's a teacher like you and her mother was a teacher."

"The world is full of coincidences."

"It sure is."

"Is your girl Italian, Vincent?"

"She's Italian on her mother's side."

"What's the other half?"

"Dutch, Mom, her father is Dutch."

"Okay Vince that'll do."

The Burning Hours
Page 181

"I'm glad it's okay with you, Mom," Vince laughed.

"You treat your young lady with respect, Vince, and be careful in this weather."

"I will I love you, Mom."

"I love you, too," Regina clicked off.

When Vince got up to leave Linda was standing in the bedroom doorway.

"I'm proud of you, Vincent, that you have such tender feelings for your mother. I see being part-Italian gets me into the Farro fraternity," she smiled.

"Yeah, you're in," Vince said.

"I never dreamed this day would be ending like this. Enough said let's get you arranged so you can go have your last cigarette, two layers of clothes, its freezing."

"What will you do while I'm outside?"

"Freshen up, change into something comfortable and resume my embroidery project."

"What are you embroidering?"

"It is an early morning sunrise over a silver ocean."

"Embroidering is tedious work," Vince commented.

"It's relaxing and rewarding to see the finished product," then changing the subject Linda reminded Vince not to track snow into the apartment.

"Okay," Vince acknowledged Linda's warning.

"No more than fifteen minutes, Vincent, and I will expect you in."

"You really are bossy," Vince opened the door and stepped into the hallway.

"Aren't you forgetting something?"

"And demanding," Vince kissed Linda's mouth.

"Fifteen minutes," she repeated.

More than an hour after Vince left the apartment Linda heard voices in the hallway. She rushed to where Vince, caked with snow, and Mr. Wagner, clad in a yellow slicker, shovels in their hands were laughing and chatting amiably.

"Vincent! I expected you would have been in over an hour ago."

"I thought I'd give Mr. Wagner a hand with the snow, sorry I lost track of time."

"Don't be angry with the boy he was a big help," Mr. Wagner clapped Vince on his shoulder causing snow to fly off his uniform overcoat."

"I'm glad he helped you, Mr. Wagner."

"A big help he was. *Danke,* Vince, now, you go with your lady I know that look I think you are in trouble."

"Good Night," Vince handed his shovel to Helmut and walked past Linda, who glared at him, into the apartment.

"Good night, Mr. Wagner," Linda said.

"Don't be hard on the boy."

"Good night, Mr. Wagner," Linda repeated, closing the door behind her.

# 57

"How did fifteen minutes turn into more than an hour, Vincent? What in the world were you thinking? You're shedding snow over my clean floor," Linda turned away and returned with a rug, "Take off your shoes and socks and stand on the rug," she commanded. "I see now why your mother whacked you the only problem is she didn't do it often enough," Linda began unbuttoning Vince's overcoat, "You're just a big kid, Vincent with a little monster inside itching to get out."

"Yeah, he can't wait."

"I didn't mean it that way you jerk."

"I'll unbutton it myself," Vince said.

Linda pushed his hand away, unbuttoned, and hung up Vince's overcoat, "Take off your jacket."

"Aren't you going to unbutton?" Vince laughed.

"Unbutton it yourself," Linda fumed.

"I thought you liked taking care of me," Vince grinned.

"You're such a child, I don't know why, but I do like taking care of you."

"What's so funny?"

"Nothing."

"Nothing! I was worried about you didn't you think about that? I looked out the window and I couldn't see you through the snow. I went to the front door and you were nowhere in sight. I'm really angry at you, Vincent. You left me in suspense for over an hour," she vented, and stormed into the kitchen.

"The only thing I want from you is an apology."

"I wanted to help Mr. Wagner I lost track of time, sorry I upset you."

"I'm mad at you, but I'll get over it. When time went by and I didn't know where you were an image of you lying in the snow in Belgium flashed through my mind and I got upset," Linda pushed Vince, "And I'm still upset. You should have told me what you were doing."

"I'm really sorry, come on, give me a break?"

"Don't make me worry like that, okay?"

"I'll be more considerate I promise," Vince crossed his heart.

"I'm sorry I was cross with you, Vincent, I didn't mean to sound like a scolding teacher."

"You're really cute when you're mad," Vince reached past Linda and turned off the gas jet she had ignited to make Vince a hot chocolate.

"Dry yourself you're drenched," she said, and then Linda felt a tug on her arm and in an instant she was scooped off the floor, cradled in Vince's arms.

"Put me down, Vincent!" she demanded.

"Does a student do this to his teacher, Miss Conover?" Vince pressed his mouth to Linda's.

"You're incorrigible, Vincent."

"That's the nicest thing you said to me since I came inside."

"Will you put me down?"

"How does it feel, right now to know I am your only connection to the planet?"

Linda rested her head on Vince's chest, "It feels nice."

"Only nice?"

"Really nice."

"Should I put you down?"

"Yes, I want you to put me down."

"Here, in the kitchen among the cups and saucers?"

"Not here."

"Then, where?"

"There," Linda pointed to the bedroom.

# 58

Linda's bedroom was dimly lit from a lamp on her bed stand. She was quiet in Vince's arms. He sat her on the edge of her bed, his hands resting on her knees a look of desire in his eyes. Linda drew his head to her chest, "Are you afraid, Vincent?" she asked.

"A little," Vince acknowledged his fear.

"I'm afraid, too," Linda said, "do you love me, Vincent?"

"I do love you."

"Say I love you, Linda, I want to hear you say my name."

Within seconds Linda felt the warmth of Vince's kiss on her mouth.

"I love you, Linda, I always will."

"Do you remember what you told me about when you were a student in my library?"

"Yes," Vince whispered.

"Tell me, again," Linda ran her hand through Vince's hair kissing his mouth.

"I tried to imagine what you looked like undressed."

Linda let her robe slide onto the bed exposing her bare shoulders and breasts, her hips and her legs, "Am I what you imagined?"

"You're more beautiful than I ever imagined," Vince pulled Linda to him, feeling her silken skin and kissing her mouth for an inexpressibly long time.

Then Linda felt herself rising and turning as if defying the laws of physics.

"Vincent," she said, breathlessly as Vince picked her up and set her on her back, her chestnut hair flaring against the white pillow on her bed.

Vince traced the contours of Linda's body with his hands and sealed her mouth with passionate kisses.

The Burning Hours          Page 186

As ecstatic waves surged through her body Linda opened her arms.

"Love me, Vincent, the way you loved me in your dreams the faraway dreams that brought you home to me."

# 59

Linda got out of bed early and put on her robe. She looked out the bedroom window at snow piled high on the sidewalk and street. Then she looked at Vince sleeping peacefully and thought how angry she had been smiling at the mental image of him pleading for forgiveness, like a chastised schoolboy. For the first time in her life Linda felt truly happy sitting on the edge of her bed feeling a rush looking at Vince. She brushed back his unruly dark hair, but before leaving Vince sleepily opened his eyes, and said, "Hello, lady."

"Hello, soldier," Linda responded, "Go back to sleep. I'm going to shower, then make breakfast before I get you up." As she kissed Vince's cheek he whispered in her ear.

"No," she shook her head.

"After breakfast," Vince negotiated.

"After you do the dishes," Linda countered.

"Can't you have someone from one of your father's estates take care of the dishes?"

"That's not funny, Vincent."

"I was joking," Vince appealed, "you're mad at me, aren't you?'

"I'm not mad at you that matter is settled," then refreshing his pillow Linda kissed Vince's forehead, "now go back to sleep."

Linda went into the bathroom, turned on the shower, took off her robe and looked into the full-length mirror retracing her body where Vince had been. She got into the shower, raised her face to the warm spray knowing she had to be the happiest woman on the face of the earth.

Vince was still asleep, but restless when Linda got out of the shower. She dried her hair, tied it back into a ponytail, went into the kitchen and put a pot of coffee on the stove. It was then moaning sounds filled the apartment. She rushed into the bedroom and found Vince thrashing violently, yelling, and trying to catch his breath.

"Vincent!" Linda shook Vince, "Wake up! Vincent! Wake up!"

Linda shook Vince's shoulders until he woke his eyes, glassy and uncomprehending, struggling to breathe.

"You were having a bad dream."

"I can't breathe," Vince choked out the words, "I can't breathe."

"Try to calm, you'll be all right, you'll be all right," Linda stroked Vince's face and within seconds his breathing resumed normally.

"I'll be okay," Vince tried to get up, but fell back on the bed.

"I'm going to turn off the coffee. Don't get up, I'll be right back."

Linda quickly returned from the kitchen and placed her hands on Vince's face, "My God, you're burning!"

"I'll be okay I have to move around," Linda pushed Vince back on the bed when he tried to get off.

"I'm going to the bathroom for towels. Don't get up, you're feverish. I'll be right back."

"I'll be okay I just need to walk around to clear my head," Vince started off the bed.

"Stay where you are! I'll be right back," Linda admonished.

In a few minutes she returned pressed wet towels to Vince's face and chest and within minutes his body cooled.

"I feel better, now."

"That was a terrible attack, Vincent, are you sure you feel better, now?"

"Yeah, I'm okay."

"Does it happen often?"

"Sometimes I stay awake all night so the dreams don't come."

The Burning Hours

"You slept peacefully during the night," Linda stroked Vince's face.

"That's because I was sleeping with you."

Vince looked away and then at Linda, "I'm damaged goods, Linda. You're young and beautiful, you deserve better than me we shouldn't have done what we did last night."

Linda got up, "I'll be right back."

"Where are you going?"

"Try to relax I'm going to refresh the towels, okay?"

"Okay."

Linda closed the bathroom door, turned on the faucet and looked into the mirror. There she saw a woman in distress who minutes before was radiant and happy. She splashed her face with cold water and went back into the bedroom.

"I'm sorry I upset you, Linda."

"Do you love me, Vincent?"

"I love you, Linda," Vince reached for Linda and she took his hand.

"Last night we made love because we love each other. That is different than just having sex. I know you're upset, but please don't ever again question our love for each other."

Vince nodded.

"You're not damaged goods. Your heart aches for what you experienced. You were nineteen years old, you should have been playing baseball or being with friends in a pizza parlor, anywhere, but where you were," she cupped Vince's face in the cool moist towel.

"I did things I want to forget," Vince said in a trembling voice.

"You had no control over that."

"I killed a soldier with a bayonet, Linda. I saw life go out of his eyes. Before he died, he said, my name is Hans," Vince started crying, "He wanted me to know he was a human being, not a thing. When I killed him I destroyed myself."

"It's all right to cry, Vincent, you have to cry to wash away the memories."

"I haven't cried like this since I was a kid."

"You kept calling for Danny, who's Danny?"

"What did I say?"

"Where are you Danny? Where are you Danny? Who is Danny, Vincent?"

Vince was quiet for a long time. Linda watched him twisting his head side-to-side, and then without looking up, he said, "I don't want to talk about it."

In a quiet voice, Linda pleaded, "Let out what's inside you, before it destroys you. I can't take away your pain, Vincent, I wish I could, but if you let me, I will help you through this."

"I can't, Linda I can't put this on you."

"I want you to," Linda stroked Vince's face.

"You must never know what happened out there."

"I won't break, Vincent, I want to fight this with you."

Vince kept nodding no when Linda shook his shoulders, "You have to confide in me. You're exhausting me. I can't bear seeing you this way," Linda cried, and then she warned, "I'm staying right here for as long as it takes, until the summer melts the snow if I have to, I'm not leaving until you talk to me, and I mean it, Vincent."

Vince didn't answer.

"I mean what I said, Vincent," Linda repeated, "You're not going anywhere, and I'm not going anywhere until you talk to me."

Vince's words caught in his throat, his body quivered and he started crying. Linda put her hands around his shoulders and pulled him to her, "Put your arms around me, Vincent, and hold onto me as tight as you can. I know unburdening yourself will be terrible, it's alright to cry, it's going to be alright, I promise you."

The Burning Hours

Vince kept twisting his head side-to-side, and then tearfully he looked up at Linda and haltingly he said -

"I hardly knew Danny. That's the way it was out there. I was with him when he got killed," Vince choked on his words, "I can't get the screaming and the noise out of my mind. One of the boys called *Mama! I want to come home!* Then he was silent, because he was dead. Christ! It rips me apart! I can't get rid of the images I can't get rid of it, Linda."

"You're safe, now," Linda pulled Vince tighter, against her body.

"I heard Danny calling for me. It was dark. I crawled to the sound of his voice and dragged him away from the fighting. He was dead half of his body was gone. I relive it over and over. In my dreams I'm screaming, where's the rest of you Danny?" Vince collapsed in Linda's embrace his body shuddering in choking sobs.

"Cry, Vincent, hold on to me, let it go," Linda said fighting back her own tears.

For a time that seemed an eternity Linda rocked Vince back-and-forth, her fragile emotional composure at its breaking point.

"Okay now?" she whispered.

Vince nodded.

"Let's get you into bed you need to sleep."

Vince's eyes were glued to Linda above him refreshing his pillow and covering him with a warm blanket. She sat on the edge of the bed, leaned in and kissed his forehead, "You're going to be fine," she said in a quiet voice.

"Are you coming in?"

"I need a few minutes to take care of the towels. Then I'll come in and we'll sleep the morning away. Then when we get up I'll make lunch and we'll do whatever you want to do, okay."

"Anything?"

"Yes, anything," she smiled at the note of mischief in Vince's voice, "now get to sleep, I'll be right back."

In the bathroom Linda's emotions crumbled. She sat on her dressing chair, holding her face in her hands trying to suppress gasping sobs that wracked her quaking body and the hot tears that burned down her face. Linda cried for Vince knowing he would bear the war's emotional scars the rest of his life. When she regained her composure, she went back to the bedroom.

Linda kissed Vince's face, she shed her nightgown and slid beneath the blanket, put her arms around Vince and they fell into an emotionally exhausted sleep.

# 60

Tommy and Darling sat in front of Major Mathias Olsen's desk. The room was quiet in the spring light that spilled through a window that overlooked the hospital campus. Nebraska born, Major Olsen was the medical director at the Army Hospital in Liege. A big man with a generous belly, he was nicknamed Keg. Major Olsen had a low opinion, as he called them, of the preening peacock officers, many of whom he believed achieved their promotions on the battlefield achievements of conscripted and enlisted men. He disdained military protocol that forced saluting ranks instead of men and enjoyed a laugh while downing a Stein of beer at the mental image of massed troops experiencing neurological quirks that caused loose elbow joints to flutter wildly to the consternation of the reviewing general.

"I wish I didn't have to read the personal parts of Rosemary's letters, Tommy, next time, I'll ask one of the nurses to read them."

"It's okay, Sarge."

"She's got some interesting plans for you."

"Sounds like it."

Tommy and Darling stood up as Major Olsen entered his office. He placed a handful of medical records on his cluttered desk, and said, "Sit down, gentlemen," dispensing with the usual military formalities.

"Where are you from, Private?" he asked Tommy.

"New Jersey, Sir."

"Call me Doctor, Doc, Major anything, but Sir."

"Okay, Doc," Tommy answered.

"Domenico is your first name do your friends call you Dom?"

"They call me Tommy."

"You're from New Jersey, where Frank Sinatra is from."

"He's from Hoboken."

"Are you from Hoboken?"

"I'm from the neighboring town."

"What's your story, Sergeant?"

"I'm a southerner, Doc, Texas, Alabama, career army."

"I'm from Nebraska the three of us cover a good part of the country," Major Olsen opened Tommy's medical record, "I'm sorry about your injury, Private, you must know what you did saved hundreds of lives."

"Thank you, Doc," he responded.

"You were with Private Tomasso, Sergeant?"

"I was down from a mortar blast, Tommy came for me," Darling answered.

"Is it alright if I call you, Tommy?"

"Sure, Doc, it's okay."

"What's your name, Sergeant?" Major Olsen's question elicited simultaneous smiles from Tommy and Darling.

"I said something funny?"

"It's a long story, Doc, you should ask Tommy."

"Let me in on it."

"Sarge's name is Carroll Darling with that name he's lucky he's a big guy, depending on your preference he will respond to honey, sweetie or dumpling."

"He's been busting me since basic, Doc."

Major Olsen leaned back, took long looks at Tommy and Darling, and then he burst out laughing, "Tommy played on your name, Sergeant?"

"He sure did, didn't you Tommy?"

"I couldn't help it, Doc; Sarge is so cute when he's mad."

"Now you know what I've been going through, Doc."

"You two are like Abbott and Costello," Major Olsen said, and then turning serious, "Tommy I want to go over your medical history and prognosis, okay?"

"That's why I'm here."

The Burning Hours          Page 195

"The ophthalmology examination revealed physical trauma in both eyes, which is the immediate cause of your loss of sight. However, as the trauma remits your sight should return, but it hasn't."

"Then what's the problem, Doc?" Darling asked.

"After your ophthalmology examinations, Tommy, you were examined by a neurologist. It is his opinion that your blindness is psychosomatic."

"What does that mean, Doc?" Tommy responded.

"It means there is no structural reason why you are not seeing. Your loss of sight is probably rooted in the extreme trauma you suffered, and that trauma has been converted into the physical manifestation of blindness."

"You mean Tommy might see, again, Doc?" Darling asked.

"That's an answer I can't give you, Tommy; there are instances where sight returns after a short time, after a lengthy period and unfortunately for some, not at all."

"If it does happen, Doc, will it be gradual or immediate?" Tommy asked.

"It could be either," Major Olsen answered.

"Is there anything Tommy can do?" Darling wanted to know.

"Go home, that's the easy part, try to forget, that's the hard part," Major Olsen leaned forward, "Is there a girl waiting for you, Tommy?"

"Yeah, her name is Rosemary."

"Do you love her, Tommy?"

"Yeah, I love her."

"But, is she devoted to you or will your blindness be a problem for her?"

"Tommy is the hard case, Major. I know because I read all of Rosemary's letters to him, she would go to the end of the earth for him."

"You feel that way, Tommy?"

The Burning Hours                                    Page 196

"Yeah, Doc, I do, Rosemary is the truest girl I will ever know, I fell for her the instant I saw her."

"That's good, Tommy, I'm glad to hear it. Rosemary's commitment will be an enormous help, okay, any questions?"

"No you explained it, Doc," Tommy said.

"The grapevine says your Medal of Honor ceremony will happen soon, and then you'll be going home," Major Olsen got up rounded his desk, shook Tommy's hand, executed a crisp salute, and said, "No need to return it, Tommy, it's the man my salute honors."

# 61

Tommy and Darling strolled the grounds of the hospital campus. They found an unoccupied bench on the edge of a pond. Since meeting with Major Olsen Tommy's mind was light years away. Darling lit a cigarette and exhaled a cloud of smoke into the air.

"What are you seeing here, Sarge?" Tommy asked.

"What do you mean, Tommy?"

"Look around tell me what you see."

"Okay, Tommy, I'm not good with words I'll give it a shot," Darling paused, "the sky is a light blue, there's one cloud up there moving slow it looks lonely, the sun is a lemon yellow, the field we crossed is a green carpet and right now we're sitting in front of a calm pond its like silver glass half the size of a football field two white swans are gliding on the surface wherever one goes the other follows they don't want to be apart the surface ripples in the breeze a few of the ambulatory guys are walking around with the help of their nurses," Darling stopped and lit another cigarette.

"It was a sunny day when Rosemary and I had our first date. After ice cream we went to Roosevelt Park. We walked along the hilly green field to a bench at the edge of a pond. The pond was different than the pond here, Sarge. Lily pads floated on the surface every once in a while frogs jumped from pad to pad. You should have seen Rosemary so excited when the frogs appeared."

"I wish you could see what I just described," Darling said.

"Yeah," Tommy said, quietly, "so do I."

"My father was a circuit preacher. I never understood the messages in the parables he preached. The night before he cut me loose with a silver dollar, he said something to a crowd of beaten-down people in the foothills of a town in Alabama that stuck with me."

The Burning Hours                    Page 198

"What did he say?" Tommy stared ahead seeing only darkness."

"He didn't thump his bible he spoke calmly. He explained to the crowd hope awakens the soul and their dreams might come to pass. Doc Olsen said your eyesight might return, Tommy, you have to hold onto that hope."

"The sun feels good on my face, Sarge, how are you?"

"Yeah, it does," Darling answered raising his face to the sun.

"It's pleasant here, Sarge," Tommy said, "reminds me of home."

"You want to walk or go back to the hospital?"

"Let's stay here for a while."

"Sure, Tommy whatever you say."

"I accept being blind, Sarge. When Doc Olsen explained the physical damage might one day resolve and I might regain my eyesight my hope went through the ceiling. It's not fair to raise Rosemary's and Mom's hopes for something that might never happen."

"I understand where you're at, Tommy, but don't give up."

"At night when I'm alone, I close my eyes, I see Rosemary, her red hair, the freckles under her eyes, her smile she is real as the air I breathe I hear her voice, Sarge. In time the shrink explained that ability will fade."

"What does he know," Darling observed.

"You're a revelation, Sarge."

"What are you getting at, Tommy?"

"Hope awakens the soul."

"It was the only biblical lesson I understood."

"My soul is awake, Sarge. When I get home I'll marry Rosemary, we'll start a family. I'll see them when I close my eyes in my day dreams. Maybe my eyesight will return. If it doesn't I'll have Rosemary and we will have a full life."

"You're alive and well."

"Yeah, Sarge, I'm alive and well."

The Burning Hours

"That's great, Tommy."

"Vince is getting married," Tommy changed the subject.

"I never thought Vince was an operator, but he moved fast," Darling said.

"I'm going to be his best man, Sarge."

"Who's the lucky girl?"

"His former teacher, the school librarian; he's had a crush on her from the first time he saw her."

"You're pulling my leg, his teacher, the school librarian!" Darling exclaimed, "She must be fifty years old."

"She's a knockout, Sarge, wait until you meet her."

"That day is coming fast, Tommy."

"Not fast enough."

# 62

**Medal of Honor Presentation**
**Army Hospital, Liege, Belgium**
**March 1946**

The Army Hospital in Liege teemed with an overflow crowd buzzing with anticipation. Attired in his regulation army uniform Tommy stood at attention, waiting for the Medal of Honor presentation to begin.

A team of military aides, public affairs correspondents and photographers followed General Alexander Wickham up the hospital stairs maneuvering through the crush of military personnel and civilians on the second floor.

In the Ward General Wickham strode in purposeful military demeanor along the center aisle to its terminus where he met and shook Tommy's hand. After a brief exchange of words General Wickham read the Presidential Citation describing Tommy's actions in the Ardennes to the hushed assemblage. A public affairs officer displayed the Medal of Honor and then handed it to General Wickham, who draped it around Tommy's neck as flashbulbs popped and the second floor erupted in ear-splitting sustained applause.

As quickly as it started the ceremony ended.

General Wickham and his staff of aides, correspondents and photographers left the ward to write and file their stories and photographs with the *Stars and Stripes* and news organizations throughout the United States.

Tommy was deluged by hospital personnel offering congratulations and examining the medal around his neck. Someone in the ward yelled let's hear it for Private Tomasso, and the crowd burst into another round of cheers. Soon afterward the electrified moments of the ceremony faded and the ward went back to its usual business.

The Burning Hours

Tommy sat back in his chair pensively holding the medal in his hand.

"You okay, Tommy?" Darling squeezed his shoulder.

"So many dead, Sarge," Tommy whispered, "so many dead."

# 63

**Garden Street Apartments**
**Hoboken, New Jersey**
**April 1946**

"Hi, Mr. Wagner," Linda smiled.

"Hello Linda, hello Vincent, do you like the replacement door?"

"It is very attractive, Mr. Wagner," Linda answered.

"I like the stain glass panels," Vince observed.

"I'll take your picture in front of the new door," Helmut took a small camera from his work cover all."

"A Minox that is a terrific little camera," Vince exclaimed.

"It is a good camera, now, smile," Helmut lowered the camera, "Vincent why no smile?"

"He's mad at me," Linda said.

"Why, Vincent?"

"She's a showoff."

"Don't pay attention to him, Mr. Wagner, we went ice skating, he couldn't stay up on his skates, he's frustrated and he's taking it out on me."

"You had to skate around the rink doing pirouettes, very funny, Linda."

"You're mad because you fell on the ice, if you didn't hold onto me, you would have set a rink record for flops, Vincent."

"See what I mean, Mr. Wagner."

"I don't like you two kids squabbling, if you don't smile for your picture I'll evict both of you," Helmut lifted his camera to his eyes, "Now that's better," he said, clicking the shutter.

"Thanks, Mr. Wagner," Linda said pushing Vince's shoulder.

"Yeah, thanks, Mr. Wagner," Vince took the hint.

The Burning Hours                                    Page 203

"I will develop the picture and put it under your door."

"I made a pitcher of lemonade, would you like a glass, Mr. Wagner?"

"*Danke,* Linda, I have beer in the refrigerator that's my beverage," his eyes twinkled, "go to your apartment and no more fighting."

"Okay, Mr. Wagner, we promise don't we, Vincent?"

"Yeah, we promise," Vince said.

Vince watched Linda take a frosted pitcher from the refrigerator, pour two glasses of lemonade and thought how truly beautiful she is, how easy it is to love her, how she had sacrificed for him and brought him out of his flashbacks knowing it would have been easier for her to run from him. He didn't have to propose to Linda that they would marry was understood. Linda spoke with Vince's mother about their marriage plans. Regina regaled her with stories of Vince growing up; Linda couldn't contain her laughter. Regina and Linda were both teachers, ironically at the same high school during different times. They hit it off immediately each looking forward to meeting the other. Vince balked when Linda said it was his turn to speak with her father and mother. Anxious he couldn't convince two of the wealthiest people in America that a barber's son, younger than their daughter, and just starting out was right for her. However, during their telephone conversation, Vince found Charles and Adalina Conover to be as Linda described, pleasant and sincerely concerned for their daughter's happiness.

"I love Mr. Wagner, don't you, Vincent?"

"He's one of a kind."

Linda handed Vince a glass of lemonade and squeezed next to him on the sofa.

"Do you like it?" she asked.

"It's okay."

"Just okay I made it from an orchard grower's recipe."

"It's a little tart," Vince said, mischievously.

"You're saying that to get even with me, aren't you?"

Linda took the glass from his hand.

"What are you doing?" Vince protested.

"I don't want you to drink something you don't like."

"Come on, Linda, give it back. I'm teasing you," Linda put his glass next to her glass on the coffee table and lifted herself on top of Vince.

"Are you still mad at me?" she asked, tousling his hair, "When you get back from Fort Monmouth I'll trim this crop, myself."

"Yeah, I'm still mad at you."

"What are you going to do about it?"

Vince sipped his lemonade, put the glass down and said," I'm going to get off this sofa and pick you up."

"Like before?"

"Yes, like before."

"Oh, God! What then?" Linda feigned.

"I will take you in there."

"Not the bedroom, unspeakable things happen in the bedroom," she cupped her face in faux horror.

"That's right, in there."

"Please, merciful," she rolled her eyes heaven-ward.

"I will fling you on your bed."

"You mean our bed," she teased.

"I stand corrected."

"Say, our bed."

"Okay, our bed."

"That's better; now proceed with your diabolical scheme."

"Who is getting even here, me or you?" Vince asked.

"Oh, go on," Linda said, "so you fling me on our bed, not just toss me, because flinging is more terrible than simply tossing me, is that right?"

"That's right I fling you on our bed, like a ragdoll."

"You're scaring me, Vincent, I'll call for help."

"No one will come to help you, you're all mine."

"Will you be merciful?"

"What do you think?"

"You're so cruel."

"Then I'll hover above you, hungry as a wolf."

"I won't be able to breathe."

"I'll take care of that."

"How will get me to breathe again?"

"Mouth-to-mouth resuscitation, I'm good at it."

"How good are you?"

"I'll seal my mouth to yours for as long as it takes for you to recover."

"You have some humanity."

"Then I will pull you to me, real tight, tangling us together, inseparable like cooked spaghetti and I will keep you that way for as long as I like."

Linda started laughing, "Is that it? That's how you will punish me for teasing you? We'll be a bowl of spaghetti. Now, Vincent that is cruel."

"I didn't say I was finished."

"I knew it you are the meanest man on the planet."

"Then I will take you in my arms."

"The way you are, now," Linda sighed.

"Yes, the way I am, now," Vince answered, "and then I will kiss you and my kisses will last a long time."

"Like now?"

"Yes, and then I will whisper you make my life worth living, and I will love you to the end of time and for all eternity."

Linda put her arms around Vince's neck her head against his chest. "I wish you didn't have to go away the only time we've been apart is when I go to school and you go to work. I love being with you. I'm going to love being your wife. I'm so proud of you, Vincent."

"It's just two weeks I'll be home before you know it and my military obligation will be discharged."

The Burning Hours

Page 206

"It's still too long, you did enough. I don't know why you have to go."

"Don't worry," Vince kissed Linda's face.

"Well, I will."

"I have something for you."

Linda took a silver heart-shaped locket from a small gift-wrapped box and held it up.

"I love it, help me put it on."

"I wish it was gold," Vince said snapping the locket chain at the back of Linda's neck.

"It's more precious than gold. I'll never take it off."

"I purchased two tickets to *Orchestra Wives* starring George Montgomery and Lynn Bari and Glenn Miller music for tomorrow at the Stanley Theatre. After the movie I will treat you to an early dinner at Robinson's Steak House."

"Now I know why your pay envelope was smaller than usual," Linda pushed Vince's chest, "You were saving for the locket and tomorrow evening."

"I wanted a date with my best girl before leaving on Monday."

"Can we just come home after the movie? Monday will come fast enough. We'll go to Robinson's for dinner when you come back?"

"Sure, when I come back."

# 64

Linda was preoccupied as she and Vince walked to the Stanley Theatre on Journal Square suspecting her malaise was due to the flu that had been going around. Vince purchased their tickets from a box office attendant beneath an enormous copper marquee. They went into a lobby with Grecian columns and a central staircase, and settled into their seats beneath a romantic sky ceiling with drifting white clouds and sparkling stars. The auditorium darkened and the film *Orchestra Wives* showed.

As the credits rolled, Linda tugged at Vince's arm, "Do you like my locket?"

"I love the way it looks on you," Vince whispered, "Who gave you such a neat gift?"

"My future husband."

"He must love you very much."

"I hope he loves me as I love him."

"He does, I assure you, he does" Vince put his arms around Linda's shoulders feeling her against him.

When Lynn Bari sang the movie's theme song *At Last*, Vince kissed Linda's mouth. As she listened to the song's lyrics: *At last, my love has come along, My lonely days are over, And life is like a song, At last, The skies above are blue, My heart was wrapped in clovers, The night I looked at you*, quiet tears unbeknownst to Vince fell from her eyes.

At home, Linda opened a laundry bag containing Vince's freshly pressed army uniform and hung it on the foyer clothes rack. In the bedroom, she packed his luggage, and then went into the parlor where Vince had organized his military documents for their album. Linda sat next to Vince hoping the fatigue washing over her in relentless waves would abate.

The Burning Hours                                    Page 208

"The impediments in our road are gone," Linda looked at Vince, "You were so concerned our worlds were so far removed that we couldn't have a lifetime together."

"I was tough to convince."

"I will be your wife, Vincent."

"The Justice of the Peace will make it legal."

"Legal is meaningless, you are my husband," Linda said struggling with her gathering enervation.

Vince put his arms around her, smoothed back her hair and brushed his lips across her mouth, "How does Mrs. Linda Conover Farro sound?"

"It's the best sound in the world."

Linda nestled into Vince's embrace and became quiet, unable to blunt her fatigue. She felt Vince's heart beat, his light breathing on her face and summoning her strength softly kissed his mouth.

"Two weeks is a long time to be apart, Vincent, I love you, and if you want to ..."

Vince stopped Linda in mid-sentence, brought her back into his embrace and kissed the top of her head, "You need to rest and get a good night's sleep there will be other days and nights."

"Okay," she nodded.

"I think you should have Mr. Wagner drive you to the doctor for a check-up while I'm gone."

"Don't worry about me, finish up there, and when you are home I'll be myself."

"I left the base command's phone number on the kitchen table. I'll call you each night while I'm away. If you need to reach me call that number. I wish I didn't have to leave you alone. These two weeks will be the longest of my life."

The Burning Hours

# 65

Linda showered and dressed before getting Vince out of bed. The thought of food provoked waves of nausea. She went to the sofa, slumped against a pillow, closed her eyes and drifted into a restless sleep.

"Hey, sleeping beauty," Linda opened her eyes, as if weights were affixed to her lids.

"Good morning, honey," she returned Vince's kisses, "You're very handsome in your uniform," she said, sleepily.

"This bug is knocking you out," Vince lifted Linda into his arms, "You're going to bed, lady. Mr. Wagner is waiting to take me to the train station I'll ask him to check on you."

"I want to see you out."

"Don't be stubborn," Vince said, sitting on the edge of the bed, "You're exhausted, and you need to rest, okay?"

"I don't want you to go, Vincent I want you home with me."

"I'll be back before you know it."

"If you say so," her eyes glazed tearfully.

"No tears, Linda," Vince ordered in a velvet voice.

"I'll try, but I won't promise."

"My beautiful Linda," Vince kissed and rested his face on Linda's, "I love you more than anything in this world and I will miss you," he said softly.

Before leaving the bedroom Vince looked back at Linda curled into a fetal position sleeping. He left the apartment, walked to its main entrance where Helmut Wagner, his 1935 charcoal-colored two-door Ford idled, ready to leave for the Hoboken Terminal.

During Vince's and Helmut's absence, Linda got out of bed. She sat recumbent on the sofa with a pillow pressed against her stomach to relieve painful cramps that magnified her general fatigue and dizziness.

"It's unlocked," she answered the ringing doorbell.

The Burning Hours                                    Page 210

"You must go to the doctor," Helmut said upon seeing Linda.

Linda didn't protest, she went to the bedroom and dressed.

When she went into the doctor's office Linda was dizzy and doubled over in pain. After responding to a long list of questions the doctor examined her. Meanwhile, Helmut waited in the reception room engrossed in a recent edition of *Popular Mechanics* magazine.

In time, Linda emerged from the doctor's office clutching an envelope in her hand. A bright smile lit her face. She shook the doctor's hand and promised to return in a month.

"You are better now, Linda?" Helmut asked a glint in his eyes.

"Much better, but please don't share your suspicion with anyone," Linda glowed.

"Your secret is safe with me," he smiled, "I will drive you home, and you can rest."

"I will tell Vincent when he's home. It will be hard to keep my news from him, but I want to see his expression."

"I will lend you my Minox to photograph his priceless expression."

The Burning Hours

# 66

Darling was deep in conversation with Tommy when he heard footsteps behind him.

"This is for Private Tomasso, Sergeant," a nurse handed Darling an envelope.

"Thanks, lieutenant."

"Who is it from, Sarge?" Tommy asked.

"Colonel McLeod."

"Read it to me."

*PFC Domenico Tomasso is approved for travel on 22 July 1946, continuing to Rhein Main, and then by air transport to Fort Dix Army Air Force Base, New Jersey arriving 27 July 1946, by train to the Hoboken Train Station. You will be accompanied by a U.S. Army public relations officer your arrival will be preceded by an announcement to the American press of your Medal of Honor. Congratulations and God's speed. James McLeod, Colonel, U.S. Army.*

"You're on your way, Tommy," Darling said, handing him Colonel McLeod's letter, "You'll be a celebrity before you get to New Jersey."

"I guess so," Tommy said in a quiet voice.

"What's the matter, Tommy? You're going home to Rosemary and your mother. You should be happy."

"Yeah, I'm happy, we survived Sarge and I'm going home. I didn't think we'd ever get out alive, but when you look death in the eye you realize how precious the people you love are."

"Yeah, Tommy, I know what you're saying."

"In the field the guys you come to love as brothers in one minute are gone in the next minute. There's something strange about this, but I can't put my finger on it. Does what we went through rewire our brains? I'll never see things the way I did. Does any of this make sense, Sarge?"

The Burning Hours

"People back home are waiting for you, Tommy that makes you a lucky guy. I've been alone my entire life, I'm just lucky to be alive."

"Where will you go, Sarge?"

"Christ! You're worried about me."

"Cut it out, Sarge! What are you going to do?"

Darling paused, reflectively, "Wait for orders and go wherever they take me."

"You have enough time in to get out, right?"

"I guess I do, but the Army has been my home for as long as I can remember."

"You could stay in New Jersey and get a job."

"So you could cut me up for the rest of my life? I have enough scars from you, Tomato-paste."

"You'd miss me, Sarge?"

Darling squeezed Tommy's shoulder, "Yeah, I'd miss you, little brother."

# 67

"Thanks for the ride, Mr. Wagner."

Linda came in from marketing with an arm full of packages and closed the apartment door with a sweep of her foot. Comfortable in her loose-fitting corn-colored dress she wore her hair in a ponytail. The apartment was bright with flowers and balls of blue and pink yarn, knitting needles, an embroidery hoop and a book titled *"Your First Baby."* Her album sat on the utility table along with a partially completed blue blanket that Linda had begun knitting. She unpacked her grocery bags and filled the refrigerator with milk, juice, fruits and vegetables. Then she sat at the table, took a deep breath, and said, "I'm tired baby, are you tired? We'll take a nap. Would you like to take a nap? I thought so," Linda's hand went to her belly, "I think you are ready for a nap. When we get up I will make us lunch. Your daddy will be jealous that I've been having my meals with a very handsome young man, but when he finds out it is you, I'm sure he will be delighted. I'll write Mr. Wagner's rent check, and then we'll go to bed."

After a brief nap, Linda woke up her cheeks pink from sleep. She kissed the palms of both hands and rested them on her slightly swollen belly confident she had never in her life been so happy.

"I think it's time we got up, baby," she said, slowly swinging her legs over the side of the bed and sliding into her slippers.

While setting the kitchen table the door bell rang.

"Mr. Wagner is earlier than usual," she thought and picked up the rent check.

"I'll be right with you."

As she opened the door the smile she reserved for Helmut Wagner dissolved in a sudden rush of apprehension and fear.

"What are you doing here? Please leave!" she began closing the door as Derek Reed pushed his way into the apartment.

"Nice apartment," he observed, looking around, walking toward the bedroom.

"Please go away you're not wanted here," Linda blocked his way.

"I want you to take me back," Derek demanded, wiping drug fueled leakage from his nose with the back of his hand.

"Our divorce is finalized. You are no longer in my life and I want to keep it that way, leave and don't ever come back here!"

Derek slithered around the apartment, eyeing and touching everything along his way, glancing malevolently at Linda, who now stood stone-like, seized by a growing sense of terror. When he saw the book Linda had purchased he shouted, "You're pregnant! Who is he?" advancing on her.

"It's none of your business," Linda said, "If you don't leave I will call the manager."

Derek brushed aside her warning roaming around the apartment in unsettling silence. Spotting Vince's army documents, he disdainfully said, "An Army Dogface knocked you up. What's his name? Tell me his name!"

"Get out of my apartment!" Linda shouted.

Derek clenched his fists, his face slathered with sweat, his nose running and his eyes a spider web of blood engorged veins.

"Go ahead, you coward! You want to hit a pregnant woman! Will that make you feel like the man you never were and will never be. You are the worst mistake I have ever made."

"What's going on in there?" Helmut rapped on the door and then pushed it open.

"You haven't heard the last of me," Derek threatened, "I'll bring your Dogface up on adultery charges. When I get through with him, he'll be in the brig for thirty years and that bun in the oven," he pointed to Linda's belly, "that's my gold mine."

"You liar, our divorce was final long ago!"

"It's a courts-martial, who do you think they will believe an officer or your Dogface?'

"Get out of my building or I will call the police and have you removed," Helmut warned.

"You and your rich daddy will be hearing from me," Derek stormed out of the apartment.

Shaken by Derek's assault and threats, Helmut eased Linda onto the sofa and went to the kitchen. He returned with a glass of water that Linda was unable to hold without spilling it.

"Try to be calm, dear," Helmut held the glass from which Linda took small sips.

"He frightened me, Mr. Wagner, I can't stop shaking if you hadn't come I don't know what he would have done."

"I'll call the doctor."

"No, don't call the doctor, Mr. Wagner, I'll be all right."

"I will stay so I know he will not return."

"Please call my mother and tell her to come for me, right away."

"What about Vincent?"

Linda burst into tears.

"He must not know I am pregnant, please don't tell Vincent, he must not know, Mr. Wagner. If he knows he will stay and fight him, but he can't win. His life will be ruined. I won't let that happen to him."

"All right, my child."

"Thank you for everything you've done for us, Mr. Wagner."

"Such wonderful children," he placed his hand on Linda's face, "I am so sorry this evil came into your lives,"

Helmut left the apartment and for a time remained in the hallway.

Linda leaned back on the sofa her hand on her belly, "Mommy won't let anyone hurt you baby," she said, quietly.

# 68

"Mrs. Conover, a Helmut Wagner is on the phone, he says it is urgent," Gladys Prescott, Adalina's private secretary announced.

"Thank you Mrs. Prescott. Is Linda all right?" Adalina listened as Helmut described what had transpired earlier that Linda was shaken, but not physically harmed and she wants to return to Connecticut.

"I will call Mr. Conover we will leave at once. Please look after Linda, Mr. Wagner."

"She should see a doctor, Mrs. Conover given her condition. I offered to take her, but she refused."

"What do you mean her condition?"

"Linda is pregnant, Mrs. Conover, she wanted to wait to tell Vincent when he came home, and then you and Mr. Conover."

Adalina paused to absorb Helmut's news, "I will have our family physician available upon our return. I can't thank you enough, Mr. Wagner," Adalina said, hung up and dialed Charles's private line at his office.

Clara Jenkins, Charles's executive secretary picked up the ringing phone, and pressed the hold button, "Mrs. Conover is on your private line Mr. Conover, she says it is urgent."

"Thank you, Mrs. Jenkins."

"Is something wrong?" Charles listened, "I am leaving right now," he hung up the phone, buzzed Mrs. Jenkins who ordered his car be brought around, he canceled all of his appointments and informed Freddie Oldfield of his unavailability until late evening.

Charles pulled his black Fleetwood El Dorado in front of the mansion. Adalina got inside and Charles sped away. On the Post Road they ran into a traffic knot. Charles and Adalina worried for Linda, now their concern encompassed

The Burning Hours                                    Page 218

the baby she was carrying. As traffic stalled their anxieties soared then the knot unwound and Charles floored the accelerator. More than two hours after Helmut's telephone call Charles pulled into a small parking lot behind the apartment house and they rushed to Linda's apartment.

Linda lay on her bed her eyes closed trying to recover from the impact of Derek's assault. Adalina pulled her into her arms and as she did Linda broke into tears.

"Daddy's here, honey, you're safe now."

Linda wiped away her tears, "I'm pregnant, Mother. I was going to tell Vincent when he came home, and then call you and Daddy with our news."

"We know, Linda, Mother and I are happy for you," Charles said, "Mr. Wagner thought it important we know. Try to calm, Linda, it's best for you and your baby."

"It was awful, Mother, he wanted to harm me, my baby and Vincent I don't know what would have happened had Mr. Wagner not come in."

"Did he physically hurt you?"

"No, Daddy, but he wanted to."

"As soon as you are well enough we'll leave for home," Adalina said.

"He threatened Vincent with court-martial for adultery."

"Nonsense you were long divorced from him," Charles said.

"He was on drugs, he said my baby is his gold mine, he said the court-martial board would take his side because he's an officer," Linda said still shuddering, "could he do that, Daddy?"

"I'll talk with Freddie we'll see what can be done, now, please Linda try to relax."

"Will Vincent be in danger if we stayed, together, Daddy?"

"He might be, honey, civilian attorneys do not have much standing in a court martial proceeding, let's wait until I talk with Freddie."

Adalina wrapped her arms around Linda, "Try to put this terrible experience out of your mind, will you do that for me?"

Linda nodded.

Charles dialed Mrs. Prescott and asked her to call Dr. Ethan Kipp and have him at the mansion at 7:00 o'clock.

"Mr. Wagner is here, Linda," Adalina said, "He will help you to the car while Daddy and I gather your things.

"I'm not leaving Vincent, Mother I won't."

"I can't know how painful this is for you, Linda, but if you want what's best for Vincent you must leave."

"You don't understand Mother we need to be together, I must be here when Vincent comes home if I leave now he might never know I am carrying his child."

"Linda, please, you and Vincent can talk when he comes home."

"I need to be with him, Mother, what will he think coming home to me and I'm not here? It will be awful for him."

"Charles."

"Honey staying together will make it easier for Derek to learn Vincent's identity. You don't want that?"

"No I don't want that," Linda began crying.

"If he learns Vincent's identity he'll ruin his life."

"I don't want Vincent harmed."

"I know you don't," Charles said, somberly.

Linda reluctantly nodded her assent.

"Leave my clothes in the closet, Mother I don't want Vincent to think I abandoned him."

"Alright, honey," Adalina consoled.

"Tell Vincent what happened, Mr. Wagner ask him to call me."

"I will help you to your father's car," emotionally numb, Linda took Helmut's hand, "Tell Vincent I love him, Mr. Wagner," Linda dissolved in tears.

"You will find one another, again, the dark clouds will part, you must have faith," Mr. Wagner put his arm around Linda's shoulder they left the apartment and Linda's life with Vince.

For several moments Adalina looked mournfully at the kitchen table, tears streaming down her face. The spirit that had enlivened the apartment was gone. She looked at the kitchen table holding Linda's preparations for the course of her pregnancy: the small wicker basket with skeins of blue and pink wool yarn, the embroidery hoop, the partially completed blue baby blanket that she was knitting, the book for first time mothers, and the start of her family album.

"Linda could have anything this world has to offer, Charles, what she really wants is right here in this apartment a wife and mother and that evil degenerate ruined it and he might have ruined our daughter's life."

"When we get home I'll talk with Freddie," Charles said, closing the door to Linda's and Vincent's apartment.

The incongruities outside were startling the sun shone brightly, refreshing breezes were blowing, except for her emotional turmoil Linda was the essence of a rare summer day in her corn-colored dress.

"Wonderful children, Mrs. Conover, Linda and Vincent will always be in my thoughts," Helmut said.

"Linda loved living here often she told me you were her second father. My husband and I shall always be grateful, Mr. Wagner," Adalina kissed Helmut, and then she slid onto the back seat of the car and pulled Linda to her.

"I will mail you a check for the balance of Linda's lease, Mr. Wagner. Call me any time if I can be of help to you."

"*Danke*, Mr. Conover."

Charles got into the El Dorado and drove away.

# 69

Dr. Ethan Kipp pressed the front door buzzer of the Conover mansion. Mrs. Prescott answered and directed him to the library. Patrician, tall, blue-eyed with a full salt and pepper mane Dr. Kipp had been the personal physician of the Conover family over twenty years. Had Charles or Adalina been the subject of a medical emergency Dr. Kipp thought he would have attended to them earlier. However, they were gone for most of the day. He theorized the urgent call involved Linda, whom he knew was living hours away, in New Jersey.

Upon his arrival Charles hurried to the library while Adalina assisted Linda to her upstairs room. Never had Charles witnessed the suffering Linda was now enduring. When he saw Dr. Kipp in the library Charles heaved a sigh of relief.

"Thanks for coming, Ethan."

"What's wrong, Charles?"

"It's Linda."

"What happened?"

"Derek Reed assaulted her."

"I thought he was long gone."

"He showed up unannounced at Linda's apartment earlier, today, drugged."

"Did he hurt her, physically?"

"She says no, she's in her room with Adalina. She is emotionally distraught, and Ethan, Linda's pregnant and beside herself with worry for her baby."

"Let's get upstairs, Charles."

"Honey, Dr. Kipp is here to see you," Adalina got off the bed where she and Linda had been sitting next to one another.

"Let's have a look at you, Linda," Dr. Kipp said.

"How is my baby, Dr. Kipp?"

The Burning Hours                                    Page 222

"Your baby will be fine," Dr. Kipp unsnapped his medical bag, removed a blood pressure gauge and a stethoscope, "You've had a rough time, Linda," he said, softly.

"It was awful."

"Let's get you better, okay?"

"Okay."

Dr. Kipp held his stethoscope to Linda's chest and back. He examined her swollen belly, slipped the blood pressure cuff onto her arm and watched the ascending and descending mercury, as Charles and Linda looked on, in silent worry.

"Let's get your blood pressure and heart rate back to normal levels," Dr. Kipp patted Linda's hand, "Okay?"

"How is my baby, Dr. Kipp?" Linda asked, again.

"Your baby is fine. Have you eaten, today?"

"I was too nauseous at breakfast to eat. I was preparing lunch when ... she stopped ... and couldn't go on."

"I understand, Linda."

"I'll call the kitchen to prepare a light broth with pasta, will that be good, Ethan?"

"Yes, that will be fine."

"I'm not hungry," Linda remonstrated.

"Please eat what the kitchen prepares, Linda," Charles pleaded.

"I don't think I can tolerate food, Daddy."

"Your baby depends on you, Linda," Dr. Kipp advised.

"I wish Vincent were with me, Dr. Kipp I need him to be with me and our baby."

"Lay back and rest. I'll check in, tomorrow."

"Okay," Linda nodded.

Dr. Kipp and Charles left the room.

"We'll be right outside, honey," Adalina kissed Linda's cheeks, "Mrs. Prescott will be here soon, promise me you will eat something."

"I will, Mother I promise."

The Burning Hours                                    Page 223

"That's my girl," Adalina smiled, and before leaving, she looked at Linda lying in her bed, lonely and lost. Never in her life had she experienced the emotion of hatred, but now, with every burning fiber of her being, she hated Derek Reed.

Dr. Kipp, Charles and Adalina met in a reading room at the end of the second floor hallway. Dr. Kipp got right to the point Linda's emotional trauma could negatively affect her physical health and her baby's well being. A further concern, he explicated is Linda and the baby's father's separation, due to circumstances beyond their control. That factor could result in an undesirable psychological effect.

"Linda is not in a good place," Dr. Kipp warned, "there are many factors working against her. The first order of business is to calm her, but I am reluctant to prescribe a sedative because of her early stage pregnancy."

"How far along is she, Ethan?"

"I guess three months. I worry sedation might produce an adverse effect on the baby."

"If there is even a remote chance that it might harm her baby she won't hear of it, Ethan," Adalina said, "she wants this baby more than anything in this world and we want her to have our grandchild."

"Is the baby's father aware of her pregnancy?"

"She planned telling him upon his return from his military obligation," Charles answered.

"After what has happened, will she tell him?"

"They are devoted to each other, and that's the problem. Linda will sacrifice to protect him. How does she recover from never again seeing the man she adores, the father of her child, even if it is to protect him," Adalina answered.

"Getting Linda's health back is our first priority, whatever happens to her, happens to her baby."

"Linda will not be in bed alone, Charles," her face flushed in maternal resolve, "When she was a little girl and had a bad dream, Ethan, I'd take her into our bed and she'd sleep peacefully. She's my little girl, again, she will sleep beside me, for as long as it takes to get her health back."

"That's better than any sedative I can prescribe," Dr. Kipp said, "Might I make a suggestion?"

"Of course," Charles answered.

"Linda should consider moving to California, to the Winery and stay at the chalet. There are too many memories here that could impede her recovery."

"The change could be beneficial," Charles answered looking at Adalina, "mother and father adore Linda, they will love having her live with them.

"If you decide on this course I will make arrangements with one of the top obstetricians in Napa City."

"It's a wonderful recommendation, Ethan we could spend as much time with her as it takes, couldn't we Charles?'

"Absolutely," Charles said, and then became contemplative.

"What is it, Charles?" Adalina asked.

"I can't imagine how broken Vincent will be and how deep will be the wounds he and Linda will carry the rest of their lives."

# 70

Vince petitioned and received an early release from duty. Helmut Wagner picked him up at the train station and drove to the apartment building. Vince unlocked and opened the apartment door it was eerily quiet inside, devoid of the spirit of Linda's playful joy. Vince wandered about in disbelief. The kitchen table usually brimming with Linda's many projects was empty. He opened the bedroom closet door touching Linda's clothes. Vince sat on their bed and retreated into an uncomprehending stare.

"Vincent," Vince felt Helmut's hand on his shoulder, "Linda left this letter for you."

"What happened, here, Mr. Wagner?"

"When I came for the rent check he was in the apartment yelling and threatening. Linda fought back. I ordered him out of the building or face the local police," Helmut answered, but kept his promise to Linda to not disclose her pregnancy to Vince.

"Did he hurt her?"

"He yelled and screamed I don't believe he hit her."

"If he hurt her I will find him and I will kill him."

"I will go, now, Vincent. Take as much time as you need."

Vince nodded.

Vince buried his face in a bed pillow breathing in Linda's familiar scents. For a long time he embraced the pillow whispering his everlasting love, too numb to cry. After reading and re-reading Linda's letter he dialed her number in Westport.

Adalina picked up the ringing phone in Linda's room answering in a somber voice. When Linda heard her mother inquire about Vincent's well-being tears rolled down her face.

Adalina handed the receiver to Linda.

The Burning Hours　　　　　　　　　　　Page 226

"Hello, Vincent," Linda's voice trembled.

"Linda," Vince said, in an equally unsteady voice, "are you all right?'

"Not entirely, where are you?"

"I'm in the bedroom."

"You mean our bedroom," Linda feebly tried to reprise their love-making banter.

"Our bedroom," Vince struggled to join in, "Are you coming home?"

An endless pause followed before Linda could answer, she wiped her tears that now flowed freely while Adalina looked on trying to control her emotions. "I want to, Vincent, God knows I want to be with you, forever, but I won't let him harm you, if we are together, that's what he intends doing."

"He's lying, Linda, a court martial will see that, please come home, we need to be together, especially now."

"But, he can get away with it I won't have him ruin your life."

"My life is ruined without you, please Linda don't do this, I'll fight for us with everything I have."

"I love you, Vincent," her hand automatically went to her belly, "I'll always love you, Vincent there will never be anyone else in my life."

Adalina took the receiver from Linda who was unable to continue.

"Vincent, Linda is very upset. My husband's attorneys made inquiries and found military boards don't give much weight to civilian attorneys. We are so sorry for you and Linda. We looked forward to having you in our family. These past four months have been the happiest in Linda's life. My husband and I are heartbroken. Please let us know if there is anything we can do for you."

Another long pause followed before Vince answered, "No, thank you. Mrs. Conover, please ask Linda to come to the phone."

"She's very upset, Vincent."

"If she can, I need to talk with her one last time."

When Vince said he wanted to say goodbye, Adalina lost her composure, she handed the phone to Linda, and said, "Vincent wants to say goodbye."

Linda put the receiver to her ear.

"I'll never stop loving you, Linda," Vince choked out the words.

"Promise me you will wear your overcoat when it snows, Vincent," Linda said, in a quivering voice.

"I promise," Vince held the receiver to his ear until he heard the click that ended their lives, together.

Linda collapsed into Adalina's arms.

"What sins did I commit, Mother, why am I being punished like this? We didn't do anything wrong. I love Vincent. I love having his baby. What sins did I commit?" she cried.

Vince remained motionless the receiver still in his hand. He stared blankly into space emotionally drained. Unable to think he had no desire to get up and go somewhere, go anywhere, everything seemed pointless. Vince offered no resistance when Helmut took the phone from his hand and hung it up.

"You can stay in the apartment for as long as you like, Vincent, Mr. Conover took care of the lease."

"Uh," Vince snapped back to reality, "Sorry, Mr. Wagner, what did you say?"

"You can stay here; Mr. Conover took care of the lease."

"I can't stay here without Linda."

"My offer is always good," Helmut assured.

"I best get going, now," Vince stood up.

"Sit, Vincent," Helmut pulled Vince down by his arm, "let's talk, maybe this old man could be of help. When my beautiful young wife died, my whole world fell apart. I think I know what you are feeling. Your life without Linda will never be the same, but you must not give up, she wouldn't

The Burning Hours                                    Page 228

want you to give up. Life works in strange ways. When two souls meant to be together are separated those souls continue searching until they find one another and are made whole, once again," Helmut experienced a pang of conscience being loyal to Linda's request not to reveal her pregnancy to Vince.

"She asked me to promise I would wear my overcoat when it snowed; she was worried about me," Vince started crying.

"A wonderful girl," Helmut squeezed Vince's shoulder, "I am so sorry."

"If I could get my hands on him, Mr. Wagner I'd kill him for what he's done to her. I can't stay in New Jersey I have to go away, far away."

# 71

Paolo Bellini scaled the steps of the mansion to the second floor and rushed to the reading room where he found Charles weighed with concern and deep in thought.

"How is Linda?" he spoke breathlessly.

"Not good, Paolo."

"Where is she? I want to see her."

"She's in her room with Adalina."

The intercom buzzed as Paolo got up to go to Linda's room.

Charles pressed its button and listened.

"Thank you, Mrs. Prescott," he picked up the extension.

"Wait a minute," he called to Paolo, "Freddie is on the phone."

"Derek Reed called a few minutes, ago, Mr. Conover."

"What does he want?"

"Ten thousand dollars."

"What's up, CC?" Paolo asked.

"Reed is looking for ten thousand dollars."

"He wants ten grand, he should be in jail."

"Freddie I'm putting you on speaker phone, Paolo is with me."

"How are you, Mr. Bellini?"

"I'll be better, Freddie when we get this garbage out of our lives."

"What else did he say, Freddie?" Charles inquired.

"He wants cash and he will go away."

"Don't do it, CC, he's an addict, he'll be back for more."

"What do you think, Freddie?"

"I agree with Mr. Bellini, he'll burn through ten thousand dollars in no time."

"You're probably right."

"What are you going to do, CC?"

The Burning Hours
Page 230

"I'll take the chance he'll honor his word and pay him," Charles answered.

"Freddie is right, CC, he'll go through ten grand like a hot knife through butter."

"What else can I do I have to think of Linda, her baby and Vincent."

"Freddie I'd like to talk with Mr. Conover, privately."

"I understand, Mr. Bellini."

"Leave Reed to me, CC, I'll make him disappear forever."

"What are you saying, Paolo?"

"I got bridges under construction he'll be in the foundation of one of them."

"I hate seeing Linda the way she is, but murder, I don't know," Charles waffled at Paolo's suggestion.

"Nobody will ever know, CC."

"I'll pay him this time, if he reneges it will be his last act on the face of the earth," Charles said, icily.

"Whatever you say, CC. Now I want to see my niece."

Paolo and Charles left the reading room. They walked along the long hallway to Linda's bedroom where she sat dazed staring out the window.

"Daddy and Uncle Paolo are here, honey," Adalina whispered.

Paolo put his arms around Linda, "We love you, Linda everything will work out."

"I'm glad to see you, Uncle Paolo," Linda lingered in the security of his warm embrace.

"Your baby needs your strength, Linda, Vincent would want it that way," Charles said.

"I know, Daddy."

"Guess what?"

"What Uncle Paolo?" Linda managed a smile.

"I'll make a construction hat for your little guy, with his name on it, like the one I made for you when you were a little girl."

The Burning Hours                              Page 231

"That's nice, Uncle Paolo."

"Mother and I spoke with granddad and grandmother last night, Linda, they are delighted you will live with them," Charles said.

"Mother told me."

"You made the right decision, Linda it's too difficult for you to stay here."

"Your father is right the change will be good for you and your baby," Paolo said.

"I know, Uncle Paolo," Linda answered in a somber voice.

"Will you go with me, Mother?"

"Of course I will."

"I'd like to go, right away, Daddy."

"Sure, honey I'll make arrangements."

"I will call granddad and grandmother before leaving."

"They will be happy to hear from you," Charles said.

"Promise Uncle Paolo you will take care of yourself and your baby," he hugged and kissed Linda.

"I promise, Uncle Paolo."

"Rest now, honey we'll pack later," Adalina said.

# 72

Tommy and Darling arrived at Baltimore's cavernous Penn Station, on a bright summer day in July. They were met by Lieutenant Harry "Happy" Huffman who would accompany them to Hoboken.

"I'm Lieutenant Huffman," he saluted Tommy and held his salute.

"The lieutenant is waiting for a return salute, Tommy," Darling said.

Tommy returned Lieutenant Huffman's salute, "It's not usual for a private to acknowledge an officer's salute."

"You will get used to officers and generals saluting you," Lieutenant Huffman lowered his arm.

"What do you know, Tommy, generals and officers saluting you."

"I'm getting even, Sarge," Tommy laughed.

"Yeah, I guess so," Darling smiled.

"I'll be handling your press and public relations contacts," Lieutenant Huffman informed Tommy, "there will be well wishers, newspaper people, and photographers on the platform in Hoboken. Your mother and fiancé will enter the railroad car from a separate entrance. It will be hectic out there so elbow me for help, if necessary."

"Okay, Lieutenant," Tommy nodded.

"Everybody calls me Happy."

"Okay Happy, call me Tommy," he's Carroll."

"You going to give me a break, Tommy?"

"Never, Sarge."

"Let's board," Happy said, "you can relax, have refreshments, and before you know it, we'll be in Hoboken."

The ride to Hoboken was uneventful. Tommy drifted into a light sleep. Darling looked out the window at a blur of houses, vehicles speeding along the state highway, factories humming and smoke stacks fuming as the train sped forward. Happy was engrossed in a handful of reports he was writing. A quiet prevailed in the car as it rolled to Hoboken.

A large crowd at the Hoboken Station buzzed and its expectation soared when a train glided to a stop in a cloud of belching steam. Happy emerged and escorted Julia and Rosemary into a waiting private car.

When Julia and Rosemary saw Tommy standing with Darling at the opposite end of the car their throats tightened with emotion. Julia pulled Rosemary into a tight embrace, "Go to him, Rosemary, it is you Tommy wants most in this world."

"I love you, Mom," Rosemary slipped out of Julia's embrace and walked slowly along the car's narrow aisle. Tommy she said quietly to herself and then in an emotionally charged voice she called his name and ran to him, and in an instant her fears of the passing years evaporated in Tommy's arms.

"Don't ever let me go, Tommy," Rosemary choked out the words, "don't ever let me go, I love you so much."

"Rosemary," Tommy whispered, "I can't tell you how many times I said your name."

"Don't ever stop loving me, Tommy."

"I want to see you, Rosemary," Tommy said, brushing his fingers across Rosemary's face, "I see you, Rosemary I love you," they held each other in the solemn quiet of the car.

"Tommy," Julia's voice conveyed a cautious plea.

"Mom," Tommy reached out and embraced Julia, "I love you, Mom."

"I prayed you would come home to Rosemary and me …," overcome emotionally Julia was unable to speak. Tommy pulled Rosemary into their orbit as Darling and Happy Huffman looked on.

"It's beautiful, Sarge, isn't it?"

"Yeah, it is," Darling agreed.

"Sorry to break this up it's time to go," Happy said, displaying and handing the Medal of Honor to Rosemary, "Please place the Medal around Tommy's neck."

"Everyone is proud of you, Tommy," Rosemary spoke softly.

"It's a big crowd," Happy observed.

"They are here for you, Tommy," Darling put his hand on Tommy's shoulder.

"Ready to go, Tommy?"

"As ready as I'll ever be."

"Enjoy the moments, Tommy. An army car will wait for us at the end of the platform. When you are home expect a gathering of neighborhood people waiting to greet you."

The anticipation of the crowd on the platform rose to a fevered pitch when Darling and Happy exited the car, and then it erupted into deafening cheers when Tommy, Rosemary and Julia on either side appeared on the train's doorstep.

# 73

The olive-colored army car stopped in front of Tommy's house and was immediately engulfed by men and women of all ages, young boys and girls, straining for a glimpse of Tommy.

"I know I'm home, Sarge, I feel it," Tommy pointed to his house, "Vince lives next door," Tommy hesitated, "I thought Vince would meet us at the station."

"Right now lots of people want a piece of you, Tommy."

Darling and Happy assisted Julia and Rosemary out of the car. When Tommy exited the gathering of people burst into sustained cheering. Benjamin Gruber embraced him, kissed Rosemary and promised them a delicious ice cream Sundae. Tommy asked if he still had the portable radio and when Mr. Gruber said he did. Rosemary responded, "So you could play with it, Tommy?" Samuel Birkman shook Tommy's hand and Tommy offered thanks for the Brady affair. Julia's eyes widened when Shamus O'Malley, dressed in civilian clothes, shook Tommy's hand and walked away without identifying himself.

Tommy, Rosemary and Julia climbed the steps to the porch platform. They waved their appreciation to the crowd and went inside. Happy drove away and Darling went into the house.

Tommy slumped into an easy chair next to the radio in the parlor.

"Are you tired?" Rosemary asked.

"Yes, but I feel good," Tommy pulled Rosemary onto his lap.

"Did I tell you I love you?" Rosemary whispered.

"Several times," Tommy laughed.

"I have to help Mom in the dining room, Tommy," and at that moment the doorbell rang. Rosemary asked Darling to help Julia set the table.

The Burning Hours          Page 236

"How can I help, Mrs. Tomasso?"

Still struggling with her emotions, Julia said, "Set the china, utensils and napkins at each chair."

"Tommy's going to be okay, Mrs. Tomasso."

"I know, Sergeant, please call me Julia."

"Okay, Julia, you will have to show me the proper way to set your table this isn't like the mess halls I'm used to."

Darling's request for instruction in dining room etiquette elicited a smile from Julia, "This is how you do it, Sergeant," she arranged a typical setting, "can you do that?"

"I'm a soldier I know how to take orders," he smiled back at Julia.

"Is that Regina?" Julia called.

"Yes, Mom," Rosemary answered.

"Mrs. Farro," Tommy jumped up, "Where's Vince and Linda? Why aren't they here?" he asked, excitedly.

Regina handed a large box containing a rum cake she had baked to celebrate Tommy's homecoming to Rosemary, and with Julia and Darling looking on, she embraced Tommy and held him for a long time.

"It's so good you are home, Tommy, we are all proud of you."

"Mrs. Farro, I'm Sergeant Darling, I was with Vince and Tommy I'm glad to meet you."

"Thank you for all you did for our boys, Sergeant. Vince wrote me often. I was comforted knowing you were together."

"Sure," Darling responded, awkwardly.

"We're not finished here, Sergeant," Darling went back to the dining room.

"Is Vince all right?" Tommy persisted, "I thought he and Linda would be here."

"Let's have cake and coffee and enjoy your homecoming. We'll talk, later."

"Sure, Mrs. Farro, Vince and I went through a lot and I need to know he's all right."

"I know, Tommy," Regina squeezed his hand.

"Coffee and cake are served," Julia announced. Tommy sit at the head of the table, Rosemary to Tommy's right, Regina to Tommy's left, Darling to Rosemary's right and Julia sat next to Regina."

Tommy ran the palm of his hand along the ivory tablecloth's intricate design, "You set the table with grandma's lace table cloth and napkins, Mom?"

"This is a special occasion, Tommy," Julia hugged him from behind, "you're home and we are all thankful."

"It's good to be home, "it would be complete if Vince and Linda were here, Mrs. Farro. What happened? Where is Vince?"

"Vince is in Los Angeles, and Linda I believe went back to Connecticut."

"What's his phone number? I have to talk to him."

"He doesn't have a phone, Tommy he'll call me tomorrow night at seven o'clock, from a pay phone. Come over then and the two of you can talk, but now, let's celebrate your return home and your prestigious honor."

"Regina please cut the cake, Rosemary, pour the coffee," Julia ordered, "Have you ever had rum cake, Sergeant?" she inquired.

"No."

"Regina makes the best rum cake in the world, you will love it."

Regina plated wedges of cake topped with whipped cream, shaved almonds, layers of dark rum and chocolate cream filling. Tommy's indulgence brought an ecstatic look to his face.

"Mrs. Farro, you are the best!" Tommy exclaimed.

Rosemary and Julia added their compliments and Regina agreed, saying coyly, "It is pretty good if I must say so."

Darling hadn't tasted Regina's cake. He had never been part of a family celebration. What he experienced were gray mess halls, rows of tables, bent utensils, stained cups, slow moving chow lines and noise that floated above hundreds of guys eating army supplied food. In the emotional warmth of the Tomasso home, its brightly lit dining room alive with easy exchanges of affection, Darling envisioned himself … and then … he stopped, because what he thought could never happen, he was, after all, a soldier, and soon, he would return to a soldier's life.

"Sergeant, aren't you going to try Regina's rum cake?" Julia broke Darling's introspection.

"Go ahead, Sarge," Tommy encouraged, "You'll love it."

"I'm sure I will, Tommy. I'm not used to a family gathering like this."

"It's okay, Sarge," Tommy understood Darling's emotions.

Then Julia broke the mood, "Sergeant! If you don't pick up your fork I will come there and feed the cake to you, myself."

"Do as she says, Sarge," Tommy advised, "You don't want to get on Mom's wrong side," Tommy's warning elicited laughter from Regina and Rosemary, and a smile from Darling.

"I've been warned," Darling surrendered and savored a piece of cake, "I never tasted anything like this," he enthusiastically complimented Regina.

"I knew you could do it, Sarge; you just needed a little push," Tommy joked.

"What I need, Tommy is another piece of rum cake."

# 74

Twilight appeared and quiet came to the Tomasso house. Darling looked at Tommy and Rosemary wrapped in each other's arms, sleeping on the sofa. He looked, but found no ashtrays and refrained from smoking. Languidly he turned the pages of the photo album on the parlor, coffee table, smiling at pictures of Tommy, his devilish smile ... Tommy who saved his life on a snowy night in Belgium. Darling watched Julia and Regina in the kitchen quietly engaged in conversation and thought they were the most desirable women he had ever known. He closed the album, looked at his wristwatch as Julia and Regina came into the parlor.

Julia stroked Rosemary and Tommy's faces, "Mrs. Farro is going home," sleepily they woke up Rosemary hugged Regina, as did Tommy.

"Still okay if I come over when Vince calls?"

"Sure, Tommy, Vince will want to talk to you," Regina responded.

"It was a pleasure meeting you, Mrs. Farro," Darling clumsily kissed Regina's cheek, "Tell Vince I said hello."

"I shall, Sergeant, good night, Rosemary."

Julia hugged Regina, "Give Vince my love."

"I will."

"You'll be leaving for the base, Sarge?"

"Yeah, Tommy."

"I'm going to wash and go to bed I'll see you before you go."

"Okay," Darling answered.

"Do you want me to help you, Tommy?" Rosemary asked.

"I'll be okay," Tommy assured, as Rosemary, Julia and Darling observed him navigating without incident to the bathroom.

Julia and Rosemary were in the dining room when they heard crashing glass. They rushed to the bathroom and found Tommy clutching either side of the sink. Darling grasped Julia's arm, "Leave Tommy to Rosemary." She knew Darling was right and with the reality that another woman would be paramount in her son's life Julia went back to the parlor where she sat quietly, if not nostalgically, on the sofa.

"I knocked over the glass when I reached for a towel," Tommy told Rosemary. The broken glass was in the basin, none of it was on the floor. Rosemary said she would clean the basin. Frustrated, Tommy crossed the hallway into his bedroom.

Darling followed Julia into the parlor and sat on the far end of the sofa. He watched Julia now deep in thought. "Tommy has a lot of adjusting to do," Darling said, "but he'll be all right."

"If you knew Tommy before the war, Sergeant, full of energy, a daredevil and now ...," Julia stopped in mid-thought.

"Tommy accepts his condition that's a difficult, but a positive thing. No one can tell you what to think, but if he's accepted it, maybe you should, also."

"I know you are right, Sergeant, but my heart aches for him."

"Tommy's my little brother. I had a hard time accepting what happened to him. I even blamed myself. If I hadn't been out there he wouldn't have stayed in the foxhole. Tommy's coming for me may have saved his life because the foxhole he and Vince were in was destroyed by artillery. It doesn't help to dwell on what you can't change instead do all you can to make his life as good as it can be."

"Thank you, Sergeant I needed to hear that."

"Call me Carroll and don't start on me like your son does," Darling shifted the mood.

"Alright, Carroll I promise."

"I'll say Good Night to Tommy and be on my way."

"It's late, stay the night the sofa isn't very comfortable, but it's better than sitting in a terminal waiting for a train."

"Which may never come," Darling joked, "I'm sure the sofa is more comfortable than most places I have slept, but I don't want to impose."

"You're not imposing I'm sure Tommy would like you to stay the night."

Tommy sat on the edge of his bed questioning himself as he had many times when he was a patient in the Army Hospital in Liege.

"Do you want me to help you with your shirt? You might be more comfortable," Rosemary asked.

"I'll take care of it."

"I can't imagine how hard this is for you," Rosemary said, her arms around Tommy's shoulders.

"I'd give my right arm and this medal to see you for just one minute, Rosemary."

"I promise we will have a wonderful life, together, you must believe that."

Tommy nodded.

Rosemary cupped Tommy's face in her hands, "Hey, mister, don't you feel sorry for yourself. I won't permit it. I want you to kiss me like you mean it," she lowered her mouth onto his and Tommy responded with equal passion. "Now lay down I'll be right back."

"Rosemary, ask my mother and Sergeant Darling to come in."

Julia and Darling sat in anxious silence when Rosemary came into the parlor, "Tommy wants to see you," she said.

"Is he all right?" Julia asked.

"A little upset."

"I think you should see Tommy, Sergeant."

"Mrs. Tomasso is right, Sergeant," Rosemary agreed.

"Mom, I want to sleep with Tommy, tonight," Rosemary announced, "I don't want him sleeping alone on his first day home, but I want your permission."

The Burning Hours                                    Page 242

"You don't need my permission, Rosemary you are the best thing that has happened to my son I love you as if you were my own daughter."

"I'm in your house I won't disrespect you, Mom, I won't take off my clothes, we'll just sleep, together, that's all."

"Whatever you two decide is your business."

In Tommy's bedroom, he and Darling revisited their discussions and Vince's visit to the hospital. While there Tommy accepted his blindness, but now at home holding Rosemary against his body and kissing her mouth more than anything Tommy wanted to see her.

Darling listened. He didn't want to give Tommy a meaningless pep talk. He reminded him that Rosemary is a terrific girl that he has a caring mother. And his life, although not what he planned would be wonderful, after all.

"You'll be leaving for the base, Sarge."

"You got me for another night. I'll be sleeping on the sofa, your mother is a tough lady."

"That's good, Sarge, your being in the house through the night."

"Your mother and Mrs. Farro treated me well, I'll always be grateful."

"After you're gone that's it, Sarge."

"I might surprise you," Darling said, "I'll get out of the way Tommy, your mother is here to see you."

Julia pressed her face to Tommy's, "I love you, Tommy."

"I know, Mom, I love you, too"

"I hope you have forgiven me."

"Nothing to forgive, I love you."

"Mom, I think you should leave Tommy with me now."

"I know, Rosemary," Julia reluctantly got up and went to the parlor where Darling was seated on the sofa.

"I'll help you undress, Tommy," Rosemary closed the bedroom door behind her.

Julia handed a pillow and a folded white sheet to Darling, who seeing Julia's swollen eyes inquired if she was all right.

"It's been an emotional time for everyone."

Darling nodded his agreement.

"I'll wash and iron your shirt before you leave, tomorrow."

"I'll get it done at the base."

"It's not a problem."

"I don't want to put you out."

"You won't put me out."

"I'll take care of it when I get back to the base," Darling reiterated.

"The shirt, Carroll," Julia demanded, holding out her hand, an exasperated expression on her face.

After a brief hesitation, Darling capitulated. He fumbled with the shirt's buttons before removing and giving it to Julia.

"Hand me your undershirt."

Darling objected.

"Let's have it Carroll I've seen a man's bare chest before."

"You got my shirt that's enough."

"I'll turn my back to protect your modesty and you can place it in my hand, okay?"

Julia held out her hand and soon felt the soft cotton undershirt.

"Can I turn back, now?"

"Yeah," Darling answered.

"I just wanted to say," Julia suppressed a spasm of laughter at Darling holding the pillow against his bare chest, "Good Night."

"Good Night and thanks."

The Burning Hours                    Page 244

"I'll wake you when breakfast is ready," Julia's eyes wrinkled in a smile.

# 75

The morning sun beat down with pitiless ferocity. At 8:00 o'clock in the morning the temperature had hit 90 degrees and was climbing precipitously. Fresh in a tan shirtwaist dress Julia had gotten up early up, washed, dried and ironed Darling's shirts.

Darling stirred awake wrapped in a white sheet when he heard the rustle of fabric in the parlor. Unbeknownst to Julia he saw her drape his pressed shirts over an armless chair, and then quietly return to the kitchen.

Unable to sleep Darling put on his undershirt, picked up his army regulation shirt and walked to the kitchen. Julia hadn't noticed Darling's presence. When he announced himself, she turned off the stove's gas jets and smiled.

"Good morning, Julia."

"Did you sleep well?"

"I did," he nervously twisted the army shirt in his hand.

"You must be the only person in New Jersey who slept under a sheet during this heat wave."

"Yeah, I guess so."

"To preserve your modesty, Carroll?"

Julia looked at Darling twisting his shirt, creating a sea of wrinkles in the fabric as if it had never been ironed.

"I was up early to wash and iron your shirt, now look at what you've done to it, give it here," she extended her hand.

"Sorry I didn't mean to wrinkle it."

"There's a razor and a soap mug in the bathroom and fresh towels in the cabinet."

"You have a razor?"

"Yes, I have a razor."

"Why? ... Forget it."

"Why do you think I have a razor?"

"I don't know, forget it."

"You think it's for a man, don't you?"

"Well ..."

"I use the razor to shave my legs if you must know," Julia said, irritated, "didn't your women folk at home tell you about the nylon shortage?"

"Last night and today is the closest thing to home I have ever had."

"I'm sorry, Carroll, that was thoughtless."

"It's okay."

"I'll go over your shirt while you get ready."

"Julia," Darling called to her, "It's okay."

"It was a dumb thing to say."

"You look nice in your dress."

"I'm glad you noticed," Julia smiled stopping short of admitting she wore it for his attention.

In her bedroom, Julia ironed Darling's shirt, hung it on a hanger and took it to the bathroom.

"Is it okay if I come in?" Julia spoke to the closed bathroom door.

"Sure, come in."

Now shirtless Darling glided his razor along his face mowing dark stubble in its path. Julia stood in the doorway, holding Darling's shirt. She saw scars on his chest from two wars aware of the reason for his modesty. Impulsively she reached up and felt his shaved skin. When Darling again complimented how she looked Julia experienced a warm flush overtake her body.

"Breakfast will be ready in a few minutes."

"Where are Tommy and Rosemary?"

"Tommy and Rosemary had an early breakfast and went out. They trapped me between them; I thought they'd squeeze the life out of me. They went to the park, then they're going to Gruber's Drug Store for ice cream, and then to the church to publish their intention to marry."

"Tommy was really down last night."

"He's much better, now," Julia smiled.

"Are eggs and potatoes okay with you?"

The Burning Hours

"Sure."

Darling watched Julia at the stove her back to him her raven hair bunched in a net that hung to her shoulders. He never thought preparing breakfast could be seductive, but Julia's movements at the stove changed all that. Everything about her was magnetic: her dark eyes, her florid skin and her voluptuous body. Darling envisioned life in a home with a true passionate woman not the paternalism of army commanders who surrender individuality for collective thought.

"Carroll, I need your help," Julia's voice punctured his mental flight.

"Sure," Darling got up.

"Put the coffee and toast on the table, I'll serve," Julia switched off the gas jets.

"Is there anything else you want me to do?"

"Put these plates on the table and pour the coffee."

"Anything else?"

Julia fixed her gaze on Darling, "Do what you've been thinking of doing."

The words Darling practiced now eluded him.

Julia waited and finally she gave up.

"Enjoy your breakfast."

"I want to kiss you, Julia, but I don't know how you will react," Darling summoned his courage, confessed his desire, and revealed his fear.

Julia looked at Darling.

"You've been through two wars and you are more afraid of a 42-year old woman in New Jersey than the Germans you fought in France."

Darling shuffled nervously.

"There's only one way to find out, Carroll," Julia locked her stare on Darling and waited.

After a long interlude Darling bowed his head, Julia stood on her toes, softly their mouths met and edgily Darling awaited her verdict.

The Burning Hours

"That was good, Carroll," Julia whispered, again lifting herself on her toes their lips meeting in a longer, more committed kiss.

"Did I pass?" Darling slid his hand down Julia's waist, along her hip, feeling the softness of her flesh beneath her dress, but on his way to her behind Julia grabbed Darling's hand ending the quest to his desired location.

"Not now, Sergeant! I'll tell you when," Julia's glare emphasized her command.

Darling removed his hand, "When?" he queried.

"When I say so, understood?"

"Understood," Darling complied.

"Good, now let's have breakfast."

# 76

Tommy and Rosemary walked hand-in-hand along the street to Roosevelt Park. Dressed in a casual white blouse and pale gray skirt Rosemary reminded Tommy that his outfit was similar to what he wore on their first date.

At the park's entrance water spouts from a massive Bernini-like fountain shot high into the air splashed into a circular pool below creating a sensation of comfort despite the day's oppressive heat. Tommy and Rosemary sat on a bench holding hands, enjoying the fountain's cooling sprays. Tommy didn't have to see Rosemary to know how radiant she looked on this spectacular summer day. He smiled at the prescience of Major Olsen's observation about his relationship with Rosemary.

"Why are you smiling?"

"Something a medical officer in Liege said, it's nothing."

"Do you usually smile at nothing?" Rosemary chided.

"No."

"Stop being mysterious, Tommy."

"A lot of things went on when I was in the hospital."

"That's all you will tell me."

"What else do you want me to say?"

"If you want this and this, Mr. Tomasso," Rosemary kissed Tommy, repeatedly, "you will tell me why you're smiling."

"You're blackmailing me, Miss McNulty."

"You got the message now speak up."

"Doc Olson, the hospital medical director asked about our relationship."

"You never told me you discussed our relationship with the doctors in Belgium."

"Doc Olson brought it up I'm glad he did."

The Burning Hours                                    Page 250

"When you didn't answer my letters," Rosemary lightly punched Tommy's arm, "you upset me, I cried night and day, if you don't believe me, ask Mom."

"I'm sorry, Rosemary, I didn't want to burden you."

"You could never burden me, Tommy."

"Anyway, Doc Olson asked me if I loved you. I told him I did. Then he asked if you loved me. I said yes." Rosemary looked at Tommy gazing blankly into the distance, "Then Doc Olson said her commitment will be a great help to you."

"And that brought a smile to your face?"

"Doc didn't know how right he was. I'm smiling because the most wonderful girl in the world loves me."

"I do love you," Rosemary rested her head on Tommy's shoulder.

"Let's go to Gruber's for an ice cream Sundae."

"With whipped cream and syrup?" Rosemary responded.

"Whatever you like."

Tommy and Rosemary quickly became accustomed to their loss of privacy. At the entrance to Gruber's Drug Store they accepted congratulations and the well wishes of neighbors and strangers. In the store they were effusively greeted by Benjamin Gruber.

"Here is your table, sit, sit," Benjamin excitedly directed Tommy and Rosemary to the table near the window they had occupied on their first date, "I'll be right back," he briskly walked away, returning within seconds with his chrome-plated portable radio.

"It seems like yesterday you came here on your first date, happy teenagers, and then the war," he choked up, "so much pain, but you're together, and ..."

"It's okay, Mr. Gruber," Tommy said, "We love you, Mr. Gruber and we love coming here, it's our special place," Rosemary added.

"I love you kids," Benjamin recovered, "now I will work on your Sundaes."

"Lots of whipped cream," Rosemary reminded.

The Burning Hours

Benjamin tapped his right temple, "I remember lots of whipped cream."

"Did you see Vince before he left for California, Rosemary?"

"I didn't, he left suddenly I wish he was here."

"Vince was going to be my best man, and now …," Tommy didn't finish his thought.

"I'm sorry, Tommy, I know how much you two mean to each other."

Benjamin came to the table holding two frosted Sundaes in each hand, "For you, Rosemary plenty of whipped cream," Benjamin set Rosemary's Sundae before her, "and for you Tommy."

"Thanks Mr. Gruber, they look wonderful," Rosemary smiled.

"Vince wrote me he and Linda were excited to marry."

"I know, Tommy."

"Vince and Linda going separate ways, I don't get it, they were crazy about each other."

"Talk with Vince, tonight, you two need to reconnect," Rosemary lifted the radio's chrome plate. Frank Sinatra was singing *You'll Never Know.*

"That's Sinatra," Tommy reached for the chrome plate.

"Don't play with the radio, Tommy."

"What if I do?"

"I'll smack your hand"

# 77

Before going into All Souls Church, Rosemary fastened a lace handkerchief to her hair with bobby pins. They blessed themselves with holy water and sat in a back pew. When the purple curtain of the confessional box swung open an elderly woman emerged. She genuflected, blessed herself, and with noticeable arthritic discomfort she walked out of the church.

"Do you want to go first, Tommy?"

"No, you go, first."

"Okay," Rosemary squeezed Tommy's hand, and went into the dark confessional box, knelt on the kneeler waiting for the priest to slide open the screen.

After several minutes Rosemary came out of the confessional box, genuflected, made the sign of the cross, and sat next to Tommy, "You're next, Tommy."

"What took you so long?"

"You'll find out, I'll start my penance."

"What's your penance? An Act of Contrition and a Hail Mary, you'll be finished before I get out," Tommy said, getting up.

"I wish," Rosemary said, bringing Tommy back to the pew.

"What's your penance?"

"I have to say the Rosary every day, for one week."

"Did you murder someone?"

"You know, wise guy."

Tommy went into the confessional box its darkness, no match for the blackness he experienced. He knelt and within seconds the screen separating the penitent from God's forgiving agent opened.

"Bless me, Father," Tommy began, "It's been three years since my last confession."

"Why the long time between confessions?"

"I've been away."

"Where were you?'

"I was in combat and then six months in an Army hospital."

"Are their sins you would like to confess?"

"I killed people."

"In war that is no sin, is there anything else?"

"You might think it a sin, but I don't"

"What is that?"

"I made love to my intended wife last night."

"What do you mean you made love?"

"That's all you'll get, Father."

"When you leave the church in the vestibule you'll see a bracket containing pamphlets titled *The Catholic Young Man in the Twentieth Century*, I suggest you read it.

"I was blinded in the war, Father I won't be able to see what you're talking about."

The priest paused, "Recite an Act of Contrition, a Hail Mary and say the Rosary each day for a week," then he slid the screen shut.

Tommy exited the confessional and sat next to Rosemary.

"Well," Rosemary asked Tommy.

"Same as you, but I don't have Rosary beads."

"I'll lend you my Rosary."

"That's a tough penance, I wonder why," a smile crossed Tommy's lips.

"I can't imagine," Rosemary giggled softly, and then said she wanted to light a few candles before leaving the church.

At the votive candles she deposited three quarters, lit three candles, and said a brief prayer before returning to the pew where Tommy was waiting.

"Who did you light the candles for?"

"One is for us, and the other two are for Vince and Linda."

"That's nice," Tommy squeezed Rosemary's hand.

"Tommy, I have something to ask you, promise you won't get mad at me," she whispered.

"I can't promise until I know what you want."

"Then promise you won't stay mad at me."

"Okay, whatever it is I won't stay mad at you."

"Now that we are in the State of Grace we should sleep in separate rooms until we are married," Rosemary held her breath waiting for Tommy's response.

"That's two months from today, that's a long time to wait."

"Tommy …,"Rosemary began.

"Do you think what happened last night is a sin?" Tommy interjected.

"No, Tommy, what happened last night was beautiful."

"In there," he pointed to the confessional box, "the priest thought killing people, was okay, but making love is a sin."

"Tommy, please, I've been with the nuns for most of my nineteen years I don't know any other way."

"What about the nun who tricked you and kept me from seeing you before I went away, was she in the State of Grace when she fell down the steps and killed herself?"

"What she did was unforgivable I believe she will answer for it."

"I don't know what kind of God says loving someone you care for is a sin, but killing thousands of people isn't; God has a strange sense of humor," Tommy whispered, "There was a chaplain who said Mass before we went into combat, he'd say if there's anything you want to get off your chests talk to your God, whoever or whatever he or she may be. I don't have to unburden myself to somebody sitting in a black box, Rosemary. The only reason I went to confession is because you asked me to go."

"Please, Tommy," Rosemary said, tremulously.

"You don't live with the nuns any longer, Rosemary. We'll be living together as husband and wife in our own home raising our children who will know their mother and father."

"Tommy, please, Mom is refitting her wedding dress for me to wear. Our wedding day will be special, Tommy, I want to receive Holy Communion the day of our marriage, please, Tommy, won't you help me?"

"You have a way of tying me into little knots, Miss McNulty."

"They're love knots," Rosemary kissed Tommy's face.

"I have a question," Tommy whispered.

"What is it?"

"If one night I go to the kitchen for a glass of water, I make a wrong turn and crawl into your bed, what then?"

Rosemary hesitated.

"What then, Rosemary?" Tommy persisted.

"There's always confession," Rosemary whispered.

# 78

That evening Tommy refused Rosemary's offer to help confident he could go unescorted to Vince's house without incident. He remembered three steps to the porch's platform. Tommy announced his presence through the screen door, and within seconds Regina greeted him.

They went into the kitchen where a phone tethered to an extension cord sat on the kitchen table. Regina explained since Vince went away, she kept the phone in easy reach. At 7:00 o'clock as Vince promised the phone rang and Regina picked up the receiver.

"Hello, Mom, how are you?"

"I'm all right, Vince, how are you?"

"I'm doing okay," Vince said unconvincingly, "Mom, has Linda called?"

"No, Vince, I'm sorry, she hasn't."

"I thought, maybe she might have called."

"Tommy is here he would like to talk to you," Regina handed Tommy the phone, and went into the parlor.

"Hello, buddy, I missed you, yesterday."

"It's good to hear your voice, Tommy, your picture with Rosemary and your mother is in every newspaper in California."

"Rosemary and Mom send their love?"

"I love them, too, Tommy, tell them I do."

"I will Vince, are you coming back to Jersey?"

"Not any time soon."

"What are you doing in Los Angeles?"

"Digging water line trenches, the pay is good and the work makes me forget."

"Come on, Vince, you can't go on like that."

"I'm in a fog no matter what I do nothing is clear, Christ, Tommy, I'm lost without Linda, I feel as if I'm just going through the motions, I think about her all the time."

"What happened, Vince? I can't believe you two aren't together."

"Her ex-husband showed up while I was at Fort Monmouth. He pushed his way into the apartment demanding Linda take him back. He threatened to have me court-martialed on adultery charges. He was getting ready to assault her when our landlord heard the commotion, and threw him out."

"That's nuts, Vince, they were divorced, long before you and Linda got together."

"He told her a court-martial would believe him over a draftee and I'd get 30 years in the brig. He scared the life out of her, Tommy. Her father's lawyers made inquiries and were told he could get away with it. To protect my identity, Linda left me. Her family is probably paying him blackmail. They are good people, Tommy. Linda left me to protect me, Tommy, it's crazy. If I could get my hands on Reed, I'd kill him for what he's done to Linda."

"Go after her, Vince, bring her back, you can't let him get away with ruining your lives."

"I've tried, Tommy, she won't return my calls, I talked with Mrs. Conover, nothing helps.

"I wish there was something I could do, Vince."

"I know, Tommy that's enough about me, what's up with you and Rosemary?"

"Is it okay if I stay on a little longer, Mrs. Farro?"

"Stay on as long as you two want to."

"Are you running out of change, Vince?"

"I'm in the apartment manager's office he'll charge the call to my rent."

"We're getting married in September."

"That's great, Tommy you're a lucky guy, Rosemary is a wonderful girl."

"She lights up my life," and after a short pause, Tommy said, "I wish things could have worked out for you and

Linda, Vince, in a way, I feel guilty that it turned out well for me, thanks to you and Sarge."

"Don't feel that way, Tommy, and don't worry about me, I'll be all right."

"We're going to stay in touch, right?"

"You know we will, Tommy."

"I'll give the phone back to your mother, now."

"Okay, Tommy, let me know your date."

"Okay, Vince, here's Mom."

"Do you need help going home?"

"I'll be okay," Tommy said, navigating the familiar floor plan out of Vince's house.

"I wish you would come home, Vince, I worry about you, all the time."

"Don't worry about me, Mom, I'm getting along."

"I pray that you and Linda get back together."

"Keep praying, Mom, maybe it will happen."

"Before that terrible trouble, Linda called me just to say hello. She sounded sweet and happy she even thanked me for having such a wonderful son."

"I didn't know that, Mom, she actually said that?"

"She loves you, Vince, but for your own good you must move on."

"Did you get the money I sent you?"

"I did, but Vince you should use your earnings for yourself."

"I'm okay, my job pays well."

"Hang up before your phone bill gets too high, go out and have a good time."

"Mom," Vince said in a quiet voice.

"Yes, Vince."

"Let me know if Linda calls you have the manager's phone number."

"I will, Vince."

"Okay, Mom, I love you."

"I love you, too," Regina hung up the receiver quietly shedding tears for her lost son.

# 79

Vince's bare chest glistened in the sultry Los Angeles sun. He wore a red bandana around his forehead to keep stinging perspiration out of his eyes. The repair of an open canal parallel to a state highway progressed at a snail's pace. Vince's crew was headed by a squat powerfully built man nicknamed Bull. No one knew Bull's true name. The standing joke among the men was Bull's last name rhymed with it.

Throughout the scorching morning Vince quarried heavy wet clay from the canal trench. The biting noise of pick-axes digging clay and the *Shhhh* sounds of shoveling it out of the trench was interrupted when Bull ordered the crew to take a break.

Vince removed his red bandana and made a beeline to the tent for shade and water. He poured the first cup from a Water Buffalo over his head, downed the second cup, poured himself a third cup and relaxed before Bull ordered the crew back to work.

"Vince you and Clancy work on the section between the stakes."

"Are you nuts, Bull, that's more than a two-man job."

"If I had all my marbles I wouldn't be working here," Bull responded.

"Clancy, it's you and me in the trench," Vince hollered.

"Is Bull out of his mind?"

"It's questionable whether Bull ever had a mind," Vince laughed.

After two hours digging a trough for a concrete wall Vince climbed out of the trench and walked back to the tent. He stood at the Water Buffalo pouring another cup of water when a red convertible zoomed past, then came to an abrupt stop, and drove backward screeching to a halt in a cloud of dust.

"I need directions," a young, tan, blue-eyed blond woman gazed seductively at Vince.

"Where are you going?"

"To your apartment."

"Oh, yeah, what's your name?"

"Astrid."

"Where are you from?"

"Beverly Hills."

"The high rent district."

"I'm willing to spread the wealth."

"No kidding."

"You'll be a perfect fit."

"Who's he?" Vince nodded to the driver.

"This is Esteban."

"Hola," Esteban winked lasciviously at Vince.

"Yeah," Vince responded.

"Esteban is my beauty consultant, he's gay."

"You don't look like you need a beauty consultant."

"What's your name?"

"Vince."

"What's your address?"

"It's too tricky to commit to memory."

"I'll write it," Astrid took a pad and pen from the glove compartment, "I'm ready."

"Forget it," Vince said.

"I usually get my way."

"Not this time."

"Here's my address and phone number," Astrid handed Vince a piece of paper, "I'm throwing a blow-out party next week, be in touch you won't regret it."

Vince put Astrid's address in his pocket, Esteban floored the accelerator and the convertible sped away.

"How many addresses do you have, Vince?" Clancy yelled.

Vince smiled and sat back at the Water Buffalo.

"The guy stands at the roadside and the babes pick him up," Clancy announced.

"Knock it off, Clancy."

Vince sensed a presence behind him and opened his eyes to a thin man in a three-piece black suit sweating profusely.

"I'm Bernie Benson," he extended his hand.

"Aren't you hot?"

"I'm from Maine we dress warm because it is cold up there."

"You're in Los Angeles it's over a hundred degrees," Vince said as the crew members looked on, mildly amused.

"For me this is cool," Bernie answered.

"You're nuts! Clancy get a cup of water for this maniac before he shrivels into a raisin."

"Coming up, Vince."

"Is your name, Vince?"

"Yeah, why?"

"I've been watching you here's my card."

"Is that right?"

"Where did you get that scar on your chest?"

"In the war who the hell are you?"

"I'm a talent scout for Worldwide Pictures you might be right for a part the studio is looking to fill."

"Yeah, sure, hey Clancy, I'm being discovered I'm going to Hollywood."

"Please take me with you, Vince, I'll carry your golf clubs," Clancy begged.

"Do you always shake like that?" Vince noted Bernie's pulsating body.

"I'm nervous all the time, maybe I should get another job."

"I have to get back to work," Vince started walking away when Bernie shouted after him.

"How does three hundred dollars for three minutes sound?"

"Are you kidding?"

"See Sheila Stone, her address is on my card, preferably, today, she respects my judgment in these matters."

"Are you putting me on?"

"You're a natural for the part," Bernie said, swigging the cup of water handed him by Clancy.

"Bull! I need to take off," Vince shouted.

"Make up the time on the graveyard shift."

"You're a prince."

"Beat it, Vince," Bull growled.

# 80

After showering Vince went to the address Bernie Benson gave him a Civil War-era building. He climbed its groaning steps to the second floor. Following instructions on the milk-white pane of the talent agency door, he knocked before entering where a dour woman who Vince thought must have come with the building greeted him. She asked his name and requested his portfolio, making no eye contact. Vince gave his name, handed her Bernie's card and said he had no portfolio. The woman swept her arm to worn leather chairs beneath two open windows and said Miss Stone will see you when she was ready.

Sheila Stone, an attractive middle-aged woman dressed stylishly in a lemon-colored blouse and rust-colored slacks motioned Vince into her office adorned on its walls with autographed pictures of Hollywood celebrities.

"Bernie said you are perfect for the part of *Mitch* in the World War II film being shot; he is usually right in casting matters. Do you have any acting experience, Mr. Farro?"

"None," Vince answered.

"Take off your shirt."

"What for?"

"The part involves a shirtless Marine on a Pacific island reviewing a map with senior officers," Sheila explained, "Remove your shirt if you want this part."

Vince took off his shirt, feeling he was in a meat market his life near to rock bottom as Sheila appraised him as if he were a laboratory specimen. She touched the scar on his chest and asked how he got it.

"In the war," Vince removed her hand.

"During the scene the camera is on you, head-to-torso for twenty seconds, then it ends and the film wraps."

"Sounds easy enough," Vince replied, putting on his shirt.

The Burning Hours        Page 265

"Leave it off," Sheila ordered, "How tall are you?"

"Six-two."

Sheila gestured Vince to a burgundy colored couch and sat next to him and placed the palm of her hand on his chest, "How much do you want this part?" Vince took Sheila's hand from his chest, put on his shirt, and said he should go.

"The young man outside would kill to get this part," Sheila's her eyes burned into Vince, "and the benefits that go with it," she waited for Vince's response.

"I'd better go," Vince stood up to leave.

"Go for a walk," Sheila advised, "think it over, if you're back in ten minutes the part is yours."

Vince nodded and left Sheila's office.

In the restroom, he looked into the mirror and saw a stranger reflected. He splashed water on his face. "Are you going to prostitute yourself, Farro?" he questioned, "You shouldn't have left me, Linda," Vince dried his face and went back into Sheila Stone's office.

"Well?" Sheila looked straight into Vince's eyes.

"Thanks for the opportunity, Miss Stone, as much as I want to, I can't accept your offer," Vince started to leave.

"Come back here, Farro! I'm not used to rejection. She must be a special woman, this girl of yours."

Vince didn't respond.

"You can't blame a girl for trying," Sheila dialed the phone and smiled at Vince.

"This is Sheila Stone tell Beau Blatz I cast the part of *Mitch*. His name is Nick Ferry. He'll be at the studio within an hour," she hung up the phone, jotted the studio address on her personal stationery and handed it to Vince.

"You are now Nick Ferry," Sheila said, "There will be other parts, now get out of my office before I change my mind."

The Burning Hours

# 81

In the days and nights since Tommy's homecoming Darling thought of Julia constantly. He sweltered in the rental car he drove to her house. Darling couldn't get Julia out of his mind, nor did he want to. He relished the small things she did for him: washing and ironing his shirts and making him breakfast, but the feel of her and the warmth of her mouth when they kissed ignited within him an unquenchable desire. In the short time Darling proposed marriage and Julia accepted.

Julia was on the porch looking fresh in her light summer dress her ruffled hair falling beneath her shoulders. Darling parked across the street, gazing long at Julia before turning off the ignition, getting out of the car and climbing the steps to the porch.

"You look lovely, Julia."

"Thank you, Carroll I looked forward to seeing you."

Darling kissed a receptive Julia.

"I expected you sooner."

"The traffic was heavy, sorry I'm late."

"Why aren't you in your uniform?"

Darling didn't respond.

"You retired from the army, didn't you?" Julia scolded.

"I received my discharge papers and pension documents last week."

"Did you," Julia spun around, opened the door and Darling followed her inside.

"Where did you get those clothes?"

"At a consignment shop."

"You do know nothing matches."

"They look all right."

"I give up," she shook her head, "Do you want something to drink?"

"Cold water is okay."

Julia poured a glass of water from a carafe in the refrigerator. She placed it in front of Darling her silence demonstrating her displeasure at not being included in his decision to leave the army.

"Thanks, it was getting hot in the car," Darling said, looking at Julia, who glared back at him, unresponsively.

"You're angry."

"Did I say I was angry?"

"You didn't have to I can tell."

"Why didn't you discuss your plan with me?"

"I should have, I apologize."

"Did you request being stationed at Fort Monmouth?"

"No, I didn't."

"Why not? We could have lived off-base if your request was approved."

"But, I'd still be in the army, orders change there was nothing to discuss."

"You're missing the point, Carroll I'm not opposed to your decision I just wanted to be included in it."

"You're right, Julia," Darling paused, "But, it was the best decision for us."

"I know," Julia relented, "In the future, please consider me in your plans."

"You have my word," then deflecting the subject, "Tommy asked me to be his best man."

"I know I was with him when he spoke to you."

"I'm honored even though Tommy would have preferred Vince."

"We'll go to Salvatore's Tailor Shop for a new suit you can't appear on the altar in those clothes."

"What's wrong with these clothes?"

"Everything, if you must know."

"Okay, when do we go to Salvatore's?"

"Next week the wedding date will be here before we know it."

"Are you still refitting your wedding dress for Rosemary?"

"I've finished Rosemary looks positively angelic in it."

"She's a pretty girl, Tommy's a lucky guy, has she selected her Maid-of-Honor?"

"Her Matron-of-Honor, that's me."

"What do you know? You and I will be standing for Tommy and Rosemary in church," Darling said, and then asked for another glass of water.

Julia went into the kitchen and soon returned, "Here," she placed a replenished glass of water on the table, sat down and folded her arms against her chest and lapsed into silence.

"You're still angry, aren't you?"

"I'm not angry, Carroll."

"You're not very happy, either."

"After everything we said to each other to not involve me in a decision that will affect our lives is hurtful."

"I don't know what it is with you Julia I can't do anything that pleases you. I'm sorry I hurt you I thought my leaving the army so we could be together without interruptions would have pleased you."

Julia cupped Darling's face in her hands and kissed him repeatedly, and softly said, "I'm sorry to be such a shrew, Carroll."

"That first day when we had breakfast, fireworks went off," Darling kissed Julia, his hand roaming to her behind, "Is it okay to proceed?" his eyes danced mischievously.

"On the condition you obey the traffic signs."

"What traffic signs?"

"The Stop, Detour and Speed Limit signs."

"What if I don't obey them?"

"I will issue you a ticket for speeding."

"What happens if I disregard the ticket?"

"I will suspend your license, subject to revoking your privileges."

"You are a tough woman," Darling patted Julia's behind.

"You haven't seen anything, yet," Julia slid her hands around Darling's neck and kissed his cheeks, repeatedly.

"We're no longer young, Julia" Darling said plaintively, "but I promise there will be good days, ahead for us."

"And some intoxicating moments," Julia quickly added.

"I guarantee it," Darling agreed.

"No more surprises, Carroll."

"There is something we need to discuss," Darling said, trepidation in his voice.

"Please Carroll I can't handle another surprise," Julia's voice was tinged with apprehension.

"Do you like plants and flowers?"

"Yes, I like plants and flowers, why do you ask?"

"I want to work with things that grow and give pleasure to people, Julia. Does that make sense to you?"

"Yes, it does."

"There's a small nursery in Long Branch for sale, and …"

"Don't tell me you bought it."

"Do you know where Long Branch is?"

"I know where Long Branch is Regina and I used to swim there when we were young."

"The owners are good people. I'd like to buy it, Julia, there's a comfortable house on the property that we can live in, a gift shop you can run while I take care of ordering flowers and plants, and working the tree farm."

"Is it what you want?"

"Yeah, it is what I want."

"It sounds wonderful, Carroll."

"You'll love this place."

"Can you afford it?"

"I have enough for the down payment, and the owners will agree to hold the mortgage."

"I can't wait to see it, I'll change."

"You look perfect as you are."

"What about the car when we get to Long Branch?"

"It's an overnight rental."

"Where will you stay when we get back?"

"I'll get a room for the night at the YMCA."

"Is the YMCA your first choice?"

"It's not my first choice."

"You really are impossible, Carroll, why didn't you ask if you could stay with me, Tommy and Rosemary for the night?"

"Well, can I?"

"Of course you can?"

"In your bedroom," Darling asked, hopefully.

"On the sofa," Julia dashed his dream.

"Is that a Detour Sign?"

"Yes, it is. Tommy and Rosemary are sleeping in separate rooms. I'm sleeping in my room, and you are sleeping on the sofa.

"The women in this house know how to drive men nuts."

"Rosemary wants to be in a State-of-Grace on her wedding day," Julia explained, "so she decided to avoid temptation and sleep in separate rooms."

"What's the State-of-Grace?"

"It's when sins are confessed and forgiven."

"I remember the chaplains in France and Belgium giving blanket absolution before battles."

"Tommy talked with the parish priest and got you a Dispensation to be his Best Man."

"What's a Dispensation?"

"It's a special permission granted to a non-Catholic to participate in a Catholic ceremony.

"Will you be in the State-of-Grace when we get married?" Darling looked squarely at Julia, mischievously.

"I don't know what do you think?"

The Burning Hours        Page 271

"I hope not," Darling answered.
"We could get married at City Hall."
"Do they care about the State-of-Grace at City Hall?"
"I don't think so."
"Let's get married at City Hall," Darling said
"Okay," Julia smiled.

# 82

The Wedding Mass was joyous and emotional. Dressed in Julia's refitted Gatsby-style ivory floor-length gown, a silk Cloche net veil that flowed down her back Rosemary was the cynosure of all eyes. She carried a bouquet of chrysanthemums and roses arranged by Julia's and Darling's flower shop in Long Branch.

Tommy was handsome in his army uniform and Julia, lovely in a cream-colored linen dress. Rosemary, on Darling's arm, smiled at guests straining for a view of her as she walked along the aisle to the altar.

At the altar Darling gave away Rosemary then assumed his role as Tommy's Best Man. Regina looked on happy for Tommy and Rosemary. She said a silent prayer for Vince and Linda. On leave from the WAC's the former Sister Maria Fidelis sang the *Ave Maria* before Tommy and Rosemary exchanged wedding vows uniting them in the state of marriage.

At the Mass's conclusion Tommy and Rosemary emerged from the church into the bright sunshine of a late September day. For their wedding gift Julia deeded them her house, and one month later she and Darling planned to marry and move to their home in Long Branch. When Tommy whispered to Rosemary that one day he would see pictures of his beautiful bride, Rosemary kissed him passionately to the cheers of the crowd outside the church.

The limousine carrying Tommy and Rosemary stopped in front of the Punch Bowl Hotel, a red brick, seven story building. The hotel's general manager escorted them into the Wedgewood Room where a gathering of family and friends greeted them. A buzz filled the room as Johnny Roma strode to the microphone.

"What's happening?" Tommy asked.

"Johnny Roma just came into the room," Rosemary answered, "he's motioning us to the dance floor."

"This is for you two kids," Johnny said before crooning *I Love You Truly*. Tommy and Rosemary clung to each other on the dance floor. Rosemary sobbed for her unknown mother and father, but with Tommy, she was reborn into a new life, with Rosemary's devotion Tommy overcame the fear of his disability.

When Johnny finished singing applause filled the room. He congratulated the newlyweds expressing pride in Tommy. He kissed Rosemary on both cheeks saying "You look gorgeous," then with a wave to the gathering he walked out of the Wedgewood Room.

Soon, the reception ended. Guests drifted away. Tommy and Rosemary left the Wedgewood Room for the seventh floor. They reminisced about the day they met Tommy running into traffic to meet the cute girl studying to be a nun.

"I reprimanded you for taking such a risk," Rosemary said.

"I'm glad you picked me instead of becoming a nun."

"I'm so happy," Rosemary threw her arms around Tommy.

In the bridal suite Tommy sat on the edge of a king-size bed. He poured two glasses of champagne, a gift from the hotel and waited for Rosemary to join him in a celebratory toast.

"What's taking you so long, Rosemary?"

"Getting out of a wedding gown is no easy matter, Tommy," Rosemary answered, adding, "take off your shoes and socks, I'll take care of the rest."

Tommy took a long draft of champagne, as he removed his shoes and socks, the bathroom door opened and Rosemary emerged.

"Hand me my glass, Tommy."

Rosemary lifted the glass to her lips, "Um, tastes good the bubbles tickle my nose," she laughed, "Now, let's get you out of your clothes," she slipped Tommy's tie from under his collar, unbuttoned his shirt and pushed it off his shoulders, "raise your arms, I'll take off your undershirt," Tommy felt his shirt sail over his head, "Sorry, honey, I messed your hair," she cooed and kissed his mouth. Then Rosemary felt Tommy's hands around her waist, sliding up her back.

"You're naked, Rosemary," Tommy said, his voice suffused with excited anticipation.

As Rosemary kissed him Tommy felt her naked breasts pressing against his chest. Then she unbuckled his belt, pulled it off and threw it on the floor.

"I have a surprise for you, tiger," she said seductively, "we'll do whatever we want to, and...," she stopped in mid-sentence.

"And what?" Tommy said, breathlessly.

"We won't have to go to confession," Rosemary whispered.

# 83

Vince followed Sheila Stone's directions to Worldwide Pictures. He arrived at the cavernous production studio where camera crews completed lighting testing ready to roll when given a green light. He stopped a harried man carrying a clipboard.

"Where can I find Beau Blatz?"

"Who are you?"

"I'm here for the *Mitch* part."

"Nick Ferry?" he confirmed after reviewing his clipboard notes.

"Yeah," Vince answered, "Who are you?"

"Production assistant, shooting is on hold pending your arrival."

"I didn't realize I was that important."

"You're not it's the final scene."

"I got here as fast as I could."

"Beau's the guy sitting in a cloud of smoke next to the dressing rooms."

"Okay, thanks."

"Good luck."

Beau Blatz tossed his consumed cigarette into an upright ashtray. He lit another inhaled and disgorged a plume of smoke out of his frayed lungs.

"I'm here for the *Mitch* part, Mr. Blatz," Vince handed Sheila Stone's card to Beau.

"What's the name Sheila pinned on you?"

"Nick Ferry."

"What's your real name?"

"Vincent Farro."

"Good name, but Sheila's got to exercise her power."

"Do you know your lines I want to wrap this film, understand?"

"Yeah, I understand."

"Smoke?" Beau extended a pack of cigarettes.

"No, thanks."

"It will steady your nerves."

"They were food in combat I don't touch them, now."

"A woman got you off them, right?"

"Right."

"I'm going through my fourth divorce. A woman got you off these things," Beau blew a stream of smoke into the air, "and women keep me on them, crazy world. Camille!" Beau hollered.

"When are you going to ditch that habit, Beau?"

"This is Nick Ferry," Beau disregarded Camille's jibe.

"Hello, Camille."

"Hello, Nick," Camille said in a slow southern drawl, "What are you doing, tonight?"

"Take an ice bath, Camille, get Vince costumed for the final scene."

"Come with me, Nick," Camille smiled.

"I want Nick back here in two minutes, Camille," Beau shouted.

"Okay, Beau," Camille answered, "he's been a real crab since his divorce proceedings."

Within a few minutes Vince, now Nick and Camille returned from costuming.

"You look good, kid," Beau appraised.

"Thanks, Camille."

"We'll do it again, Nick," Camille smiled.

"You will be standing next to Dick Flynt, who plays your commanding officer. The visual effects crew did a great job to make the scene appear to be filmed on Guadalcanal."

"It's a make-believe world in here," Vince observed.

"It's the art of escape, Nick do you know who Dick Flynt is?

"Sure he's a big Hollywood star."

"He's starring in this movie," then Beau whispered, "Flynt's a real Prima Donna, a celluloid war hero, in the scene he asks what you saw on patrol, and …"

"I'll point to the map and say, the guns are there," Vince interjected.

"Let's go!" Beau stuck another cigarette into his mouth, "Wish this divorce was done; I'm really stressed."

As Bernie Benson and Sheila Stone said the shot took three minutes. Before leaving the set Dick Flynt glanced at Vince, said nothing and walked away, followed by his entourage.

"What's with him?"

"He's scared of you," Beau said.

"You're crazy, he's a big star I'll be a faded memory, after today."

"In this business star power is everything you got it in spades, Nick and Flynt senses it."

"Thanks, Mr. Blatz, I appreciate it."

"Mr. Blatz is my old man," call me, Beau.

"Okay, Beau."

"Pick up your check in the accounting office."

# 84

Regina Farro sat in the quiet of her living room knitting a pair of wool gloves on a brisk, autumn day. She awaited Vince's call wondering the reason for changing his telephone routine. At 2:00 o'clock the phone rang, Regina put down her knitting and picked up the receiver.

"Hello, Vince you are right on time."

"How are you, Mom?"

"I'm fine."

"How is the weather in Jersey?"

"It's lovely I visited your father, and now I am knitting gloves for the Guild's charity."

"Did Tommy and Rosemary get my telegram?"

"The hotel manager read it at their reception. Everyone asked for you. The Wedding Mass was splendid. Rosemary was lovely in Julia's wedding dress. Johnny Roma surprised everyone when he dedicated a song to Tommy and Rosemary," Regina paused, "I wish you were here, Vince. I wish it could have been the same for you and Linda."

"It wasn't meant to be, Mom, I'm adjusting to that reality."

"I'm sorry, Vince, I know how much Linda means to you."

"Did you get the money I wired?"

"It's a lot of money, how did you get it? You did nothing illegal."

"No, Mom I earned it," Vince laughed, "I changed jobs."

"You're not working for the water company?"

"I got a job in a film I'm in the last scene standing next to Dick Flynt. In the credits I'm listed as Nick Ferry, that's me, Mom, I'm Nick Ferry."

"You'll always be Vincent Farro, my son," Regina scolded.

"I know, Mom," Vince laughed.

"It's good to hear you laugh, Vince, I'll go to the Stanley Theater when it opens and at long last I will see my son."

"That's good, Mom, it has been a while."

"Are you coming home, Vince? I miss you, everyone misses you."

"Not right away, Mom."

"I bumped into Mr. Birkman at the market, he asked for you. He remembered your plan to study to become an English teacher."

"That's a lifetime ago, tell Mr. Birkman I said hello."

"You haven't given me an answer, Vince."

"I won't be returning to New Jersey, Mom I'm staying in California."

"Oh," Regina said, sadly, "When will I see you? You were gone during the war, and now you're far away, again."

"After the movie's release women called the studio asking who played *Mitch*, it resulted in a successful on-camera speaking audition."

"That's wonderful I'm not surprised women want to know about my handsome son."

"Mom," Vince hesitated, "move to Los Angeles."

"No, Vince I couldn't leave papa."

"I bought a house in a quiet neighborhood. It has a back yard and a garden it's in walking distance of a Catholic chapel. As soon we settle in we'll bring Pop here and you'll be able to visit him whenever you want to."

"I don't want to burden you?"

"Mom, I signed a three-movie contract there's enough money to cover expenses."

"To move at my age, I'm not sure, Vince."

"You're still a young woman, if you say yes, then you, Pop and I will be together, again."

"Are you sure, Vince?"

"Yes, Mom I'm sure."

"Then tomorrow I will go to the cemetery and tell papa our plan, but I feel he knows."

# 85

"Mr. Conover, your father is on your private line, it's an emergency," Clara Jenkins's voice crackled through the intercom.

"What's wrong, Dad?"

"Linda was rushed to the hospital this morning."

"What happened?"

"She suffered a weak spell and fainted. Adalina is with her at the hospital. Mother and I are going, now."

"I'm leaving, now, Dad," Charles hung up the phone.

"Mrs. Jenkins please call the garage and have my car ready, call Trumbull Airport and book a flight plan to Napa County Airport, contact Paolo Bellini and ask him to meet me at the airport, call Dr. Kipp and ask him to call Dr. Mancini at the Valley Clinic, and ask Mr. Oldfield to manage affairs until I return."

"Yes, Mr. Conover, right away I hope all is well."

"Thank you, Mrs. Jenkins," Charles released the intercom button his heart pounding.

Suddenly the demands of his corporation miniaturized in importance; now Linda, her baby and Adalina were all that mattered. He dashed out of his office, took the executive elevator to the garage where his chauffeur waited. He jumped into the idling vehicle, and it sped off to the airport where he would meet Paolo.

Charles and Paolo were in a fog of physical and emotional exhaustion on the plane to the Napa County Airport. Each had spent the flight in preoccupied silence, occasionally assuring each other that Linda and her baby would be all right and hoping their speculations were correct. Arriving at the airport Charles rushed to the nearest public telephone and called the hospital. He spoke with Adalina who was distraught that Linda's weak spell had not satisfactorily resolved. She did not tell him that Linda had been scheduled for an emergency Cesarean section.

"Valley Clinic, and step on it," Paolo demanded.

Charles and Paolo stared straight ahead, oblivious to the autumn colors that lit up the valley as the taxi sped ahead. The fifteen minute ride to the hospital seemed an eternity. When the taxi screeched to a stop in front of the hospital Paolo handed the driver a fifty dollar bill, told him to keep the change, and he and Charles walked briskly into the hospital.

Charles Sr. and Laura Conover waited in the middle of the lobby, Charles stoically, his arm around Laura's shoulders who had succumbed to tears. Laura broke away from Charles Sr. and ran crying into Charles's arms.

"Linda was enjoying her wait time," she spoke somberly, "talking to her baby, the changing colors in the valley, preparing the nursery, always smiling, and then ...," Laura paused to compose herself, "then she couldn't get out of bed, she's terribly sick, Charles."

Charles pressed Laura against him, "Don't worry, Mother, Linda and her baby will be fine."

"Linda is prepared for surgery, Charles, she waited to see you," Charles, Sr. said.

"Surgery," Charles uttered in disbelief.

"Her labor slowed, and then it stopped completely, Dr. Mancini suspects internal bleeding. Adalina is with Linda, she donated a unit of blood."

"As soon as I visit Linda I'll go to the blood bank."

"I'll go with you, CC," Paolo said.

The Maternity Ward was as bright as the milk white uniforms of the nurses charting patient records and carrying out doctors' orders. When the elevator door opened Charles rushed to Linda's room.

A charge nurse and a patient transporter waited impatiently to take Linda to the operating room where Dr.

The Burning Hours

Mancini, the nurses and technicians were ready to go ahead with the Cesarean section.

"Try to relax, honey, daddy will be here any minute."

"What's happened to me, Mother?"

"Bellini women have difficult pregnancies, honey, but we deliver beautiful babies, and you will have a beautiful baby, I love you with all my heart," Adalina consoled.

"I'm scared I try not to be, but I am."

"It's natural to be scared, honey."

"I want Vincent's name on the Birth Certificate."

"Of course, now try to be calm."

"If my baby is a boy, name him Vincent, and if a girl, Regina for Vincent's mother. Is it alright that she be named Regina?"

"Yes, honey it is alright."

"Mother if I don't wake up find Vincent and tell him I tried hard to have his baby."

"Don't think that way, Linda," Adalina rested her face against Linda's, "You will be fine, your baby will be fine, and you will be the most wonderful mother in the world."

Then Adalina felt Charles's hand on her shoulder.

"Daddy's here, honey," Adalina got up, her face wet with tears.

Charles took Linda's raised hand, "How's my girl?" he sat on the edge of her bed and kissed her forehead.

"A little groggy."

"It's the medication, Linda."

"Daddy, I asked Mother if it doesn't go well ..."

"Honey," Adalina interjected, "You will be fine, and your baby will be fine, Charles, please tell our daughter all will work out well."

"Listen to your mother, Linda, believe me, you and your baby will come through with flying colors."

"If you say so, Daddy."

"Uncle Paolo is here," Charles whispered.

"You and your baby will be okay, you trust Uncle Paolo, don't you, honey?"

"Yes, Uncle Paolo, I trust you," Linda said, lapsing in and out of consciousness.

"It's time, let's go!" the charge nurse commanded. The patient transporter snapped the bed rails in place and pushed the bed into the hallway. Coming out of her stupor Linda said she wished Vincent was with her.

"Vincent is with you, honey."

Linda lost consciousness as the patient transporter pushed into the operating suite the swinging doors closing behind him.

Adalina stared at the closed doors of the operating suite. She felt trapped in a vacuum where only fear existed. She experienced an overpowering sense of impotence. She wanted to lash out at a God that caused her daughter and her yet to be born baby such suffering. Adalina fit herself into Charles's embrace and for a while remained consoled in his arms. And then without warning she pounded Charles's chest with her clenched fists, and in a flood of anguished tears, she cried out, "My daughter and our grandchild must not die, Charles! They must not die!"

# 86

Regina relaxed in the garden of her new Los Angeles home. She closed her eyes, realizing a life-changing event had occurred. The warm sun on her skin felt revitalizing as did the gentle breezes softly through her hair. The sea of sealed boxes awaiting her attention intruded on her respite. Reluctantly, Regina got up and went into the house.

Inside Vince checked his watch. There was time for a nap before meeting with Beau Blatz and Ivy Townsend. When Regina came in her face was pink from the California sun.

"Do you like it, here, Mom?

"I love it, Vince; I couldn't have picked a more comfortable house."

"That's good, Mom I'm glad. Since pop died, I dreamed of doing something special for you, and maybe this house and bringing you to California, fulfills that wish."

"You're a good son, Vincent Farro," Regina mussed Vince's hair.

"Come on, Mom, I have an appointment at the studio," he protested with a smile.

"You are aware combs and brushes were invented to keep hair in check."

"Okay, Mom, you win."

"I went to early Mass, today the chapel is lovely. I filed an application for a cemetery plot for papa and me."

"When you're settled, we'll go to New Jersey and bring Pop back with us."

Regina nodded, nostalgically, "I miss Vincenzo.

"Do you pray for me, Mom, when you go to Mass?'

"I say prayers and light candles for Papa, for you," Regina paused, "and for Linda."

"Linda will always be a part of me."

"I know," Regina touched Vince's face, "When will you go to Mass, Vince?"

"Soon, I guess."

"Well, I hope so Mister."

"I talked to Tommy, Rosemary is doing well."

"Rosemary is in full bloom, she and Julia helped me pack."

"How is Mrs. Darling?"

"Julia loves her gift shop, she arranged a delightful flower piece as a going away gift," and after a momentary silence, "Everything changes, Vince, nothing ever stays the same."

"Yeah, I know, I'm going to take a nap, don't let me sleep more than thirty minutes."

"I'll set my alarm."

"Okay."

"Why are you meeting Ivy Townsend?"

"I don't know."

"Does the star usually meet with supporting players?"

"I don't think so but the studio told me to report to the meeting."

"Get some sleep I'll wake you in time for your meeting."

Vince stretched out on his bed and drifted into a deep sleep. Regina started to unpack taking from cartons objects that evoked memories of years gone by. When her alarm clock rang Regina went to wake Vince and found him sitting on the edge of his bed breathing unevenly.

"It's Linda, Mom; she's been in an accident. It wasn't a dream. There's blood everywhere. I held her hand, I told her to fight. And then her hand slipped away. It wasn't a dream. I saw her. I have to know she's safe."

Vince fumbled for his address book in his bed stand. As he withdrew it Linda's book of poems fell to the floor. He dialed her room in Connecticut; a stranger answered, and said he had a wrong number. No one answered Adalina's phone. He phoned Charles Conover's number, and a receptionist at his corporate office answered.

"May I speak with Mr. Conover," Vince asked in an excited voice.

"May I have your name, please?" the receptionist answered.

"Vincent Farro, put me through, it's important."

"What is your business with Mr. Conover?"

"It's a personal matter."

"I will take your information and give it to Mr. Conover's executive secretary."

"It's important Mr. Conover call me," Vince said before hanging up and preparing for his meeting with Ivy Townsend and Beau Blatz.

"Mrs. Jenkins, I just had a caller asking to speak with Mr. Conover."

"What is the caller's name?"

"He said, Mr. Farrell."

"Did he give a first name?"

"I believe his first name is Victor."

"Are you sure?" Mrs. Jenkins asked, skeptically.

"Yes, I believe he said Victor.

"Did you get his phone number?"

"I asked him," the receptionist dissembled.

"Well did he or did he not give you his phone number?"

"Yes, he did."

"What is it?"

"I answered another call and forgot to record it."

"How long have you worked here?"

"This is my first day I'm a temporary replacement."

"In the future record all incoming calls first that is the main focus of your responsibility," Mrs. Jenkins admonished thumbing through her records, "I see a Fenlon, a Farro, and a Frost on Mr. Conover's *Telephone Put-Through List*, but there is no Farrell listed."

# 87

Vince's hand trembled as he shaved. He covered a razor nick on his throat with a piece of toilet tissue to staunch the bleeding. Then he showered, dressed and prepared to leave for the studio.

"Remember, Vince, it was a dream," Regina advised.

"Yeah," Vince said, "call me if Mr. Conover returns my phone call."

"I will, you look very handsome, Miss Townsend will go to pieces when she sees you."

Vince kissed Regina, "You know how to lift my spirits, Mom."

The drive to the studios of Worldwide Pictures brought Vince a modicum of distraction. Perhaps it was a dream born in his desire to be with Linda, as they were in Hoboken. Before the war, at Regina's insistence Vince attended Mass regularly, but his experiences in Europe and his loss of Linda created doubts that he couldn't reconcile. As he drove along palm tree-lined roads to his meeting he found himself bargaining with God to assure Linda's safety.

Vince pulled into the studio's overflowing parking lot. He got out of the car and entered the imposing administrative building. He asked a receptionist if his mother had called. She nodded negatively, smiled at Vince and escorted him into a conference room where Beau was waiting blowing smoke rings from a large cigar.

"What's going on, Beau? I got a call from upstairs. Will Mr. Big be here?"

"Are you kidding?" Beau exhaled a thick cloud of smoke.

"You gave up cigarettes for cigars?"

"This Cuban," he looked at his cigar, adoringly, "this baby represents a double celebration; my divorce has finalized, and I will be directing Ivy's new film."

The Burning Hours                    Page 289

"That's great, Beau, congratulations."

"Yeah, Nicky, I need the cash," Beau fanned pictures of his former wives on the table simulating a Las Vegas dealer, and said, "These four dollies bankrupted me, Nicky."

"You're a marrying guy," Vince laughed.

"I'm in love with being in love."

"What am I doing here, Beau, meeting with Ivy Townsend?"

"You mean British Royalty via a Pennsylvania coal town."

"What are you talking about?"

"Come on, Nicky, you're in Hollywood, Ivy Townsend was born Ivana Tornowski, she invented herself and her British accent. She's smart and positively ruthless, she gets whatever she wants, and ...," Beau paused, and whispered, "the word around town, Nicky, is she wants you. The entire male population in Hollywood wants to bed her, and she wants you. I don't know whether to envy or feel sorry for you."

"You're nuts, Beau?"

"When you did the screen test you didn't know you were auditioning for the role of Ivy's love interest in her film, *Yesteryear*. It was part of the studio's Star Search for Ivy's film. She asked specifically for you, she selected you for the part."

"Dick Flynt has the part."

"Flynt doesn't have the part," Beau waved a file before Vince, "this is your new contract, read it, sign it, and deliver it upstairs to Mr. Big's office, maybe he'll deign to say hello."

"What new contract?"

"After this meeting, Flynt will be on an epic rampage," Beau observed the conference room door opening, "She's here, get up, Nicky, and remember what I said."

Fashionably late for her meeting Ivy Townsend made a memorable entrance. Tall and slender with platinum blond hair, large blue eyes, and a wide seductive mouth, she was more striking in person than her appearances on the silver screen. She exuded sensuality and the power that goes with celebrity. Attired in a burgundy-colored dress Ivy wore white gloves, a glittering diamond necklace and a pair of matching earrings. She dazzled in a Hollywood firmament of bright stars; everything about her, the way she walked, the challenge in her gaze and her precise British accent were intimidating reminders of the power she wielded in selecting scripts and her co-stars.

"As usual love, you look marvelous," Beau lightly kissed her cheeks.

"You reek of cigars, Beau. Get rid of it the smoke is getting into my hair and my clothes," Ivy demanded fixing her gaze on Vince, now Nick Ferry.

"This is Nick Ferry," Beau introduced.

"I know," Ivy peeled off her glove and to Beau's utter surprise, knowing her penchant to avoid skin contact she held her naked hand out to Nick.

"Pleasure meeting you, Miss Townsend," Nick shook and held Ivy's hand, transfixed by the stunning woman standing before him, before releasing it.

"Shall we begin?"

Beau pulled out the chair at the head of the table.

In a fluid motion Ivy slid into it and motioned Nick next to her.

"Have you read the script, Nicky?"

"I read most of it."

"Then you know the story centers on lovers in Victorian England.

"I'm aware of that, Miss Townsend."

Ivy patted the top of Nick's hand, "Call me, Ivy, Nicky," and turning to Beau whose eyes widened in amazement at Ivy's affectionate interplay with Nick, she said, "Cast introductions tonight at my place, Beau, rehearsals at the studio for the rest of the month, and then we depart for location filming in London, is that okay with you, Nicky?"

"Sure, Miss Townsend, whatever you say."

"Ivy, Nicky, my name is Ivy."

"Beau has the details," Ivy rose to her full height, smoothed her dress and shook Nick's hand, "See you tonight, Nicky, don't be late," Beau rushed to the door, and with a look over her shoulder at Nick, she left the conference room with a flourish.

"That's one for the books," Beau shook his head.

"What do you mean?"

"She's aloof with her male co-stars as a warning not to upstage her."

"I thought she was pleasant."

"You have a lot to learn, Nicky. I never saw her act toward a co-star the way she did with you. Be careful, Ivy's a Queen Bee, she stings.

# 88

A fog of uncertainty filled the waiting room at the end of the hallway opposite the surgical suite. Emotionally spent, Adalina rested her head against Charles his pained face showed his concern for Linda and her baby. Charles Sr. stared at his clasped hands in his lap as Laura dabbed her eyes with her handkerchief. Paolo paced the hallway trying to dispel his worry for his adored niece.

Charles's hallmarks of power and control abandoned him; Linda was in the hands of Dr. Enrico Mancini, Ethan Kipp's medical school classmate. Gripped with gnawing fear, Charles prayed to a universal power to protect his daughter and her baby.

Then a shrill voice from the hospital public address system declared an emergency in the maternity ward. In the hallway doctors, nurses and medical technicians dashed to the surgical suite.

"What's happened, Charles?" Adalina asked frantically.

Laura felt her heart leap into her throat.

"Stay with Adalina, Paolo."

Charles ran into the hallway past the nurses' station and at that moment a softer voice on the public address system canceled the emergency. He knew a cancellation could mean the patient expired. He rushed to the surgical suite. When its swinging doors opened Dr. Mancini emerged. Charles's thoughts ricocheted between images of Linda as a happy young girl to the woman fighting for her, and her baby's life. He would gladly trade his vast empire for the safe return of his daughter and her baby.

"How is my daughter?" Charles felt his heart throb and his pulse pound.

"Linda is in intensive care," Dr. Mancini answered.

"And her baby?"

"He's is in the Neonatal Intensive Care Unit."

"A boy," Charles managed a slight smile.

"Yes, a boy."

"Will they be all right?"

"Let's go to the waiting room, and we'll all talk."

# 89

"Where the hell are you?" Beau yelled into his phone, "Ivy's asking every five minutes."

"I'm waiting for an important call," Vince responded.

"What's more important than announcing Ivy Townsend's new discovery and co-star?"

"Yeah, okay, Beau, I'll leave now," Vince hung up his phone.

"Mom, if Mr. Conover calls, call me," Vince wrote Ivy's phone number on a pad in the kitchen."

"Vince, honey, listen to me; I know Linda will always be first in your heart, but you can't undo what is done."

"I know, Mom, but ..."

"When Linda called me and we talked, it was if I had the daughter I always wanted. She is a sweet girl I believe she would want you to go ahead with your life."

"All this good fortune and she's not here to share it with me."

"I know how you feel, but time passes and before you know it it's gone, unrecoverable. You have an exciting life ahead of you, Vince, thanks to Miss Townsend. She could have selected anyone to co-star with her, but she picked you. Life turns in cycles, honey you must go where your life's currents take you."

"I wish I had your faith, Mom," Vince kissed Regina and left.

At Ivy's mansion Vince drove its long driveway and parked in an available space behind an imposing Italian porcelain-clad 15-bedroom mansion, which on the Boulevard of Stars is known as Ivy Tower. The balmy night brought Ivy's guests outside where they talked, laughed and milled around a kidney-shaped swimming pool from which piped music played and multicolored lights danced on its blue water.

The Burning Hours

"It's about time," Beau grabbed Vince's arm.

"Where's Ivy?" Vince asked, looking around the sprawling patio.

"She's circulating, I'll run interference for you, I don't know what the hell you were thinking, Nicky, the biggest moment in your life and you show up late."

"I'll explain to her."

"Here she comes," Beau announced, "I've seen her eviscerate people for far less than your stunt, Nicky, be contrite and apologize profusely."

"It wasn't a stunt, Beau; it's a serious personal matter."

"Okay, Nicky, sorry."

Dressed in an orange blouse and white slacks, delicately holding a glass of bubbling pink champagne, Ivy deftly navigated the crowd to Vince.

"So, the prodigal has returned," Ivy said, icily, while Beau looked heaven-ward, thinking, "Here it comes."

"Sorry I'm late, Ivy, it was a ...," Vince began apologizing.

Ivy held up her hand, her ice blue eyes held Vince's, "No apology needed," she said, and then she turned to Beau, who shifted, nervously.

"What's the shooting schedule, Beau?"

"Next week, script reading, and then we leave for London three weeks later, shoot the Victorian scenes, approximately three months, return to New York, three months of shooting before wrapping up to meet Oscar's deadline."

"Can you handle that, Nicky, and be on time?" Ivy said, coolly.

"Sure, I'll be ready, and I'll be on-time."

"After I announce Nick as winner of Star Search, and my co-star, present the film's shooting schedule Beau."

Ivy turned to Nick her face illuminated in a sparkling smile, "It's all good, Nicky, let's meet your public and those annoying entertainment reporters, how does that sound?" she squeezed his arm.

"Couldn't be better," Nick returned Ivy's smile. Beau rolled his eyes bewildered by Ivy's out of character display of affection.

"Ladies and gentlemen, before I ask Beau to present *Yesteryear's* shooting schedule," Ivy said, "Let's toast the winner of Star Search, and my romantic co-star, Nick Ferry."

Following Ivy's announcement cheers filled the night, guests gathered around Vince, now publicly anointed Nick Ferry, men slapped his back and women threw themselves at him.

"Where's the kiss to seal the deal, Ivy?" someone in the crowd yelled.

"Kiss me, Nicky," Ivy whispered and Nick responded with a passionate kiss, as flashbulbs popped and cheers rose into the balmy evening.

"Umm, Nicky," Ivy wiped lipstick off Nick's mouth, "Again, for luck."

"True to our kickoff custom," Ivy paused, "Throw Beau into the pool."

Within minutes, a cigar clenched in his mouth, Beau sailed through the air into the blue water of Ivy's swimming pool to the raucous delight of the crowd, and particularly to Ivy and Nick who looked on enjoying the moment.

# 90

Known to his professional colleagues and friends as "The Renaissance Man," Dr. Enrico Mancini, now in his mid-fifties, winner of an Olympic Gold Medal in fencing, composer of original operatic arias, and valedictorian of his medical school class and inventor state-of-the-art surgical instruments strode with Charles into the waiting room.

Dr. Mancini asked everyone to sit around a circular table in the middle of the waiting room. Without hesitation, Adalina wanted to know the condition of Linda and her baby.

"Linda and her baby had a difficult time," Dr. Mancini began, "the baby was in a transverse position, and both mother and the baby were in distress. What should have been a relatively uncomplicated Cesarean procedure turned into an emergency.

"Are they all right?" Adalina interrupted.

"Linda is in intensive care. She experienced heavy blood loss during surgery and is now undergoing transfusions. I had to perform a hysterectomy to remove any risk to Linda and her baby."

"My God, she's only 26 years old," Adalina cried out.

"I'm sorry, Mrs. Conover it was unavoidable."

"Did the emergency code have anything to do with my daughter?" Charles inquired.

"It did, Mr. Conover. Something unexplainable happened. On her own Linda came back, her blood pressure and cardiovascular rhythm returned, enabling us to remove the baby and stabilize Linda," Dr. Mancini shook his head, "There are things that medical science can't explain, perhaps a force beyond us or somebody brought your daughter back."

Laura Conover began weeping. She pictured Linda as a little girl playing among the grape arbors in sunlit days she refused to accept the image of her lying in an intensive care unit scarred and unconscious, tubes sticking out of her body.

Adalina went to Laura and hugged her, both crying.

"Shall I order you a sedative, Mrs. Conover?" Dr. Mancini asked.

Laura shook her head no and dabbed her eyes with her handkerchief.

"What is Linda's outlook?"

"Right now she is critical, Mr. Conover. When the transfusions are complete her strength should return and her prognosis will hopefully change in a positive direction. Linda will have a rough road ahead, her life will change, she will need a great deal of support," Dr. Mancini paused, "Can you contact the baby's father? He will be a great help."

"I have Vincent's mother's phone number in New Jersey," Adalina fumbled in her pocketbook and took Linda's address book from it, "I'll phone her."

"I'll call," Paolo said, "you stay here, Adalina."

Adalina handed Paolo Linda's address book.

"Her name is Regina Farro, Paolo."

"How is Linda's baby, Dr. Mancini?" Charles questioned.

"It is beneficial for baby and mother to bond after delivery. Hopefully that will be soon."

Adalina buried her head in her hands and rocked back and forth. She refused Dr. Mancini's offer of a sedative. Realizing the emotional toll on Charles Sr. and Laura, Charles recommended they go home. Reluctantly they agreed. Paolo returned to the waiting room he nodded negatively; Regina's phone number was reassigned and her house was sold, no forwarding phone number or address was left.

"Linda and her baby will be fine," Charles embraced Adalina.

"I asked the charge nurse to have a bed brought to Linda's room."

"Yes, thank you, Dr. Mancini, I want to be with Linda when she wakes."

"I'll look in on her and the baby, later tonight."

"She named her baby, Vincent, for his father," Charles said.

Dr. Mancini acknowledged with a nod.

"Thank you, Dr. Mancini, Ethan Kipp holds you in highest esteem."

"I will update, Ethan, try not to worry."

"Dr. Mancini Linda suffered an emotional shock early in her pregnancy could that have contributed to the problems she and her baby are experiencing?"

"Whatever occurred probably didn't help."

# 91

Street lamps cast an orange glow on the dark boulevard outside the hospital. Linda was in a twilight state when she arrived back to her room. Except for illumination from a small light above her bed and a lamp in the corner, the room was bathed in a subdued quiet light.

"Mother," Linda moaned.

"You're going to be well," Adalina said, "Isn't that right, Charles?"

Charles kissed Linda's forehead and brushed his hand on her face, "Try to sleep, honey, Mother and I are staying with you."

"My baby, Mother, where is my baby?"

"You have a son, honey, he's resting."

"A boy," Linda managed a smile, "A boy," she repeated, drifted away, and then returned to consciousness, "Where is Vincent? Is he outside?"

"You were dreaming, honey, try to rest," Adalina said.

"It wasn't a dream, Vincent was with me, he was in the operating room, I saw him, and he held my hand, he kept telling me to fight."

And then, with a small sigh Linda fell asleep. She lay still breathing evenly as Charles whispered encouragement. Adalina slumped into a chair at Linda's bedside, her eyes glued to the bandages and intravenous needle inserted into her arm.

She went to Charles and slid her arms around his shoulders and rested there.

"She's so sick, Charles, our lovely daughter, so bruised."

"I know, honey," Charles held Adalina, and then walked her to the bed arranged by Dr. Mancini, "You're worn out you need to sleep. I'll wake you when Dr. Mancini arrives."

Overwhelmed by physical and emotional exhaustion Adalina slipped into a restless sleep. Charles sat at Linda's bedside, his hand on hers watching his daughter battle to recover while imagining his infant grandson lying in an incubator fighting for his life.

Charles floated in and out of sleep; each time he woke he touched Linda's arm. He thought of the valley and imagined Linda's life there with Vincent and her baby. In the dim light of her hospital room, as beeping machines and the chatter of nurses punctuated the night, Charles experienced a mixture of fear for his daughter and grandson and a boiling revulsion for Derek Reed.

"Charles, is Linda all right?" Adalina's eyes fluttered open.

"Yes, she is resting comfortably," Adalina didn't answer and went back to sleep.

With the approach of midnight the clicking sound of the wall clock seemed to thunder in Charles's head. He went to the doorway and looked to the surgical suite hoping to see Dr. Mancini. He reclined in a chair at Linda's bedside and closed his eyes for what seemed a few minutes, and then he felt a hand on his shoulder.

"Mr. Conover," the voice was subdued.

"Dr. Mancini," Charles sprung awake, "What time is it?"

"It's 1:00 am."

"I was out longer than I thought."

"Have the nurses looked in on Linda?"

"Yes, I'll wake my wife; she'll want to see you."

Dr. Mancini reviewed the nurses' notes and took Linda's vital signs."

"How is she?"

"As well as can be expected, Mrs. Conover."

"Have you looked in on the baby?"

"He's comfortable, Mrs. Conover ..." at the sound of baby Linda stirred and then drifted away.

The Burning Hours

Dr. Mancini motioned Charles and Adalina away from Linda's bed.

"The baby is in the Neo-Natal Intensive Care Unit; he is weak and refuses to take formula; his status is critical."

"Are you saying …," Charles started asking.

"The baby's prognosis is uncertain, without nourishment he will weaken; we're doing everything possible to avert that possibility."

"My God, Charles, she can't lose her baby."

"She won't lose her baby," Charles promised, "Linda won't lose her baby, Adalina," he repeated, emphatically. Now, only the well-being of his daughter and grandson mattered, and yet Charles couldn't dismiss his loathing for Derek Reed.

# 92

Armed with two garment bags and a tote containing toiletries Paolo Bellini arrived at the hospital in the early morning. He set them on the spare bed arranged by Dr. Mancini and went to Charles, at Linda's bedside, holding her hand, stroking her face.

"Your mother packed a change of clothes, for you and Adalina."

"How are they?"

"They're still upset my staying the night provided them some comfort."

"Thanks, Paolo."

"How is Linda?"

"Dr. Mancini believes she rallied during the night."

"That's a relief. How's the baby?"

Charles shook his head, "He's getting weaker, Adalina is with him, now."

"What does Dr. Mancini say?"

"Vincent refuses formula, without nourishment he'll continue to decline. Linda is his best chance, but she's too weak."

"I'll go to Adalina."

"Mr. Conover, there is a call for you."

"Thank you, nurse. Paolo, wait."

Charles was at the Nurses Station for several minutes. In his absence, Paolo went to Linda and held her hand. He watched Charles, hunched over talking quietly, and then he hung up the phone, and walked back into Linda's room.

"Is everything all right?"

"That was Mrs. Jenkins," Charles said, a quizzical expression on his face.

"What's wrong?"

"Yesterday, a call came in that Mrs. Jenkins found odd."

The Burning Hours                    Page 304

"What do you mean?"

"A temporary receptionist in the front office took the call, but she didn't put it through to Mrs. Jenkins. After hanging up, she called Mrs. Jenkins and reported a Victor Farrell wanted to speak to me."

"Do you know a Victor Farrell?"

"No," Charles shook his head.

"Do you think the caller was Vincent?"

"She didn't write down his contact information she assured Mrs. Jenkins the caller's name was Victor Farrell."

"Freddie Oldfield called the chalet last night."

"What did he say, Paolo?"

"Derek Reed is back scratching for more money."

Charles shook his head in disbelief.

"All that matters is Linda and her baby. Reed caused this, Paolo. Had it not been for him Linda and Vincent would be married and the birth of her baby might not have been so risky," Charles paused; he went to Linda and softly kissed her face. Returning to Paolo, Charles said, "My daughter doesn't know how rough the road ahead will be for her."

"What do you want to do, CC?"

"I want Reed to disappear, Paolo."

"You're sure."

"You and Freddie were right, yes, I'm sure."

"I'll take care of it," Paolo squeezed Charles's shoulder and as he did Linda stirred.

"Mother."

Charles rushed to her bedside.

Paolo dashed into the hallway and returned with a nurse.

"Mother is with Vincent, honey."

Linda pushed herself up her pain elicited a stream of tears.

"I want to see Vincent, he needs me I know he needs me."

"You should rest, Miss Conover," the nurse advised, "You've had a difficult time and need to regain your strength."

"I want to see my baby," Linda disregarded the nurse's advice."

"Please, Miss Conover it's not advisable, your condition …"

"My daughter is going to her baby, nurse," Charles's voice rang with authority.

"We should check with the doctor, first, Mr. Conover."

"Yes, now help me get my daughter into the wheelchair."

Linda smiled through her pain.

"Nurse, please call Dr. Mancini and tell him my daughter has gone to see her baby."

"I will, Mr. Conover, right away I will alert the resident physician to meet you in the Neonatal Intensive Care Unit."

"Thank you, nurse."

"Are you ready, honey?"

"Yes, Daddy."

"Good, we're on our way."

The Burning Hours

# 93

Adalina stared into the Neonatal Intensive Care Unit her thoughts awash in a sea of uncertainty. She knew Vincent's life depended on the incubator, but she couldn't shake a foreboding sense the clear plastic box produced within her. The sight of Linda coming to her cleared Adalina's emotional fog.

"I've come to see, Vincent, Mother," Linda announced.

"Yes, honey," Adalina cupped Linda's face in her hands.

"The resident physician is coming," an intensive care nurse said, "Would you like to wait, Miss Conover?"

"I want to see my baby, now."

"Please, follow me."

Charles pushed Linda's wheelchair into the Neonatal Intensive Care Unit and stopped at the incubator. Linda touched the plastic cover and turned to Adalina.

"He's so small, Mother, he's not fussing; shouldn't he be fussing?"

"When he is stronger, he will."

Linda placed the palm of her hand on her breasts, "I have nothing for him."

"You will, honey, soon, you'll be able to take care of him."

"I want to touch him, nurse."

"There's a risk of infection, the doctor will explain."

"Your baby is frail Miss Conover it is imperative he be kept warm and resistant to possible infection."

"I want to touch my baby, doctor."

"If you insist."

"I insist," Linda responded.

The doctor looked at Charles, who nodded his approval.

"Nurse, bring a surgical mask."

"I don't want a surgical mask I want my baby to see my face."

The Burning Hours       Page 307

The doctor assented and the nurse lifted the incubator lid.

Linda stroked Vincent's face. She brushed her hand along his arm to his hand. "Mommy is here, Vincent," she whispered, "remember when I read stories to you and described the flowers and butterflies in the garden and when I sang to you, Linda pleaded in a soothing voice, "Please, Vincent, Mommy needs you to come to her."

Observing Vincent's lack of response and fearing a heightened risk of infection the doctor suggested closing the incubator.

"If you close the incubator I'll never see my baby in this life," Linda remonstrated, holding Vincent's tiny hand.

"A few minutes more," the doctor conceded.

Linda desperately wanted to see Vincent fuss, to hear him cry, but he continued to lay still and unresponsive. She felt Adalina's and Charles's hands on her shoulder. Unable to bear Linda's emotional pain, Paolo left the room.

As the doctor started to close the incubator Vincent's hand tighten around Linda's finger. She watched his face scrunch into a pink ball and then she heard a soft cackle that exploded into a chorus of rhythmic cries.

"Bring a bottle of formula," the doctor directed.

"Give me my baby," Linda demanded.

The doctor took Vincent from the incubator and placed him into Linda's outstretched arms, he covered him with a blanket and handed Linda a bottle of formula.

"I knew you would come to me, Mommy loves you, Vincent. What a funny face you're making," Linda smiled, tears stung her eyes, "and this strong little hand that won't let go of me," she kissed Vincent's fingers, "you're such a beautiful baby, you're my baby," Linda rattled on while Vincent continued wailing."

"Honey," Adalina patted Linda's shoulder, "the bottle I think Vincent wants the bottle."

The Burning Hours

"I'm sorry, Vincent. I'm so thrilled you came to me," Linda offered Vincent the formula, which he refused, her second attempt met with another refusal, after Linda kissed and rolled the petite nipple in her mouth, Vincent eagerly accepted the formula.

# 94

Charles Conover gaveled the Audit Committee meeting to a close and asked Freddie Oldfield to stay.

"Did you transfer the funds we discussed to Paolo Bellini?"

"I did, the day you called, Mr. Conover."

"Before you leave for your Canadian hiatus, Freddie, stop at our North Central District Office to review their regulatory reports."

"I'll make the necessary arrangements."

"Why you take Canadian winter vacations when you could soak up Miami or Havana sunshine mystifies me."

Freddie shrugged his shoulders and smiled.

"To each his own," Charles said, "When will you leave?"

"Mid-week."

"Have a productive meeting and a restful vacation."

On his way out of the conference room Freddie stopped and blurted, "My wife is in Canada, Mr. Conover."

Freddie's declaration elicited surprise followed by a broad smile from Charles.

"You old dog, I didn't know, who's the lucky girl?

"Her name is Kimi Fairweather."

"A solid English name. When did this happen? You should have let me know? We could have celebrated at the mansion," Charles fired question after question at Freddie, "Adelina will not be pleased," Charles jokingly wagged his index finger, "But, I am sure she will get over her pique."

"Kimi is an Algonquin Indian, Mr. Conover," Freddie announced, "We married fifteen years ago, in the Algonquin tradition, and we have a fourteen year old son."

"I see," Charles responded.

"I'm proud of my wife and many times I wanted to shout our marriage from the roof top. Kimi and Freddie would not be accepted in our society and I couldn't put them through that."

"Sit here, Freddie, let's talk," Charles exhorted, "tell me about Kimi, how you met, how your love blossomed."

Freddie didn't hesitate. After fifteen years of secrecy, he gladly discussed with Charles the happiest moments of his life, and so he started:

"Algonquin men and women helped build my cabin. That's when I met Kimi. The minute I saw her I fell in love with her. Kimi is a beautiful and caring woman. Our son Freddie was born a year later; he's a smart and inquisitive boy. If you recall eleven year-old Freddie you will have a mental image of Freddie, Jr."

Charles processed Freddie's surprise announcement for a long time, "Good for you," he slapped Freddie's shoulder, "I'm happy for you and I know Adalina will be, too."

"Thanks, Mr. Conover, it means a lot coming from you."

And then, Charles said, "We almost lost Linda and Vincent."

"It must have been a difficult experience."

"Linda hemorrhaged and her heart stopped during surgery and Vincent teetered on the edge of mortality. An emergency code was called. Linda was clinically dead, but she came back, on her own."

"Linda came back to protect her baby."

"Do you think so, Freddie?"

"Yes, I do, it's the indefinable power of love, but for me, it's as real as the ring on my finger."

"All this, Freddie," Charles swept his arm around the conference room, "would be meaningless if they didn't survive."

"How are they?"

"They're home, now. Linda has a difficult road ahead. Vincent is thriving. The women compete to hold and feed him; Linda wins that competition, most of the time," Charles smiled.

"Hopefully, all will continue well."

"I echo your sentiment," Freddie.

"It is regrettable that Reed turned up, again."

"Yes, it is. Have a wonderful vacation with Kimi and Freddie, Jr."

Freddie nodded and started walking away when Charles called to him, "Kimi and Freddie, Jr. are always welcome at the Conover's.

"Thank you, Charles."

"After all these years you have called me Charles."

"The time is right."

"Yes, the time is right, Freddie."

Freddie nodded and closed the door behind him.

Charles looked out the window at the subtle signs portending another New England winter. He thought about his brief conversation with Freddie about the power of love and wished at that moment he could be at the chalet with Adalina, Linda and Vincent.

As he swiveled back the intercom buzzed.

"Mr. Conover, Paolo Bellini is on your private line," Mrs. Jenkins said.

Charles picked up the receiver.

"Freddie tells me he transferred the funds you requested."

"I have them. Reed didn't show for our meeting in Las Vegas."

"Did you hear from him?"

"Nothing."

"Do you think he suspected?"

"Maybe, but it won't keep him from making another arrangement."

"What do you suggest?

"We wait. If he hasn't fallen off a cliff, we will hear from him."

# 95

Vincenzo Farro's mahogany casket rose out of its resting place. Four gravediggers pulled up their straps and stepped back from the open grave. A priest blessed the gleaming casket. He read the prayer for the departed from his breviary, offered words of consolation to Regina and Vince, accepted their cash gratuity and drove away in his black Chevrolet.

Regina ran her hand along the casket's cool surface, and then kissed its gold plate inscribed with Vincenzo's birth and death dates.

"I am living with Vince, now in California. Soon, we will be home and you will rest in the shade of a magnificent tree adjacent to a small chapel. It's sunny most of the time, like your village in Italy. So much has happened in the past year. Tommy married a sweet Irish girl and they had twin girls. Julia married Vince's and Tommy's sergeant and they are living in Long Branch," Regina patted the casket's surface, and then she whispered, "I sound like a newspaper reporter. Vince is with me, Vincenzo."

"Hello, Pop, I've been in London for the past five months. I'm working in motion pictures. Mom says I'm an accidental actor," Vince paused, "Before we leave for California, Mom and I will have lunch at Tommy's with Julia and her husband. I love you, Pop," Vince kissed his hand and held it on to the casket. At his direction, the gravediggers lifted Vincenzo's casket onto a gurney, slid it into a waiting hearse, and within seconds the hatch door closed and the hearse drove off, to the Hoboken train station.

The four gravediggers stood in respectful silence as Vince and Regina their heads bowed reflected at the site where Vincenzo's headstone had been. Then Vince offered each gravedigger a gratuity; all declined.

"Please accept, to show our appreciation," Vince insisted.

"It is our privilege to honor your father," the crew leader waved off the gratuity.

Vince stuffed the cash into his pocket and extended his hand in thanks.

"Our hands are dirty," the crew leader held up his hands.

"It is my privilege," Vince said, and shook hands with each man, as did Regina, and then they left the cemetery.

Regina and Vince walked along the familiar main street of the neighborhood. For Regina her brief return to the old neighborhood proved rich in memories. She passed the restaurant where Vincenzo treated her and young Vince to pizza on meatless Fridays. On the corner where Mr. Mueller from Sparta, New Jersey displayed his spruce trees for sale at Christmas time. When she and Vince rounded the corner in the distance across the street, Tommy and Rosemary's house came into view.

"You're smiling, Mom?"

Regina put her arm through Vince's and looked up, "You've grown so tall, Vince. When you're a father and have a son of your own, you will know why your mother is smiling."

"How would you like to visit Pop's village in Italy?"

"I'd love to, but …"

Vince interjected, "Filming has been interrupted I have the time, we can go in September when the weather is cooler."

"Why has filming stopped?"

"Artistic differences with the book's author."

"When will you go back to work?"

"I only know what I hear a year, maybe more."

"Then your earnings will stop."

"No, my salary will continue."

"How is that possible?" Regina asked, "I don't understand what you are saying."

The Burning Hours                                    Page 314

"It's the way Hollywood works, Mom, my contract ensures my earnings will continue, so what do you say?"

Regina nodded yes, "You're such a good son," she pushed him as they walked to Tommy's and Rosemary's house.

# 96

"I'll get it," Julia responded to the ringing front door bell and greeted Regina with a warm embrace.

"It's good seeing you, Julia."

"I hope the cemetery wasn't too difficult for you."

"Vincenzo will soon be home with me for that I am comforted."

"Tommy's been waiting for you," Julia wrapped her arms around Vince.

"How have you been, Vince?" Darling cuffed Vince's shoulder.

"Can't complain, Sarge, how are you, how's Tommy treating you?"

Darling smiled at Vince's inquiry, "He calls me daddy, now."

"I guess daddy beats sweetie pie," Vince laughed.

"Yeah, I guess so," Darling rolled his eyes.

"Don't start in, Carroll, Tommy teases you, because he loves you," Julia said.

"I'm anxious to see Margaret and Veronica," Regina said, excitedly.

"They look like Rosemary."

"How can you know, Julia, they're only three months old," Darling challenged.

"I can tell. You'll see the resemblance, Regina, they're beautiful and healthy and they have red hair, just like Rosemary."

"Tommy's a red-head, Julia," Darling interjected.

"I'm aware of that, Carroll he is my son, after all."

"I can't win with these two, Vince," Darling sought commiseration.

"Stop trying, Sarge."

"You'll get to see the twins, Regina, if you can get past Tommy, he's a real mother hen," Darling advised.

The Burning Hours                                    Page 316

"You and Tommy are like children, Carroll," Julia scolded, "Rosemary is anxious to see you and Vince."

"Mrs. Farro and Vince are here," Julia's announcement brought Rosemary from the kitchen. She threw her arms around Regina, kissed her and stayed in her embrace, before greeting Vince with equal fervor.

"Where are your gorgeous babies?" Regina inquired.

"In the bedroom, Tommy is with them."

"Come, Vince, let's meet Margaret and Veronica," Regina said.

"Let me go in, first, Mom, I want to surprise Tommy."

"Here we go, again, Regina, just like when they were kids," Julia bemoaned.

Tommy sat on the bed making silly sounds to Margaret and Veronica. Vince silently approached and pulled Tommy into a bear hug.

"The father of twin girls, the world is full of wonders.

"Vince, I'm glad you're here, good hearing your voice."

"It's great seeing you, Tommy."

"Are you okay, Vince? You know, Linda."

"Yeah, Tommy, I'm getting along."

"Aren't my angels beautiful, Vince?"

"They're visions, Tommy," Vince stroked the babies' faces with the back of his hand.

Regina kissed Tommy's cheek, "Hello, Tommy," she whispered.

"Hello, Mrs. Farro. Rosemary dressed the babies in the monogrammed Bodysuits you sent."

Regina picked up Margaret, and then Veronica, she kissed their round faces, and then returned them to the bed where they lay side-by-side.

"Your daughters are adorable, Rosemary, you are a lucky girl," Regina said.

"They're delightful babies, Mrs. Farro, and they sleep through the night."

"Rosemary got awfully big," Julia said, "When she delivered uneventfully we were relieved."

"I'll get lunch ready."

"We'll help," Regina and Julia said in unison.

"I'll lend a hand," Vince offered.

"Wait a minute, Vince; I want to talk to you."

"Sure, Tommy."

"Are we alone?"

"Yeah, we're alone."

"You have to keep this to yourself."

"Okay," Vince said, quizzically.

"I'm getting flashes of sight," Tommy whispered.

"That's great, Tommy."

"They don't last long. I saw Rosemary and the babies."

"Does Rosemary know?"

Tommy shook his head no.

"I don't want to get her hopes up."

"Lunch is ready," Darling announced from the doorway.

"We'll be right there, Sarge," Vince answered.

"What's going on?"

"Nothing, tell Rosemary we'll be right out," Tommy said.

"Don't hand me that, Tommy, I know when something is up with you," Darling challenged.

"I'd like to tell you, Sarge, but …"

"But, what?"

"You can't keep anything from my mother."

"You don't think I can keep a secret?"

"Not from my mother she'll torture you and then you'll sing like a canary."

"Thanks a lot, Tommy."

"Sorry Sarge, you have to swear to say nothing to my mother."

"Alright, Tommy, you have my word."

"Go ahead, Vince, tell him."

"Tommy's getting flashes of sight, no one knows, not even Rosemary."

"That's great, Tommy, Doc Olsen said your vision might return."

"It stays in this room, Sarge," Tommy demanded.

"You can trust me, but ..."

"I knew it, what, Sarge?"

"Can you trust Margaret and Veronica, they heard everything, and they're pretty tight with Rosemary, do you think they will keep your confidence?"

"Sarge has a point, Tommy," Vince laughed.

"Don't say anything to your mother, girls, okay?" Tommy rubbed Margaret and Veronica's stomachs to their delight.

"Let's go before the women get suspicious," Darling said.

"Lead the way, Daddy."

"You won't give me a break, will you, Tommy?"

"Not in this life, Sarge."

# 97

In the dining room Darling and Vince placed a love seat beside Rosemary while Julia and Regina set Margaret and Veronica on it. Tommy smiled broadly when told the twins were near Rosemary and when she inquired about Tommy's smile he brushed it off as nothing.

"You outdid yourself, Rosemary," Regina surveyed the dining room table, brimming with varieties of cold cuts, breads, rolls, olives and cold beverages.

"Thank you, Mrs. Farro, enjoy your lunch."

"Pass the salami," Darling requested, and Julia obliged.

"*Grazie*," he said upon receiving the platter.

"*Grazie*, Sarge?" Tommy jumped in.

"Carroll is teaching himself Italian, Tommy," Julia said.

"You're kidding, Sarge, tell me you're kidding."

"I'm giving it a try."

"Grandpa is trying to speak Italian, girls," Tommy whispered to the twins.

"Stop teasing, Tommy," Julia warned, "They're always winding each other up, Regina, grown men acting like immature boys when they're together."

"You should have seen them in France and Belgium," Vince laughed, "This is nothing."

"Say something else, in Italian, Sarge."

"That's enough, Tommy," Rosemary said, "now eat your lunch."

"Good idea, Tommy that will keep your mouth busy," Vince taunted.

"Here's another line in Italian," Darling said, "*Tommy e fastidioso*," and as Tommy and Rosemary looked on, Regina, Julia and Vince burst out laughing.

"What did he say, Mom?" Tommy asked.

"He said ..." Julia's laughter precluded her from continuing.

The Burning Hours                                    Page 320

"What did you say, Sarge?"

"Ask Vince."

"What did he say, Vince?"

"He said Tommy is annoying."

"Serves you right, Tommy," Rosemary laughed.

When they heard Rosemary's laughter Margaret and Veronica giggled and stretched their arms and legs.

"Grandpa made my baby girls laugh at daddy," Tommy smiled.

"When will your movie be in the theaters, Vince?"

"That's anybody's guess the studio suspended filming."

"Why?" Julia asked.

"Artistic differences with the book's author."

"When will it re-start?" Rosemary asked.

"When the legal matters are settled; it might take a year, maybe more."

"That's a long time," Darling joined the discussion.

"It's not unusual," Vince said.

"What do you do in the meantime?" Tommy inquired.

"We sit around and wait; it's like the army."

"I have an announcement to make," Regina said, "While Vince is waiting for filming to resume, we are going to Italy for a few weeks, to visit Vincenzo's village."

"That's wonderful, Regina," Julia got up and kissed Regina.

"I've wanted to visit Vincenzo's village for a long time," Regina added.

"When will you go, Vince?" Julia asked.

"In September."

# 98

Paolo Bellini dined alone in a Five Star San Francisco Hotel restaurant. He sliced into the pink flesh of the Angus sacrifice on his plate and chased each bite with sips of a California Cabernet. He guarded a multimillion dollar check payment for the completion of a multi-story building project. Bellini Construction was on the cusp of entering the lucrative international restoration marketplace. While in California Paolo visited Linda and Vincent at the Conover Winery. He delivered a small blue construction helmet monogrammed with Vincent's name. Vincent now a robust little boy looked nothing like the frail baby more than a year ago. He smiled to himself at the image of Linda making funny faces and Vincent laughing heartily at her playfulness. Paolo sensed sadness in Linda born of Vincent not being with her, and the surgery, no matter how necessary that had forever altered her life.

Capping his meal Paolo quaffed a French cognac rolled the caramel liquid on his tongue before delivering its warmth down his throat into his sated stomach. He paid his bill; left a handsome tip, purchased newspapers in the gift shop, and took the elevator to his penthouse for a satisfying night's sleep, before returning to Connecticut in the morning.

Paolo showered and dressed for the night. He sat in a comfortable chair and scanned the newspapers, he purchased in the lobby. He read several articles dealing with the Hollywood Black List and Jackie Robinson joining the Brooklyn Dodgers, but the article he read and re-read dealt with the Marshall Plan and the European recovery from the devastation of the war years. Paolo made a mental note to check the progress of his application for funds to enter the foreign markets. He went to the bar, poured another cognac and returned to his reading. With mild interest Paolo read the *San Francisco News's* front-page story detailing the defeat of Mayor Lapham's crusade to junk the city's cable cars and finding nothing else of interest he tossed the newspaper onto the coffee table. When he reached for his cognac a headline of lesser importance captured his attention. Paolo devoured the story and when finished he chugged his cognac, picked up the phone and dialed Charles Conover.

"This is Paolo Bellini, may I speak with Charles Conover."

"Mr. Conover is in a Board meeting, Mr. Bellini, I'll let him know you called," Mrs. Jenkins answered.

"Here's my number, it's important, ask Charles to call me as soon as he can."

"I will give him your message," Mrs. Jenkins jotted Paolo's phone number.

Paolo again read the story appearing in the *San Francisco News*. He poured and in a celebratory expression held high his glass, and then downed it in a single toss. Then, Paolo picked up the ringing phone.

"I know why you're calling, Paolo, but first, how are Linda and Vincent?"

"Vincent is getting to be a little bruiser; he's a happy little guy, and Linda ..."

"Hold for a second, Paolo, Adalina," Charles called, "Paolo is on the phone."

"Paolo, how is Linda and Vincent?"

"Vincent is growing like a weed Linda adores the little guy, when they're together, her eye's shine brighter than the sun, but ..."

"What is it, Paolo? Is anything wrong?"

"She's lonely without her young man, she didn't say so, but she is and not being able to have children weighs on her mind."

"I'm glad you visited, I'm sure it was beneficial for Linda seeing you."

"Your mother and father are doing well, CC, they send their regards."

"The Board of Directors approved your funding application, Paolo, congratulations."

"Thanks CC," Paolo said, unenthusiastically, "that's not the reason I called, he's dead."

"What do you mean?" Charles said.

"Reed, he's dead."

"How, Paolo?" Adalina asked.

"I just read it in the local paper I have the paper in front of me."

"Read it to us, Charles said, coolly."

"Slowly, Paolo, I want to hear every word," Adalina said, an Arctic edge in her voice.

"Okay, here goes-Dentist found Dead in Condemned High Rise … No Foul Play Suspected … The decomposed body of Dr. Derek Reed, an army dentist who had been Absent Without Official Leave was discovered by construction workers preparing the abandoned building for demolition. Dr. Reed apparently died from an overdose of adulterated drugs, a syringe was found at his side. His identity was determined through an examination of army dental records. Further investigation revealed while under the influence of an illegal substance Dr. Reed fractured the front tooth of the base's general officer causing its loss. He was released on his own recognizance pending court martial proceedings before disappearing over one year ago. The army and local police attribute Dr. Reed's death to an accidental drug overdose and have closed the case. That's it," Paolo concluded.

A stunned silence prevailed for a long time until Paolo, asked, "Are you, okay? Adalina, CC, are you okay?" Paolo repeated.

"Now, Linda can get peace," Charles said.

"Yeah," Paolo said, "I wish I had the pleasure of dispatching him."

"Are you all right?"

"I hope he suffered the way my daughter and grandchild suffered. If there is a hell I hope he's burning in it," Adalina exclaimed, hot tears streaming down her face.

"It's done, it's over, and we go on," Charles tried to console Adalina.

"It's never done, Charles, the saints in heaven forgive I don't, for as long as I live I curse Derek Reed to the fires of hell for what he did to my daughter and grandchild."

# 99

Vince and Regina parked their rental Fiat in front of the corn silk-colored municipal building in Avellino, Italy. They climbed its cracked stone steps, entered the main entrance, and inside they perused an office directory fixed to a worn plaster coated wall.

"Is this it, Mom?" Vince pointed to *Cancelliere di Record, Piano Terra, Sala #3.*

"Registrar of Records, Ground Floor, Room #3, I guess we start there," Regina answered.

They found room #3 at the far end of a dimly lit hallway and went inside where a middle-aged man, missing his left leg greeted Vince and Regina.

"Good afternoon, my name is Carlo."

"Good afternoon," Vince responded.

"May I help you?"

"Certificate of Birth for Vincenzo Farro," Regina requested.

"Year of birth?"

"1896," Regina answered.

"A moment, please," Carlo picked up his cane, but before he got off his chair the voice of an unseen female came from the archive room.

The woman who appeared cradled a large leather bound book in her arms. She was elderly, most likely an octogenarian. She placed the volume on the counter and turned the yellowed pages to the section annotated 1880 to 1900; she stopped at Vincenzo's certificate and rotated the book affording Regina and Vince a view of the document.

"Here," she pointed a gnarled, arthritic index finger, "Vincenzo Farro."

Regina ran the tips of her fingers across each line of Vincenzo's birth, the names of his parents and the attesting signature of the custodian of the city's records.

The Burning Hours                                    Page 326

"Your father," she turned the book to Vince.

Vince placed the edge of the yellowed pages between his thumb and index finger as if caressing the spirit of the man in the page in the antique book.

"Finito?" the woman asked.

"Mom?" Vince inquired.

"Yes, I'm finished," Regina answered.

"Your husband, *senora*?" the woman asked.

"Yes, my husband," and gesturing to Vince, "Our son."

"I knew Vincenzo, he was a happy boy and young man, always smiling, helpful to anyone who needed help. He worked hard for his transit money to America. I accompanied him, with his mother and father to the Naples pier the day he left for America. That was a long time, ago, only memories remain," she said and closed the book.

"I am grateful to speak with you," Regina said, after a brief silence.

"Do you have my father's boyhood address? We would like to visit it," Vince requested.

"He lived at *147 Via Monte Del Gallo*, but the building no longer exists, it was torn down to make way for children orphaned by the war. Vincenzo made his First Holy Communion and his Confirmation at the Cathedral; you may want to visit there."

"How much do we owe you?" Vince asked.

"There is no charge," Carlo answered.

"May we know your name?" Regina asked.

"Anna," the woman responded.

"Thank you, Anna," Vince said.

Regina patted Anna's hand, "Thank you."

"Are you okay, Mom?"

Regina managed to smile and said goodbye to Carlo and Anna. She and Vince walked in silence along the drab hallway out of the building into the bright Italian sun.

Anna didn't move her hand from the closed book. She looked distractedly at the door when Carlo called her.

The Burning Hours

"Why didn't you tell the woman and her son you are Vincenzo's aunt?"

Anna stared straight ahead before answering.

"Vincenzo is dead, Carlo, his mother and father are dead, my brothers and sisters are gone, and soon I will be gone. It is best their memories are free of that ancient order," Anna cradled the book in her arms and walked to the archive room.

The ride to the Avellino Cathedral took fifteen minutes.

Before entering the cathedral Regina fixed a lace handkerchief to her head. At its entrance, she dipped the tips of her fingers into a Holy Water font, and admonished Vince to do the same. An aroma of incense permeated the cathedral. Beyond a row of burgundy veiled confessionals flames from votive candles flickered in the cathedral's somber light while a rotund priest celebrated Holy Mass. With a handful of worshippers Regina went to the altar railing and took Holy Communion. She lit candles for Vincenzo, Vince and Linda, and then she returned to the pew where Vince was seated. She closed her eyes and reflected on Vincenzo and their lives, together.

Regina grasped Vince's hand, and whispered, "Thank you, Vince."

"What for, Mom?"

"I can't tell you how much coming here means to me."

Vince nodded and squeezed Regina's hand.

The Burning Hours

# 100

The overhead fixtures in the Naples Train Terminal, most dull, some dead, and others sputtering, cast a gloomy gray light. Vince looked around the terminal at people rushing in all directions many carrying battered suitcases held together with rope, small boys begging, and a woman of obvious wealth a poodle on her leash, walking slowly through the crowd creating in Vince's mind a sense of the surreal.

"I'll check the schedule, Mom."

"I'll rest it's been a busy day."

"I'll be right back."

No sooner had Regina closed her eyes, she felt a tug on her dress.

"Mama."

A small boy stood before her, his cheeks grimed with dirt, his clothes, nothing more than unwashed rags. He extended to her a yellow rose he had stolen from a casket awaiting transportation.

"For you, mama, take me to America with you."

"What is your name, dear?"

"Franco."

"How old are you, Franco?"

"Nine."

Regina dug into her purse and handed Franco a dollar bill.

"For you," he insisted Regina take the flower.

"No, Franco, you keep the flower."

"Who is your friend, Mom?"

"This is Franco, Vince."

"You G.I.?"

"No longer," Vince answered.

"She your mama?"

"Yes, Franco, she is my mother."

The Burning Hours                                    Page 329

"I go to America with you."

Vince looked at the small boy wearing torn shoes too big for his feet. He reflected on the stories he heard in Belgium about *I Bambini Perduti di Napoli*, "The Lost Boys of Naples," who avenged their families killed by the Germans by stealing their weapons. They attacked the Germans with such a ferocity that its offensive stalled. The oldest was sixteen. Too many of the lost boys were ruthlessly executed by the infuriated Germans. Today," Vince thought, "many G.I's owe their lives to kids like Franco.

Vince sat on the bench, next to Regina, "I wish we could, Franco, but we can't."

"Oh," Franco said, dejectedly.

"Who cares for you, Franco? Where do you sleep? Where do you eat?" Vince asked.

"My big brother, Angelo, we sleep here, sometimes in the church when it is not locked, and sometimes nice people, like you and mama give us money to buy food."

"It's good you have a big brother," Vince said, "How old is Angelo?"

"Angelo is eleven."

"Oh, God!" Regina felt her heart leap into her throat.

"The conductor is calling us, Franco, we'll have to go."

"I go with you, G.I.," Franco took Vince's hand, and they walked to the waiting train.

"Mom, I want a minute with Franco."

"Goodbye," Regina kissed Franco's dirty cheek, boarded the train and sat at the window where she was able to see Vince and Franco.

Vince took a twenty dollar bill from his wallet and bent down.

"This is for you and Angelo, don't let anyone know you have it, or they will steal it from you," Vince pulled Franco against him and whispered, "You will do wonderful things, one day," and then released Franco from his embrace and boarded the train.

"What will happen to him?"

"I don't know, Mom."

Franco ran alongside the rolling train his eyes riveted to Regina's and Vince's window until it disappeared in the far distance. In the dull gray light of the station Franco looked a long time at the empty stretch of track and imagined one day a train will take him to America.

# 101

Easy breezes rolled off the mountains in the Napa Valley and sang softly through lines of grape trellises at the Conover Winery. Adalina primed her camera and prepared to take pictures of Vincent, now an active and inquisitive three year old child.

"Mom, Dad, ready, I'll take the first picture of you and Vincent," but before Adalina snapped the photograph Vincent slid off the lounge swing and smiled at his successful escape. Charles whispered a promise to Vincent, who settled while Adalina snapped the picture she had planned.

"Good boy," Laura kissed Vincent's cheek.

"That's my boy," Charles mussed Vincent's hair with the palm of his hand.

"Dad, I can't take Vincent's picture with his hair like that."

"Linda can fix it, can't you, Linda?" Charles smiled, sheepishly.

"Sure, Granddad, come here Vincent," Linda held out her arms and combed his hair, now an anthracite color.

"You are such a handsome boy," Linda kissed Vincent repeatedly on both cheeks, "Who bought you this handsome outfit?"

"Grandma," Vincent answered.

"Where's Grandma?"

"There."

"What is Grandma doing?"

"Pictures."

"Where's Pop-Pop and Great Grandma?"

"There," Vincent pointed to Charles and Laura on the lounge swing.

The Burning Hours
Page 332

"Very good, honey," Linda picked up Vincent, placed him on her lap for his photograph, which Vincent thwarted when he slid off her lap.

"Well, that won't work," Adalina mused.

"Honey, you have to stay on Mommy's lap if Grandma is going to take your picture."

"This picture is for your daddy," Linda whispered.

"What did you say, Linda? He's a little angel, now."

"Take the picture, before he becomes a whirlwind, again, I'll tell you, later."

Adalina photographed Vincent sitting contently on Linda's lap.

"Since you're being good, Vincent, I'll take another picture," Adalina snapped the camera's shutter a second time.

Vincent squirmed off Linda's lap, ran to Charles and grasped his hand.

"What's going on, Dad?" Adalina asked.

"Did you promise to take him to the wine cellar," Linda said.

"Vincent enjoys playing hide-and-seek with vintner assistants," Charles explained.

"Isn't it dangerous, running around the vats?" Adalina said.

"It's a well-lit restricted area the men know where he is at all times," and looking at Vincent, Charles added, "Vincent knows the names of some of the men. Tell Mommy who you play hide and seek with, Vincent?"

"Julio," Vincent said.

"Who else, Vincent?"

"Sammy."

"Who else?"

"Pop-Pop."

"When we find Vincent the game is over we will be back in a few minutes."

"You mind Granddad," Linda said, "When you come back you can take your nap."

"Don't worry, Linda, he will be fine, the men look out for him and they enjoy Vincent's visits," Charles took Vincent's hand and the Mayflower patrician and his great grandson happily trekked the path surrounded by blooming grape vines to the wine cellar.

"What did you say to settle Vincent, Linda?" Adalina rewound the film in her camera.

"I told him the picture is for his daddy; it just came out."

"Well, it worked."

"I'm going to take a nap," Laura rose from the lounge swing.

"Are you all right, Mom?" Adalina asked.

"I'm fine," Laura answered, "don't worry the men will look out for Vincent."

"We won't worry," Adalina responded, "Enjoy your nap."

"Have you given further thought to what daddy proposed?" Adalina asked Linda.

"It's a wonderful idea, but there are others more qualified than me."

"If your father thought that he wouldn't have asked you."

"I don't want to be away from Vincent."

"You can manage from here. You will only be required to chair a semi-annual trustee meeting in Connecticut, and now Vincent can travel with you. Daddy and I know how deeply you feel about the disabled veterans, Linda, this is a wonderful opportunity to assist them, now and in the years to come."

"Alright, you're very persuasive, Mother," Linda agreed

"I will call your father with your acceptance and Freddie will prepare the legal documents to establish The Linda Bellini Conover Charitable Trust."

For several moments Linda reflected, unable to speak.

"I am a lucky woman, Mother," and as quiet tears flowed from Linda's eyes, Adalina took her into her arms and whispered, "We're the lucky ones, your father, Vincent and me."

"It's just that …," Linda wiped her eyes.

"What is your heart telling you, Linda?"

"I should be happy. Vincent and I have everything life has to offer, and we have the love and support of a most marvelous family."

"But, something is missing?"

"I'm lonely, Mother, I can't overcome feeling alone."

"Without Vincent?"

"I miss him every day I wonder where he is and what he is doing. Not being with him is an incurable void in my heart."

"Have you thought of trying to contact him now that Derek Reed is no longer a threat?"

"There are too many complications; I don't know where he is, if he is married and has children. I don't want to disrupt his life, but I want him to know he has a son. It's a knot I can't unravel."

"Daddy could have a bank investigator try to locate him, and …"

"I don't want his life examined that way; it wouldn't be fair."

"You will let me know if there is anything I can do."

"Mother, what went through your mind when you could no longer have children?"

"Why do you ask, Linda?"

"There are times I feel less a woman."

"Is it because you can no longer bear children?"

"Yes," Linda nodded.

"If a man truly loves a woman it doesn't matter, it might even bring them closer together, as it did with your father and me."

The Burning Hours

"There is no man other than Vincent that I would ever want to have children with, and that's not going to happen … and … and … Oh, I don't know what I'm trying to say."

"I think I do I experienced the same conflict, Linda, knowing I could no longer bear children, but wishing what fate took away from me could be restored."

With a nod Linda agreed.

"I know how you feel, honey. It took me a long time to recover, but I did and you will, too. Your femininity isn't diminished. You are a woman in every sense of the word and you also happen to be among the loveliest of the lovely, and that's not just your mother talking, it is apparent to anyone who knows you. What woman wouldn't want to possess your virtues?"

Linda managed a small smile.

The hide-and-seek game in the wine cellar lasted less than ten minutes. Charles thanked the men who had participated in the game. He took Vincent's hand and they walked along the path to the house. Nearing the house, Vincent shook loose and ran to the patio where Linda stood.

"Up, Mommy," he extended his arms.

"You are getting to be a big guy," Linda picked up Vincent who rested his head in the crook of her neck and shoulder.

"Who discovered your secret hiding place?" Linda inquired.

"Pop-Pop."

"Pop-Pop found you?"

Vincent shook his head and struggled to keep his eyes open.

"Mommy, go in, now," Vincent said, and then fell asleep in her arms.

# 102

Nick Ferry studied his final scene of *Yesteryear* a close-up with Ivy Townsend, the movie's romantic characters reunited after separated by war in a passionate kiss on a bridge in a rainstorm. Crews repositioned cameras and wheeled scenery into place their noise echoed through the cavernous studio. Soon the excitement of the pending conclusion of an Academy Award-quality film settled into an expected silence, which the sound of an artificially produced rainfall interrupted.

"Nick," Walter, an assistant producer knocked twice, "Tommy Tomasso is on the phone."

"Transfer the call to my dressing room."

"Will do," Walter answered.

Vince picked up the phone on its first ring.

"Tommy, how are you and the family?"

"We're good, how are you?"

"I'm okay, getting ready for the film's final scene, and then I'll have time off."

"The dollhouse and the furniture kits arrived yesterday; where did you find it?"

"In a small woodworking shop here in Los Angeles, I hope Margaret and Veronica enjoy playing with it.

"They love it, Vince and so does their mother."

"Did the order arrive in good shape?"

"Everything is perfect."

"How's your vision, Tommy?"

"Still getting flashes of sight, but they aren't sustained."

"Sorry, Tommy, but I'm still hoping for a positive result."

"Anyway," Tommy perked up, "we're waiting to see my buddy on the silver screen."

"After today I'll have time off, come to L.A. with Rosemary and the girls. I'll arrange an appointment with a specialist, what do you say, Tommy?"

"Thanks, Vince, I'm going to let it ride, if it's going to happen, it will happen," Tommy said, resignedly.

"The offer stands if you change your mind."

"It's Vince," Tommy handed Rosemary the phone."

"Hi Vince, how are you?"

"I'm fine, Rosemary, Tommy tells me you and the girls are enjoying the dollhouse."

"The dollhouse is charming, its detail is exquisite, and Margaret and Veronica love it."

"Vince said a few more kits are in the mail," Tommy interjected.

"The girls put the miniature figurines of the father, mother and their two daughters, whom they've named Margaret and Veronica, in the kitchen and now they're pestering me for a brother."

"When will that be, Rosemary?"

"Don't give them ideas, Vince, they have fertile imaginations."

"Okay," Vince laughed.

"Uncle Vince is on the phone, girls," Rosemary called to Margaret and Veronica.

"They're climbing on my lap, Vince," Tommy said, "Thank Uncle Vince for the dollhouse," he positioned the phone between Margaret and Veronica.

"Thank you for the dollhouse, Uncle Vince," they chirped in unison.

"You're welcome, do you like the dollhouse?"

"We love the dollhouse, Uncle Vince."

"What else do you want to say to Uncle Vince?" Rosemary said.

"We love you, Uncle Vince."

"Now, say goodbye."

The Burning Hours

"Bye, Uncle Vince," Margaret and Veronica climbed off Tommy's lap and ran back to the dollhouse.

"Rosemary wants to say hello, Vince."

"We're excited and proud of you, Vince, and we look forward to seeing your movie."

"It's just a job, Rosemary."

"In a few months you will be a household name."

"I'd trade it for what you and Tommy have," Vince said in a quiet voice.

"Here's Tommy," Rosemary said, "We love you, please give our love to your mother."

"Love you, too, Rosemary."

"Five minutes, Nick," Walter rapped on the door.

"I have to go, Tommy, we'll talk, again"

Walter poked his head into the dressing room, "Beau's a nervous wreck, Nick; he wants a fast wrap-up to the film."

"Tell him not to worry."

"Tell the pope not to pray," Walter answered and went back to the set.

Vince finished his mental preparation and got up to leave. When he opened the door Ivy Townsend stood in its space her hair and clothes soaked from the artificial downpour for the movie's final scene. She pushed Nick back into his dressing room and closed the door.

"A scene of our own, Nicky," Ivy whispered seductively.

# 103

The chalet's living room of the Conover Winery was library quiet. At his request Charles handed a *Wall Street Journal* to Charles Sr. who turned to a section titled *Corporations-on-the-Move*. Charles sat back in a wood carved club chair and perused the local news reported in the *Napa Valley Buzz*.

"The *Journal* features Conover Bank, Charles."

"What does the article say, Dad?"

"Your gross and net profits surpassed expectations."

Charles smiled, "You made the right choice, Dad."

"I guess I did."

"What are you two up to," Adalina asked easing into a club chair.

"*The Wall Street Journal* spotlights your husband."

"Favorably?"

"Favorably," Charles Sr. responded.

"I expected nothing less, Charles."

"Where are Linda and mother?"

"Upstairs jousting as to will take care of Vincent."

"That little guy is my sidekick," Charles Sr. smiled.

"He knows mother is more indulgent than Linda," Charles observed.

Charles Sr. folded his *Wall Street Journal* and placed it on the coffee table, "Linda should get back into circulation."

"Another man in her life is a non-starter, Dad, if that's what you mean."

"How can you know?" Charles Sr. responded.

"Linda made up her mind; she wants no one, but Vincent in her life."

"What's new in the local press?"

"Nothing much," Charles handed Adalina the newspaper.

"See anything of interest?"

The Burning Hours

"There's a movie in town."

"Go to the movie; Linda deserves a night out," Charles Sr. interjected.

"What do you say?"

"It's good with me I'll check with Linda."

As Adalina began her ascent she met Linda descending the staircase into the living room.

"Are you up for a movie, tonight?"

"I don't think so, Mother," Linda answered.

"How's my little sidekick, Linda?"

"Here's an update on your sidekick, Granddad," Linda said, a veneer of frustration in her voice, "When Vincent's nap time arrived, he ran to Grandmother, and with a triumphant look on his face, he dared me to take him from her."

"He's a natural negotiator, Charles," Charles Sr. laughed.

"I agree, Dad, we can use the little scamp at the bank," Charles joined the laughter.

"What is he doing, now, Linda?" Adalina asked.

"He is playing with the train set Grandmother gave him, and," she paused, "and he is singing *Down by the Station*."

"What is *Down by the Station*?" Adalina asked her eyes crinkled into a smile.

"It's a kiddie song that came with the train set."

"How does it go?"

"Do you really want me to sing it, Mother?"

"Just a few lines."

"Vincent is singing it now, he'll be glad to entertain you."

"We prefer hearing a few lines from you, Linda, don't we Dad?"

"Yes, Linda, please indulge us," Charles Sr. said.

"I don't know why I'm doing this, nobody laughs?"

"Okay," Charles and Charles Sr. agreed.

"What about you, Mother?"

The Burning Hours                                    Page 341

"I agree, Linda."

"Alright then … Here are the opening lines … *Down by the station early in the morning … See the little puffer bellies all in a row … Chug, Chug, Puff, Puff … Off they go.*

Okay, are you satisfied?"

"That's very good, Linda," Adalina laughed.

"It's not funny, Mother. I'm trying to keep him on a schedule, you're all spoiling him," Linda paused, and then she started laughing at the mental image of her son and Grandmother singing *Down by the Station*.

"You need a break, Linda," Charles said, "a new movie is premiering in town."

"Go, Linda, enjoy a night out, join the bustling energy of the valley, it will be good for you," Charles Sr. counseled.

"Look," Adalina showed Linda the newspaper.

"*Yesteryear*, it stars, Ivy Townsend. The studio will unveil the winner of its Star Search competition. What do you say, honey?"

"Okay," Linda nodded, "I could use a night out."

# 104

The marquee's bright light illuminated the Napa Community Theater's entrance. The line of movie-goers crawled to the ticket window commanded by a wizened crimson-lipped woman. Linda remembered the last movie she saw with Vincent the night before he left for Fort Monmouth. She recalled feeling sick, resting her head on his chest, his arm around her shoulders to provide comfort. The day of his departure Linda discovered she was carrying Vincent's child.

Charles purchased front row, Mezzanine tickets. Adalina rebuffed his gesture of ladies first and sat next to Linda, who sat, on the aisle. As the theater darkened Adalina took Linda's hand and they exchanged smiles. A shaft of white light splashed across the silver screen and a church-like quiet presaged the start of the main feature.

On the screen, John Quartermain walked to the side of two leather bound chairs and introduced himself as Vice President of Production. He described the movie's plot, and then he said, "Welcome, *Yesteryear's* female lead."

Ivy Townsend shook hands with John Quatermain and eased into one of the leather bound chairs. She wore a vermillion pencil style dress with Bolero sleeves, a string of pearls and her blond hair in an up swept motif.

"You look spectacular, Ivy, as usual," John Quartermain gushed.

"Thank you, John," Ivy smiled, her blue eyes shone.

"Ivy, what drew you to *Yesteryear*?"

"The story's plot captivated me, John."

"What in particular caught your attention?"

"That love and devotion are the same irrespective of generations."

"There has been a growing buzz around the male lead of the movie."

The Burning Hours                                    Page 343

"I'm aware of that, John," Ivy smiled.

"Will you now introduce the winner of Star Search and your co-star?"

"With pleasure, John," Ivy stood up, "Here he is, ladies," Ivy greeted Nick Ferry with a warm embrace and an even warmer kiss.

Disbelieving her eyes and then grasping the reality of Vincent Farro transformed by Hollywood into Nick Ferry every fiber in Linda's body numbed, her heart raced and her throat tightened before she caught her breath.

"Are you okay, Linda?" Adalina whispered.

"Yes, Mother."

"Linda," Charles whispered past Adalina.

"I'm all right, Daddy."

"How did you get involved in movies, Nick?" John Quartermain asked, "Did you have training in acting?" he continued.

"No, John, I'm an untrained actor. While working construction for the Los Angeles County Water Department a talent scout invited me to try out for a part in a war movie. I had nothing to lose, so I auditioned and I got the part."

"What did that part call for?"

"Wearing a torn shirt that showed a scar on my chest. Speaking three or four words, nothing more."

"Were you in the war, Nick?"

"Yes, I served in Europe."

"How did you get involved in *Yesteryear*?"

"I'll answer that, John," Ivy interjected, "When I saw Nick's part," she cast an affectionate glance at Nick, "his screen presence was magnetic. I knew right away I had my romantic co-star."

"That's the way it happened," Nick affirmed.

Linda's head swum, her eyes fixed on Vincent, now Nick Ferry. She took her hand from Adalina's and held it to her mouth. As she watched Hollywood's leading lady and Vincent exchange affectionate glances Linda's emotions

The Burning Hours                    Page 344

crumbled. She had to get out of the theater, but before she got up to leave John Quartermain announced he had one last question for Nick.

"Everyone has mementoes given us by special persons in our lives, here is my father's watch," John showed Nick a gold watch, "I'll treasure it always. Do you have any mementoes you'd like to share with your public?"

Nick's pause prompted John Quartermain to repeat his question. Ivy looked perplexed. Linda couldn't take her eyes off Vincent, the father of her child; she took deep breaths and fought back tears.

"I do."

"Care to share details, Nick?"

"Sure," Nick said, and paused before answering, "It's a book of Lord Byron's Poems."

"Who gave it to you, Nick?"

"It was a gift from a high school teacher."

"Do you still have that book?"

"Yes, I still have the book."

"Are you in touch with your teacher?"

"No longer, but I often think of her."

"Maybe someday the two of you will reconnect."

"Yes, I hope so."

"I have to go, Mother."

"But, the movie is starting?"

"I want to be home with Vincent."

"Granddad and Grandmother are taking care of Vincent," Charles said, "Stay Linda, enjoy your night out."

"Vincent's a handful when he wakes up, Daddy."

"You're sure?" Charles asked.

"I'm fine I'll see you when you later."

# 105

Within an hour Linda arrived home. She watched Charles Sr. and Laura quietly enjoying each other's company and reflected on her time with Vincent in Hoboken. Back then she envisioned their future together and when their burning hours cooled in the inexorable passage of time they would enjoy each other in the devoted way of her grandparents. But, that dream was shattered.

"Linda, did you enjoy the movie?" Laura asked, "I am so involved in my embroidery I lost track of time."

"I left early Grandmother."

"Why dear? Didn't you enjoy the movie?"

"I left before it began. I thought it best to be home with you and Vincent."

"That little guy plays hard and sleeps soundly. You need a diversion, Linda," Charles said skeptical of Linda's motive for leaving the theater.

"A cup of tea, Linda?" Laura asked.

"No, thank you, I'll check on Vincent, read, and then go to bed," Linda ascended the staircase to Vincent's room. For a time she looked at her son sleeping peacefully. She knelt beside his bed and whispered, "I saw your father, tonight, baby. You're the image of him," Linda kissed Vincent's cheeks and went to her room.

Arriving home Charles and Adalina went to the living room where Charles, Sr. and Laura were awake past their usual retirement time for the day. As soon as they entered the room, Laura asked, "Why didn't Linda stay for the movie?"

"She wanted to be home in the event Vincent woke up," Charles answered.

"Why do you ask, Mother," Adalina inquired.

"Something is wrong," Charles Sr. interjected.

"Linda put on a brave face, but she was crying," Laura said.

"I'll go see her, Charles," Adalina went to Linda's room where she found her sitting in the glow of an upright lamp, a book in her lap. Linda managed a smile when Adalina entered her room.

"Honey, is there anything you're not telling me?"

"No, Mother, I'm just tired."

"Grandmother thought you were crying."

"I wasn't crying."

"Why didn't you stay for the movie?"

"Is this an inquisition, Mother?" Linda said, petulantly.

"We know how difficult these past years have been for you."

"I'm sorry, Mother I didn't mean to sound cross."

"It's okay, honey, you will tell me if something is weighing on your mind?"

"I will I promise."

"Good, girl," Adalina kissed Linda's cheek and turned to leave.

"Mother."

"Yes, dear."

"Nick Ferry, the actor."

"He's a handsome young man."

"He's Vincent's father."

"What?" Adalina's face registered surprise.

Linda's glazed eyes met her mother's.

"I'm not crazy, Mother, you do, believe me."

"I'm astonished, but yes, I believe you."

"Before he was Nick Ferry he was Vincent Farro. I bought the book of poems he mentioned as a gift for him. He was a student in my library class. When he returned from the war he visited me that's when I gave him the book. He wouldn't tell me why he didn't visit me before leaving, even though I asked him. He just thanked me for the book and left. I saw him at the cannon mount when leaving for the day, his back was to me. I touched his shoulder. He said I should go home before the snowstorm worsened, and then he looked away.

As I started to leave, he said something about dying in the war that upset me. I made him promise not to entertain such thoughts. I took his arm and we walked to the trolley. We exchanged smiles. In those moments on his arm I was a complete woman. When we got to the platform Vincent wouldn't get on the trolley with me. He had a hard time dealing with my social position and being Charles Conover's daughter. After I boarded the conductor said he was still on the platform. I went outside and told Vincent I wanted him to come home with me; I said home Mother. I didn't say my apartment, I said home, it was the feeling he stirred in me. On the trolley ride we fell in love."

"I know, Linda, love blooms on trolley rides," Adalina smiled.

"The storm worsened by the time we arrived home. Mr. Wagner was shoveling, but the snow fell faster than he could clear it. I repaired a button on Vincent's overcoat and we had hot chocolates. He went outside for a cigarette promising he would be back in fifteen minutes. Without telling me he helped Mr. Wagner and was outside for a long time. When he came in, he was soaked from head to toe shedding snow over my newly cleaned floor. I was furious with him, Mother. I didn't know if something happened to him. I pictured him lying wounded in the snow as the newspapers reported. I told him I was angry with him. He stood before me like a mischievous kid. My son takes after him, Mother; if I reprimand him, his smile breaks my heart. I felt ashamed it was only a wet floor. I should have realized Vincent was eighteen when they sent him to war. I apologized and went to the kitchen to make him a hot chocolate as a peace offering, but he had another idea. I believe Vincent was conceived that night."

An uneasy quiet prevailed after Linda finished speaking. Adalina didn't know what to say.

Charles appeared at the doorway.

"Vincent is fast asleep," he announced, "Are you all right, Linda?"

"Charles, please come in," Adalina said.

"Are you unwell, Linda?"

"I'm well, Daddy."

"Sit down, Charles."

"What is going on?"

"Tell your father why you left the theater, Linda."

Linda hesitated, and then she said, "The actor, Nick Ferry."

"What about Nick Ferry?"

"He's Vincent's father," Linda said in a barely audible voice.

"I don't understand what you are saying, Linda."

"Nick Ferry is Vincent Farro, Daddy, they changed his name."

"Adalina,"

"It's true, Charles."

Linda showed her locket to Charles, "Vincent gave me this before he left for Fort Monmouth," and then she snapped it open.

"My goodness," Charles exclaimed.

"Mr. Wagner took this picture when we returned from ice skating, the other picture is Vincent's Army photograph."

"How long have you known, Linda?" Charles asked.

"I didn't know until tonight I couldn't bear to watch him with another woman."

"I understand, honey," Charles consoled.

"Vincent and I will never be together the way we were," Linda lamented, "but I want him to know he has a son."

"Don't ever say never, Linda."

"I'd like to believe that Mother, but we are worlds apart, now. He owes his career to Hollywood's most desirable woman and it's obvious she's in love with him; that's his world now."

"Why do you say theirs is more than a professional relationship?" Charles asked.

"Ivy Townsend looks at Vincent the way I looked at him, it's the look of a woman in love it is all over her. I know that look, Daddy, a woman knows that look."

"Adalina."

"I saw what Linda saw, Charles."

"I'll always love Vincent, Daddy. I miss him every second of every day. I'm in pain, for myself, and for my son, who is growing up without his father."

"Charles, can anything be done?"

"Vincent or Nick is a valuable economic property for his studio. He will live in a gilded cocoon protected by a beachhead of lawyers and publicists. Getting through to him will be near impossible. I'll see if we have common financial dealings with the studio. If we do perhaps a channel of communication could be established, but it's an extremely difficult situation."

"Daddy, I want Vincent to know he has a son, and I want my son to know his father."

"We love you, Linda," Charles said, a quiver in his voice.

"Mama."

"You haven't called me mama for a long time."

"I want you to hold me, Mama."

Adalina wrapped Linda in her arms, "You will be fine, honey," she said, in a low voice.

"What I want most in this world is denied me," Linda cried, quietly.

# 106

Linda Conover completed her first six months as board chairman of the Linda Bellini Conover Charitable Trust Fund. In the quiet of the chalet's library she prepared recommendations for funding from several veterans groups. She set aside files for delivery to Freddie Oldfield preparatory to the Trust's semi-annual meeting in Connecticut, which she chairs. Her charitable trust work was rewarding and at times she forgot her emotional pain only to feel it reemerge in quiet moments with a sharper edge.

When in Connecticut Linda dined with Charles and Adalina at the country club. She went on a few solo dinner engagements with successful men accepting good night pecks on her cheek, but rebuffing intimate kisses. Now five years old Vincent traveled by plane with Linda to Connecticut and back to California.

The valley was serene beneath a cloudless blue sky. Linda looked through the library window at Vincent playing catch with Julio, a vineyard worker and his son Ricardo. She reflected on the anxious hours before Vincent's birth and delighted at his startling resemblance to his father. Within minutes Julio and Ricardo departed for the day, leaving Vincent alone, bouncing his ball.

"Toss me the ball," Linda clapped her hands.

Standing a few yards away, Vincent complied.

Linda dropped the ball, picked it up and tossed it wide.

"Mommy, you don't know how to play catch," Vincent critiqued Linda's performance.

"Try, again, honey," Linda pleaded.

"Okay," Vincent tossed his ball to Linda.

"I caught it," she exulted.

"Toss it high to me, Mommy."

"Here goes," Linda lobbed the ball in the air and Vincent caught it.

The Burning Hours                    Page 351

"You're pretty good for a girl."

"A girl, that's the best compliment I had all day," Linda said, "Let's do pictures and words before your nap, okay?"

"Okay."

Vincent took his book from a lower shelf on the bookcase and sat beside Linda.

"Remember your ABC's, Vincent?"

"Yes," he answered.

"Now, then, what do we have here?" she said, "A picture of a ship. What are these letters?" she pointed to the letters S-H-I-P.

"S-H-I-P," Vincent responded.

"Now, honey, say after me," Linda pronounced the word Ship

"Ship," Vincent articulated.

"Very good, honey," Linda kissed Vincent's cheek.

"Mommy, are you going to kiss me every time I give a right answer?"

"Should I?"

"Not all the time."

"Okay, it's a deal."

"What's a deal?"

"A deal is when two people agree on something."

"Okay, it's a deal," and then Vincent brushed his hand over the ship's main and mizzen masts, "Are these sails?"

"Yes, they are. When the wind gets in them the ship sails."

"Can I see a ship like that?"

"Sure can, when we go to Connecticut in July. After my meeting, we'll go to Mystic Seaport. There you will see a real sailing ship and before we come home, I will treat you to a Boston Red Sox game. Do we have a date?"

"Yes," Vincent's eyes brightened, "What's a date?"

"A date is when two people agree to do something together."

"Like when Julio and Ricardo played catch with me."

"Yes, honey, like that," Linda said and observed Vincent suddenly quiet.

"Why don't I have a daddy to play catch with the way Ricardo has?"

As each day passed Vincent became increasingly inquisitive. Linda wrestled with how to explain an adult complication to a five year old boy. Charles's inquiries to establish a channel of communication proved unsuccessful. "Will your son ever know his father, Vincent?" she wondered.

"Do you know how babies are born, Vincent?"

"When their mothers get round, they go to a hospital and come back with a baby."

"That's good, honey," Linda said placing the palm of her hand on her stomach, "When your daddy and I parted he didn't know you were in here. If he knew nothing would keep him from you," Linda stroked Vincent's cheeks.

"When will he know?"

"I hope soon," Linda saw the gleam in Vincent's eyes vanish, "Do you want to do more pictures and words?"

"I'll go for my nap, now," Vincent said.

"Do you want me to tuck you in?"

"No," Vincent answered returning his book in the bookcase.

"Come here, honey," Linda hugged Vincent and whispered, "Mommy loves you."

After Vincent left Linda took several minutes to collect her emotions. She culled press releases on funding awards made by the Trust. As she clipped and removed an article in the *California Clarion* a picture of Vincent and Ivy Townsend appeared in the window made by her incisions. Its caption read: Academy Award winners Ivy Townsend and Nick Ferry take a break from filming *Matthew and Abbey* sequel to *Yesteryear.*

Linda perused another newspaper.

# 107

Spring debuted at the Tomasso household. Rosemary ironed laundry reeled in from the clothesline that in the past served as Tommy's and Vince's secret means of communication. Tommy napped in his favorite chair while Margaret and Veronica played with their tea set, a birthday gift from Julia and Darling.

When the phone rang Tommy picked it up.

"This is Samuel Birkman, Tommy."

"How are you, Mr. Birkman?" Tommy said sleepily.

"I'm fine, Tommy, did I wake you?"

"A springtime nap."

"Do you have a few minutes for me?"

"Off course I do it's always good hearing from you."

"The Board of Education wants to honor you and Vince in a ceremony at the high school."

Tommy hesitated.

"It is a well-deserved honor, Tommy can you get in touch with Vince?"

"Sure, I'll call him."

Rosemary stopped ironing and went into the living room followed by Margaret and Veronica.

"It's Mr. Birkman, Rosemary."

"Hi, Mr. Birkman," Rosemary spoke into the phone.

"How are you and your little angels?"

"Angels, I'm not sure."

"Enjoying every moment I wager."

"They are a joy. How are you?"

"I am faring well. The Board wants to honor Tommy and Vince Farro in a ceremony at the high school, Rosemary. Please urge him to accept the invitation."

"Say yes, Tommy," Rosemary exhorted her eyes shining.

The Burning Hours                                    Page 354

"Say yes, Daddy," Margaret and Veronica mimicked Rosemary.

"I guess it's unanimous," Tommy smiled at Margaret's and Veronica's celebratory clapping.

"I'll inform the superintendent."

"When will the ceremony take place?"

"Sometime in July."

"As soon as we hear from Vince the Board will set a date."

"Thank the Board members for me, Mr. Birkman."

"I shall."

"Thanks, again," Tommy said and hung up the phone.

"What a wonderful honor," Rosemary threw her arms around Tommy.

"When will you call Vince?"

"I'll try now."

"Where are you two going?" Rosemary asked.

"To play with our tea set," Margaret announced.

"Will you pour me a cup of tea?" Rosemary asked.

In unison, Margaret and Veronica said yes and dashed into the kitchen.

"I thought you dressed the girls in the blue outfits Mom sent."

"I was going to, but since today is the first day of spring," Rosemary stopped, "How do you know they aren't in their blue dresses, Tommy?"

"They're in yellow sun suits."

"Tommy," Rosemary's eyes teared.

"I can see, Rosemary, not great, but I see you and our daughters."

Rosemary threw her arms around Tommy her tears now freely flowing.

"I see you and Margaret and Veronica," Tommy stroked Rosemary's face.

"When, Tommy?"

The Burning Hours         Page 355

"Last week. I needed to know it was permanent before telling you."

"Margaret! Veronica!" Rosemary called, "Come here!"

"We're playing, Mommy," Margaret answered.

"Mommy and Daddy want you in the living room, now."

"Will you have tea with us later if we come?" Veronica asked.

"Yes, but now Mommy wants you here with me."

"Come here my angels," Tommy beckoned and Margaret and Veronica climbed onto his lap.

# 108

Nick Ferry heard the familiar sounds of production crews preparing the *Matthew and Abbey* set for his climactic scene with Ivy. Then it was quiet, outside. Nick looked in the dressing room mirror in another futile attempt to discover himself. I have the world at my disposal, he thought, but that doesn't seem to matter. I'm unfulfilled and I know it, but I can't reverse that emotion. Nick picked up the latest edition of *Hollywood Happenings* its headline blared *Nick Ferry and Ivy Townsend Nuptials Imminent.*

The ringing phone brought Nick back to reality. He knew only three people had his private line: Ivy, who was outside with Beau Blatz, Regina, who at this hour was at Mass, and Tommy.

"I knew it was you, Tommy."

"Got a couple of minutes, Vince?"

"Sure, how are Rosemary and those two cuties?"

"She wants to say hello," Tommy handed Rosemary the phone.

"We had a wonderful time in California, Vince. I'll let Tommy tell you his news."

"Next time we'll tour the studio. Margaret and Veronica will get a thrill seeing how cartoons are filmed."

"Don't breathe a word to them, Vince, they're little conspirators, they won't give me a moment's rest until they get their way."

"Okay," Vince laughed, "I'll keep it to myself."

"Should I ask how you are doing or pick up a newspaper to find out?"

"In Hollywood nothing is sacred."

"Good talking with you Vince, here's Tommy."

"Samuel Birkman called. The school board wants to honor us."

"After the trouble we caused."

The Burning Hours                                          Page 357

"We're illustrious alumni," Tommy said facetiously.

"You mean illustrious delinquents."

"That's closer to the truth," Tommy laughed.

"When?"

"Mid-July at the high school."

"Sure, it's okay with me."

Tommy grasped Rosemary's hand, and after a pause, he said, "I can see, Vince. It's not the best, but it's consistent."

"That's wonderful, Tommy."

"When I hang up and say I'll see you, Vince, I'll mean it, literally."

"They're knocking on my door. Let me know the date when you have it. I couldn't be happier for you, Tommy," Vince hung up and went outside to the set.

Beau Blatz chomped his unlit cigar with the vigor of an omnivore. His eyes shone with enthusiasm of wrapping up another Academy Award-quality film. He set camera angles, and then motioned Ivy and Vince to him.

"Are you ready, Ivy?"

"As ready as I'll ever be," she responded.

"Nicky."

"Let's go," Nick answered.

Ivy and Nick exchanged smiles.

Beau stretched wide his arms, "Let's hear it for Ivy, Nick and our next Oscars," and the crowded studio erupted into sustained applause. When it subsided Beau took to his director's chair and called for filming to begin.

The rolling cameras honed in on Ivy and Vince alternating close-ups from front and side angles. As quiet gripped the studio Ivy initiated Abbey's dialog.

*"It won't work, Matthew, heaven knows I want it to, but it won't,"* Abbey looked into Matthew's eyes.

*"You belong with me, Abbey, what my family thinks doesn't matter."*

*"In time it will and you will come to resent me."*

The Burning Hours                                    Page 358

*"I'll never resent you I love you, Linda I'll never let you go."*

"Cut! Cut!" Beau yelled. He threw his cigar on the floor stomping on it and waving his arms like a Flamenco dancer.

"Who the hell is Linda, Nicky? You're making love to Abbey. Get that through your Dago skull; it's Abbey, not Linda, damnit" Beau lit another cigar.

The set quieted at Beau's outburst.

Ivy glared at Nick, but said nothing.

"Five minutes, Beau," Nick held up five fingers.

"Five minutes, Nicky, get your lines straight," *capito*.

"Okay, Beau."

Ivy followed Nick into his dressing room and slammed the door.

"Who's Linda, Nicky?" she demanded sharply.

Nick looked away without responding.

"Look at me, damnit!" Ivy commanded.

"It was a slip I'll get it right in the next take."

"What's going on, Nicky?"

"Nothing, I said it was a slip."

"It was no slip."

"Give me a break, Ivy."

"Who's Linda, Nicky?"

"A woman I knew before the war."

"A woman you knew before the war," Ivy repeated.

"That's what I said."

"Do you love her, Nicky?"

"It was a long time ago."

"That's not what I asked you."

Nick looked away without answering.

"You make love to me, Nicky, but you never said you love me?"

Nick looked into Ivy's blue eyes, a combination of anger and hurt, "There are many kinds of love."

"Is that so? Where do I fit into your love continuum?"

"I'll always care for you, Ivy."

"Not once after we made love, Nicky, did you sleep in my bed. I begged you. I wanted to feel you beside me in the night. Do you have any idea the pain you caused me, do you?"

"I didn't mean to hurt you, Ivy."

"You slept in Linda's bed after you made love, didn't you, Nicky? You made her feel loved and safe, didn't you?"

"Yes, I slept in her bed, I loved her then."

"Do you still love her, Nicky? Hold me the way you held Linda, kiss me the way you kissed Linda, whisper you love me the way you whispered your love to Linda."

"What do you want from me, Ivy?"

"I want what you and Linda had."

"Cut it out, Ivy, we have a scene to film and Beau is foaming at his mouth."

"Nicky, please listen to me. I thought love was an emotion manufactured by movie studios; maybe it is, I don't know. They call me a diva. I'm not proud of the things I did to get out of the coal town and stay on top," Ivy paused, "The studio wants to coronate us the royal couple of Hollywood. We have the world in our hands. We can't go back to who we were, Nicky, we're good, together, don't throw it away," she implored.

"What's going on in there?" Beau banged repeatedly on the door.

"We'll be right out," Nick answered.

"You can't live with a ghost Nicky, its unfair competition for me and it's unfair to you. Find your Linda; see if the flame still burns, then you and I will know if we are lovers or devoted friends."

Beau rapped repeatedly on Nick's dressing room door.

"If you aren't out in the next two minutes, Nicky I'll cancel today's shooting," he threatened.

"We're coming, Beau."

"For the good times, Nicky," Ivy raised her face and closed her eyes.

"For the good times," softly Nick kissed Ivy's mouth.

# 109

Linda's two week visit to Connecticut ended on a high note. Subsequent to the charitable trust's semiannual meeting, she enjoyed luncheon in the executive dining room of the Conover Financial headquarters with Charles, Adalina, Freddie and Freddie's wife, Kimi. Then, as promised, Linda treated Vincent to an outing at Mystic Seaport and a Boston Red Sox game at Fenway Park.

In a lazy afternoon, at the Conover estate in Westport, Charles perused *The Wall Street Journal,* Adalina thumbed through *Life Magazine* and Linda searched newspapers for press releases of financial grant awards announced by the charitable trust to selected veterans groups.

Vincent pulled his Radio-Flyer wagon, a gift from Charles and Adalina, laden with souvenirs and *Superboy* comic books Linda had purchased for him into the living room. He placed a model schooner, a chest containing miniatures of uniformed sailors and a stand-alone statue of a regally attired British Commodore on a table between Charles and Adalina.

"This is a sailing ship Mommy bought for me," Vincent handed the schooner to Charles.

"It is a magnificent ship, Vincent."

"Here are the foresail, the mainsail and the mizzen sail," Vincent pointed to each sail.

"That's very good, Vincent. Who taught you?"

"Mommy."

"Mommy is an excellent teacher."

Vincent nodded his agreement.

"Who gave you these toy sailors, honey?" Adalina asked.

"Mommy," Vincent answered."

Adalina picked up the stand-alone figurine, "Did Mommy buy this sailor for you?"

The Burning Hours                                   Page 362

"Grandma," Vincent whispered in Adalina's ear.

"He did," Adalina smiled.

"Yes," Vincent nodded.

"Vincent, are you and Grandma keeping secrets from me?"

"I told Grandma Captain Bill said you were pretty."

"Your Mommy is pretty," Charles chimed in.

Vincent leaned into Adalina and whispered, again.

"What did he say, Mother?"

"He said, Captain Bill asked you for a date."

"You shouldn't tell tall tales to Grandma."

"Is it a tall tale, Linda?"

"Captain Bill invited us to tour the schooner when it returns to port."

"A private tour?"

"Yes, Mother, a private tour."

"What did you say?"

"Nothing, I just smiled."

"Sounds like a date to me," Charles expressed his opinion.

"I agree, Charles, that's a date if ever there was one," Adalina laughed.

"This is the only guy I date," Linda tickled Vincent.

"Must you leave tomorrow, Linda? Take a few more days," Adalina asked.

"I can't, Mother, I need to shop for Vincent's school outfits. He starts pre-school in July and school in September."

"We can shop in New York City."

"I'd love to, but I can't."

"You're doing wonderful work with the Trust, Linda."

"Thank you, Daddy, it's been personally rewarding."

"I will make it hard for you to leave, tomorrow, Linda," Adalina picked up the *New York Daily News* and began paging through it.

"What are you doing, Mother?"

"I'm looking for back-to-school sales at Macy's and Bloomingdales that you won't be able to resist. We'll shop and have lunch at Jack Dempsey's so you will have to delay your return to Napa."

"Your mother is very determined, Linda."

"I know she is."

Adalina paged through each section of the newspaper, and then she stopped and handed the newspaper to Linda.

"Did you find irresistible bargains, Mother?"

"Look at the article and pictures in the lower section of the newspaper, honey."

"What is it, Linda?" Charles asked.

"A ceremony honoring Vincent and Tommy Tomasso at the high school, tomorrow," Linda answered.

"You're leaving for California, tomorrow," Adalina said.

"What do you want to do, Linda?"

"It might be my last chance to let Vincent know he has a son."

"You must go, Linda, God knows it will be difficult, but you must go," Adalina counseled.

"I know, Mother."

"I'll call Paolo, and we'll drive to New Jersey," Charles said.

Linda turned to Vincent.

"Honey, would you like to see where Mommy worked before you were born?"

"I don't know," Vincent shrugged his shoulders, "Can I bring my comic books?"

"You can look at them in the car."

"When will we go home?"

"Sunday, honey."

"Okay."

"Shall I reschedule your flight for Sunday?" Adalina asked.

"Yes, Mother, thank you."

"What will you do, Linda?" Charles asked.

"The newspapers say Vincent and Ivy Townsend's wedding is any day, now; she might be with him at the ceremony. I can't get back what we once had, I know that, but if it's possible I want Vincent to know he has a son."

"It is a public ceremony, Linda, approaching him with such a sensitive matter will not be easy," Charles assessed.

"The newspaper article says Samuel Birkman is coordinating the ceremony. If you can see him and tell him who you are I'm sure, he will help."

"What if Vincent wants to see you?" Charles asked.

"He will know where to find me."

# 110

Samuel Birkman waited at the center of the crescent-shaped cannon mount. Before him a standing microphone and behind, fixed to the grayish wall two plaques covered with burgundy veils, the high school colors. He looked up at the pale blue cloudless sky and rich lemon colored sun and thought it a marvelous day for a well deserved celebration. Vince and Tommy with Regina and Rosemary at their sides moved through the crowd accepting congratulations and good wishes. Margaret and Veronica, their usual friskiness checked by the large crowd, clung to Julia and Darling.

Charles Conover, Paolo Bellini, and Adalina, held Vincent's hand dressed in an open collar, white shirt and short blue trousers, his dark hair neatly combed stood on the grassy edge of the cannon mount. Linda was not with them.

Samuel looked at his watch. The outpouring of interest stalled the start of the ceremony. He tapped the microphone, which emitted a shrill sound.

"Congratulations, Tommy," Benjamin Gruber said, in obvious arthritic discomfort.

"Are you well, Mr. Gruber?" Rosemary asked.

"It is age, Rosemary."

Tommy shook Benjamin's hand, "Thank you, Mr. Gruber," he said, and then continued to the cannon mount.

Vince saw Helmut Wagner deep in the crowd his face showed the etchings of his advancing years.

"Mr. Wagner."

"Good to see you, Vincent," Helmut's voice lost its once booming quality.

"Mom, this is Helmut Wagner, Linda, and I lived in his apartment in Hoboken."

"Thank you for helping Vince, it was a difficult time for him," Regina kissed Helmut's cheek.

"*Danka*," he put his hand on his cheek, and then handed Vince a photograph, "I took this when you and Linda returned from ice skating."

Vince looked at the photograph and after a brief pause, he said, "Thank you, Mr. Wagner," and put it in his pocket.

"Be kind to take my picture with these two people," Helmut handed his camera to a teenage girl standing nearby.

"Yes," she said, excitedly.

Helmut stood to Regina's side, Vince put his arm around them and the young girl clicked the camera.

"One more, please," Helmut requested.

The young girl snapped the shutter a second time.

"*Danka,*" Helmut bowed his head, courtly.

"You're welcome," the young girl handed her camera to Regina, "Please take my picture with your son," she implored.

"Certainly, dear."

Vince put his arm around the excited girl, smiled and Regina snapped their photograph.

"One more," Regina snapped the picture and returned the camera to the young girl who with her friends dashed through the crowd, screaming, "I have a picture with Nick Ferry."

"Good seeing you, Mr. Wagner."

"I'm happy you remembered me, Vincent."

"I'll always remember you, Mr. Wagner," Vince said an emotional quiver in his voice.

"You have a good son," Helmut turned and disappeared into the crowd.

"Ladies and Gentlemen," Samuel began. "Today we celebrate the lives of two sons of Hill Top High School. Domenico Tomasso, Tommy as we know him and Vincent Farro, who we now know has been renamed Nick Ferry by Hollywood, both were students of mine. This coming school year will be my fiftieth and my last year. I enjoyed a fulfilling career at Hill Top, but it is time to reflect on the legions of students who have passed my way. Before beginning, congratulatory letters and telegrams came from New Jersey's governor and senators and our mayor; they will be published in the local press and Hill Top's school newspaper.

"Here are a few things about Vince and Tommy that you might not know."

As Samuel finished his opening statement the microphone emitted a loud shriek. Its piercing sound brought Tommy to the microphone.

"The mike warns you not to go there, Mr. Birkman," Tommy said and the crowd cheered.

Vince followed Tommy to the microphone.

"I second Tommy's motion," eliciting a second round of cheers.

"I'll inform the assemblage of only the good stuff," Samuel retook the microphone engendering another wave of cheering.

"Remarkable young men," Charles whispered to Adalina.

"Yes," Adalina responded squeezing Vincent's hand.

As the laughter subsided Samuel's demeanor became serious. He tilted the microphone to his comfort zone, and began, "Vince and Tommy are two sides of the same coin. They were born minutes apart on the same day. They grew up in houses separated by a narrow breezeway. From their earliest days as young schoolboys through their harrowing days in combat they remained devoted friends. Tommy returned home grievously injured and for his actions in the Ardennes Forest he received the Medal of Honor," sustained cheering brought Samuel's opening statement to a momentary halt.

When the cheering ended, Samuel resumed his remarks, "Vince sustained wounds in the same action as Tommy. He recovered and went back into combat where he remained to

The Burning Hours                                    Page 368

the end of the war." That revelation caused a buzz through the crowd.

"Linda didn't tell us, Charles," Adalina whispered.

"Vince called me before he left for California, he said to find himself. As we know fate found him. Our Vincent Farro is now known to the world as Academy Award winner Nick Ferry," Samuel paused and the crowd cheered.

"I now ask Tommy and Vince's family to come forward. Rosemary Tomasso and Regina Farro please unveil the plaques honoring your husband, and your son."

Rosemary and Regina removed the veils covering bas-reliefs of Tommy and Vince. Each plaque displayed their likenesses and inscribed below, Tommy's Medal of Honor and Vince's Academy Award.

Vince hugged Regina.

Tommy corralled Rosemary, Margaret and Veronica and then held his hand out to Julia and Darling.

Samuel called Tommy to the microphone.

"Thanks, Mr. Birkman and the school board for this day. I'm overwhelmed. There are many more people more deserving than I am. I love my wife, my two little angels, my mother and her husband, my platoon sergeant who escorted me home. I don't know what else to say. I'll leave the deep thoughts to Vince. He's good with words, always in the library reading, but I knew better. He had his eyes on the pretty librarian."

Charles and Adalina smiled at Tommy's last statement.

"Thank you, Mr. Birkman," Vince said, "I echo Tommy's appreciation to the school board, he paused, "I love you, Mom. I wish Pop were here," he looked at Regina who struggled to hold back her tears. I'm home. This day means more than Academy Award night," then someone in the crowd yelled, "Where's Ivy?"

"Ivy is in Los Angeles."

"Why isn't she with you?"

"She's busy reading scripts."

The Burning Hours
Page 369

Adalina looked at Charles, feeling pain for Linda.

"Since Tommy revealed my crush on the attractive librarian," Vince changed the subject, "I'll now tell you how he and Rosemary met."

"Come on, Vince, give me a break," Tommy hollered.

Vince flashed a roguish smile, "Tommy and I left a track and field event at Roosevelt Park. Tommy spotted Rosemary walking on the opposite side of the boulevard. He dashed into traffic zigzagging between screeching vehicles. When he got to the other side of the street, Rosemary told him he was crazy, but Casanova wasn't deterred he begged her for a date. Rosemary told him to get lost. Tommy persisted. Rosemary consented, and they met for an ice cream Sundae at Gruber's," Vince paused thoughtfully, the crowd waited, "We know how it turned out. My brother, Tommy, his lovely wife and their two beautiful children," then Vince left the microphone.

Samuel placed his hand over the microphone, "You okay, Vince?"

"I'm good Mr. Birkman."

Samuel thanked the people in the crowd for their presence, wished all a wonderful day and clicked off the microphone.

"Thought you might be here," James McLeod tapped Klaus Richter on the shoulder.

"It's been a long time," Klaus responded, "I read the announcement in *The New York Times*."

"Shall we?"

"Yes, I'd like to meet these young men," Klaus answered.

"Colonel McLeod," James saluted, Tommy, "Now civilian James McLeod."

"Rosemary," Tommy exclaimed, "this is Colonel McLeod, my commanding officer in Belgium."

Tommy has spoken often of you," Rosemary said, "These two little ones are our daughters, this is my mother-in-law, Julia and this is…"

"Carroll Darling," James interjected, "Good seeing you Sergeant."

"Same here Colonel," no salutes were exchanged.

"Tommy, meet Major Klaus Richter. Before the war we roomed together at Columbia. Klaus was the German Officer who found you, Farro and Darling."

Klaus Richter saluted, "It is an honor meeting you, Private Tomasso and your family."

"We are happy to know you, Major," Tommy said.

Regina sat on the cannon mount's lower wall, exhausted from the day's excitement. Even when surrounded by fans and signing autographs Regina knew Vince was lonely. Often he confided how solitary life is on the top of the world.

James McLeod and Klaus Richter waited at the cluster of people around Vince. As soon as it thinned James introduced himself and Klaus. They shook hands and chatted, and then Vince returned to signing autographs.

James and Klaus walked the green to the campus's main entrance.

"What are you doing these days, James?"

"Real estate law in Bergen County."

"And you, Klaus?"

"Teaching philosophy at Columbia."

"Any plans for lunch?"

"None."

"Let's go to Petrocelli's for pizza and wine."

"An appealing menu, James."

"You remember Pete Petrocelli?"

"An unforgettable character."

"That's an understatement," James said as he and Klaus walked off the campus.

"Tired, Mom?" Vince signed his last autograph and sat with Regina.

The Burning Hours
Page 371

"A little, the sun feels good on my face."

"I made reservations at the Hotel Plaza for us and Tommy's family, you can rest before dinner, and we'll leave for California in the morning."

"I'm having a Mass said for your father in the chapel. I'd like you to attend with me."

"Of course I'll go with you, Mom."

"You have a fan, Vince," Regina said.

"Where did you come from?" Vince asked.

"Grandpa and Grandma," Vincent pointed to Charles and Adalina.

"You're a handsome little fellow," Vince smiled, "What can I do for you?"

"Sign my program."

"I am happy to," Vince took a pen from his breast pocket.

"Sign on your picture," Vincent requested.

"Okay," Vince smiled, "Tell me your name?"

"My name is Vincent."

"Vincent is my name, do you have a nickname?"

"No, Mommy said my name is Vincent, she calls me Vincent."

"Want to know a secret, Vincent?"

"Yeah," Vincent's eyes shone, conspiratorially.

"My mother called me Vincent when she was mad at me."

"Mommy doesn't get mad at me."

"That's because you're a good boy, stay that way, Vincent."

"Okay, I will."

"What is your last name, Vincent?"

"Conover, write it after my first name."

Vince looked up from the program at the boy standing before him dismissing his name as an odd coincidence.

"Where do you live, Vincent?"

"California."

"I live in California, too," Vince said writing Conover on Vincent's program.

"Sometimes I live in Connecticut," Vincent said to Vince's astonishment.

"How old are you, Vincent?"

"Five, going on six."

Charles and Adalina came to Regina's side.

"He is a darling boy, is he with you?" Regina asked.

"We're his grandparents," Charles answered.

"Hello," Adalina said.

Regina acknowledged with a smile.

"Is your mother with you, Vincent?"

"She brought me, she used to work here."

Vince stared for a long time at the boy waiting for his autographed program. Regina perceived an unusual occurrence transpiring between Vince and the boy who had sought his autograph. She saw Vince wrap his arms around Vincent whispering, "My son, my son."

"Why are you crying?" Vincent asked.

"I didn't know I was," Vince responded unwilling to put Vincent down.

"Give the boy to me, Vince," Regina demanded.

Charles and Adalina rushed to Regina's side.

Vince either didn't hear or he ignored Regina. He felt Vincent's heart beating against his chest and refused Regina's entreaty to give him up.

Finally, Regina wrenched Vincent away, sat him on her lap and held him tight.

"I didn't know, Mom, I didn't know," Vince repeated.

"I can't imagine what you are feeling, Vince."

"Is he my father?"

"Yes, Vincent, my son is your father."

"Then you're my grandmother, right?"

"Yes, dear, I am your grandmother."

"Where's my other grandfather?"

"He's in heaven, Vincent," Regina answered, "but he will always look after you."

Charles and Adalina went to Vince.

"Mr. Ferry," Adalina began.

"Vincent, my name is Vincent."

"Linda is a loving and devoted mother," Adalina said, "There has been no one else in her life," unable to continue she rested her head on Charles's chest.

"She tried to find you," Charles explained, "We tried to find you the day Vincent was born. We couldn't get a message to you no matter how hard we tried."

"Linda is a good girl and ...," again, Adalina's composure failed.

"The past six years have been difficult for her," Charles said.

"Is Linda here, Mr. Conover?"

"She said if you inquired you would know where to find her."

Regina handed Vincent to Adalina.

"Will you see, Linda?"

"I want to see her, Mom."

"I know you are upset, Vince, but I am telling you not to hurt Linda, she gave you a beautiful son," Regina admonished.

"Don't worry."

"I mean it, Vince, be gentle with her."

"Okay, Mom."

"Mrs. Conover, may I have Vincent?" Vince asked.

"Grandma," Vincent threw his arms around Adalina.

"Don't be frightened, honey, go with your father, he loves you."

"See those two girls? Would you like to play with them?" Vince asked.

"I don't know, they're girls," Vincent said, "Okay," he changed his mind.

The Burning Hours
Page 374

"Hold my hand and Grandpa's hand and we'll go there, okay?"

"Okay."

"Would you like to swing?" Vince asked which brought an enthusiastic yes from Vincent.

Charles and Vince coordinated a lift and Vincent swung back and forth between them laughing heartily.

Regina and Adalina sat on the low wall of the cannon mount.

"What will happen to our children, Regina?"

"I trust my son will do right by Linda, Adalina, but I don't know."

"If Linda had a girl she wanted to name her Regina."

"Thank you for telling me, Linda and I had pleasant telephone conversations, she is a sweet girl," Regina squeezed Adalina's hand.

"I spoke by phone with Vincent he was terribly upset at losing Linda; I hope it works out for them," Adalina said, and then she and Regina lapsed into silence.

"Are you ladies all right?" Paolo asked.

"Just two Italian mothers worrying over their children," Adalina answered.

Paolo looked at Regina waiting for an introduction.

"Regina, this is my brother, Paolo."

"Pleased to meet you," Paolo bowed his head.

"Regina is Vincent's mother."

"Nice meeting you, Paolo," Regina said.

"May I sit beside you?"

"Yes," Regina said.

"This is Margaret and Veronica," Vince introduced, "would you children like to play?"

Margaret nodded yes; Veronica objected, "He's a boy, Uncle Vince."

"Soon they won't be able to stay away from each other," Charles laughed and Vince nodded his agreement with a smile.

"Will you try, Veronica?" Vince asked.

"Yes," she agreed reluctantly.

"You look alike," Vincent said.

"That's because we're twins," Margaret answered.

"Don't you know what twins are?" Veronica challenged.

"It's when two babies are born together and they look the same."

"Then why didn't you say we're twins?"

"I don't know," Vincent shrugged his shoulders.

"They're off to a good start, Vince," Rosemary laughed.

"It looks that way," Vince replied.

"Are you going to Linda, Vince?"

"Yes, Tommy I need to see her."

"I'll walk a while with you, if you want me to."

"I'll be okay, Tommy, thanks, anyway."

"Vincent," Charles said, "remember once you loved Linda."

# 111

A simple peach-colored dress cinched at the waist by a coordinated fabric sash highlighted Linda's still youthful figure. Now thirty years of age, she wore her hair pixie-style. From the window, she watched Vince walk the familiar path to the library. Throughout her lonely days of desiring him, Linda now experienced a chill of fear. She wanted to run away, out of the library and live her life in anguished solitude instead of bearing Vince's disdain. And then she remembered the good times and the love they once shared.

Linda's fright reemerged when she looked at Vince standing in the doorway. She buried her face in her hands, tears streaming down her face. She sensed Vince's presence; as he came close to her she backed away until she could retreat no further.

"Hey, lady," Vince said, prying Linda's hands off her face, "let me see your beautiful brown eyes."

"I'm too ashamed, please Vincent, it's my fault."

"You have nothing to feel guilty over," Vince pulled Linda to him.

"I couldn't bear it if you hate me, Vincent."

"Look at me, Linda."

"Won't you forgive me, Vincent?" Linda implored.

"There's nothing to forgive."

"I never wanted us to be apart."

Vince and Linda held each other and during their silent moments Linda's tears subsided, and then she stopped crying.

"Okay, now?" Vince asked, softly.

"I think so," Linda shook her head.

"No more crying, okay?" Vince helped Linda to a colonial-style bench.

"Okay," Linda agreed.

"You have a handsome little boy," Vince lit up.

The Burning Hours

"We have a handsome little boy," Linda corrected.

"Yes, we have, always the teacher, Miss Conover."

"Always the teacher, Mr. Farro."

"You're wearing your hair short."

"Vincent is to blame; when I picked him up, he'd grab a handful."

"It's becoming," Vince ran his hand over Linda's hair.

"I stopped wearing earrings for the same reason."

"Tell me about our son."

"He's a wonderful boy, Vincent, he is inquisitive and funny and affectionate. I have his baby album with me," Linda paused, and then her emotional dam burst, she wrapped her arms around Vince and cried.

"Let it go," Vince whispered.

"When I found out I was pregnant, I was beyond happy. I couldn't wait to tell you, and then evil came into our lives. He said awful things. I wouldn't let him harm you and our baby," Linda's voice faded away and she became quiet, "There were times I couldn't breathe for being without you."

"He can no longer hurt us."

"I know, but I can't forget."

"I'd like to see Vincent's album, promise me no more crying."

"I'll try, but I won't promise."

"Okay," Vince smiled, then we have an understanding."

"We have an understanding."

Linda placed the royal blue album with Vincent's name embossed in gold leaf onto her lap and turned to the first page, a copy of Vincent's Birth Certificate.

"You listed me as Vincent's father," Vince said, proudly.

"I wouldn't have it any other way," she said, and turned the page.

"Here I am with Granddad and Grandmother Conover shortly after my arrival to Napa."

"You've been living in Napa?"

The Burning Hours                                    Page 378

"At the family winery, in the chalet."

"Mother wanted to show my baby bump so she took this picture."

Vince traced the picture of Linda's abdomen with his fingers.

"You're beautiful, Linda," he said his eyes watering.

Linda squeezed Vince's hand and turned the page.

"This is Vincent at six months."

Vince's face glowed, "Wow, he is plump."

"I took good care of your son," Linda's mouth curled into a smile.

"I can see that," Vince returned her smile.

"Here is Vincent at two years; Mother took the picture."

"You both have bright smiles."

"It wasn't easy to get him to sit still."

"You're wearing the locket I gave you."

"I wore it every day."

Vince clicked open the silver heart-shape locket hanging around Linda's neck and saw his Army portrait and their picture taken by Helmut Wagner. He snapped it close and it settled on Linda's chest.

"I saw Mr. Wagner at the ceremony he gave me the picture in your locket."

"We were happy then, Vincent weren't we happy?" Linda began crying.

"Yes, we were, you promised not to cry."

"I didn't promise," Linda answered searching her purse for a handkerchief.

Vince took a handkerchief from his pocket and shook it open.

"Give it to me," Linda held out her hand.

"I'll take care of it," Vince said mischievously.

"Give me the handkerchief, Vincent," Linda demanded.

"Come now don't be stubborn."

"You're tormenting me."

"C'mon, blow."

"There, are you satisfied?" Linda pushed Vince's shoulder.

"For now, tell me about Vincent's photograph."

"As mother snapped the camera, he slid off my lap, and then he did it, again."

"He got away, twice?" Vince grinned.

"It's not funny, Vincent, he's quick and has energy to burn."

"I had a mental image of you chasing him around the vineyard," Vince laughed.

"You think it's funny because he's the way you were. Your mother told me stories about you growing up and the trouble you and Tommy Tomasso got into. You're laughing at my expense, aren't you?"

Vince shrugged and continued laughing.

"I said you were a big kid, and nothing has changed with you."

"It's good seeing you laugh, Linda."

"It's easy when I'm with you."

"Linda," Vince said his tone serious.

"Yes, Vincent."

"I want you and Vincent to come home and live with me."

After a painful pause Linda said what she dreaded.

"I wish it could be the way it was for us, Vincent. You're an international celebrity, you are recognized everywhere. I am thrilled for your success. Ivy Townsend is young and beautiful and she adores you. Your place is with her. I came here today because I wanted you to know your son, beyond that I have no expectations. I wish it could be the way it was, but that's our past. The time we had, together will always be the happiest of my life."

"I meant what I said, Linda."

"There are things you don't know, Vincent."

"Nothing you can say could change my mind."

Linda looked away and didn't speak.

The Burning Hours

"What don't I know?" Vince touched Linda's shoulder.

"I wanted to experience the pain of bringing my child into the world. I loved feeling him inside me. The day before Vincent's birth, he stopped moving. He was in a transverse position and natural childbirth was out of the question. He was taken out of me, surgically," Linda drifted into a protracted silence.

"I didn't know," Vince grasped Linda's hand.

"During surgery my heart stopped. Before the emergency team came to the operating suite, it started beating, again. Before I went dark I saw you, you held my hand, and you told me to fight and then you said..."

"Don't leave me, Linda," Vince choked up.

"I heard you, Vincent, and I came back. When I woke, Vincent wasn't with me, he was...," Linda broke down crying.

"Don't say anything more," Vince held her.

"They told me Vincent was in the neonatal intensive care unit. We were fighting to stay alive. I was unconscious for more than a day. I lost so much blood I couldn't care for my baby. The doctor said he was hours away from...I won't say it, I won't say it," Linda's voice trembled, "I insisted on seeing him. He was so fragile lying still in the incubator. When I touched his tiny fingers he moved and started crying, you can't know how I felt when I heard him cry," Linda looked at Vince, "to save my life the doctor performed a hysterectomy. I can't bear children, I'm no longer young, I am scarred from here to here," she traced a line across her abdomen, "I can't give you what Ivy can. You must see your place is with her."

Vince got up and walked to the window and looked out. Linda followed him and they exchanged sad smiles. He put his arm around her shoulders and they stood that way for what seemed a lifetime.

"Do you know who that is at the commemorative plaques?"

"That's Captain O'Malley."

"Captain O'Malley is Tommy's father."

"I didn't know," Linda said.

"Shamus O'Malley never knew his son. All he knows of him is a plaque fixed to a cold concrete wall. Tommy didn't experience the joy of growing up with a mother and father. We talked when we were in combat when our lives were measured in seconds. Tommy told me having supper at my house with me, mom and pop is one of his treasured memories."

Vince paused.

"I love Ivy Townsend, Linda."

"I know you do," Linda said in a quiet voice.

"But, I don't love Ivy the way I love you. Vincent and I need you. I want us to be a family. You have to make up your mind, Linda," Vince said, and went back to the bench where he sat looking straight ahead.

"Vincent, you live in a culture of glamour and excitement. That isn't my world. I'm a good mother and I want to enjoy a quiet life surrounded by people I love.

"Does that include me, Linda? Is a good mother sufficient for you? What about a wife to your son's father? You said you liked the sound of Linda Conover Farro."

"Please Vincent, I'll love you forever, I want what's best for you."

"What did you tell me when I was sure your wealth and social position would stand in our way?"

"I said it didn't matter, because I loved you."

"Nothing has changed in here, Linda," Vince placed his hand on his chest.

"But, your life has changed, Vincent. I'd be in your way, and I won't do that to you."

"Are you listening to me, Linda?" Vince took Linda's shoulders. Do you hear what I am saying to you?" he shook her, and then softening his grip he pulled Linda to him.

"I'm sorry, Linda," Vince whispered, "I'm sorry."

"You didn't hurt me, Vincent I know you would never hurt me."

# 112

As Linda's tears fell Vince kissed the top of her head, and then he closed his eyes, trying to recapture their happy times, but he couldn't expel from his memory the telephone click that ended their lives, together. Then, the sound of the library door, sweeping open, punctuated the silence of their minds

"I can do it, myself, Grandma," Vincent said, and closed the door.

"How did you get here, Vincent?" Linda broke away from Vince.

"Grandpa and my grandmas brought me."

"Why did they bring you?"

"I wanted me to see where you worked."

"This is where I met your mother, Vincent."

"Did you work with all these books, Mommy?"

"Yes, honey, I did."

"And, your mother taught us how to use the library and kept it quiet so we could study."

"Mommy taught me my words and pictures; she's a good teacher."

"What have you been up to, mister?" Linda scolded, "Look at you, your hair is mussed, your shirt is hanging out of your trousers, and you have grass stains on your knees."

At Linda's request Vince rummaged through her handbag for a comb, "It looks like you have the last ten years of your life in here; I can't find it."

"Give me the bag and refrain from further observations," Linda took a comb from her handbag and jiggled it, "This is a comb."

"How did you get these grass stains, Vincent?"

"Margaret pushed me when we played tag."

"Who is Margaret?"

The Burning Hours                                   Page 384

"She's Tommy's and Rosemary's daughter," Vince answered.

"I didn't know Tommy and Rosemary had a daughter."

"There are two of them, Mommy," Vincent informed, "Veronica is the other one."

"Really."

"They are twins," Vince clarified, "little redheads, cute as buttons."

"I'd like to see them and Tommy, and meet Rosemary," Linda stuffed Vincent's shirt into his waistband, "Where did you get the idea to play tag on such a hot day?"

"From Daddy," Vincent pointed to Vince.

"Oh, it was daddy's idea?"

"Yes," Vincent shook his head.

"When I dressed our son this morning he was as crisp as an early morning autumn day, look at him, now, see what you've caused."

Vince continued smiling.

"You find this amusing? If you think you're going to change my son …"

"Our son," Vince corrected.

"Our son," Linda said, "into a Jersey boy so you can relive your misspent youth through him, you should think, again."

"C'mon, Linda, he was playing, the kids were having fun, and anyway your father thought it was a good idea."

"Daddy thought it was a good idea," Linda said, incredulously.

"Yes, he encouraged it."

"He encouraged it."

"That's what I said, ask him."

"Mommy, can I go sit with Daddy?"

"Of course you can."

"Come here, buddy," Vince held out his arms.

Vince lifted Vincent onto his lap, "Did you like playing tag?"

The Burning Hours                    Page 385

"It was fun."

"Do you like Margaret and Veronica?"

"They're okay, for girls."

"Why did you stop playing?"

"Margaret and Veronica didn't want to play anymore; they said I run too fast."

"I'm sorry you stopped playing," Vince said.

"Grandpa said we could play hide and seek in California."

"Did grandpa say that?" Linda asked, surprised.

"Yes, he talked with Margaret's and Veronica's mommy and daddy."

"Do you think you will enjoy playing hide and seek in the vineyard?" Linda asked.

"That will be real fun."

"What are you whispering, Vincent?"

"I'm not whispering, Mommy."

"I'm sorry, honey I was talking to your father."

"Daddy wants to know if we are going home with him."

"Now you have our son speaking on your behalf, Mr. Farro?"

"Ask your mother, again," Vince whispered.

"Mommy, are we going home with Daddy?"

"You're scheming, Mr. Farro the way you and your father schemed," Linda smiled.

"Well, what's it going to be?" Vince asked, and then he whispered to Vincent, who parroted Vince, "What's it going to be, Mommy?"

"If I say yes, you both have to promise no scheming."

"Give us a minute," Vince requested.

"A minute, Mr. Farro, you want a minute?"

"I need to discuss your request with Vincent."

"You want to discuss my request with our son?"

"Just one minute, okay?" Vince repeated.

"Sure, take a minute, take two or three I'm beginning to feel isolated."

"Okay, thanks," Vince took Vincent's hand and they walked to the middle of the library.

"Where are you going?"

"I'm going to show Vincent where I sat when I was in your class."

"Whatever you say," Linda answered, smiling at Vince and Vincent whispering and laughing while Vince picked up their son and hugged and kissed him.

"I bet you can't catch me, Daddy," Vincent challenged.

"Let's see."

Vincent got up and dashed around the table eluding Vince, who pursued him at each turn. Linda shook her head and beamed at the sight of her son and his father playing like kids in a school yard.

"I said you couldn't catch me, Daddy," Vincent said, triumphantly.

Then Vince feigned right and Vincent ran into his arms.

"You tricked me."

"You are fast."

"Let's do it, again."

"Okay," Vince replied.

"That's enough, boys; libraries are for reading and studying, they aren't playgrounds and they should be quiet, now stop playing."

"I think we owe your mother an apology, buddy."

Vincent nodded his agreement.

"You go, first."

"Okay, sorry we were noisy, Mommy."

"And you, Mr. Farro?"

"I'm sorry, too."

"I assume you have an answer for me."

"Tell Mommy what we decided."

"Sorry Mommy we can't promise we won't scheme."

Linda's face lit into a glowing smile.

"You two know how to break my heart," Linda rushed to Vince and Vincent, and threw her arms around them her long nightmare ended.

Printed in the USA
CPSIA information can be obtained
at www.ICGtesting.com
LVHW011326051023
760085LV00063B/1647